Derek Nelson, born in 1977, lives in Kells, County Meath, Ireland. Known affectionately as Del, he carries the nickname since the age of 14. Derek hails from a family of 11 children and his parents tell him that when he was a child, he'd often wander off to other worlds in his imagination, possibly for a bit of peace and quiet! Derek's carried this vivid imagination with him into adulthood for us all to enjoy here in this, his first book, *Well-Keeper Island*. When he's not writing, Derek works in the shipping industry.

To my son, Nathan, who taught me to wander the timeless paths of imagination.

Derek Nelson

WELL-KEEPER ISLAND

AUSTIN MACAULEY PUBLISHERS™

LONDON • CAMBRIDGE • NEW YORK • SHARJAH

A CIP catalogue record for this title is available from the British Library.

ISBN 9781398421271 (Paperback)
ISBN 9781528954983 (ePub e-book)

www.austinmacauley.com

First Published (2020)
Austin Macauley Publishers Ltd
25 Canada Square
Canary Wharf
London
E14 5LQ

I'd like to acknowledge everyone from the Austin Macauley team that worked on this book and sincerely thank them for selecting my manuscript for publication. I'd especially like to thank my son, Nathan, for never giving up on me; my wife, Niamh, for her (almost) endless patience; and Sophie, my beautiful daughter, because she is an angel.

Chapter 1
Well-Keeper Island

It was a beautiful sunny morning, so Sara and Daniel Taylor dashed out the back door before they were barely finished with breakfast. The sound of their mother yelling something about staying where she could see them dwindled in their ears as they bolted down the garden.

The pair loved the summer holidays and during them they often spent time together in their big country-garden. Sometimes they'd play catch, other times they'd play skipping and sometimes they'd play football all day long. In the corner of the garden there was a swing that was made from a rope and tyre, hanging from a great old oak tree. The rope was threadbare from overuse. Frogs and newts swam in the stream that ran down the side of the garden and sometimes Daniel and Sara would see who could spot the most. The stream ran out under the big fence at the end of their garden to places they imagined must hold great adventures. They'd often catch butterflies among the flowers or play hide and seek in the bushes. They loved living in the countryside, and because they didn't have many close neighbours, Daniel and Sara whiled away the days together. The last few days the pair had been packing in fun as they knew school would start back in a week's time.

'There's nothing to do, let's play football,' said Daniel as he raced up and down the lawn dribbling his ball.

'No, absolutely not,' replied Sara. 'We did that yesterday. It's a perfect day for skipping rope.' She spun her rope in a loop. 'C'mon Dan, I'll jump and you count.'

'Not a chance,' said Daniel. 'We did *that* yesterday and the day before. We've only a few days left before schoolbags and homework, and I want to have as much fun as possible before then.'

'Well I'm not playing football again; you can do it yourself,' said Sara, with certainty.

Suddenly, with mischief in his eyes, Daniel grabbed Sara's favourite skipping rope and ran towards the stream.

Sara screeched, *'Come back here!'* and raced after him, hot on his tail.

Daniel, delighted with Sara's reaction, dodged in and out of the bushes. 'I'm going to build a tight rope across the stream with this old string,' he edged towards the stream.

Sara followed, 'It's not a string, it's my best rope; now give it back or else.' She had stopped a few feet away as her brother was now standing right at the edge of the stream.

'Or else what?' said Daniel, waving the skipping rope in loops through the air.

'Or else...or else...' said Sara, looking at Daniel then around the garden. Her eyes fell on Daniel's football. 'Or else,' she said once more, and broke into a sprint for the ball. Daniel raced after her, but just before he caught up Sara drew back and kicked the ball with all the power that her legs could muster. Daniel collided into her, and the two rolled on the freshly cut lawn. Together they watched the ball going up, up and right over the fence at the end of the garden.

'Now look what you did, you lost my ball,' said Daniel as he stood up.

'It's your own fault,' Sara stood too. 'You shouldn't have been teasing me. Anyway, you're just jealous because I kicked it farther than you can.'

A voice called down the garden to them, 'Is everything all right you two?' Their mother was standing outside the back door putting some paper in the recycle-bin.

'Yes, Mum,' they both replied, waving as their mum retreated back inside to answer the front door to someone who had just rang the doorbell.

'Let's see where the ball went,' suggested Daniel. The disagreement was already forgotten. Daniel was thirteen years old and tall for his age so he had no problem reaching up into the branches of the old oak tree. He gave Sara a leg up onto the first branch and quickly followed after. Together they climbed way up into the leaves so they could see over the high fence.

'Look!' cried Sara. 'I can see it bobbing up and down in the water.' The ball was drifting down the stream on its way to Appledown Orchards.

The pair gazed across the meadow to the trees in the distance. This was not the first time they'd looked over the fence towards Appledown Orchards, and now as before their minds took flight.

I'd just like to see what's over there, even just once, thought Sara. They couldn't see the old abandoned cottage that sat in the middle but they knew it was there.

I wonder what the orchards are like up close, thought Daniel, looking longingly at the green horizon. Their parents had warned them often enough not to go into the meadow as sometimes the farmer that owned it let a bull and some cows out to graze. The orchard was quite a distance across the meadow, and nobody had been over that way in years.

Their father often joked, 'Besides, that orchard is enchanted. It has an old wishing-well in it and strange things happen if you get too close.'

And their mum would add, 'Don't tease them. Still, if you want fruit, there is plenty in the fruit-basket. Stay away from the meadow *and* the orchards. And another thing, the stream is deeper at the far end of the meadow. It could be dangerous.'

This would only leave Daniel and Sara more curious, and they often wondered what it would be like to visit Appledown Orchards.

The sun rose in the sky as they remained in the tree looking to the horizon when suddenly Sara brightened up. *I've got it,* she thought, and clicked her fingers. 'Are you thinking what I'm thinking?'

'Yes, my ball is gone and now I'll be even *more* bored.'

Sara giggled, 'No silly, we'll follow the stream as far as Appledown Orchards and see if we can find your ball.'

Daniel's brow furrowed. *Hmm,* he thought. 'I don't know. You know we're not supposed to go into the meadow, not to mention near the orchards. Besides, what about the bull?'

'It doesn't matter if you're afraid of the bull,' said Sara, grinning.

Daniel frowned. 'I'm not afraid of the bull, I never said *that.*'

'Okay then, the bull that you're *not* afraid of won't be in the meadow. Just look at the length of the grass, there hasn't been cows in it for ages. Come on, Dan, it'll be an adventure before school.'

Daniel paused to think. *Hmm, school or adventure. No contest really.* He brightened up and began to climb across the branch that leaned over into the field. 'Okay, Sis, but I'm in charge.'

'We both are,' Sara replied. 'I might be one year younger than you but it's a well-known fact that girls are smarter than boys. We mature quicker.'

Hmm. 'I've never heard *that* fact,' said Daniel suspiciously.

'Point proven,' Sara nodded firmly and followed her brother out onto across the branch. Daniel dropped from the tree and helped his sister down too.

Sara rubbed her knees. 'Oh shoot, I've gotten bark stains on my favourite blue dungarees.'

Daniel put his hand to his mouth. 'Oh dear, bark stains. The world is coming to an end.'

'Very funny, Dan. Shut up, just because you've the fashion sense of a scarecrow.'

Daniel looked around the meadow. 'You're right about the grass it comes up to my knees. Let's walk beside the stream where it's a bit shorter.'

'Close but not too close so we don't fall in,' said Sara.

'Fine, as that's a good idea I *suppose* we can share leadership, as long as you can keep up of course.'

'Agreed,' they shook hands on their arrangement, and set off at a merry trot along the course of the stream.

Daniel selected a long blade of grass to chew on and Sara a thin branch that she swished occasionally at a fluffy dandelion or into the stream just to make a splash. The pair wandered happily soaking up the summer sounds. From time to time they caught echoes of bleating lambs in the distance. Crickets chirped, the grass rustled in the gentle breeze and many different birds were whistling and calling to one another.

'Bet you can't name that bird,' said Daniel, when they heard a cooing noise in the distance.

'Simple,' said Sara, 'It's a pigeon. Okay you guess next.' They only had to wait a few moments till a sweet whistle floated by on the breeze.

Daniel thought for a moment. *Hmm.* 'Could it be…no wait, it's a lark, I'm sure of it.'

'You're right. One each then, it's a draw.'

Next Sara guessed the magpie and then Daniel the curlew. They listened out for the next bird when suddenly a loud cackle sounded very close to them. They both leaped with fright.

'What was that!' cried Sara.

Daniel recovered quickly from the fright. 'It was only a pheasant. There's no need to be scared, Sis.'

'I'm not scared, I *just* got a fright,' said Sara, 'You jumped too.'

'Shut up, I didn't jump. I just reacted, it's different.'

'*Sure* it is.'

'Anyway, that's the end of the game,' Daniel decided, 'We've named them all.'

After walking for some time, the pair turned around to see how far they'd gone. Their garden fence looked small in the distance.

'Wow,' said Daniel, 'I didn't realise the field was this big. We've been walking ages.' When they turned again to continue, the bright beams of the sun fell on the stream creating a dazzling shine that bounced off the surface. 'Gosh,' continued Daniel, 'see how bright it shines. I don't think this stream has a name; how about we call it the Silver Stream?'

Sara considered the name for a moment then nodded. 'Okay, Silver Stream it is,' she said, without sharing her next thought. *I'm definitely naming the next thing that needs a name.* The pair hurried along, following the turns of the Silver Stream. Soon after they came to a sudden stop, for there looming before them was a great dark shadow.

Sara looked up, 'I don't see any apples.' In front of them stood a row of great big fir trees with the darkest of green foliage, full of the strength of summer.

'Well we've come this far; we might as well keep going,' said Daniel, 'C'mon, we'll just stick to the Silver Stream. I bet it leads to the old wishing-well.' The stream's path coursed between two of the fir trees and the pair followed, something in the air urging them onward. Daniel kept his eyes on the water. 'Notice how brightly the stream shines despite the shadow cast by those big fir trees.'

'That is odd,' replied Sara. *I wonder what causes it.* Leaving the line of fir trees behind them, they followed the stream towards a high row of bushes a short distance ahead. Sara shuddered. *There's that strange feeling again, creepers.* She stepped closer to her brother.

When they reached the bushes, Daniel looked upward. 'Gosh, these bushes are twice as tall as me.'

Sara studied the bushes. 'See how they spread in either direction, just like a wall,' she said, 'Let's follow the stream further as it may lead us to the other side.' A little further on the stream changed course to the left and spread out wider, still joined by the high wall of bushes on the opposite side. Sara gazed at the clear water. 'Gosh, see how deep the stream is down here?'

'Yes, it does look a little deep,' said Daniel, 'Perhaps we'll find a way across farther on.' They continued in the direction of the flowing stream.

Sara finally felt they'd walked far enough. 'It's leading nowhere; maybe we should go back. Besides, my legs are getting tired.'

'Ah, Sis, don't be such a girl. Just a little farther; it's got to lead somewhere,' said Daniel.

Sara stopped and looked at him sternly. 'But I am a girl!' She huffed and walked a few paces ahead, but she had only taken a few steps when she cried, '*Look!*' and tired legs forgotten she broke into a run. Daniel was right behind her as they dashed down the stream till they reached a rickety bridge made from wood and rope. The pair stared curiously across the bridge which was met on the other side by a high wooden gate that interrupted the line of bushes. The gate was almost completely covered in thick green ivy but for the weatherworn bottom, where some of the wooden rows were still visible. Together they gingerly crossed the rope bridge that swayed to-and-fro with each step the pair took.

When they got to the other side, Daniel pushed hard on the gate. 'It's locked,' he said with disappointment, 'What'll we do now?' Sara didn't answer; instead she ran her hand up and down the gate, gently pressing her palms into the ivy leaves. 'If pushing it won't open it, I don't think rubbing it will,' said Daniel, impatiently.

'Shush,' replied Sara with equal impatience, 'I'm checking is what I'm doing.'

'Checking for what?' Daniel asked, puzzled.

Sara's hand suddenly disappeared through the ivy and she broke into a smile. 'A latch brother dear, every gate has a latch.' She twisted her wrist and they heard the scrape of metal. Sara withdrew her hand and pushed on the gate; it opened with a groan. With a smile of satisfaction she glanced at Daniel and stepped through the gate.

Wait for me. Remember I'm in charge!' cried Daniel. *I can't have her making all the discoveries,* he thought, and quickly followed her. On the other side of the gate they stood side by side.

'Wow,' they chorused together as their heads turned this way and that—for they knew they'd found Appledown Orchards. They smiled to one another with delight. The grass, overgrown and seeding on top came up to their knees and dotted around the orchard were clumps of tangled briars. Daniel and Sara looked around, dizzy with the sweet smells of ripening fruit.

'Look!' shouted Daniel, 'There's a huge bed of strawberries.'

'I see them,' replied Sara excitedly, 'And alongside those are rows of gooseberries and, next to those, raspberries!' Thrilled to finally be in Appledown Orchards they raced over to the berry beds. Straight away the pair picked the reddest, juiciest strawberries, as these were their favourite. The stream meandered through the orchard and Sara knelt down beside it.

'Wash your strawberries in the stream,' she said, 'You don't want to be eating insects.'

'Ha, insects don't scare me,' replied Daniel. He washed them all the same. With juice smeared on their grinning faces, they passed through the orchard to the apple and pear trees. The apples were shiny green and rosy red.

Daniel picked a stick off the ground and spun it in the air. 'Crack-shot Daniel they call me.' With a perfect aim he brought down a huge apple from the nearest tree.

'I wouldn't eat that one,' said Sara, smiling. She too picked up a stick and made for the tree bearing the juiciest, yellow pears. Ignoring her, Daniel bit into the apple and just as quickly spat it out, his face twisted. 'You should've listened,' Sara continued. 'Your eyes are bigger than your belly. Anyone can see they're sour apples.'

Daniel moved to a different tree, this time taking down two purple plums. 'Delicious,' he declared, with juice running down his chin. 'Want one?'

'No thanks,' said Sara, 'I'm trying for a nice apple, the sweet kind.'

Daniel unbuttoned one of his pockets and popped the other plum away to enjoy later. *Glad I wore my combats, can't have enough deep pockets, that's what I say.* He joined Sara at the next apple tree and prepared for another throw.

As Daniel drew back his arm to throw Sara cried out excitedly. 'There it is Daniel. There it is. It's the wishing-well, we've found it.' She was pointing towards a shaded corner of the orchard.

Daniel frowned. *Oh shoot, I'd been hoping to spot the wishing-well first.* He kept this thought to himself but his face showed disappointment. Forgetting the apples he followed Sara along the path of the stream which led towards the well. 'I wish it knew where my ball was,' he said as he reached Sara beside the well.

The well was made of grey stone. It was round and had a small apex roof supported by two wooden stilts. The whole thing leaned to one side.

'It looks like it's been here for a long, long time,' said Sara.

Daniel was thinking. *Hmm.* 'Isn't it curious that the stream just disappears when it reaches the well.' The water shone brightly, reflecting the afternoon sun. A small splash in the stream next the well caught their attention. Daniel's ball had popped up from under the water and bobbed on the surface against the side of the well. 'Hey, my ball,' he said. 'Fancy that, maybe it's a real wishing-well after all.'

'Not likely,' said Sara, matter-of-factly. 'The ball obviously floated down the stream till it reached the well. The water must run under ground here, hence why the stream disappears.'

Daniel looked at his sister, smiled and shook his head. 'Hence why the stream disappears,' he said, trying to copy her voice. 'You're always so

16

serious Sara,' he teased as he fished his ball from the stream. 'I know it's not a *real* wishing-well, but why not make a wish? Just for the fun of it. I wished for my ball and what do you know, here it is!'

'Don't be ridiculous, Daniel, there are no such things as wishing-wells!'

'Go on, Sis, let yourself go, wish for anything in the world, go crazy like.'

Sara rolled her eyes. 'Okay then, I will. Anything to shut you up.' She fell silent and looked at the ground, thinking. *What interesting wish could I make? Something fun, something daring.*

'Hurry up, wish for no more school,' said Daniel, tapping his foot.

Sara frowned. 'I certainly will not.' *I quite like school, although I must admit I enjoy the holidays even more.* 'I wish for...I wish for...I know,' she stopped. 'No, not that either.' Once again, she looked thoughtfully at the ground.

Daniel grew impatient. 'Come on slow coach, today maybe.'

'I wish for something adventurous to happen,' Sara chimed, 'something exciting like.'

Daniel rolled his eyes skyward. 'What kind of silly wish is that?'

'Well you asked,' said Sara, slightly annoyed, 'Besides, it would be nice for something fun and exciting to happen, before we go back to school.'

'Wasn't coming here exciting enough for you?'

'Something else *other* than this.'

Daniel turned to go. 'Come on, we better be going home, Mum will be cross when she realises we've left the garden.'

'Well you got your wish,' said Sara stubbornly. 'Visiting an old abandoned orchard is okay, but it's hardly an adventure. Besides, we're back to school next week, what will we tell our friends?' she pointed to imaginary people. 'What did you do? Went sailing, how cool, well guess what me and Dan did? We ate fruit, yep, I'm serious,' she nodded her head dramatically.

'Hey,' said Daniel, 'I like fruit.' Sara folded her arms and stayed put. She bit her lip, deep in thought. *He's right of course, we should go, but for some strange reason I feel like sticking around.*

Daniel's football suddenly fell from his hands. Sara turned to see why he was statue-still and gazing behind her. Her mouth fell open and her eyes almost popped, for blasting out of the well in a great fountain were millions of sprinkling flakes.

'Oh Creepers! What in the world is going on?' cried Sara.

'I've no idea,' said Daniel uncertainly, 'I think it's snowing, sort of. It's freaky.'

'It *is* snowing,' said Sara astonished, 'Its multi-coloured snow, and see how they sparkle in the sunlight. How weird is that.'

'It's freaky *and* weird!' Daniel decided. The stream almost sang as the flakes touched it, and all around the air, whispered of magic. Suddenly the pair were lifted off the ground and floated amidst the rainbow shower.

'Daaaniel! What's happening Daniel?' shouted Sara.

'Freaky and weird, Sis, freaky and weird!' Daniel called back while looking at the ground several feet below him. They swayed aloft in the air as the magic gathered strength. Suddenly the flakes, the siblings and the stream itself lifted and all spun around above the wishing-well, and then with great speed everything was sucked into the well.

The pair hardly had time to think as they zoomed down the well. The water spread before them, rolled back and disappeared.

Sara tried to concentrate. *We're surrounded by multi-coloured, fluffy clouds. Daniel, are we flying or falling?* she shouted.

'Flying, no wait, we're falling, hang on, I actually think we're flying!' Daniel shouted back. They stretched out and joined hands as the walls of the magic well widened just for them. Then just as suddenly as they were sucked in, they came shooting out again, landing in a roll along soft ground.

'Okay, *what* just happened and *where* on earth are we?' said Sara, astonished.

'Good questions, Sis. I *assume* we're on earth as we've landed on green grass,' Daniel was equally bewildered. A well just like the one in the orchard rested on the grass beside them and beside it sat a big saucer-shaped rock. Daniel and Sara turned away from the wishing-well and gazed all around them. In the distance to the north they could see a great big forest swaying with dark colours.

'That doesn't look like any forest I've ever seen on earth before,' said Daniel, 'It looks like the trees are continuously changing colours.'

Sara shook her head in disbelief. 'It couldn't be, it's a trick of the light, it's got to be. Look beyond the forest, a *normal* rocky mountain.'

Daniel turned west. 'I think I can hear the ocean.'

'Yeah, me too. It must be over those purple hills,' replied Sara, pointing. Some distance to the west they could see rows of sand dunes coated in purple flowers and rushes. Turning south they saw a shimmering lake with plains of flowers, plants and grass running either side. Next, they looked to the east and saw crests of gently sloping hills. The wishing-well itself sat in the centre of a beautiful, green meadow.

'Where do you suppose we actually are then?' wondered Sara.

'Welcome to Well-Keeper Island.' The pair swivelled their heads to find the source of this deep eerie voice.

'Well-Keeper what?' said Daniel, as they turned to see a strange man walking towards them across the grass. He was very tall and pale, with bushy, silver eyebrows. Strands of black and silver hair poked out from

18

under his black top hat. As he moved, his long black coat crackled as though of magic.

Sara moved closer to Daniel. 'He looks eh…unusual.'

'Should we run?' But then the man smiled, his wide faded-red mouth opened to show snow-white teeth, and suddenly his fresh-looking skin showed wrinkles that seemed to map countless journeys. It was a kind smile. Sara felt herself smiling back at him.

'No,' replied Daniel quietly, 'Where would we run to?' *Why did I say that?* he found himself wondering as he locked eyes with the tall man in black.

The stranger's eyes were jet-black and danced with the energy of youth, yet pierced with an ancient depth. The stranger reached them and extended big hands that gracefully emerged from his sleeves, hands sporting extraordinarily long fingers.

'Welcome to Well-Keeper Island,' the stranger repeated and patiently waited for Daniel and Sara to shake his hand.

Sara thought about the man before her. *His voice is haunting, yet kind. It comes from far away yet, close by at the same time. I best let Daniel lead, just in case.* 'Daniel, you're in charge,' she decided, firmly.

Daniel too was mesmerised by the strange voice that trailed with random echoes. *Hmm. It's not a normal voice, that's for sure. Mystical maybe, but I hear no threat in his tone.* Daniel shook the stranger's hand but remained silent. Sara followed suit.

'It's nice to meet you,' said the stranger, 'At last you've answered my summons. Greetings, one and all.' The stranger gave a bow.

'What is this place? *Where* is this place?' said Daniel, finding his voice.

Taking courage from Daniel, Sara quickly added, 'Who are you?' *He could be a dark sorcerer if I believed in such things. Then again, he could be a sad clown.*

'My name is Tobias Wells. I am the keeper of this well and this is Well-Keeper Island.' The stranger gestured with his hand to the surrounding island. 'This is a place where magic of the heart comes to the fore.'

Daniel looked puzzled. 'I don't know anything about magic of the heart but the way we arrived here certainly felt like magic.'

Sara's brow furrowed. 'We didn't answer any summons. We'd know if we did. What are we doing here? What do you want from us?'

The well-keeper tipped his top hat with his long finger, squared his shoulders and stepped sideways to reply, 'A summons can take on many forms: the call of a bird, a whistle on the wind, a feeling from within calling you forwards. The summons was sent out and was answered, hence why you are here.'

Sara suddenly thought, *I wonder if that strange feeling egging me on was the summons. No, it couldn't be.*

Daniel's thoughts echoed his sisters'. *Hmm. There was definitely something in the air willing us on towards the orchards.* 'So you summoned us by magic, or whatever. Why?'

Tobias continued in a friendly but commanding tone, 'You wished for an adventure did you not! And now you are here to be granted your adventure. As keeper of the well, I give you the task to search the island for three treasures and return to the well with all that you find. To succeed on your quest for these treasures you will need the most important magic of all to aid you.'

'I…I was only playing around wishing for an adventure,' said Sara uncertainly, torn between confusion and disbelief. We don't even believe in magic.' She turned to her brother, 'Do we, Daniel?'

'Eh, eh of course we don't,' said Daniel unsurely, 'None of this makes sense.'

'And yet here you are. Your destiny awaits you,' offered Tobias with a knowing smile. 'It doesn't matter whether you believe in magic or not. It doesn't matter whether it makes sense to you or not. You answered the summons, you made the wish and here you are. *This* is what's important. Your adventure starts now, and *time* is of the essence.'

The pair looked at one another silently.

Daniel frowned. *Hmm. I know that look, Sara's curious. We can't deny that we're here on this unusual island. Tobias Wells seems nice in a weird sort of way. And how stranger could things get?*

Sara rested her chin in her hand. *There's that excited look he gets. If I know Daniel, he's eager to accept the charge. I must confess I'm curious too, but we can't rush into it without finding out more details. Wishing-wells, treasures, magic. It's just not normal.*

Daniel's face brightened. 'We'll do it,' he declared.

'*Daniel!*' snapped Sara, 'You speak for yourself, but don't forget we're both in charge.' *Why does he always act without thinking things through? Boys.*

'What?' asked Daniel, confused. Tobias stood by patiently.

'Shush,' said Sara, 'I'm thinking.' *Tobias seems nice in a strange sort of way. He's most likely a clown of sorts. But still, we need to be careful.* She turned to the well-keeper, 'Mr Tobias sir, we'll do it. We will accept your quest, but first you must give us more details.'

Hearing this, Tobias nodded once, his face showing no surprise, as though he knew all along that they would agree to the task. 'More details, of course, I will give you all the direction you need,' said the well-keeper with a sweeping gesture of his hand that sent sparkles through the air.

'Good,' replied Sara, satisfied, *leave it to a girl to take charge.* 'So what *are* the treasures, and where should we begin?'

Standing to his full height Tobias crackled with more sparkles of magic and pointed north. 'The first of the treasures that you must find is the hag's staff. Travel towards those colourful woods yonder.' As he spoke, the questers were mesmerised by his hand motions and enchanting tone. 'The second, of course, is the shard of the dragon's tooth. And the third can only be the nourishing stone.' He stepped back holding three fingers aloft after delivering the charge.

'What kind of strange treasures are they?' said Daniel.

Probably clown treasures, Sara thought suspiciously.

Tobias began to shimmer in and out of focus, while at the same time a fountain of colourful magical flakes gushed from the well and swirled all around them.

'I must warn you, at times the path will be perilous and you will face many dangers. Be guided by magic of the heart, for this is the stuff upon which this world thrives, and without it surely you will fail.' And so saying, Tobias faded towards the wishing-well into the colourful flakes and almost out of view.

'Wait,' cried Sara, 'you said time is of the essence; how long do we have?'

'Four nights you will spend on this island fair. Five days from now, we will meet again in this place.' The colourful flakes exploded in every direction then swirled in a whirlwind around the well. 'Be sure to return before sunset on the fifth day, for the wishing-well rests nowhere for long.' Suddenly Tobias and the well were no longer visible through the thick of the multi-coloured magical snow.

Ignoring the flakes, Daniel raced into the thick of them. *I can't see a thing.* Confused by the magical flakes, he just spun and called out, 'But where will we find the treasures?'

Sara joined him in the blur, but neither Tobias nor the well could be seen, and all they heard was the voice of Tobias, deep, magical and coming from all directions at once.

'Be guided by magic of the heart and all will be revealed.' As the fading voice dwindled into silence, the questers watched with awe as the magical flakes disappeared into nothingness. And as suddenly as Tobias appeared, he, the wishing-well and the magical flakes were gone.

'He's gone. So is the well,' said Daniel.

'You don't say brother,' said Sara, 'One minute we're eating strawberries, the next we're on a magical island talking to a clown in a top-hat! *What* is going on?'

'Honestly I've no idea,' said Daniel, 'I can only think of one course of action. Let's begin the search. What do you make of this magic of the heart business?'

'I haven't a clue. I'm more concerned about the many dangers he mentioned.'

'Actually I think it's all getting very exciting.'

'Getting weirder more like. But I suppose you're right, we should begin the search. What do you make of the treasures?'

'Very odd; what do you suppose they're for?'

'Most probably for clowns.'

'Clowns?'

'Oh nothing. Let's go then. The sooner it's over, the sooner we can get home. I'm more worried about the time it will take.' Sara circled around and scanned the horizon.

'That did occur to me,' said Daniel. 'We're gone ever so long already. Mum will be going crazy if we're not home before dark, not to mention four nights.'

'I guess there is nothing we can do about it now, we'll worry about it later.'

'The first thing to do is decide which direction to head for; the second is to find some food. I'm getting a little hungry; we should have eaten more strawberries.' Daniel rubbed his tummy.

Sara rolled her eyes. 'You're always thinking of food. Weren't you listening to Tobias? The first of the treasures that you must find is the hag's staff; head towards the colourful woods yonder. So let's go that way.' *Although now that I think about it, I'm a little hungry too.*

Daniel brightened. 'That's it, Sis. We'll ask the hag if we can borrow her staff, she might even give us some food too, if we ask her nicely like.'

Sara looked at him doubtfully. 'I hope it'll be that simple.'

'Course it will,' beamed Daniel. 'Let's get going. I love adventures. It's great being in charge.'

'We're both in charge.'

Daniel wasn't listening. 'Yep, it sure is great.' *Ha-ha I've a good one.* 'Hey Sara?'

'Yes?'

'Are you the hag by any chance?'

'Shut up Daniel. Idiot.'

The pair trekked in the direction of the dark woods.

Chapter 2
Moody Woods

The questers entered under the canopy of trees.

Daniel studied their surroundings. *These woods are nothing like those around Appledown Orchards.* 'Hey Sara, see how the plants and trees are constantly changing colours. Told you, didn't I?'

'It's just not normal,' said Sara, shaking her head, 'Nothing around here is normal.'

'Why are you whispering?' asked Daniel.

'Because you are.'

'Oh. Oh yes I am. Hush then till I sus out this place.'

With no Silver Stream to follow this time, the pair left the forest edge for the deep shadow of the trees. The woods were very dense, so they travelled slowly, hopping over rotten branches and trudging through piles of fallen leaves. Like all forests, there were many noises meeting them, flapping, scampering and sometimes running. It was quite dark, for the trees were very tall with wide spreading branches blocking out much of the daylight.

'So many strange plants,' said Sara, looking around cautiously.

'Yes. I recognise some, but others I've never seen before,' said Daniel.

'It *is* quite creepy here Daniel, isn't it? It's not just me.'

'No Sara, it's not just you. There's a strange feeling, as though the forest itself is nervous.' *I can't help but feel as though we're being watched.*

'That must be it.' *I'm feeling nervous myself. Creepers!* A loud rustle sounded from the brush just a few paces behind them. They looked back only to see more forest. 'I must confess I'm a little scared,' said Sara and reached for her brother's hand.

'Don't worry Sis, there's nothing to be frightened of.' He took her hand and gave it a gentle squeeze. Suddenly a dark-green vine with small, spiked leaves shot out from a bush and coiled around Sara's ankle.

'*Aaahh!*' Sara screamed, '*Daniel, it's a snake. Help!*'

'*Hang on,*' cried Daniel, taking her by the arms and pulling her away from the vine. 'It's not a snake, Sis, it's some kind of plant. Pull your leg away as hard as you can and I'll pull your arms.' *Please don't look back.*

Sara was looking towards Daniel so she couldn't see the many other vines snaking from the bush and reaching for her. Daniel pulled with all his strength and Sara came free. As the pair tumbled backwards atop a hard mound, they caught a glance at the retreating vines slithering into the bush.

Sara gasped. 'Daniel, there were lots of them, you didn't say!'

'Oh, I didn't see the others. Just as well eh?' Daniel grinned.

'You did so Daniel Taylor… Thanks Dan,' said Sara, relieved. 'What do you think they were?'

'No idea, but from now on we keep our eyes peeled. No more surprises.' Suddenly they felt the ground lift from under them before they tumbled to the forest floor. Stumpy legs and a long snout emerged from under the mound they had landed on.

'Stay still,' hissed Daniel. The creature turned its snout towards Sara and took a few wet sniffs of her face.

'Oohh,' said Sara, unable to help herself. Uninterested the humped creature rumbled off into the forest. 'That was just gross. Eyes peeled eh Daniel. Pity it didn't slobber you.'

Daniel couldn't help but laugh, 'You scared it away, Sis. Are you sure you're not the hag?' Sara scooped up a handful of forest clay and threw it at him.

They continued through the forest and after some time came to a small clearing.

'Wait Daniel,' said Sara, 'Perhaps we should go back the way we've come. We've been searching for quite a while now. If we go too deep into the forest, we might not find our way out again. We don't know how big the forest is, so let's retrace our steps and try entering from a different point.'

'Good idea, Sis, which way *is* back though? I could swear I've seen this clearing before,' said Daniel. A chilling howl came through the branches from behind them and echoed through the canopy.

'Well it's not back that way anyway, come on,' said Sara, trembling. Hand in hand they ran with all haste, breaking through low hanging twigs, dodging trees in and out and tripping in burrows only to leap up and run all the faster.

Daniel called out as they ran, 'Was it my imagination or did the entire forest turn navy-blue during that howl?'

Sara skidded to a stop, halting Daniel with her. 'Possibly Daniel, but *that's* certainly not my imagination.' She pointed straight ahead.

Daniel's eyes widened. 'Don't move Sara. It's some kind of big lizard,' his voice betrayed more than a hint of fear.

'That thing is as big as you Daniel *and* it's got claws,' Sara's voice quivered. 'A few more paces and we'd have run into it.' The creature lay horizontally across their path. It was shaped very much like a lizard but had a scaly body and its feet forked out into three menacing claws. Turning its lizard-like head the creature regarded the questers through its slanted yellow eyes. The thin black pupils within thinned further as it flared its nostrils to test their scent. The questers gasped as one when the creature's mouth opened displaying rows of sharp teeth.

Sara rasped through the side of her mouth, 'What do we do now?'

'We, eh, we—' The canopy swayed in a wave of deep navy-blue as the chilling howl rang out across the forest again. The creature sprang up and darted off into the underbrush. Daniel and Sara looked at each other for a split second only then together they ran. They ran with reckless care for their own safety. Branches slapped them in their faces, vines snapped at their ankles and twice they charged through shin-deep pools of dark liquid. They kept going, driven by fear of the unknown. The forest whizzed by them in a blur of changing colours. Sara's red cotton cardigan snagged on a bush and tore as she ran on regardless.

Sprinting for as far as their energy would allow, they eventually slowed to a trot. They both looked skyward when they heard a rustling in the trees but all they saw was the canopy.

'Just a little further,' said Daniel breathlessly, 'I think we've put enough distance between ourselves and whatever is howling.'

'I hope we've left that scaly creature back there too,' Sara panted. She stared up into the canopy. 'This place gives me the creeps.' Finally the trees began to thin out enough to let the daylight fill their surroundings. The pair stopped and bent their arms to their knees, breathing hard.

'Thank goodness for this sunny glade,' said Sara, through deep breaths.

'Yes.' Daniel swallowed deep gulps of air. 'We've a good view in all directions. Let's rest a moment or two.' He looked at his trainers covered in muck and slime. 'So much for my trainers, they used to be grey!'

Sara studied her own. 'Mine *were* white. Not anymore though.' A light-brown hairy shape fell from overheard and stopped inches from Sara's face. *'Aaahh!'* she screamed and fell to her knees with fright.

'Aaahh!' the shape screamed back.

Daniel was standing just a step away from Sara's side and instantly made to protect her. He reached out and grabbed the creature by the throat. The creature thrashed to-and-fro but Daniel held it at arm's length. Sara quickly rolled on the ground and stood away to the side.

'Daniel,' Sara called, 'it's some kind of a monkey I think. It's hanging by its tail.' The creature broke free of Daniel's grasp and sprung back up the tree he had dropped from. He then hopped to the next tree onto a lower branch and regarded the questers through small jet-black eyes. He rubbed his paws over and back across the top of his small head while throwing cautious glances at Daniel.

'It *is* a monkey!' exclaimed Daniel, 'It doesn't look dangerous, but we best be careful.'

The small brown monkey rubbed his white-haired face once more, swung once around the branch on his long tail and sat upright. ''Course I'm a monkey, ain't I. You're a human, in't yeah, we all gotta be something.'

'It speaks!' gasped Sara.

'It speaks!' the monkey mimicked.

Daniel was wide-eyed but stayed calm. 'Magic wells, woods that change colour, plants that attack you, now a talking monkey. Sara, you know what to say.'

'Creepers.'

'Creepers is right.' *Hmm, well only one thing to do. I can't believe I'm about to do this.* 'Hey monkey, eh, what, em…' Daniel was stuck for words. *What do I say to a monkey?*

Sara came to his aid. 'Hi, em, Monkey. I hope you're okay. We don't mean you any harm.' The monkey stared at them in silence. Sara took this as permission to continue. 'This will sound strange,' *well maybe not giving that you're a talking monkey.* 'We're not from around here at all.'

'That ain't strange, obvious in't it,' the small animal interrupted.

Sara rested her hand in her chin. *He seems harmless. Worth a try.* 'Okay this is it. Maybe you can help us. We're here on a quest, in these woods I mean. We were looking for a hag. Wait, no. Actually we only want her staff. Perhaps you know where we could find her?'

'Wait,' cautioned Daniel. *He might be small but that doesn't mean he's harmless.* 'She's right, we mean you know harm. I didn't mean to hurt you. It's just that you gave us, well you gave my sister a fright. Not me though. How do we know you don't wish us ill?'

The monkey regarded them quietly for a few moments. He seemed to have reached a decision. 'Wouldn't be sitting here if I meant you harm, would I?' So saying he quickly rubbed his head and somersaulted on the branch.

Daniel still undecided stood beside Sara. *Hmm.* 'These woods, the plants and trees, the ground, everything changes colour. Can you tell us why?'

The monkey jumped and twitched nervously on the branch. 'They sense your mood, don't they? Sense the mood of all the creatures.'

'How strange,' said Daniel.

'Strange to you maybe. Strange why?' said the monkey. 'You change colour, don't you? Just now you were red in the face when you tried to kill me, now you're pink. Pink human.'

Sara giggled, 'You *did* go red Daniel.' She turned to the monkey, 'Have you got a name monkey?'

'Aahh, aahh,' cried the monkey as it scampered up the tree and back down again. 'Of course I gotta name. Ain't you?'

Sara rolled her eyes but couldn't help but smile. *I'm beginning to like this strange little fellow.* 'My name is Sara and this is my brother Daniel.'

The monkey glared at Daniel and opened his mouth, showing rows of small pointy teeth. 'Aahh, aahh. Met your brother din't I.'

Daniel was warming to the little animal too. 'Yes about that. I *am* sorry. We've had a few surprises since entering the woods. None were pleasant.'

'Shouldn't be here should you. Not safe for people. Not safe for many.' Daniel and Sara exchanged a worried look but got distracted when the monkey hopped from the tree and landed at their feet. 'Ashar's the name. Hanging monkey ain't I.' He extended his paws in a gesture of friendship. The questers shook his paws and when they let go the monkey somersaulted and leapt back up the nearest tree. He called down from the branch, 'Know where the hag is don't I. Aahh-Aahh.'

'Oh can you please tell us?' asked Sara.

'Yes,' added Daniel, 'We'd be truly grateful.' The forest rattled as another ferocious howl blasted through the trees. Leaping with fright the questers joined hands and prepared to dash but paused after a couple of steps. Ashar had hopped down from his branch and sat on the ground, unconcerned with the howl and the ripple of dark colours shimmering all around them. Unsure whether to run or not Daniel stepped back then forwards again. 'Want to come with us Ashar? That thing could be close.'

Sara pulled at Daniel's arm. 'C'mon Daniel, whatever it is it sounds simply awful. Let's get out of here.'

'Aahh, Aahh, that's just Harry. He ain't no threat to nobody,' said Ashar, 'Except flowers maybe.' The questers hesitated.

'Harry?' asked Sara, 'But why does he howl so?' Ashar's head snapped up, alert and listening.

He sniffed the air and bared his teeth momentarily. 'He's a howler in't he, howlers howl.' The monkey seemed distracted.

Sara didn't notice. 'It sounds so awful.'

'Wouldn't you if you forgot who you were? Aahh,' said Ashar.

'How did he do that?' asked Daniel.

'Ate some lilac vipers, din't he,' said Ashar, 'thought they were tulips he did.' Ashar grew more unsettled but when the questers exchanged a puzzled look he continued. 'The vipers make you forget what you were doing, where you were going, even who you are!'

'That sounds simply terrible,' said Sara, 'I've never heard of lilac vipers.'

'Humans call them forget-me-lots,' said Ashar.

'Forget-me-lots?' said Daniel, 'I've never heard of *those* either.'

'I think he means forget-me-nots,' offered Sara helpfully.

Ashar bounded several leaps back the way they had come from, spun in a circle and bounced back again. 'Forgotten have ya? Flowers ain't they. Forget, forget-me-nots, forget-me-lots are what Harry ate. Aahh-aahh.'

Daniel leaned into Sara and whispered, 'He's a little crazy Sara.'

Ashar spun in a circle. 'You say. I ain't the one wandering around drawing nasty attention to myself.' Daniel's face reddened with embarrassment. 'Got good hearing too, don't I,' the monkey added. Ashar's head turned quickly and he stared back through the woods in the direction the questers had come.

Daniel noticed the monkey's movements. *He seems concerned about something back there.*

Sara still hadn't noticed. 'So what will happen to poor Harry if he can't remember who he is?'

Ashar bared his teeth. 'Who can say? The vipers wear off eventually don't they, familiar surroundings, familiar faces always help. Maybe when he hears his own kind, he'll remember who he is.'

'His own kind, you mean howlers then?' Sara asked, ever curious, 'Are there others hereabouts?'

Ashar became frantic. 'Holwers don't belong in Moody Woods, do they? The open plains is their home. Aahh-Aahh, chit-chat yap, yap. Forest isn't safe.'

Daniel frowned. *Does he mean for us or for Harry, I wonder… He's getting impatient, something is definitely bothering him.*

Sara continued, 'Where *are* his own kind?'

'Aahh-aahh, too many questions girl. His herd's gone roaming ain't they.'

'I'm sorry Ashar,' said Sara, startled, 'I won't ask any more about the howlers.'

Ashar leaped up into a tree, back down and spun in a circle while waving his paws in the air. 'The howler is no threat to you. No threat, Aahh. Can't say that about the others though, can I. Danger, dangerous. Aahh-aahh.'

'*Others?*' the questers blurted together.

'Being tracked by a group of gizord, ain't ya. Following your scent they are. Not hard is it.'

Sara took a moment to be offended. 'We don't smell. Well I don't anyway.'

Untroubled with the notion of smelling Daniel's mind worked quickly. *Gizord, Lizard-like creature. Coincidence? Hardly.* 'These gizords, scaly things are they? Green with long tails and claws?'

'Gizord looks like a gizord. Aahh,' said Ashar, 'But if you must waste time with chit-chat you can say it the long way.' Ashar's head darted to-and-fro.

Sara quickly forgot the smelling insult at the mention of the gizords. 'A group of them? We only saw one and that was way back.'

'Saw a scout din't ya, one is trouble, many is death. Not way back now. Close, ain't they. Nasty gizords.' An unmistakable hissing snarl followed from the direction the siblings had come to the glade.

'If that's them, they still sound some distance away,' said Daniel rather doubtfully.

Ashar leapt up and down frantically. 'Aahh-Aahh. Closer than you think ain't they. Away now and find your hag. Quickly, give me something with your scent.' Without waiting the monkey scrambled up Sara's shoulders and took a light scarf she'd been wearing around her neck.

'What are you doing?' asked Daniel as Ashar came to him and started tugging at his blue hooded-top.

Sara already guessed. *He's going to lead the gizords away. Brave little monkey.* 'Quickly Daniel, give him your t-shirt. Keep your hoody.'

Daniel quickly removed his hooded top and t-shirt. Ashar grabbed the t-shirt and ran several paces back towards the snarling which sounded much closer now. Stopping in a clear patch the monkey pressed the scarf and t-shirt to the ground and began dragging them round in a circle.

Ashar called back to the siblings. 'Aahh. No time. I'll distract them, go now. See those two chestnut trees over there?' The questers looked to their right. In the distance two large chestnut trees grew side by side, the trunk of each tree bending towards the other. Ashar continued, 'Go between them and follow the silk trail. That'll take you to the hag. She don't speak, mind. Aahh-aahh. Not all is as it seems in these woods. Go now.'

Sara fretted, 'What about you?'

'Don't worry 'bout Ashar. They never got me, yet did they? Go now, hurry.'

Daniel looked at Sara. *Hmm, it doesn't feel right leaving him but I won't risk Sara's safety if I can help it.* 'We'll go. And Ashar, thank you for doing this. How can we repay you?'

'Ashar don't need repaying do I. Go now. But if you see howlers on your travels maybe you can come find Harry. This ain't no place for a gentle giant like him.' Ashar continued running in circles dragging the clothes along the forest floor. With each circuit he'd spread the circle bigger.

'We will. We promise,' said Daniel. The sound of loud vicious snarling made the questers jump and together they turned and ran towards the chestnut trees.

After a few paces Sara shouted, 'Wait a moment.' She turned back towards Ashar and called out, 'What do howlers look like?' But the monkey was gone. The questers just caught a fleeting glimpse of him scampering in the opposite direction to where they were headed. He disappeared into the distant undergrowth, still dragging the t-shirt and scarf behind him. Wasting no more time they turned and dashed for the chestnut trees.

Reaching the chestnut trees Daniel looked back once more, just in time to see several gizords in the distance leaping into the underbrush exactly where Ashar had disappeared.

Chapter 3
Silk and Silhouettes

The questers stepped between the two trees and into a denser area of the woods.

'Gosh,' said Sara, 'It's as though the trees mark an entrance into this part of the forest. There's hardly any daylight getting through this side.'

Hmm, an entrance to what though, thought Daniel. 'We'll just have to make do. Ashar said to follow the silk trail, once we find it that should take us to the hag.'

Sara worried. 'Daniel, what do you suppose Ashar meant about "not all is as it seems in these woods"?'

'I don't know, Sis. The hag probably changes colour too, or something like that! Nothing would surprise me in this place.'

Sara bit her bottom lip. She was not entirely convinced. 'Daniel?'

'Yes Sara?'

'Will he be alright? Ashar.'

'Let's hope so. He can climb, can't he? Those gizords only seem to move along the ground. Don't worry, he'll be fine.' *I hope you're okay brave little Ashar.* 'C'mon, let's find this silk trail then.'

All around them trees of every shape and size grew close together. The branches spread and twisted in all directions and locked together with branches from neighbouring trees. The undergrowth was heavy too, packed with clusters of thorny bushes, leafy plants and giant nettles. There was very little bare ground for the pair to walk on.

'Stay behind me,' Daniel said as he navigated around trees and between dense brush.

I've no other choice do I, thought Sara. There wasn't room for them to walk side by side.

After a short while of ducking below branches, scrambling through gaps and getting stung and pricked, Daniel paused, 'Finally, the path is a bit wider here. C'mon Sara, keep up. Still no sign of the silk trail though.'

'Grrr,' Sara snapped, 'How do you expect me to keep up when you seem bent upon dragging me through every nettle patch in this awful forest?' She struggled between two twisted branches. '*Aaahh.* Now look what you made me do.' She had lost her grip, slipped and lay on her back on the forest floor.

Daniel giggled, '*Come* on Sara. We *only* have four nights to complete the quest.'

'It's not funny,' said Sara, annoyed, 'I'm pricked and stung, I'm tired and hungry and I'm not getting up!'

Daniel rolled his eyes. 'Sara this is no time for you to go all stubborn. Want the gizords to catch up with us, do you? Let me help you up.' Daniel reached an arm down to help her.

Sara's expression changed to one of surprise and she slapped Daniel's arm aside. 'Wait, Daniel. I said I'm not getting up yet.' She stared into the branches overhead.

'What are you playing at Sara? I'm serious, we don't have all day.'

Sara pointed up at the treetops. 'So am I Daniel. Come down here and look up into the branches.'

Daniel joined his sister on the ground. 'Well, what am I supposed to be looking at? Trees in a forest? Surprise-surprise!'

'There's no need to be smart Daniel. Look there just below the canopy. There's a thin silky thread joining branch to branch. It could be the silk trail Ashar was talking about.'

'Gosh, you're right. Sorry Sara.' The pair fell silent for a few moments and followed the path of the thread with their eyes.

Sara made to get up. 'Let's follow it to see where it leads.'

Daniel rose slowly, staring intently at the thread. 'Wow. Look Sara, there's movement on the thread. It's actually a web and there are tiny spiders crawling along it.'

'Wow,' echoed Sara, on closer inspection, 'Silk spiders! Their little feet are weaving tiny strands of silk. Amazing.' The silk spiders were barely visible as their tiny feet zoomed back and forth over the silken strands of web.

'We follow the web then. Good work Sara, I knew you had some use!' said Daniel, good-naturedly.

Distracted, Sara replied, 'Thanks Dan.' *I wonder what mood the spiders are in.* She was fascinated watching the spiders; as their legs spun the web-strands, the branch underneath danced with tiny silver sparkles.

They followed the web around trees and under branches, along thorny briars and through a bunch of blooming flowers. The web-strands led them into a patch of strange purple plants with long stingy shoots and bulb-head tops. The bulb-heads hissed as the questers passed, giving off a pungent smell that stung their eyes and caused them to sneeze. Still they went on.

As he walked Daniel watched the tiny creatures at work. *Amazing. I must remember never to stamp on a bug again. Well I'll never stamp on a spider again anyway!*

After a stretch of particularly dense undergrowth they rounded a large oak tree to find a small enclosed clear patch.

'The silk trail stops at this tree,' said Daniel, puzzled. He studied the surrounding branches closely. 'It's a dead end,' he groaned, 'The only way to go is back.' To the left and right the bush was too thick for them to go through. All that was in front of them was an old gnarled tree with no leaves. The tree was a mass of twisted branches.

Sara rested her chin in her hand. 'Back *seems* to be the only way to go. But remember what Ashar said "things are not always what they seem in these woods."'

Daniel was doubtful. 'Well I don't see any hag, or her staff. The web definitely stops here and all *I* see is a dead-end.' Suddenly from behind the old tree came a brilliant shining light.

'Wow,' the questers chorused together as they looked at the fantastic sight before them. Behind the tree was a massive silk spider-web, woven in the most detailed patterns. The patterns stood out as the light shone through the web's many designs.

'It's beautiful,' said Sara.

'It's sunlight,' said Daniel as he stared at the spider's masterpiece. 'It's like a curtain made purely from silk web.'

Sara's brow knitted into a frown. 'I'm guessing the other side of that web is our way out, yet we still haven't found the hag's staff. We can either leave now or go back and keep looking.' *We've been in here quite long enough though.* 'Those gizords Daniel. Poor Ashar,' she added, her tone sad.

'Now-now Sara,' said Daniel. Ever protective he walked over to Sara and put his arms on her shoulders. 'Ashar wouldn't have risked himself to those gizords only to send us this way for nothing. We've not had sight nor sound of one in ages, have we?'

Sara sniffled, 'No, s'pose not.'

'Right then. I say we retrace our steps and see if the silk trail branched off anywhere in another direction. Eh?' *I'm worried about Ashar too. But when she's upset, I'll only make her worse by showing it.*

'S'pose,' Sara reluctantly said again. *He thinks he fools me. He's sorry for the monkey too.*

'Good. C'mon then, we'll pick up the trail in no time.' Daniel made his way back to the big oak tree and turned to beckon Sara to follow. His eyes widened with surprise. 'Quickly, come over here a moment. What's that you said about not finding the hag?'

Curious, Sara hurried over beside him. Daniel, eager, took her arm and stepped back a few more paces. He didn't take his eyes off the silk web with the beams of light breaking through.

'Now take a look at the outline of that old tree; what does it look like?' asked Daniel. As the beams of light shone through the web, they broke around the old twisted tree. 'See the shape of the trunk along with those twisted branches? It creates a silhouette of a cloaked old woman hunching over.'

Sara's bottom lip dropped. 'Gosh. And where the light breaks over that particular branch, it looked like she's leaning on a staff! You're a genius Daniel,' she squealed excitedly.

He grinned. 'Well I don't like to brag.'

With a run and a dive, the pair went for the branch at the same time. Colliding into each other they fell, arms outstretched and grabbed it. The branch gave easily with the force of their fall and together they crashed forwards, fumbled, and broke through the silk web.

Lying on the grass with the sun in their eyes the questers brushed strands of web off their clothes with one hand, and with the other hand they both still clutched the hag's staff. They looked at it and then at each other and smiled with delight.

'Gosh,' said Sara, surprised, 'It feels quite strong considering that it broke so easily when we fell on it.'

'Indeed,' agreed Daniel. *It should be rotted through.* 'And see how it gleams in the sunlight, so smooth and brown, not rotten at all. What a strange treasure. A staff, it's really just a stick.' He helped Sara off the ground.

'Yes, it is a strange treasure,' said Sara, 'Jewels and gems, that's treasure, but a staff! Hey, perhaps Tobias wants it for himself. He did seem kind of ancient!'

'Ha-ha, true.' *Although I meant the rich smooth texture of the wood is strange. The way it feels.* 'Hey Sara, that Ashar was a crafty monkey eh? Remember he said the hag doesn't speak; he knew it was a tree all along.'

At the mention of Ashar Sara's lip quivered and she looked at the ground. 'Poor Ashar.'

Daniel frowned and looked down too. *Shoot. I shouldn't have mentioned Ashar again.* 'We have a lot to thank him for,' he said quietly. Daniel didn't like to dwell long on gloomy thoughts. 'Hey Sara, I guess you're not the hag after all. Fancy that!'

Sara smiled at her brother's efforts to cheer her. 'You...you pink, human clown,' she jeered back and punched him in the arm.

Daniel returned her smile. 'Easy now.' He rubbed his arm in mock pain. 'That's my good arm.'

Sara smirked. 'Show me the other one.'

Daniel rubbed his stomach while scanning his surroundings. 'Well now we have the staff; where to next? I'm starving. It really is a shame that we didn't eat more in the orchard. I'd nearly eat that cooking apple this minute.'

'I'm hungry too, but there doesn't look like much to eat around here.' Sara looked all around her.

Behind them were the woods spreading far into the distance in both directions. In front a small shrubby meadow was all that separated them from a huge rocky mountain. Peaks and plateaus climbed away to the sides and up as far as the eye could see.

Hmm. 'Looks like we've only two choices, up the mountains or back through the woods,' said Daniel. A distant chorus of growls and snarls came to the questers' ears from somewhere within the woods. Daniel looked back through the trees and quickly changed his mind. 'Correction, we've only got one choice. I'm not going back in there.'

'Then it's not a choice is it,' replied Sara, gloomy once again.

'Huh?'

'Oh nothing. I s'pose we'll have to go up the mountain then. Although, it doesn't look like the kind of place to find food, or anything else for that matter.'

'What's up Sis? We've left those creepy woods, haven't we? We have the hag's staff already and it's only a matter of time before we find the other treasures. We're having a real adventure, isn't that what you wanted?'

'Don't remind me! Next time I'll play football.'

'Chin up, Sara. We're bound to find the nourishing stone somewhere on the mountain; it seems like just the place; mountains are made of stone after all.'

Sara rolled her eyes. 'Your genius knows no bounds brother.'

Daniel wasn't listening. 'Or maybe even the shard of the dragon's tooth; it could be up here either.'

'That's what I'm afraid of,' Sara mumbled to herself. *Gizords and howlers are bad enough, a dragon doesn't bear thinking about.*

'What's that Sis?'

'I said when we find the dragon you can take the tooth Daniel, I'm easy with that.'

'Gee, thanks.'

'Don't mention it.' The pair began across the shrubby meadow, not rushing, as they didn't really know what direction to go.

Chapter 4
The Rocky Rise

The air was fresh and the sun was shining brightly, so it was not long before Sara's humour brightened. To further cheer her, just as they approached the foot of the mountain, she found what she thought to be a patch of baby onions.

Daniel scrunched up his nose. 'Don't expect me to eat those; they taste worse than garlic.'

'No one is asking you to eat anything, it just means more for me.' Sara stooped to pluck herself one. 'Oh, how strange,' she said, surprised, as her hand closed around thin air. She tried again, and again the leafy stalk vanished. One by one the stalks vanished as though they were sucked into the ground. Daniel laughed as Sara chased around the disappearing onion patch trying in vain to catch one.

Soon they were all gone and she sat on the ground defeated. 'I don't like onions much anyway,' she said.

'I don't think they like you either,' giggled Daniel, 'Come on, let's keep moving.'

After a few paces the questers could hear a sound like bubbling water. Turning, they saw the whole patch of small onions out of the ground and following them on tiny little legs. The onions stopped still.

'How cute,' said Sara, as she studied their tiny features; each of them had little black dots for eyes, no noses and little circular mouths.

Daniel gazed in disbelief. 'Who'd have thought there was such a thing as walking, talking onions, and what a funny sound they make.'

The little-legged plants all made their bubbly noises together and moved as one in the direction of a boulder that rested close by. The noises got louder until from up behind the boulder stood an old man. The adventurers stared in silence at the man who supported himself with a wooden hook and was dressed in a long, brown robe.

'What is it my little ones, is danger afoot?' said the stranger with urgency. The old man raised his hands out, as if to calm the strange, little plants. With this one motion the onion-like creatures fell silent. Alert, the old man turned slowly and raised his eyebrows when he saw the questers. 'My goodness, so you're what all the commotion is about.' He relaxed and walked towards them, still talking, 'I'm Zac the goat herder. We don't usually see people hereabouts, especially young ones.'

Sara's eyes were fixed on his long white hair and beard. She leaned into Daniel and whispered, 'He must be ancient, his beard is down to his waist.'

'At least he's human,' Daniel whispered back. *And if need be, judging by those skinny ankles and sandals we'll out-run him easily over these rocks.*

Despite his sandals and skinny ankles, the old man quickly reached them with sure-footed strides and extended a bony hand to Daniel. 'I'm Zac,' he repeated, 'Welcome to the Rocky Rise.'

Cautiously Daniel shook his hand. 'I'm Daniel Taylor and this is my sister Sara.'

Zac let go of Daniel's hand and shook Sara's. 'Hello young lady. Sister and brother eh? I'd wager you're here on serious business, that or you're lost. The Rise is no place for wandering youths.' Unsure whether they could trust him Daniel and Sara exchanged a cautious glance.

Sara changed the subject with the first thing that came into her head, 'Where are your goats?'

The old man smiled a friendly grin. 'Why they're sleeping, out there in the shrubs.' He pointed out towards the shrubby meadow. 'And that's what I'd be doing too if not for my loyal bonions who came and woke me. They're so alert, don't you think?'

'Surely you mean onions?' asked Daniel. The bubbly murmur rose again and the old fellow laughed.

'Hee-hee, forgive my laughter,' said Zac, 'even the bonions think that's funny. Surely, you've never seen a walking onion before, or a talking one for that matter. No, these are my patch of bubbling bonions; a goat herder's pride and joy.'

'No,' admitted Daniel, 'I've never seen a walking, talking onion before, but I've never seen a *bonion* either. What do they do exactly?'

'They help me tend the goats. By sinking their heads into the earth, they can feel vibrations of anything approaching. This is why my patch is so useful while the goats are snoozing in the shrubs. If there is anything unusual or dangerous, the bonions alert me straight away.'

The questers listened keenly.

'And you say they talk, Mr Zac; is that what they're doing when we hear that bubbling noise?' asked Sara, 'And do you know what they're saying?'

'Why yes, that noise you hear is their speech,' replied Zac, 'and while I don't speak their language, we understand each other well enough. This patch has been with me since I was young, Daniel's age.'

Sara raised her eyebrows. 'You can remember that far back?'

This won a warm chuckle from the old man. 'Ho-ho, and a lot more besides. Say, would you like to see them in action?'

Sara looked to Daniel who shrugged, then back to Zac. 'Sure, why not. They are kind of cute. In the last while we've dealt with slimy, snouty creatures, hanging monkeys and gizords, I think we can handle a few little bonion thingies.'

Zac suddenly turned serious. 'What did you say young lady? Gizords. When? Where?'

Sara swallowed, shocked by the sudden change of tone.

Alarmed by Zac's reaction, Daniel sensed worry in the old man's words. 'Not long ago. Back there in the woods. A group of them were tracking us until…' he hesitated, 'until we lost them.'

Zac's brow furrowed as he regarded the siblings intently for a few moments. 'You did well to lose a group of gizord, but gizord are determined and vicious predators and it won't be long till they pick up the scent again. We have to get to higher ground quickly.'

The questers' faces betrayed their feelings.

I was hoping we saw the last of those gizords, thought Daniel fearfully.

Oh dear, they're even worse than I imagined, poor Ashar, Sara fretted.

Zac noticed their expressions and seemed to guess their recent experience must have been a frightening one. 'Worried eh? The slopes are no place for wanderers whatever your business, you two would be safest coming with me.'

Daniel protectively stepped closer to Sara and nodded. 'We'll come.'

Slapping his hands together, Zac announced, 'Good, it's settled. We'll just wake up the goats and make haste.'

The old man's eyes twinkled as he outstretched his hands and whistled a few low notes from his lips. Following the whistle, the bonions leaped to attention, they spread out in a line either side of him and faced the shrubs. He then raised his arms and dropped them again and blew a shrill whistle. At this signal the bonions took off into the shrubs at a speed surprisingly fast for their small size. The bonions could be heard making their bubbly noises while darting between the plants; and it wasn't long before goats could be seen getting to their feet and shaking their sleepy heads.

'The bonions will round them up. We'll make our own way,' said Zac as he turned towards the mountain.

'Where are we going?' wondered Daniel.

'Higher ground young man, where the gizords can't reach us. You're welcome to my cave for supper if you wish, that's further on again. But first things first, let's get out of here.'

Sara stopped. 'Cave! You live in a cave?'

'Oh yes, the best shelter on the mountain, I live in a cave with my wife Gertie; you'll like her, she's a great cook and the cave is quite cosy, I assure you.' The goat herder paced ahead.

Sara threw Daniel a questioning look. He stepped close to her and whispered. 'I know, you're wondering if we can trust him. We don't need to go to his cave, but we'll follow him to higher ground at least. He seems as worried about the gizords as we do.'

'Fine, but if anything goes wrong it's your fault,' Sara whispered back. 'You're in charge after all.'

'We both are. Besides, you never know, he might be able to lead us to the dragon.'

'Marvellous.' *Not.*

Zac had moved several paces ahead of them. He stopped and called back, 'Are you coming then? Time passes.' The questers marked the urgency in his voice and began to follow.

The goats had already begun the climb and were easily hopping across the lower, rocky slopes. Each goat had a small patch of bonions at their hind legs herding them along. A gentle, bubbling noise murmured in their wake.

'Wait,' said Sara after a few paces. 'What about this little one?'

Zac turned to see one of the bonions swaying on its tiny legs in front of Sara; he picked it up and stroked it affectionately before putting it down again. 'Why I do believe this one has decided to be your guide; make sure and follow carefully, as these rocks can be very unsafe.' The little bonion darted from rock to rock and the questers quickly realised it was directing them where to place their feet.

'Amazing,' said Daniel aloud.

Sara was fascinated watching Zac, as from time to time he'd tap an odd stone with his hook. *Wow, he's so sure-footed for such an old man. And he doesn't even need a bonion to guide him. I must ask him how-,* her train of thought was suddenly interrupted by a chorus of vicious hissing and snarling. The goats bolted up the mountain in great big leaps.

'*Gizords!*' Daniel and Sara cried together.

'And dangerously close,' warned Zac. 'Your choices are few. Join me for supper or *be* the gizords supper.' There was no humour in his tone. The questers needed no encouragement; they leapt from rock to rock till they reached Zac's side.

'What about your goats?' asked Daniel.

'Mountain goats are among the best creatures at climbing rock,' offered Sara.

'Your sister is correct about the goats,' said Zac. 'And you would both do well to copy them. They'll make for the next plateau which is above that rise of rocks.' Zac pointed ahead. 'The gizords are fast on the flat stone, but their claws get caught when they climb and it slows them down. Be warned though, it doesn't stop them.'

Not far ahead of them the flat stones gave way to a wall of chiselled rocks rising straight up twenty feet in the air. As they approached the wall the questers leapt with fright as gizord snarling sounded right behind them.

Zac spun in a full circle and urged the pair on. *'Don't look back, just run to the wall and climb!'*

Daniel and Sara looked back. *'Aaahh!'* they both screamed.

They stopped were they stood, momentarily frozen to the spot with terror. The gizords were almost upon them; six in all, snarling, hissing and gnashing with their slimy tongues darting in and out between razor-sharp teeth.

'Run!' roared Zac from halfway up the wall. His roar snapped the questers from their shock and they bolted after him.

Daniel glanced to Zac's position and thought to himself, *Gosh, the old man can certainly climb.* Zac was racing up the wall of rocks with arm-leg to arm-leg movements. Reaching the wall ahead of Sara, Daniel threw the hag's staff like a spear up to the plateau above. He jumped and wedged his foot into a gap at waist height and launched himself up after Zac. Sara tried to copy Daniel's jump but her foot just came short and she hit the rock and fell backwards, landing hard on her back.

Sara screamed. *'Aaahh!'*

'Sara!' roared Daniel as he jumped back down and quickly knelt beside her. 'Sara, are you hurt?' He put one hand on her shoulder and took her hand in the other. 'Let me help you up.'

'I'm okay, I just got a fright,' replied Sara, rubbing her knee.

Daniel raised his head in horror. One gizord had broken ahead of the group and was stopped inches away from him. Its yellow eyes glared, its forked tongue dripping with foamy ooze sped in and out between sharp teeth and a low hiss rasped from deep within its throat.

'Stay very still,' whispered Daniel.

The blood drained from Sara's face, terrified as she locked eyes with the creature.

The gizord bared its talons and pounced. Out of somewhere a shepherd's hook smashed into the side of the gizord's head, so close to Daniel's face that he felt the wind on his nose.

'Climb you two, climb!' roared Zac. The old goat herder had leaped down from the wall to their aid. 'Young lady, are you okay to climb?'

'I'm just a bit bruised,' Sara managed, her voice wavering.

'Quickly then, we'll give you a boost up.' Daniel and Zac boosted Sara up to the foot wedge and she began the assent. Daniel immediately followed.

Zac turned to face the group of gizords which were now upon him. 'Back off mud-breaths,' he cried and swung his hook at the advancing creatures. They scattered a few paces back and Zac stole the moment to leap up the wall and climb after the questers. He reached the plateau just as Daniel hoisted his legs over the last rock.

Sara was sitting back from the edge and breathing hard. 'Mr Zac sir. Thank you, that's all I can say. Thank you.'

Daniel spun to see the old man crest the rock beside him. 'You made it, and so fast. How?' he said, puzzled.

'We're not out of the woods yet young man. See to your sister and I'll put a stop to these ghastly beasts.'

'You all right, Sis?'

'I'll live Dan.'

Dan nodded. 'She'll live. Can I help?'

Zac was peering over the edge and poking his hook down between some of the outer rocks. Daniel joined him and peered over too. He leapt back with fright. The gizords where making their way up the wall, slowly but surely.

'It slows them down, but doesn't stop them,' Zac reminded them. 'But you *can* help young man. Fetch that stick you threw up here, we can use it as leverage.'

'Leverage?' asked Daniel as he retrieved the hag's staff, still in one piece despite been thrown on the mountain.

'No time for questions,' said Zac. 'Give it here.' Zac had locked his hook between two sizable rocks on top of the wall. Daniel handed him the staff, which he placed horizontally across the top of his own hook. The two sticks made a cross shape. Zac rolled up his sleeves and swung his beard over his shoulder. 'Now Daniel, take the other side of your stick and when I say pull, pull!'

Daniel obeyed.

'Pull!' shouted Zac.

Nothing gave.

'Maybe I can help,' offered Sara. She joined Daniel.

Zac nodded. 'Again, *now pull!*'

The hook bent slightly and the rocks that held it gave way. They rolled loose and tumbled down the wall catching several other rocks on the way down.

Zac held his arm out directing the questers back from the edge as the crash and tumble of rocks could be heard below followed by choked hisses and snarls. The noise ceased and a small cloud of dust sailed up the mountainside. All three stepped forwards and cautiously peered over the edge.

Zac counted the bodies among the fallen rocks. 'Two, three and wait, four and five, yes I make it five.'

'Six Mr Zac,' said Sara, pointing back the way they'd came. Retreating towards the shrubs was one gizord. Its body was bloody and it limped along slowly.

Zac smiled with relief. 'And a broken leg for his trouble. Good show folks. He won't be bothering us again, I'll see to that.'

Daniel and Sara exchanged glances and nodded to one another.

'Eh Zac, sir,' Daniel began.

The old man's eyes twinkled. 'I know lad. No need to say it. You're welcome.' The siblings couldn't help but smile. The goat herder had won their trust.

'Now what about that supper?' said Zac. 'With all that action I've built up quite an appetite. What do you say?'

Knowing what her brother would say Sara spoke for both of them. 'That would be lovely Mr Zac. We *are* a little hungry.' *Cave or no cave, I'm famished.*

'And fed you'll be. Now fetch that stick of yours and we'll be on our way.'

The plateau was mostly flat and spread about ninety paces front to back. At the back the mountain rose up straight again, many times higher than the wall they had just scaled. Jutting out above the back of the plateau was a large outcrop of rock which served as a roof and huddled beneath it were Zac's goats. Next to the goats sat the patch of bonions, their green appearance standing out against the grey of the rock.

Sara was curious. 'Excuse me Mr Zac, how come you didn't need a bonion to guide you over the rocks?'

Zac stopped, leaned on his staff and sighed before answering. 'Well my friends it's like this: I've been on these mountains for many a long year and know them well; this great rock has revealed to me many secrets, but you must remember that my wisdom of the mountains is not complete nor will it ever be. These mountains change just as we do. It may be a slower process, but it changes just the same. From the smallest insect to the darkest storm cloud, from the greenest leaf to the rocks on this mountain everything is on a journey each to their own. This is why even I, Zac of the Rocky Rise, must check the stones along the paths that I've walked on all my life, to make sure they are still okay for me to use on my journey.'

Daniel and Sara listened silently, impressed by Zac's wisdom.

The goat herder smiled warmly. 'Now then, almost there, and not before time. Gone is the day when I'd be up and down these slopes three times before breakfast, and that would be just for fun.'

The questers followed him under the outcrop of rock and through the herd of goats.

'They seem quite content,' noticed Daniel.

'Why wouldn't they,' replied Zac. 'My good friend Bison stands guard at the cave entrance first and foremost, but if he senses a threat to the goats on the plateau, well let's just say he makes his presence known.'

A deep, throaty growl sounded and the questers leapt with fright.

Zac didn't seem to notice. 'Bison is a Rockwilder. He's with me since he was a pup. Mark though, never his master only his friend.' The goats parted to let the group through and standing at the entrance to the cave was an enormous black dog. His head was large and round, fronted by powerful jaws.

Daniel gulped. 'He's…eh he's huge. Twice as big as your biggest goats. Don't you mean Rottweiler? Although, I've never seen a Rottweiler this big.'

'Eh?' said Zac. 'No young man. Bison is a Rockwilder and that's no mistake.'

'Creepers,' said Sara, staring at the bulging muscles on the dog's torso.

'No, definitely a Rockwilder,' Zac said a third time. Then shaking his head he muttered, 'Strange children.'

The massive dog sat without a fuss when Zac patted him on the head as they entered the cave. Daniel and Sara followed nervously. Zac held the hook out to the dog's nose. Bison sniffed eagerly and his ear pricked up.

'Hiss-hiss. Go get 'm boy,' said Zac, pointing back the way they had come. The Rockwilder took off in great bounding leaps and within a few strides disappeared over the edge.

'Will he hunt down the last gizord?' Sara guessed.

'The last of that group anyway,' said Zac. 'A lame gizord can be even more dangerous. Bison will make short work of it. I can't have it lurking down there in the shrubs.'

'Why don't you bring Bison along to graze?' wondered Daniel.

Zac raised a finger. 'When danger is close a worthier companion you could not ask for, but the Rocky Rise is a dangerous place. Gizords are not the only threat hereabouts. Bison guards the cave and the plateau from many unwelcome visitors. Only at times such as this will I ask him to leave his post.' The questers exchanged a worried look.

Zac noticed their faces. 'Don't fret though. Nothing will trouble us while he's away, his scent is strong and he won't be long. Come now, supper awaits us.'

It grew darker with each step the further they got from the cave's mouth and Sara was just reaching for Daniel's hand when there was a bright flash. Their surroundings lit up to reveal Zac holding a bulrush with its head on fire.

The group took three steps onward when a swarm of small, black creatures flew through the cave and past their heads. Daniel and Sara crouched down as the flutter of leathery wings whizzed by.

'*Aaah!*' Sara screeched.

'*Bats!*' Daniel shouted as the last of them flew past.

'Aye. Bats, confirmed Zac, not alarmed. 'The mountain is full of them. They mean you no harm, not those kind anyway.' The goat herder gave the siblings no time to consider his words. 'Come along then. You can carry the torch young man.' Zac handed the burning plant to Daniel.

Daniel beamed with his new responsibility and held it sure and steady. He noticed the dark stone in Zac's hand. 'Did you light the torch with that stone?'

'Well spotted, Daniel.' Zac was clearly enjoying the company. 'This is flint and when smacked against the cave wall it creates a spark. The spark lights the head of the bulrush, which is soaked in oil.'

Daniel glanced at Sara. *Hmm. She's still nervous, can't blame her in these creepy caves. Best if she has something to do.* 'Say Zac, could you let Sara carry the flint; she'd be very careful.'

'What a splendid idea, you can both help.' Zac handed Sara the flint.

Sara brightened instantly with her new task. She leaned up to her brother and whispered, 'Thanks for remembering we're both in charge.'

Daniel grinned. 'I thought I was now?'

'We both are.' Sara smiled back.

Zac overheard them and smiled too.

They ventured through the cave, stopping occasionally to light more torches that were fixed to holes in the cave wall.

'It must be strange living in a cave,' said Sara as they approached a turn in the cavern.

They rounded the turn and heard a lady's voice humming mildly.

Zac raised a hand to his ear. 'My Gertie has the most beautiful voice, don't you agree?'

The cavern opened up into a large chamber, lit up by a small fire in at the rear that threw out plenty of light. More entrances could be seen dancing in the flickering shadow around the edges. Sitting on a cushion a small distance from the flames sat a lady; she was stirring a large pot and smiled as she looked up.

'It's not so strange pretty one,' she said to Sara. If she felt any surprise at the arrival of two adventurers in her cave, her face hid it well. 'There were once many cave dwellers; too few now though alas.' She stood and motioned them over. 'I heard your footfalls echo through the cave. It's rare for Zac to bring company. Please, sit.'

Zac nodded to the pair and gestured towards cushions on the floor. 'I wish it was under better circumstances my dear. Gizord attack, my young friends here showed great courage.' The questers blushed with the praise.

'We did nothing really. It was all Zac,' said Daniel, extending his hand to Gertie. 'I'm Daniel, and this is my sister Sara.'

Sara was enchanted by Gertie's appearance. *What long, beautiful hair she has, so white and full,* she thought. *And her green eyes sparkle like jewels.* Gertie wore sandals similar to Zac's and a long woollen frock from shoulder to ankle, and tied round her waist was a blue, silken scarf. 'It's nice to meet you Ms Gertie. May I say you have lovely hair,' she said as she shook Gertie's hand.

'Yes and a sweet voice,' added Daniel, blushing afresh, equally captivated by Gertie.

At this Gertie waved her head and laughed mildly, showing perfect snow-white teeth. 'Why it's nice to meet you too; what pleasant folk you are. Please sit and take a bowl. We'll all have stew, and I'll tell you why we live in a cave.'

The questers watched as Gertie spooned out the delicious-smelling stew. *It's impossible to guess her age*, thought Daniel. Soon they were enjoying the food, each sitting on a cushion side by side.

Gertie placed her bowl in her lap and began. 'We're two of the last cave dwellers on the island. We once belonged to a community of cave dwellers, but most have since moved on.'

'Where to?' asked Daniel while chewing on a tender piece of meat.

Gertie's eyes turned sad. 'Some fled to the lowlands. Some disappeared over the Rise never to be seen again. And some died in their caves.'

Zac continued, 'The slopes are dangerous nowadays my new friends, but that wasn't always the case. The Rise was a safer place once upon a time, where we cave dwellers lived in peace.'

Sara searched the eyes of the old couple. 'Gosh, was the peace threatened somehow?'

'Indeed my pretty one,' replied Gertie as she put down her bowl. 'Danger fell on us unawares from the other side of the Rise. There were many attacks. We the cave dwellers lost much of our livestock, our homes and many dear friends.'

'Was it gizords?' asked Daniel.

Zac replied in low tones. 'Gizords, aye it was, and many more creatures besides.'

Sara's brow furrowed. 'It sounds awful. Why didn't you flee to the lowlands?'

Zac welcomed the question. 'The goats are why we stayed. We're goat herders plain and simple; it's what we know and love. We'll stay here as

46

cave dwellers for as long as we can protect our flock.' The questers waited expectantly so Zac continued with a twinkle in his eye. 'The goats need the mountains. They climb the rocks of the Rise to have their young. There's plenty of shelter for their kids among the rocks, and the springs of fresh water that flow down the slopes are the best on the island so there's always plenty for them to drink. The goat's main food is the wild shrub that grows at the foot of the mountain. They live for the mountains and so for them we stay, despite the many dangers that threaten our way of life.'

Gertie smiled while Zac spoke of the goats, sharing her fondness for their chosen way of life. 'It's not any easy life especially for old timers like us, often dangerous and sometimes lonely, but we love it all the same,' she said while taking Zac's hand in her own.

Sara was intrigued. 'You look happy for sure but it *must* be ever so lonely up here.'

'We've got each other for company,' said Gertie. 'The goats to keep us busy and I've got Bison nearby when Zac is tending the flock. Still, we do see other people occasionally when we venture down to the lowlands to trade. While we're there we catch up on all the news from around the island.'

Between mouthfuls of stew Daniel asked, 'So there are other people on the island?'

Smiling, Gertie replied, 'Of course, you didn't think we were here all alone did you? Well-Keeper Island is home to many. The village of Hawksdale is the centre of trade, but people are spread throughout the countryside too.'

'Are there any other cave dwellers living near here?' Sara asked.

'No pretty one,' said Gertie. 'There aren't any other cave dwellers hereabouts. There remain a few, the nearest in the eastern slopes beyond Cascade Falls; a long way from here.'

A thought occurred to Sara and her cheeks reddened.

'Are you too warm?' enquired Gertie caringly.

'No not at all,' said Sara, blushing. 'This will sound childish, only meeting Zac was a surprise but when I saw you first, I thought you were some kind of enchantress or old princess. Or something! And living high up a mountain in a cave, it's quite amazing.'

At this Zac and Gertie broke into a hearty laughter.

'Old yes, but I wouldn't call myself a princess. And there is no need to be embarrassed pretty one, for while I'm no enchantress either I've seen many strange things in my time.'

Zac grinned. 'She'll always be my princess.' He winked at the questers in the firelight.

Daniel gobbled up the last of his stew. 'Well you certainly look like one. There isn't any more stew by any chance?' They all laughed together now. With the mood lightened Gertie dished out more bowls of stew.

The siblings ate contentedly for a time without comment till Gertie asked, 'Well, now that you know why we're here, perhaps you young ones could tell us what brings you to the Rocky Rise.' She looked at Zac knowingly. 'Pleasant as it is to have nice company we're deeply concerned for your safety; you must know that great risk awaits you around every boulder up here.'

Daniel recounted their journey from their garden to the wishing-well and up until they entered the colourful woods. The goat herders remained silent for the telling but when it finished their faces, lit up in the firelight, were bright with interest.

Gertie lowered her hands from her mouth. 'You came here through a well,' she said, her voice full of surprise. 'Could it really be true, Zac?' she turned to her husband.

Zac looked at his wife for a moment, deep in thought then nodded and turned back to the questers. 'Well travellers eh? Fascinating. And after so many years.'

Shocked, the questers gasped in union.

'There have been others?' asked Daniel, wide-eyed.

'Have you known them?' Sara added eagerly.

Gertie ignored the questions. 'Tobias, did he mention the cave dwellers at all?' she asked, hopefully, while throwing another glance at Zac.

'No, he didn't,' said Daniel, 'He just started us off by sending us to the colourful woods, he didn't mention anyone really.'

Gertie seemed to accept this. 'Ah, I see.'

'Should he have?' asked Sara, curious. 'Have *you* known other well-travellers?' she repeated.

Zac shook his head as though clearing a thought, then chuckled. 'Goodness no, there are tales from over the centuries past. We're old but not *that* old! But those tales are for another day.' He gestured with a bony hand. 'Please go on, what happened in the woods?'

Fancy that, we're not the first, thought Sara. She took up the story from the woods up till they met Zac in the shrubs at the foot of the mountain. She hung her head sadly when she finished, thoughts of Ashar fresh in her mind.

Zac seemed to sense the source of her fears and made to ease them. 'True, the forest is a dark and eerie place, with many strange inhabitants residing within; they're drawn there by the lingering of dark magic. This Ashar must be a very resourceful creature to live there.' Zac raised a finger.

'And remember, he chose to help you willingly. Besides, dwelling on the past won't change it. You must look ahead if you're to succeed.'

'S'pose,' mumbled Sara.

Daniel put one arm on Sara's shoulder for comfort, *'Don't dwell on it, Sis,'* and he finished off the telling. 'The only direction we could go was up the mountains or back into the woods, so we chose the mountains as the most likely place to find the shard of the dragon's tooth, or possibly even the nourishing stone.'

'A sensible choice,' reasoned Zac, 'So that stick you carry is the staff eh?'

Daniel handed Zac the hag's staff.

While Zac studied the staff, Gertie turned to Sara, 'What a wonderful journey you're on, full of magic and mystery, and still far from over.' Then with a faraway look in her eyes she said, 'Ah to be young again.'

'Have you ever had a magical journey?' Sara asked Gertie.

'Pretty one, I believe everyone has magic in their lives if they just take time to realise it. It exists in people's hearts and minds and is full of never-ending mystery. As for me, well I'm still on my journey; long may it last.' She smiled and moved a piece of fallen hair out of Sara's eyes.

Zac examined the staff by the firelight and Daniel waited eagerly for his opinion.

'This truly is a magical treasure,' said Zac. He ran his finger up and down the staff.

'It must be,' Daniel replied, 'It was rotten when we broke it from the tree, but now look how it shines and feel how solid it is. Still though, it wouldn't be much of a treasure where we come from.'

Zac held it up and admired it once more before handing it back. 'Perhaps the gift lies not in the treasure itself but in those who wield it.'

A low growl by the cavern entrance startled the questers and they jumped with fright. Bison was standing there panting with his tongue hanging out to one side. The siblings inched away, terrified as the giant dog padded over to Zac and Gertie. His nose was smeared with blood and there were big grey feathers stuck to his face.

Sara sat mute, frightened to stillness.

50

Gertie noticed their discomfort. 'Don't fret my dears. I'll clean it off his nose and he won't seem so fierce. Bison is our friend and he'll protect you like one of us.' She picked up a bowl of water that had a piece of wool soaking in it and began washing the blood of the hound's nose.

Daniel gulped, nervous around the beast despite the herder's ease. 'Gizords don't have feathers, do they?'

'Indeed they don't,' said Zac, 'It appears Bison has killed a gostridge.'

'An ostrich?'

'No, we have ostriches in the lowlands though. Up here we have gostridges, quite similar in appearances, distant cousins I suspect. Both big, dumb flightless birds, but gostridges have much bigger *and* sharper beaks.'

Daniel was curious. 'Wow, they sound interesting. Will we get a chance to see one?'

'Perhaps, perhaps not,' said Zac, 'It's not something I'd invite. Gostridges are solitary birds, nesting here and there on the mountain ridges. They attack anything they see, usually out of fear or stupidity. They are no match for Bison here.' Zac patted the hound's head. 'But be warned, gostridges are faster than people. They can leap from rock to rock and if you're not careful you could quickly lose a finger or worse an eye.'

Daniel's brow furrowed. *What a strange place this is. So many similarities and yet so many differences.*

Sara frowned too. *I never liked ostriches.*

Gertie clapped her hands together to call attention. 'Now my dears, although you've come this far, you've still quite a way to go. Zac and I will help you with what little we can. Isn't that right, Zac?' She turned to her husband.

'Indeed it is, my sweet,' said Zac, turning to the siblings. 'Sorry to say we've never heard of this nourishing stone, however-,' he paused and raised a finger. 'We *can* point you in the right direction to find the shard of the dragon's tooth.'

Sara sighed. 'I was hoping that we could avoid the dragon.'

The old pair smiled and Gertie said, 'Don't fret dear. While there are *many* dangers on our mountain, the shard of the dragon's tooth is just exactly that, the piece of a tooth! The dragon himself has faded into legend long ago.'

'And quite a legend it is too,' said Zac, 'There's still time yet. Stay awhile and I'll tell you the whole story.' Daniel and Sara exchanged an unsure look.

I'm not sure, thought Daniel. *We've been here quite a while already.*

I do feel safe with them, thought Sara. She gave Daniel a subtle nod. *You decide.*

51

'It may be useful to know as you continue your journey,' Zac encouraged.

'Okay then,' said Daniel, 'If there's time.'

Gertie poured some warm fruit juice and all four settled on their cushions.

Taking a moment to recall the tale Zac raised his eyes upward, drew in a long breath and began.

Chapter 5
Magic in the Air

Many ages ago when the world itself was young and magic of the heart was bold and beautiful, everywhere danced with energy like a fresh morning in spring. Each day new inhabitants appeared on Well-Keeper Island; plants, people and creatures alike flourished from the foot of the Rocky Rise to the edge of the Botanic Beaches. A beautiful harmony existed and it was a great time to be alive. There was an air of goodness and excitement all around. Well-Keeper Island is as old as time, and as long as there is magic of the heart here, the island will be sustained. Anyway, it came to pass that a great shadow slowly descended on the far side of the Rise. It was not known why at the time, but this was because not all who live are guided by magic of the heart; some follow a darker path, shrouded in fear. And so it was that those living things that loved harmony, peace and fairness came over the Rise away from the falling darkness, and those living things disturbed by eerie thoughts and dark longings stayed and gathered under the shadows.

It came to pass with the unfolding of time that the island was divided in two: this side, bright and colourful, and the dark side, grey and murky. The mountains marked the border, and it was very rare that anyone or anything would cross to the opposite side. It happened that one peaceful day a pitch-black cloud could be seen hovering above the mountain; all of the island stared up, for never before had such a strange cloud appeared. Suddenly and with staggering speed, the cloud began to swoop down the bright side of the Rocky Rise. Goats, rabbits, birds and all of the creatures that used the Rise as their home fled before the descending force, because alas, it was no cloud but a fierce dragon. The beast was a giant with spiked wings and a tail the length of his body, the end pointed like a spear. His eyes were blood red, and the scales covering his body were black as the darkest night. This mighty creature had flown over from the dark side of the Rise, and all who saw it quaked with fear. The most striking feature of all was in the dragon's mouth, for sitting at the end of his gaping, bottom jaw was a massive diamond-shaped tooth; it sparkled like an ice crystal and stood out against his other teeth that were jagged and yellow. It is said that although this monster had a dark soul, some good exists in every living thing and so the purity that remained in this magical beast resided in his diamond-tooth, refusing to fall foul to the ever-threatening shadow.

Soaring through the sky, the dragon circled the island, scanning all with his blood-red eyes. After a time, heads reappeared from out of burrows and from behind bushes. People came out of their dwellings and birds left their nests but stayed low, for the dragon was returning in the direction of the Rise. His mighty bulk filled the sky while his shadow scoured the ground as he passed. Growing at the foot of the Rise was a large wooded area, home to many plants and creatures. As the dragon flew over these woods he swooped down to just above the treetops. He arched his back, drew back his head and let out a monstrous growl. Terrible as the noise of the growl was, it was nothing compared to the furnace of flame that launched from the beast's throat. The flame shot far across the treetops and they were instantly engulfed in fire. Panic and confusion followed for the creatures of the woods as they tried to flee amidst thick smoke and the furious fire. Now high above the smoke, the flames and the woods the Dragon hovered, looking down on the disorder that he had created; with one last swing of his tail, he took to flight once more and flew back over the Rocky Rise from whence he came.

The whole of the woods was in chaos, but the most peculiar thing was happening; as the flames rolled across the forest floor and licked up the trees and bushes, not all of them burned as they would in a normal fire. Some *were* burning for sure, but others though surrounded by flames did *not* burn, though they twisted and gnarled amidst the heat. And although many creatures got caught in the flames and the blinding smoke, they did not burn either, but they screamed and thrashed as though something had crawled inside them and was trying to break out through their skin. Just like the dragon, this was a magical fire; it came from the depths of the dragon's soul, a raging fire sent to blacken the heart of all it touches. The flames were a crimson-red that embraced all around them in their fiery grasp.

Meanwhile, as the dragon's fire raged through the helpless woods, there were strange stirrings on the far side of the island. On the plains beside the Botanic Beaches something was exciting the animals. The wild horses faced the dunes and rose up on their hind legs, a herd of buffalo faced the same way; they stamped the ground and snorted. A chorus of birdcalls could be heard as each type called and whistled, all the while getting louder. Darting forwards and back across the plains was a herd of roe deer, as if aware of a presence but not yet seeing it. Even the insects were excited as they all rose up at once, buzzing and zooming in all directions around the animals. It was a mild, windless day, and just beyond the dunes the ocean could be heard, but instead of the gentle lapping of the water against the beach it sounded like monstrous waves crashing against high cliffs in the height of a storm. But there was no storm, it was something else entirely. Suddenly the ground started to shake as rising up over the dunes came a mighty pair of wings filling the horizon, and with the sunlight beaming off them they shone white as snow. The animals went wild with frenzy, kicking and stamping, as up from the ocean to the Botanic Beaches and over the plains flew a giant, flying stallion.

It was a magnificent creature to behold; the span of his wings filled the skyline. At first glance he dazzled all eyes, for his coat was such a brilliant white. The tail and mane were glittering; silver and multi-coloured sparkles shimmered from them as he moved gracefully through the air. He shook his mighty head and magical flakes sparkled and poured from his mane and rained down on the plains, glimmering as they fell. Lifting his mighty head, the majestic beast with enormous wing-beats flew in the direction of the flaming forest.

The flight of the flying stallion across Well-Keeper Island had the opposite effect of the dragon. Instead of everything hiding in fear, eyes and faces appeared from everywhere to gaze upon the shimmering beauty racing through the sky. Hooves could be heard like thunder as the wild horses of the plains galloped for a while underneath the shadow of the flying horse, but they could not keep up for long because his speed was too great. People left cottage and cave to peer with shielded eyes at the flying wonder as though they were staring at the sun. The birds took to flight alongside the mighty steed only to be left behind moments later.

Smoke could be seen from all over the island coming from the woods, and the frantic cries of terror could be heard from the many creatures great and small trapped within. The flying stallion approached the inferno high above the rising smoke; there he hung for the smallest of moments, motionless in the sky. Then he spread his mighty wings as far and wide as they would go, and indeed it was a glorious sight, for his wingspan seemed to dwarf the flaming forest. Raising his front legs, he kicked the air and with a thunderous shake of his head he began to beat his wings. First slowly, and for a moment it seemed to fan the flames. But within seconds his wings were beating so fast that they were a blur, driving a wind like no other wind before down atop the fire. The flames grabbed at what they could, but the strength blowing down on them was too great and soon the fire had nowhere to go; it was trapped with the force of a hurricane pounding down upon it.

The flames soon turned to smoke and as the smoke coughed from the woods, the flying horse began to climb skyward in a spiral flight, still beating his mighty wings as he flew. Caught in the wind trap, the smoke became one twisting line following the magical, white beast high into the sky. Suddenly he stopped his flight, turned on the smoke, and beat his wings and thrashed his legs with all his might. The smoke turned inward, shrank, rolled, fell and melted into a whisper. Clear skies could be seen once more. The smoke was gone and the flying horse shimmered brightly in the sunlight.

Gazing down from the sky the white steed saw the mark left by the dragon's fire from the dark side of the Rocky Rise. Trees and plants were black and twisted. Animals rolled on the dark earth frantically scratching and clawing at themselves, their eyes bloodshot and fevered looking. Once again, the giant wings spread and the mighty beast flew skyward. Up and up till he was almost out of sight, when in a graceful arch he turned around; wings stretched out to full, he began to dive straight down. He fell so fast that he looked like a shooting star. All on the island stood still and gazed up at this white flame falling from the sky. Just before the flying horse met the treetops, he straightened up and soared over the ruins of the once-beautiful forest. Gliding elegantly through the air, silver sparkles shimmered from his mane and tail and left a trail of magical flakes in his wake, pouring over all beneath.

As the magic rain touched the surface of the trees explosions of colour could be seen. The forest floor became like a river when the colourful flakes landed on the darkened earth and began to swirl. Creature's skin, fur and feathers shivered when the sparkles fell upon them. They called out in surprise at the strange feelings going through them, their eyes blinking rapidly, no longer bloodshot, their faces losing the fevered look. But stranger still, the creatures seemed to understand each other. The forest was being transformed, and all within it as the two magic's met. Ripples of colour and light swam through the leaves. Birds of black feather took to flight only to return moments later with feathers blue. A yellow doe hopped over a purple log, but when she landed, she was red again; a red hare and green squirrel sat talking about the strange goings on. All around the forest whirled in a tapestry of noise and colour as the echoes of the magic danced through the forest. A golden horizon shone over Botanic Beaches, and in the distance flying towards it, the mighty flying stallion could be seen returning to the ocean, a shining white, beautiful and strong against the sky.

All rejoiced as the tale of the white horse spread throughout the island. As it happens, with the passing of time the magic settled and routine was restored. The woods that had been set alight took on a strange and colourful existence and over time became known as Moody Woods. Many thought the dragon was gone, but some counselled that it would return and once again unleash terror unto the island. Nobody knew where the dragon had come from. Nobody knew why he was here. Nobody knew where he was gone. Rumours began that the dragon was from another world altogether, and had returned there, where he reigned as a king of terror.

Alas, not long after, the worst fears were realised, for the black dragon appeared again and swooped over the island spreading his lethal fires. But as before, the mighty flying stallion rose up from the sea and quenched the dragon's flames. And so it continued, sometimes a day would pass when the black shadow could be seen high up the Rise ready to swoop again, and as sure as it would so, too, would the great white wings appear rising over the dunes of Botanic Beaches. Sometimes, many days or even many moons would pass before the black dragon would appear, but appear he would, blazing with flames of fury and striking fear into all who dwelt here. And as always, the great white horse followed, thundering through the sky restoring order and hope to the island.

The visiting creatures destroyed little, but just like Moody Woods, the whole island was slowly transforming as both magic's mingled. Animals flew that had never flown before, some plants grew legs, water could be seen flowing uphill and many creatures and plants could communicate in strange and wonderful ways. And always after the great winged creatures left their mark on the island, before the sun set that day in the west with the oncoming of night, the black dragon would be the far side of the mountain and the flying horse returned across the sea. One day rolled to the next, and the island continued to change amidst the comings and goings of the mystical creatures, but high up on the Rise there was a new strangeness in the air and the shadows were stirring. Unknown to all but the tiny insects burrowed within the moss on the mountain rock and the bats that dwelt in the high caves of the Rise, the dragon sat waiting, poised on a ledge between two peaks and hidden from the view of the lowlands. His eyes burned blood red as he pondered what lay before him. Because a dark heart is always in turmoil, and the black beast was growing restless with desire to lay waste to all on the island that was happy and colourful. Such is the way of it with a dark soul; greed and fear ever try to extinguish hope and light. In the half-light of dusk as his nemesis flew out to sea, instead of returning over the dark side of the Rise, the dragon was perching in the shadows of the highest ledge waiting for night to fall.

Night soon fell and the island rested under a blanket of stars. Late into the night the mighty dragon raised his head and gazed down the slopes before him. Raising his long neck to the sky, the black wings began to beat and once again the dragon was swooping down the Rocky Rise, this time using the cover of darkness.

With the coming of dawn, two fires from the dragon blazed on the island, one in the East where the Tor-Folk dwell, the second to the South, across the grassy plains where the grazing herds came to feed. Rising with the sun, the flying stallion appeared on the horizon, and it was not long before the fires were quenched and harmony was restored. This was the way of it in the days that followed; the dragon's terror reigned by night, and by day the flying horse brought peace and calm to the island. And each day as the magical horse went about his good work, high up nestled in the peaks of the Rise, the black dragon lay on his lonely ledge consumed by rage and shrouded in a cloak of darkness.

Alas, one sunless day arrived to herald a moonless night and a heavy storm; it was on this very night that the black dragon set off and unleashed his final terrible fury upon Well-Keeper Island. Fear and despair rang out across the land as the loathing dragon torched much of the island fair. Such was the dragon's ferocity and his consuming desire to breathe his menacing, red flames that he did not return to the mountain with the coming of the morning, but continued to glide round and round looking for patches still not ablaze. The flames leapt up house and hill and the very ground boiled. Thousands of birds had taken to the air, desperately trying to flee the cries and screams of panic and terror, only to start choking in the smoke-filled skies and fall helplessly to the ground. Amidst a sweeping arch, the dragon froze momentarily and stared towards Botanic Beaches. A wall of white had appeared on the horizon, growing in size and speed as it raced towards the coast. As the white wall got closer to land, the dragon turned tail and flew in the direction of the Rise, for now he could see what approached; a whole herd of flying horses. And leading the charge, towering over the others was the giant, flying stallion, shining and magnificent as he came. The herd of smaller, flying horses flew straight to whatever patches of fire were nearest and immediately started tackling them using wind and magic. Such was the flying stallion's rage at the devastation brought by the black dragon that he pursued the dark beast with lightning speed towards the mountain. The dragon was still only halfway up the Rise when he turned to face the oncoming steed; the two beasts clashed, and the whole island shook as an explosion of fire, wind and magic rang out across the skies.

A great battle ensued that was to roll right across the island. Rocks tumbled down the mountainside, caused by the tremors that were shaking all around. So too did the mighty beasts, locked in a fierce embrace as they fought while rolling down the Rocky Rise. They crashed into a river, and the water boiled one moment and froze solid the next. Rising and falling through valleys, plains and marshes they were tangled, two mighty foes matching each other strike for strike. Crashing into the high hills to the east, the pair became surrounded in a swirl of magic crystals unleashed from the stallion's mane followed by a screaming cry from the dragon that engulfed them both in a ball of crimson fire. The battle lasted all day and into the night, and still neither beast gave quarter. The smaller, flying horses had done what they could and began returning towards the ocean when the clouds opened and the rain fell like lakes from the sky. Once again in the air, the giant beasts passed across the island. The scene below them was a wretched one of chaos and turmoil; anywhere that was not in flames was soggy and wet, and the air itself was damp and smoky. Moody Woods quivered in a tantrum of dark colours as the two giants passed over them once more.

Slowly the night ached on and although the rain had stopped and many of the fires had been quenched, it seemed that the night itself would never end. The beasts had fought down the mountain, all around the island and now they were back on the Rocky Rise. Both creatures were balancing on the highest ledge as the dragon was driving the flying stallion back against a jagged peak with blast after blast of flaming, red fire. The horse was trapped between peaks with no room to spread his wings. The flying steed back-stepped on his hind legs in a desperate effort to take flight when disaster struck; the rocks beneath him gave with the tremors of battle and the beasts pounding down upon them. In that instant, as the horse lost his footing, the dragon saw his chance. Drawing deep into the cavity of his chest, invoking all that was dark from his soul, he unleashed one final and terrible inferno. The flames burst forth in a raging blaze of fury. The air was consumed and so too was the flying horse, surrounded in a fireball and lost from sight. A sphere of fire hung in the air and the dragon looked on through his deep, red eyes. Seeing the defeat of the white steed, the dragon opened his mouth and howled a chilling scream of victory into the night that echoed across the island. All who heard it looked to the Rise and wept with despair, as they knew what it meant. The champion of light and hope had lost. The flying stallion had fallen foul to the fires of black dragon.

As the black beast craned his neck and howled to the skies, a new dawn arrived, and with it came the sun. The sunlight appeared in the east, rising over the hills and its shining rays shot out far and wide across the island. The dragon turned his head in surprise at this sudden change from shadow to light, and in that instant the mountainside transformed. The dragon stared defiantly at the morning sun and opened his mouth further. He summonsed a chilling roar of rage at the intrusion of dawn on his victory when a ray of sunlight fell on the diamond-tooth set deep in his bottom jaw. Light of sheer brilliance suddenly exploded from the tooth, lighting up the mountain. The dragon reeled and his massive bulk swayed on the ledge. The dark creature froze to the spot. He felt a pounding in his head and his eyes were blinded by the flash. From the tooth a beam of pure, white light arrowed its way through the air and pierced the blazing inferno that had consumed the flying stallion. As the beam of light and the sphere fused, the fire began to grow in all directions, but as it grew it also changed colour from red to a blinding white. The dragon broke from his trance, frenzied by the burning brightness, but he could not shake free of the glowing beam that locked him fast to the dazzling white inferno. With one last monstrous cry, the black beast twisted his neck in an effort to wrench himself free from the blazing beam. The cord of light flashed like lightning, arched up and snapped, and at that moment the white inferno exploded in a thunderous flash.

Thousands of crystal shards hurled through the air, sparkling with magic. The clouds rattled and the mountain shook as the mighty, flying stallion charged forth from the blast. Rising on his hind legs, he met the black dragon with both the front hooves kicking, one square in the jaw, shattering tooth and bone, and the other square in the chest. The dragon felt his chest collapse but at the same time felt his body fly without wing beat, because such was the force of the stallion's strength that the dragon was driven from the ledge and high into the air. Now falling with his red eyes facing the sky, the black beast knew that he was doomed. He strained to utter a defiant cry, but no sound came from his crushed chest or through his shattered jaw. His writhing body landed on the highest peak of the Rise, pierced through by the jagged rock. There it hung for the briefest of moments, then sagged. The lifeless tail hung down the dark side of the peak while his sagging neck and head hung out in the light. The black scales stood out against the morning sun. Not one of the yellow teeth remained in the broken jaw, as all were smashed with force of the horse's hoof. But still there hanging from the gaping jaw sat the diamond-tooth, undamaged and shining bright as the sun itself.

Taking to the skies, the flying horse flew up and backwards from the ledge till he was level with the jagged peak and its lifeless victim. There he hovered as once again the magic sparkles flowed from his mane; they danced in the air and swirled in coiling loops around the body of the dead dragon. There was another small explosion of light, and the diamond-tooth simply fell from the open mouth and bounced down the side of the peak to rest on the very ledge where the final battle had taken place. Bowing his head, the flying stallion beat his wings with all his might and flew towards the peak. His giant head smashed against the rock and the peak gave with a mighty crack. Stone, dust and rubble crashed down the side of the mountain, and amongst the fallen was the dead body of the black dragon returning for the last time to the dark side of the Rocky Rise from whence he came.

The stallion returned to the ledge where the diamond-tooth lay and with a great stamp of his hoof he shattered it into ten pieces. Magic crackled from his hoof as the shards of the dragon's tooth clinked underneath. Taking the shards in his mouth the victorious stallion flew back up to the tip of the shattered peak that still towered high over the rest of the mountain and there he placed one piece. The shard sat upright and glistened brightly in the light of the new morning. He flew to the other highest peaks of the Rise and placed a shard on the tip of each. Nine shards in all, shone on top of the peaks. They stood as a beacon to one and all that good will triumph in the end, and also as a warning to the dark creatures from the far side that any who crosses the Rocky Rise with mischief in their hearts will bring great peril unto themselves. The stallion kept the tenth and final shard for reasons that have forever since remained a mystery.

Soaring over the island, the flying horse gazed down upon the aftermath of the great battle. The magical flakes poured forth as he swooped over land and lake, man, beast and plant. There were some places in which the dark magic of the dragon had burrowed deep, some places that neither the rainwater had quenched nor the servant horses had found; some places that the flying stallion himself had not reached in time. In these dark, creepy pockets of the island grey mists swirled, plants gnarled and twisted and fevered beasts groaned. In such places as these where the shadow now dwelt, the white horse laboured to leave defences against the dark magic of the dragon. And so it was that after restoring much of the wonder and beauty to the island and protecting it from whatever dangers may still lurk in hidden corners, the mighty flying stallion circled the skies for a time while the magic took effect. But towards the coming of evening as the sun was setting, the giant wings spread wide once more and the white steed returned over the dunes of Botanic Beaches, never to be seen again.

In many ways the island just picked up where it had left off before the strange beasts had ever appeared. People were still people, plants still plants, and animals still animals, but many of the same had changed and strange new happenings occurred all around; they now shared a magical existence. Yet even in this change, an order of sorts developed as it does with time. Soon one day was much like the last as all of life settled into its own routine. Shortly afterward, the smaller, flying horses reappeared on the island. They, like their giant leader, were also magical beasts and could communicate with all other creatures. From time to time they could be seen high up on the Rocky Rise circling the peak where the shards of the diamond-tooth stood. Some said that the flying horses were the protectors of the island; others said they were the guardians of the shards of the dragon's tooth till such a time as the magic within the shards could be wielded for good.

Legend has it that when the need arises, if the bearer of a shard is pure of heart, the magic contained within will reveal itself to their aid before returning to nature to begin anew.

Chapter 6
Magic on the Ground

Silence filled the cave but for the crackling of the fire. The questers stared at Zac, captivated by the story. The old man sighed and looked up. 'My goodness, I have gone on. It's way past dusk. You'll just have to wait till morning before continuing on your quest. The Rise can be a treacherous place by night.'

Still spellbound, Daniel didn't mind. 'Wow. What a legend. So there are nine shards of the dragon's tooth. I wonder which will be the easiest to get to.'

Zac stoked the fire. 'No young man. There is but one left alas. It remains on the highest peak of the Rise.'

'What became of the others?' asked Sara.

'Each has a legend of its own,' said Gertie, 'Let's just say they were sought over the centuries when the need arose.'

'*Please* tell us more,' begged Daniel.

Gertie clucked. 'I'll prepare beds, and Zac will tell you a *little* more about the island. You'll need all your strength in the days ahead. You should rest while you can.'

As Gertie rose from her cushion Sara turned to Zac. 'So Moody Woods became sort of enchanted because of the magic from the dragon and stallion, right? Is that what you meant earlier about the lingering of dark magic?'

The goat herder nodded. 'Correct you are.'

'Gosh, that explains why the place was so creepy.'

Zac nodded. 'Many a dark creature has crossed the Rise over the centuries. Some make their homes in the woods, others elsewhere.'

With fresh memories of the woods coming back again the siblings exchanged sad glances.

Daniel quickly moved the conversation along. 'The hag's staff we've found, would it have come from the first fire? I mean when the dragon came and set the woods alight. It's kind of a strange treasure don't you think, a staff. It's just a stick really.'

Zac smiled. 'Ah back to the stick, eh? I thought you wouldn't let that one go. You're very sharp indeed. I can tell you by just the feel of the stick in my hand that it wields a magic of sorts. And it is as you say, from the first fire, as are many of the wonders of Moody Woods.' Zac looked intently at the hag's staff and ran his fingers along it once again. 'As to what it is for, I cannot say. But know this: magic endures till such a time that it is called upon. When or how this will happen I cannot tell you, but when it does, its true purpose is revealed. After which the magic is no longer bound and can return to nature.'

Gertie returned to the fireside carrying fresh cups of hot fruit juice and the conversation continued late into the night.

Bison ambled lazily over and sat beside Zac. The old goat herder patted the hound affectionately. 'The peak you seek is on this part of the mountain range. You must follow the mountain up and easterly to a dangerous part of the range known as Nightmare Reaches.'

'Is that because it's a nightmare to reach it?' asked Sara doubtfully.

'You could say that my dear.' Zac raised three fingers. 'The area got its name for three reasons.' He flicked his fingers as he listed them. 'The treacherous heights, the Whirlwind Ravine, and the drooling bats.'

Concern etched on Daniel's face. 'The treacherous heights I understand, but if our recent encounters are anything to go by I don't much like the sound of these drooling bats. Let me guess, bigger and fiercer than those bats we saw earlier?'

Zac nodded solemnly. 'Bigger, fiercer and deadly I'm afraid. You hear them before you see them. The caves they live in are under the very same ledge where the black dragon used to lay and wait for nightfall. Once these bats were quite ordinary, but the dark magic of the dragon seeped into them night after night unchallenged, and so over time they shaped into ferocious creatures.'

Sara looked troubled. 'Couldn't the flying stallion save them?'

'Alas, no,' said Gertie, 'The stallion was too late. So instead he used his magic to keep the doomed bats at bay. He created a magical whirlwind in the ravine below their caves. The whirlwind whips up from below many times a day and spreads out, engulfing the ledge and the entire ravine.'

'Oh, so are the bats trapped?' Sara asked, hopefully.

'Not completely, but they'll only risk the whirlwind to make a kill. Instead, they brood in the caves reserving their strength, always listening for signs of life. The whirlwind is said to be unpredictable, so only when the bats sense movement near will they brave the ravine.'

Sara shuddered. 'Bats are creepy.'

Daniel turned to Zac. 'So these things drool. Is the drool poisonous? Is that what makes them so deadly?'

Zac pressed his lips and nodded. 'Aye lad. Their drool is venomous. A drooling bat will sap the strength from anything it bites, drawing that energy into itself, while the victim will quickly weaken and die. Passing birds often perch on the ledge and from time to time a mountain goat or hare might stray up that high. And others, all to their doom.'

Worry lines creased Sara's brow at the thoughts of the bats, so out of her earshot Zac secretly warned Daniel that few humans have travelled to Nightmare Reaches and fewer have ever returned.

Daniel nodded gravely. 'So what other defences did the stallion leave against the dark magic of the dragon?' he asked loud enough for all to hear.

The old man stoked the fire again. 'Well let me see, he did spread much of his magic on the ground, hmm. Yes, there's the tale of the blind wolves of the Parched Valley but that is a legend the Tor-Folk tell.'

Daniel pleaded. 'Do tell us.'

Zac sighed. 'The full story escapes me right now. I can only say that a once beautiful valley was burnt to char by the fires of the dragon. And the wolves that lived in the valley turned ferocious. So much so that they attacked the flying stallion and he in turn blinded them.'

Sara gave a little shiver. *I'm not even fond of big dogs, no offence Bison, not to mention ferocious, blind wolves.* She hugged herself tightly. 'What became of the valley and the wolves?'

'I bet I know what became of the valley,' ventured Daniel. 'The horse sprinkled magical flakes from his mane and the whole valley was restored.'

Zac drew on his pipe. 'Strangely enough, in this case he didn't. He just left the valley as he found it. With the passing of time and the comings and goings of the seasons, the black soot and charred clay was washed away, and all that was left was dry desert, arid and scorched. And so it stands till this day; that's why folk call it the Parched Valley.'

Sara moved closer to the fire for warmth. 'What about the wolves? Did they get washed away with the comings and goings of the seasons too?'

Zac chuckled. 'If only, my dear, if only. No, the wolves stayed and indeed endured. They are still there; well, their descendants at least, still blind and still as dangerous as ever. They come out only at night, hunting in packs, using sound and smell to detect their prey.'

Sara was worried. 'Let's hope we don't encounter them.'

Gertie patted her on the shoulder. 'If you do, you'll have travelled far, for the valley is a long way from here.'

Zac went on. 'Folk who live close to the Parched Valley keep many fires burning by night, for light is the thing the blind wolves fear most.'

Daniel looked puzzled. 'It's strange that they fear light if they're blind. So do the fires keep the wolves at bay?'

Zac shook his head. 'Aye, strange it is lad. And alas no, sometimes the fires are not enough; much too often the wolves make a kill, and they are not fussy about their victims: animals, birds-,' the goat herder leaned in so only Daniel could hear him again. 'And I'm afraid sometimes even people.'

Sara stretched her arms and yawned. 'I'm glad it's not a wolf's tooth we're seeking. The wolves are a lot like the bats in Whirlwind Ravine.'

Gertie stood up from the fire. 'Indeed they are young lady, but even wolves and bats sleep, and that's what you should be doing now. You'll need your energy for the journey ahead.' She helped Sara up and patted the blanket round her shoulders. 'Come on, you'll sleep over here.'

Over near the wall of the cave there lay two beds laid out made from straw and wool.

Sara tried to keep her eyes open. 'Thanks for everything, Ms Gertie, you're so kind.'

'Don't mention it, Darling, here use this.' Gertie tucked Sara in and handed her the cushion that she'd been sitting on. Sara was asleep as soon as her head touched the cushion.

'*I'm* not tired yet. I usually stay up later than Sara. Can't you tell me a little more?'

Zac grinned over at Gertie but then his tone turned serious. 'How right you are young man, and you'll do well to remember this along the way, because you have both an exciting and perilous journey ahead of you.'

Gertie joined them back at the fire and the old pair of cave dwellers told Daniel more about the history of Well-Keeper Island and some of the strange creatures that resided on it. The night wore on and they discussed a great many things. Eventually the flames turned to embers and Daniel didn't remember nodding off to sleep.

Chapter 7
Preparations

The smell of eggs frying drifted across the cave. Daniel woke as his nose caught the scent. Glancing around the cave he noticed that he lay next to the place where he sat the previous night, except now he was covered with a thick, woollen blanket.

Gertie entered the main cave from a side cavern where the smell of cooking was coming from. 'Look who's decided to join us. Good morning young man, how did you sleep? I'm afraid you were too big for Zac and me to move without waking you, so we left you asleep where you lay. It looks like you needed it too; it's past noon.'

Daniel stood and rubbed his sleepy eyes. 'Thank you, Ms Gertie, I slept fine.' He looked towards the side cavern. 'I didn't realise you had other rooms.'

'Oh we have many hereabouts; the mountain is riddled with caves and chambers, and one must be ever vigilant not to stray into the wrong ones. We use that one as a small kitchen as it has a natural vent to take out the smoke and steam. Sara is in there now helping me prepare you some breakfast.'

Just then Sara entered carrying a board with brown bread and goat cheese. 'Hey sleepy head, I'm glad you're awake, maybe now we'll get some peace.'

'What do you mean?' asked Daniel, puzzled.

'You kept us awake from the early hours; you were snoring like a bear.' She giggled and started making loud snore noises.

Gertie smiled at the exchange. 'Nonsense, you slept like a lamb; your sister is only teasing. She is fed and fresh, and you should be too.' She patted Daniel on the head and began folding his blanket.

Not too sure which was worse, snoring like a bear or being referred to as a lamb, Daniel rubbed his eyes again and yawned. *Hmm, I'll let Sara tease. It's just too early in the morning.* He looked around. *I wonder where Zac is.* Suddenly the memories of last night came flooding back to him. 'Hey Sara, wait till you hear this, after you fell asleep—'

Gertie interrupted, 'Enough time for chit-chat later, let's get this breakfast into you. Come along Daniel, as it's for you, you can help carry it,' clapping her hands firmly so as not to be disobeyed.

Daniel fetched his breakfast from the kitchen-cavern and the hunger after a long night's sleep quickly took over. *Great*, he thought, *I'm famished.*

To accompany the brown bread and goat cheese, Daniel was busy getting stuck into a plate of fried duck-eggs, mushrooms and roast rabbit. He looked up to the echo of footfalls when around the main cave entrance strode Zac with purpose in his step.

Zac didn't wait to be greeted. 'Ah you're up. Good. And not a moment too soon; the wind has changed, and I sense fog in the air. Time is short.' He gripped Daniel on the shoulder. 'If you're to have any hope of getting to the peak before nightfall, you must leave immediately. The peak is quite a distance from here and that's travelling under clear skies.'

With a look of regret, Daniel stood up from his breakfast, half the meal still uneaten.

Gertie read his face. 'Now-now, there is still time for you to finish your food; there's always time for breakfast in *my* cave.' Daniel brightened at once and sat back down.

Zac continued, 'Eat up then Daniel, for the fog may be the *least* of your troubles.' Zac shot a worried glance to Gertie. 'Campfire smoke in the lower passes. I suspect from a band of marauders.'

Alarmed, Gertie's hands shot to her mouth. 'Oh dear.' She gave Zac a grave look before hastening off towards a side cavern. 'I'll fetch the pigeons,' she called back.

'Marauders?' asked Daniel through a mouthful of mushrooms.

'Aye lad, marauders, and no good can come of it.'

Worry lines creased Sara's brow. *I don't like the sound of these marauders.* 'What exactly are marauders?'

Zac's tone took on an edge of warning. 'Not only fell creatures cross from the dark side of the Rise, but bad men too, with mischief in their hearts. They make raids on flocks, plundering and dare I say it, kidnapping.'

Gertie returned in hurried strides, carrying a cage with three pigeons inside. She placed her free hand on Sara's shoulder. 'These marauders are a dangerous bunch. Please promise me you'll remain extra vigilant, as help is hard to come by up here, and more often than not arrives too late.'

Daniel and Sara both gulped. 'We promise,' they said in chorus.

Gertie placed the cage on the cave floor. Distracted by the soft cooing, Daniel was suddenly curious. 'What're the pigeons for?'

Zac rummaged in his cloak and took out some twigs and small, white pebbles. 'Messenger pigeons,' he said while handing a pebble to Gertie.

Gertie gently removed a pigeon from the cage and using a small piece of thread began tying the pebble to its foot. Meanwhile Zac had produced a blade and was marking the twigs with small scratches. Intrigued, the questers moved closer to watch what the goat herders were doing.

Gertie saw them watching. 'The white pebble is our symbol for the west side of the Rocky Rise. That's here,' she explained.

Zac held up a twig to show the questers the scratches he'd made. 'This grid is a net. It's our symbol for the marauders. They sometimes use a throwing net to catch-, he paused. 'To catch their prey,' he added finally.

The questers knew what he meant.

Oh creepers, thought Sara, biting her lip. *I don't want to go any further, not the two of us on our own anyway.*

Daniel crunched up his forehead, deep in thought. *Running through the woods away from gizords is one thing, but a band of cutthroats up a mountain is another. How will I protect Sara?* He saw the anxious look on his sister's face and pressed his lips tight. *I just will.* 'What about those other scratches?' he asked Zac, pointing to the rows of three wave curves scratched into the twig.

'Smoke,' said Zac. 'Marauders smoke seen on the west side of the Rise, that's our message.' The goat herders had fixed a pebble and a twig to each of the three pigeons' feet.

'Who will you send the message to?' asked Sara, her voice etched with worry.

'Friends and comrades,' said Zac. 'Others on the island too, those who would want to know that marauders might be afoot in the region.'

'Those who *need* to know,' added Gertie, her tone serious.

Daniel considered their words. *They're really worried, so we should be too!* he thought, though remained silent.

Gertie saw his frown. 'Enough about the marauders now,' she said encouragingly. It was only smoke and we're sending the messages *just* as a precaution.'

Zac nodded. 'Gertie is right, but you two should get going, *just* in case.'

There was tension in the cave as the questers sensed the concern of the goat herders.

Sara swallowed a lump in her throat. *Just in case they kidnap us!* She looked to the ground and spoke quietly. 'Won't you come with us, Zac? No one knows the mountain like you.' She looked up, pleading. 'I know it's unfair of me to ask, only, we've had some big scares already. I don't know if I can take much more danger.'

Daniel quickly put an arm around Sara's shoulder for comfort and looked at the goat herders. 'We would be grateful, not that we aren't grateful already, but if you *could* join us it would improve our chances of…' he hesitated, 'eh, of making it off the mountain in one piece.'

Gertie looked at Zac, her face sad. 'I'll release the pigeons,' she said quietly, and popped the pigeons back into the cage before hurrying down a side cavern.

Zac looked at the questers affectionately. 'Alas I cannot join you. Much as it pains me to say it, you must go alone. The well-keeper chose you two; this is your quest and not mine.'

'Even just a bit of the way?' pleaded Sara.

'I'm sorry Sara. My place is here with Gertie and on the slopes with my goats. Some things are just meant to be a certain way.'

Sara nodded, meekly. *I'm not going to cry,* she told herself, although she felt her eyes watering.

'Besides,' said Zac light-heartedly, 'the journey would take it out of me for I'm an old man despite my youthful looks—'

Sara sniffled then giggled at Zac's efforts to cheer her up. 'Sorry Zac, please go on.'

Zac's tone became serious again. 'Of course your path will be perilous, but stay together and be of stout heart and you *will* get through it; be sure of that my brave climbers.'

The siblings listened and both nodded with an air of renewed determination.

Daniel glanced at Sara. 'We can do it, Sis, eh?'

'Yeah… Yes we can.' Sara stood up straight. 'We *have* come a long way, I guess we can go a little further.'

'Good,' said Zac to the sound of Gertie's footsteps returning. He raised a bony finger. 'For a start, we know a shortcut that will shorten your journey considerably.'

Gertie joined them. 'The pigeons are sent,' she said to Zac.

Zac looked at her and nodded. 'Good, good.' He turned his head sideways. 'Now, where was I?'

'You were going to tell us about a short-cut,' offered Sara.

'Ah yes, of course. But wait there a moment. First I have some items you may find useful along the way.'

Zac walked to a shadowed corner of the cave to an old, wooden chest. He lifted the lid and it groaned with complaint. The questers looked on while Zac leaned over the chest and rummaged through the contents.

Gertie made her way towards the kitchen cavern. 'And I've prepared some food for you both,' she called as she walked. 'It may be a while before you see a hot meal again.'

When the goat herders were out of earshot, Sara turned to Daniel. 'What's a stout heart?' she asked quietly.

Daniel crunched his forehead. *Hmm.* 'It's all to do with balance, it'll be slippery and wobbly out there on the rocks and we must be *stout*-hearted not to fall over.'

Sara was doubtful. 'Are you *quite* sure?'

'Certain. Beyond a shadow of a stout!' Daniel laughed.

'It's hardly the right time for your silly jokes.' But Sara couldn't help it and a short smile escaped her lips. 'Idiot.' Her smile faded and she fell silent for a moment, thinking. 'Daniel?' she asked quietly.

Daniel had stopped grinning. 'I know, Sis, the marauders. Let's cross that path if we come to it.' *Let's hope we don't come to it!*

Zac called out from the chest. 'Ah, here we go. This is a length of rope woven from the beards of wild climbing goats.' He strode back to the waiting questers. 'Their hairs grow to withstand the harshest of weathers. I've platted strands together and coated them with special bees wax taken straight from Moody Woods.'

Daniel regarded the rope. 'It's tough to the touch.' The rope was a faded-yellow colour and gave off a weak shine.

'I grant that it's not much to look at,' offered Zac, 'but a stronger cord will not be found this side of the Rise.'

Daniel took the rope and looped it over his shoulder.

Zac handed Sara a small leather satchel. 'This satchel contains some pieces of black flint. Strike them off any rock and you'll get a spark strong enough to light small twigs. You never know when you may need a fire.'

Sara took the satchel from him and peeked inside. There were six pieces of flint in all, of varying shapes and sizes. 'Thank you so much, Zac, sir. We're ever so grateful for everything.'

'Yes,' agreed Daniel. 'Thank you for the food and shelter, the advice *and* this stuff.'

'Nonsense,' Zac replied. 'No need for thanks, nor time for that matter. There are a couple more items yet. Here now, take one of these each.' He removed two small, white whistles from around his neck that were attached to pieces of leather cord and hung them over their heads. 'These are bone whistles, carved from gizord bone. Tuck them into your clothes to keep them safe.'

Sara tucked hers in beneath her blouse. 'What are they for?'

'If you find yourself in grave danger, blow this whistle as hard as you can. If Bison is within range to hear it, he'll soon be by your side.'

Daniel's face was solemn. *He must be certain danger awaits us.* He looked to Sara and smiled reassuringly. 'Hopefully we won't be needing these, but useful to have, *just* in case.'

Zac raised another bony finger. 'There's one more thing young man. Here. You take this.' He handed Daniel a small, leather pouch. 'Inside you'll find flint powder. The powder is compacted into balls and wrapped in oil-soaked skins. Throw them at the rock and you'll get a burst of flame. These little gems can gain you precious moments in a fight.'

Daniel nodded and quickly tied the pouch to his belt.

Sara looked worried. 'With all this stuff you must be expecting big trouble for us then?'

Oh shoot, thought Daniel.

'Prepare for the worst, hope for the best. Eh?' said Zac.

'S'pose,' replied Sara. 'I mean how much worse could it get!'

Gertie returned carrying two bundles, one in each hand. 'Fix these to your backs, I've rolled up two fleeces for you and prepared some food. It's just some bread and cheese and a canteen of fruit juice to drink.' The fleeces were thick but soft and not too heavy; she had them rolled up and tied with cord, with two loops left to fit on the shoulders.

Daniel took the leather satchel containing the food from Gertie and put it around his neck. He fitted the fleece to his back. Sara tried to get her arm through the loop and spun full-circle twice in the effort.

'Here, let me help you with that,' said Gertie, and she hooked the loops over Sara's shoulders. She then looked at the sibling's faces and although she smiled her eyes remained sad. 'And now brave adventurers, it's near time to say goodbye. We'll show you the short cut. It's not far.'

Zac raised his hand. 'Hang on, what's this?' At Sara's feet stood the same little bonion that had guided them up the mountain. 'It seems this little dear has decided to adopt you.'

Sara raised her eyebrows. She looked from Zac to the bonion and back again.

'Go on then,' Zac encouraged. 'Aren't you going to pick up your little friend?'

'You mean I can keep her?' asked Sara, suddenly delighted.

Zac grinned with his now familiar grin. 'I think *she* means to keep you young lady. Keep her in your satchel, she'll be quite safe.'

Sara stroked the bonion's tiny head affectionately. 'I'll take the greatest care of you little friend.' She looked to the goat herders. 'Can I give her a name?'

'How do you know it's a she?' asked Daniel.

'I just do is all, a girl's intuition!'

Daniel rolled his eyes and the goat herders chuckled at the exchange.

Gertie joined Sara's side and stroked the little creature. 'Of course you can name her, make it official.'

'I'll call her Bobbin.'

'Bobbin the Bonion. Just perfect,' said Gertie.

Sara stroked the little creature once then popped it into the satchel with flint.

Zac rubbed his hands and took the hag's staff. 'Right so, just one more thing. We can't forget this old stick, now can we?' He quickly fixed the hag's staff under the ties of Daniel's fleece. 'Now, follow us.'

Daniel and Sara followed the old couple to the back of the cave and through a long, narrow crack in the cave wall. They stood in almost pitch-black darkness for a moment until Gertie struck a flint and lit a bulrush. With the light they found themselves inside a small, empty cavern but for a large lump of tree bark that was propped up against the wall. Gertie and Zac held one side each and lowered the bark to the floor. From behind where the bark had stood, they revealed a hole in the side of the cavern which the questers studied with curiosity.

Sara frowned, deep in thought. *I assume we're going through this somehow. I can see how I might fit, but I'm not so sure about Daniel.*

Daniel's thoughts echoed his sisters'. *Hmm, from bottom to top it's about up to Sara's shoulder in height, and half that in width. She should be ok, but it'll be a tight squeeze for me.*

The hole was completely blocked with tightly packed wool. Together Zac and Gertie wrenched at the wool from the middle of the pack and it soon began to loosen.

'Keeps out the draught,' said Zac as he worked a clump of wool free.

Daniel frowned slightly. *I wonder what else it keeps out.*

Seeing what the goat herders were about, Daniel and Sara began to help, and soon all the wool was removed. Before them was the entrance to a dark passageway that led deep into the heart of the mountain.

'*This* is as far as we can take you,' said Zac. 'This passageway will take you to a higher plateau east from here. When you get out the other side, you'll see the peak that holds the shard of the dragon's tooth in the distance. There are gullies and cracks along the way, and the passageway is narrow so try and stay steady. The air is thin, so stay quiet and don't stop till you see daylight. Halfway through you will find another bulrush. Light it, as this one will be fading if not already gone out. That's all I can say; good luck, my brave climbers, my heart is with you.'

Sara stepped up to Zac and threw her arms around him in a hug. 'Oh thanks for everything Zac. You've been so kind and helpful.' She turned to Gertie and hugged her too. 'Will we ever see you again?'

Gertie closed her eyes and held Sara's embrace. 'Who is to say, but know that you're in our thoughts and hearts and we'll always be part of your journey; that will never change.'

Daniel turned to Zac. 'What will we do when we get the shard of the dragon's tooth?'

'Well young man, you've come this far and farther you shall go. Just trust your wits and may magic of the heart guide you.'

Daniel shook his hand, thanked him again and turned to Gertie. 'Thank you too, Ms Gertie, you've been wonderful.' He hesitated shyly, then extended his hand.

Gertie shook it and smiled though her eyes were still sad. 'Don't mention it Daniel.'

'Come on then, Sara, let's go,' Daniel urged. As Sara climbed through the entrance, Daniel turned quickly and threw his arms around Gertie in a warm embrace, then without another word he jumped through the gap and was gone.

Chapter 8
Rocky Burrow

The fire from the bulrush illuminated the walls of the passageway as the questers leaned low making their way along.

Sara went in front, as she carried the flame. 'I can only see a few feet in front of me Daniel,' she whispered. *And I dread to think what might be lurking up ahead.*

All Daniel could see was Sara in front and the shadows that danced and flickered off the stone walls of the tunnel. 'Do you notice it's harder to draw breathe down here? Best shush now Sara.'

Sara inhaled deeply. 'I guess,' she replied and crawled on carefully. *Shush yourself, easy knowing you're not leading.*

The going was slow. After some time Sara noticed the shadows deepening. 'Hey Dan, the passageway is widening, although the ridge in the centre isn't, but see the walls to the sides, they're farther apart.'

'It's a pity the ridge isn't widening too, as *it's* all we have as a path.' Daniel glanced to one side and then to the other. 'I wouldn't fancy falling down there.' Deep gullies fell away into the blackness on either side.

Sara was nervous and fought the urge to talk; but when she felt the rock beneath her getting smoother, she decided to. 'Steady, Daniel. It's getting slippery; stay in the middle.'

Daniel followed her lead and took each step carefully. The going got slower.

A few more paces and Sara's natural curiosity returned. 'You know, this reminds me of school,' she blurted, a little too loudly for Daniel's liking.

'What? School! How can you think of school at a time like this?' he hissed back, but quickly thought again. 'Actually, Sis, I see your point. School is the last place I'd want to be right now, apart from here of course.'

'No, don't be such a numbskull, that's not what I mean, and *you* know it. What I meant is this reminds me of something I *learnt* in school.'

Sara couldn't see Daniel rolling his eyes in the dark. 'Here we go again. Dazzle me with your knowledge then.'

Sara, quite used to his reactions, ignored his smart tone. 'I think in the past water seeped down through the mountain and spilled across this part of the passageway; that's why the rock is so smooth hereabouts. I learnt about it in geography class.'

Daniel frowned. 'Hmm. I mustn't have been listening in that class.' *Why does she have to be so smart? Clever clogs.* He grinned in the dark. 'Say, Sara, by any chance did they teach you anything about magical islands in that class? Coz it sure would be useful right about now.'

'I wish they did,' said Sara. 'Actually I don't wish. Let's *never* wish for anything ever again.'

They both laughed together now, forgetting momentarily their bleak surroundings.

Sara screamed. *'Aaahhh!'* She jolted upright and banged her head off the roof of the tunnel.

Meanwhile Daniel, who had lost his concentration while laughing, collided into her and slipped to the ground. His laughter quickly turned to panic as he found himself hanging on with both hands over a pitch-black crevice. The crevice fell away into the heart of the mountain.

'Sara, Sara, what's the matter?' he gasped, 'You'll have to help me up. Quickly, it's too hard to get a grip.'

Sara held the back of her head in one hand and the torch in the other and turned to her brother. Her voice quivered in fear. 'Oh Daniel, I saw it; the most *awful, big brown rat*. Right in front of me it was, and its red eyes and its yellow teeth sticking out. It was right there in front of me, *staring at me.*'

Daniel struggled to tighten his grip. 'Listen to me, Sara, *forget* about the rat; you're going to have to pull me up. Otherwise you'll be going on alone.'

Sara turned back and waved the bulrush flame in a loop, illuminating the passageway as much as possible. 'Phew, it seems to be gone. I *hate* rats, filthy vermin.'

Daniel gritted his teeth. 'Sara, I can't hold on for much longer.'

Sara was shaking. She placed the burning torch down and took a deep breath to gather her wits. *Swallow your fear girl, he'd do it for you,* she told herself, and stepped back to help her brother. She reached over with one hand and grabbed a hold of the hag's staff that was fixed to the fleece on Daniel's back. She pressed her other hand against the roof of the passageway for support and tightened her fist around the staff.

'Right Daniel, when you feel me lift, you try to pull yourself up.'

The struggle of holding on was almost too much for Daniel. He just nodded his head and strained to keep a grip.

Sara braced herself and heaved with all her might. 'Grr,' she growled with the effort. But her growl turned to wonder when she felt a warm sensation passing through her arm. 'Oh my, what's happening?' she asked as Daniel seemed to float up effortlessly.

Daniel wide-eyed with surprise quickly stood up behind Sara. 'Did you feel it, Sara? Did you?'

'Yes, said Sara. 'It went *right* through me. What do you suppose it was?'

Daniel smiled. 'Magic Sis, what else could it be? Magic of the heart maybe.'

'There must be magic of the heart in this tunnel. Remember Tobias said it's all around us.'

'Sure. I guess, or perhaps it's in the staff itself. It felt *so* strange, almost like floating through the wishing-well again.'

Sara wore a stunned expression. 'I guess Zac was right, the magic in the staff *has* come to our aid. I was sure it was just a normal stick. Nothing would surprise me in this place anymore.'

'Yeah, I guess he was. Anyway, let's keep going. I'd take school any day over this rocky burrow.'

'Me too.' Sara turned and picked up the torch. *Oh shoot. The filthy rodent.* She paused again. 'But what about the rat? Maybe *you* want to go in front for a while?'

Daniel waved her forwards. 'You just said nothing would surprise you in this place anymore!'

Sara almost shouted. 'Yes, surprise, not terrify!'

'Look around you, Sis, the ridge is too narrow for me to risk passing you here. You'll have to continue to lead for now. Maybe the path will widen further on and I can get by you then.'

Sara started to sob. 'Daniel, you know I hate rats. I even hate mice, and rats are giant mice! And these are giant rats! That makes them giant, giant mice!'

Daniel couldn't help a chuckle, but did his best to sooth Sara. 'Come now, it was only one rat and the light probably played tricks on your eyes.'

'It was as big as a badger!'

'Are you sure it *wasn't* actually a badger?'

'Don't be an idiot Daniel, I know the difference between them, and this was a rat the size of a badger.'

'I suspect it wasn't as big as all that. Try to stay brave and we'll be out of here in no time. You'll see.'

'But I'm not brave. I've been scared senseless countless times since we got here and things just keep getting worse.' Sara hung her head and sobbed again.

'Hey, you listen to me now.' Daniel's tone was gentle. 'The opposite of brave is not scared, it's cowardly, and you're no coward. If you do something that puts yourself in danger even though you're scared, it makes you even braver than if you weren't scared in the first place. Do you get me?'

Sara sniffled and wiped her nose with her sleeve. 'I think so. I never thought I could be brave and scared at the same time. I *guess* I can lead for another bit then, seeing that I'm *so* brave!' She turned slowly in the passageway to continue in the direction they had been moving. 'Hey Daniel, it's not like you to say anything so clever.'

'No its not, is it. Hey, wait a second. What do you mean it's not like me?'

Despite her fears Sara smiled in the shadows. 'Shush now Daniel. Remember what Zac said about talking too much.'

'Hmm.' *Hmm. I'll let her away with that Jibe. At least she's calmed down about the rat.*

They continued on in silence for a time. Daniel tried not to think about hanging over the crevice and Sara tried not to think about the giant rat. The effort it took to crawl on all fours made it easier to forget but it was starting to take its toll on them. The lack of air didn't help and they soon began to tire.

The questers crawled onward till eventually they came to the spot where the second bulrush sat in a hole on the wall of the passageway.

'Thank goodness,' whispered Sara. 'This one has almost burnt out.'

'See if you can light it up and we'll keep on going,' said Daniel, quietly.

Beside the bulrush was a small alcove full of dark oil. Sara dipped the head of the new bulrush in the oil till it was soaked through. She then lit it using the end of the first torch.

She held the first bulrush out and half-turned to Daniel. 'What will I do with this one?'

Daniel pointed. 'Toss it on further.'

Sara placed the second bulrush back into the hole in the wall for a moment and with as big a swing as she could manage, she threw the first one up the tunnel. The pair watched the flame arc through the air and land about twenty paces ahead.

'Good shot, Sis, considering you didn't have much swing room,' offered Daniel.

'More like considering how tired I am,' replied Sara. 'See there where it's landed? The ridge has widened out.'

'So it has.' Daniel paused to look around. 'And guess what, we can stop crawling. Take a look up, the tunnel is deeper hereabouts.' He stretched out his arms and legs. 'Gosh, my bones do ache. Maybe we can rest for a spell, *then* I'll take the lead.'

'No,' said Sara, firmly. 'Remember what Zac said "do *not* stop." Besides, we've been in this rocky burrow long enough already.' *Eh, hello Daniel. Giant rats, let's not be hanging around!*

Daniel nodded. 'Okay then, I'll take the lead now. Hurry on there to where the torch has landed and we'll swap over.'

Sara turned slowly and walked towards the space where the first torch lay burning on the passageway ridge. She had only taken a few steps when she stopped suddenly and gasped with a sharp intake of breath.

Daniel collided into her again but managed to keep his footing. 'Sara,' he snapped. 'What is it now? Are you trying to knock me over again?'

Sara was frozen to the spot. 'Rats, *a swarm* of giant rats,' she rasped, barely able to get the words out.

Daniel pushed past her to see several pairs of eyes peering through the flames of the torch that lay burning on the path. The torch had almost burned out and its dying flames flickered frantically.

Sara was starting to panic. 'Daniel, what'll we do Daniel?'

'Easy, Sis, there *is* a lot of them but they don't seem to be passing the flame, perhaps they're scared of it.'

Sara looked on, terrified, as the dying flames of the torch cast huge shadows from the rats. The shadows danced up the tunnel walls in the flickering light. A black nose pointed through the flames and the giant rat it belonged to shrieked loudly as its whiskers melted. The questers jumped with fright at the sound of the shriek.

Sara started to cry. 'Daniel, do something Daniel,' she shouted.

Daniel fumbled around his neck with his fleece but couldn't get at his whistle. 'Sara, blow your whistle,' he shouted. 'Blow it now.'

Sara, stricken with fear quickly pulled her whistle off from around her neck and threw it towards the dying torch and the rats. It was a poor throw and the whistle disappeared over the side of the ridge and into the blackness.

'What on earth,' cried Daniel, losing his temper. 'You idiot, what did you do that for?'

'You said throw your whistle,' Sara shouted back. 'So I threw it.'

Daniel fumbled furiously with his fleece and found his own whistle. 'I said blow your whistle, b-l-o-w blow.' Daniel blew hard on his bone whistle and a long, shrill note sounded through the tunnel.

The sound of the whistle startled the rats and they all began to shriek wildly. More and more noses where poking through the shrinking flame.

Sara became frantic. 'Oh creepers, Bison isn't coming and we're about to be eaten by giant rats. The only thing between us and them is *that* torch and it's about to go out.' She waived the torch in her hand and shouted, 'We're going to die Daniel.'

'Snap out of it,' Daniel yelled back at her just as the torch on the ground burned out. 'Quickly throw some light down the tunnel so we can see the rats. As long we have the second torch, we can hold them off.'

But Sara didn't hear him properly. The sight and sound of the giant rats filled her with terror. The torch on the ground had just burned out and the last thing she saw was the swarm moving in the shadows. All she heard Daniel say was "throw" and "light". With an arch of her arm she tossed the second torch just as she had the first.

Daniel watched in horror as the torch sailed through the air and landed on the ridge. The shrieking rats jumped back from the burning bulrush.

Daniel couldn't believe it. 'Sara, *what* did you do? Have you lost your mind? I said throw some light, not *the* light!'

Sara screeched back, 'Shut up Daniel, you said throw and I threw! We're stuck in a hole in a mountain about to be eaten by giant rats. Why don't you do something instead of giving me stupid orders!' Her face was red with temper.

Daniel was furious. 'Stupid? I'm not the stupid one that threw our last light away. We can't back track in the dark, if we don't fall to our deaths the rats will catch us when the torch burns out.' He took a deep breath to collect his thoughts. *Focus Daniel, focus.* 'Look, they're getting braver. The flame won't hold them for much longer.'

Hundreds of red eyes could be seen glowing through the flames. Sara burst into tears afresh but Daniel made no move to comfort her, he just watched on as more and more rats burnt their snouts as they tried to advance past the fire.

Daniel had an idea. 'I'm going to grab the torch back.' His jaw was set as he shuffled the fleece-pack off his back.

'No Daniel, no,' Sara pleaded. 'You'll be too close to them. They'll get you.'

Daniel held her roughly by the arm and looked her in the eyes. 'Sara, they'll get us if I don't.' He let go and dashed for the burning bulrush.

Sara watched in fear as Daniel raced towards the torch and the giant rats. She saw Daniel dive with one arm outstretched. She saw a pair of red eyes and yellow teeth appear through the fire. She saw the pointed snout and brown body of a rat leap over the flame. She put her hands on her head screamed at the top of her lungs. 'Daaaaaniel, watch out Daniel.'

Daniel skidded along the rock and looked up just in time to see the menacing rodent land inches from his hand. He lay on the ground and stared into the rat's eyes. The rat's back arched and it bared its teeth, ready to pounce. The questers were frozen to the spot, Sara watching from back down the tunnel and Daniel where he lay. The black hairs on the rat's body stood up like bristles. Time stood still. The rat pounced.

Daniel rolled as the rat pounced and it landed in the space where Daniel had been. A monstrous growl sounded through the tunnel. Sara dropped to the ground with fright just in time to see Bison jump over her head. The big hound reached Daniel in one more bound and came to a stop. Bison's bulk filled the passageway as he stood over Daniel and lowered his massive jaws down to meet the rat in the face. The rat, tiny compared to the Rockwilder, shrieked and turned to flee back past through the burning flame. But it wasn't quick enough. With a flick of his neck Bison tore the throat of the rat and flung the lifeless body over the flame.

A deafening chorus of shrieking rang through the tunnel when the dead rat landed amongst the swarm. Bison matched the noise with a thunderous bark and charged through the flames of the burning torch, headlong into the swarm.

From where he lay, Daniel helplessly saw Bison's hind leg clip the bulrush as he passed it. The force of Bison's charge sent the torch flying across the tunnel, where it crashed into the wall. It fell away down the deep crevice, beyond the safety of the ridge that ran down the middle of the passageway. Sparks flew and the shadows danced frantically as the light failed. The last thing the questers saw clearly was Bison taking the giant rats two and three at a time between his massive jaws. Crush, tear and fling. And the chaos as the swarm turned on each other in a desperate attempt to escape the ferocious charge of the Rockwilder.

In the failing light Sara found the nerve to crawl up beside Daniel. Together they lay motionless while the sounds of shrieking, snarling, crunching and tearing pierced their ears. The noise continued close by but after a time it started to sound further away.

Sara leaned into Daniel's ear and spoke above the din. 'That was Bison. He's chased them further up the tunnel.'

Daniel said nothing.

The snarling of the great hound and shrieking of the giant rats had turned to echoes and finally faded away to nothing. The siblings lay in the darkness. There was only the faintest of light coming from the crevice where the bulrush had fallen. It was barely enough light to make out shapes in the dark.

Sara sighed. 'Thank goodness for Bison. Remind me to get a dog when we get home. A big dog, ha.' It was the nervous laugh of relief.

Daniel grunted, 'Humph.'

'What Daniel?'

'You think this is funny?'

'Daniel, I'm only glad it's all—'

'Shut up, will you?' Daniel jumped up and glared at Sara. 'First you knock me over. Then you leave me hanging while you *rabbit* on about mice! Then you lose the torch. *Who's* the numbskull now?' There was no humour in his tone.

Sara was too taken aback by his fury to cry again. 'I…I didn't lose the torch, Bison kicked it. And you *weren't* hanging when I mentioned the mice. It was when *you* didn't believe me about those disgusting rats. *You* said they were badgers!'

'Whatever.' Daniel waved his hand in front of his face. 'Just don't talk to me. In fact don't say anything at all unless you've something useful to say. Because of you, we're stuck. We can't go back because the ridge is too narrow back there to risk in the dark. We don't know how wide or narrow the ridge is up further either. We could still fall to our deaths further along. And *even* if we don't you've blinded us. We've no idea how Bison faired against the rats, if we continue forwards, we could easily end up as giant rats' supper!'

'That's not fair!' Sara shouted back. 'The rats would have been in front of us anyway torch or no torch. And if we tried to go back to the cave, they'd have gotten us from behind.'

'Whatever. Just shush while I think.'

'Daniel?' said Sara meekly.

'Didn't you hear me? I don't want to talk to you right now.'

Sara pleaded for his attention. 'I've an idea Daniel.' She fumbled with the satchel Zac had given her. 'Here, take a piece of flint. We can crawl along and bang pieces off the rock as we go. The spark should be bright enough for us to see a few paces ahead each time. At least we'll have some small light.'

Daniel was about to shout at her again but stopped short. *Hmm, it's actually a good idea.* He stared at her for a few moments, his eyes intense. *I'm not going to tell her though.* 'Fine, give me a piece then.' He was still angry. 'We'll follow Bison. I figure if he's won the fight, we'll get out the other end, wherever it is. If he's lost, well then the rats will get us anyway.'

Sara gulped in the dark. *Let's hope he won. Creepers, let's hope.*

Daniel scrambled past Sara to where his fleece-pack lay and fit it back over his shoulders. 'Let's get going,' he snapped and roughly crawled by her again to lead their way through the tunnel.

Sara smacked her piece of flint off the rock behind him. 'I'm coming already,' she snapped back. *I should've left him in Moody Woods. You'd swear he never made a mistake himself.*

They continued on in silence. The only noise was the crack as they struck their flints off the ground and the sounds of their gasps and grunts as they struggled onward. The peace and safety they had felt in the warmth of the goat herders cave was a distant memory.

Further on they found no trace of the rats or of Bison. Sometime after taking the lead, Daniel noticed a shift in the shadows and looking ahead he saw the reason why.

'There's daylight ahead.' He stood, put the flint in his pocket and hurried forwards with newfound strength.

Sara stood and followed slowly; she was too exhausted to share Daniel's haste.

At the end of the tunnel there was a hole in the side of the mountain and the daylight was pouring through it. The hole sat in the wall at Daniel's chest height and was big enough for the pair to scramble through. Daniel reached it and jumped up to climb through but dropped down again when he heard Sara wearily call out.

'Daniel, wait for me will you. I'm…I'm so tired Dan. I'll need a leg up.'

The tension from their row was still in the air but Daniel waited for Sara to reach the hole.

Daniel took the straps of Sara's fleece. 'Here, take this off from your shoulders. Look. We can use it as a step for you, and once you're up I'll pass it up to you.' He helped her remove the fleece-pack from her back.

'Thanks Daniel,' was all Sara managed.

One after the other they made their way through the hole and emerged out into the cool, fresh air of the Rocky Rise.

Chapter 9
A Murky Mist

The questers stopped next to a big boulder just twenty paces from where they had exited the tunnel. Next to the mouth of the tunnel the wall of the mountain turned at a right angle and continued eastward. The plateau stretched out east along the base of the peaks and south towards the plateau's edge. There were many boulders dotted across the plateau, though the main feature was the thousands of small, sharp, grey rocks and smoother, brown stone stumps, both of which covered the plateau as far as the eye could see.

Sara sat on a stump to rest, her strength drained. Daniel walked to-and-fro surveying their surroundings. The tension between them lingered.

Daniel glanced at Sara briefly and then directed his gaze across the mountain range. 'That must be it, two peaks over.' His voice remained tense.

Sara lifted her head. 'What's that Daniel?'

'It must be Nightmare Reaches. See how the peak is higher than the other peaks? It's exactly like Zac described it.'

Sara stared. 'Yes, yes I think you're right. Do you think that sparkling on the top could be from the shard of the dragon's tooth?'

'I hope so, otherwise what on earth are we doing here.' Daniel turned in a half-circle. 'We'll make our way along this plateau and hopefully it'll take us to the base of the peak.'

Sara stifled a yawn. She stretched her arms and spoke through it. 'What will we do when we get to the base of the peak?'

Hmm. 'We'll work that out when we get there.' He stared towards the highest peak once more then turned back to Sara. 'We best push on then. Are you ready?'

Sara had just wrapped herself in her fleece and was nestling in against the large boulder. 'Oh Daniel, must we go right this moment? Can't we rest for just a *short* while? Please Daniel, I'm *so so* tired.' She looked at him, her face sad.

Daniel frowned but read the pleading in her eyes. *She does look exhausted…but if she hadn't thrown the light we wouldn't have had to crawl in the dark, and that's what made us so tired.* 'Tell you what, you have a rest. I'm going to look around hereabouts to see what I can see.' His voice had softened only slightly. He turned to go

'Please Daniel, why don't you rest with me?'

Daniel ignored her and continued to walk across the plateau.

'Wait, Daniel.'

'What is it?' his reply was gruff.

'Don't leave me Daniel. Not now.'

'I won't be gone far.' He turned to go again.

Sara called out again. 'Daniel. Dan, I've been thinking about home.'

Daniel stopped and called back. 'What about home Sara? It's a long way from here, wherever here is.'

'I know Daniel, only I was wondering about Mum. She'll be frantic. We've been gone for two days almost. Maybe it wasn't such a good idea to take up this quest.'

'Maybe, maybe not.' *Hmm.* 'Well it's too late now either way. We're here and that's that.'

Sara lowered her head again. 'I guess.'

'Don't worry about it, Sara. The best thing we can do is complete the quest, maybe then we can think of home.'

'Stay and rest with me Daniel, please.'

'You stay put. I won't be long.' Daniel jumped over some loose rocks and set off across the plateau.

Sara watched Daniel trundle off for a few moments till it was clear he wasn't going to rest with her. *Why are brothers such stubborn idiots? Well I'm taking a nap and he'll be the tired one later.* She began to make herself comfortable and wrapped her fleece more tightly around her. With a slight shiver she felt her eyelids getting heavy and looked at the clear sky. *Oh time is getting on, it'll be evening soon. I think I'll just take a quick power nap, then Dan will be back for me.* Tiredness soon got the better of her; she yawned and her eyes fell shut.

Daniel, deep in thought, wore a frown as he strode across the rocks. *Why do sisters have to be so, so girly! Hmm. I suppose the flint was a good idea though, I'd never have thought of that. I'll tell her later.* He felt the chill in the air. *Gosh, this wispy mountain breeze can give you the shivers.*

The plateau was covered with crags and sharp rocks jutting up here and there which Daniel navigated around slowly. He looked ahead and saw that the wall of the nearest peak turned further on. *I'll just walk in this direction for a bit to see what lies around the next bend.* He continued on for a short while but the bend turned out to be farther away than first appeared. *Hmm. I'll be going this way later with Sara anyway, so maybe I'll walk out to the plateau edge instead and check out the view.* He turned right and began making his way to the edge, stopping only for a moment to remove the hag's staff from his fleece-pack. He smiled, pleased with his idea. *The staff will be handy for balance.*

Halfway across the plateau, the island below came into view. Daniel gasped in wonder. *Wow, what a view! Sara will be sorry she missed this.* A wave of remorse came upon him. *I guess I was hard on her; she is only twelve after all. I'll say sorry to her when I get back. She'd love to see the island from up here.* With a look of regret he glanced back the way he had come. *Yeah, I'll tell her how sorry I am soon.* He turned again and began to hasten, eager to drink in the beautiful sights before him.

On the horizon Daniel could see a lake with the sunlight bouncing off it and before that what seemed like a river of green, but he knew it to be grass blowing in the wind. To the east he could make out gentle hills scattered with white specks, and he wondered: *Are they houses or sheep? Oh it doesn't matter what they are, the view is breath-taking.*

Daniel approached the edge and caught his breath as he peered downward. *Gosh, I didn't realise how high up we are.* The foot of the mountain was far down below, so much so that Daniel stepped back as he felt a little dizzy. *Zac's short cut must have been a steady climb. No wonder Sara is exhausted. I'm sorry, Sis.*

Staring down the mountain, he could see the mysterious Moody Woods dancing with a myriad of magical colours. And far off to the west a row of purple mounds that he knew could only be Botanic Beaches, and beyond that again the ocean blue stretching as far as the eye could see. *This reminds me of the story of the flying stallion.* He stared at the sea for a long time wondering with each turn of the foam if he might see the mighty white wings for himself.

Gazing into the distance, Daniel continued to daydream letting his imagination take flight, hypnotised by the beauty of Well-Keeper Island. There he stayed wandering the timeless paths of imagination till something caught his eye. A shadow quickly spread across the island and Daniel suddenly felt cold. Turning around, expecting to see the sun blocked by a cloud, he gasped. A thick, misty fog had rolled in from the far side of the Rise, and Daniel could only see a few paces across the plateau. He could feel the moisture in the air and shivered. *I think I'll throw on my fleece. Lucky for me I didn't leave it back with Sara. Sara!*

'Sara!' he cried aloud.

Daniel wrapped himself in his fleece, worry adding to his haste. *I really hope I can find her in this murky fog. I never should have left her.* Facing away from the edge he walked into the mist and began calling his sister's name.

***

Sara had woken with a chill and quickly realised that she was embraced in a blanket of fog. *Oh shoot. I must've overslept and now look at this mist. I can hardly see anything. Come to think of it, Zac had mentioned fog in the air.* She shivered and rubbed her shoulders for warmth. 'Brrr.' *It's quite nippy. I wonder where Daniel is.*

'Daniel. Hey Daniel, are you out there?' she called aloud.

But to her dismay the sound fell where she stood. She tried again.

'Daniel. Daaaaaaniel. Answer if you hear me Dan.'

The echo that usually sings over a mountainside was lost. *Double shoot, my voice won't carry through the fog. It must be very thick.*

Sara slowly turned full-circle to find her bearings. *Let me see, I'm pretty sure we came out of the tunnel over there so I could go back that way.* With a sharp gasp she suddenly thought better of it. *The rats! No maybe not. Daniel did tell me to stay put.* She lowered herself slowly down against the boulder again.

Hurry up Daniel. Uncertainty washed over as she tried in vain to peer through the fog. She reached out and swung her hand through the air, leaving trails in the mist. *Creepers, it's everywhere.*

Sara stayed where she was with her hands pressed behind her against the boulder. Every now and then she called out looking for Daniel, but after a while without replies the worry set in. *What if something's happened to him? He's probably looking for me right now out in the fog. Oh it will be completely dark soon and I don't fancy spending a night on these slopes on my own.*

She roared. 'Daaanieeellll!'

Nothing. Against her better judgement, she decided to move from the spot she was in and started to talk to herself in a nervous but determined tone. 'Right, I'm not waiting here any longer. I'm coming to find you Daniel, and when I do, you'll get a piece of my mind for wandering off. Idiot.' She gulped and turned east. *This is the direction I seen him go so I'll do the same.* She began making her way along very carefully and every few breaths she'd cry out. 'Daaanieeellll!'

With every unanswered call her worry increased and her steps became less careful. Her foot snagged in a crack and she tripped and rolled across the rocky plateau.

'*Aaahhh,*' she cried as her hands scrapped off the stones. The fleece had cushioned her fall so she wasn't seriously hurt. But the fall had disorientated her and when she stood again, she had no idea what direction she was facing. *Oh no, please no. Where am I now?* She fought back the tears as her panic was quickly turning to fear. '*Daniel, Daniel, where are you?*'

When no reply came, she wrapped up tightly and plunged on into the fog trusting in luck alone to guide her.

***

Even with the aid of the hag's staff Daniel stumbled as he wandered blindly through the thick mist. Remorse gnawed at him. *Why did I leave her? I had no right to be mad with her. Zac had warned me to watch out for her. If she was here, she'd tell me what an idiot I was, and she'd be right. I'm sorry Sara.*

With no idea where the edge was, what direction he was going or where there might be a deep crevice, he was filled with fear. He frantically looked to-and-fro and every few moments he'd roar.

'Saarraa, stay where you are Sara!' *Don't worry, Sis, I'll find you.* But he didn't know where or how.

Time and time again he stumbled, fell and got back up. He struggled on through the swirls of grey. After countless trips and falls he stopped to catch his breath. At the same moment a birdcall pierced the fog. He looked up as a blurred shape fluttered over his head. Then another by his side and then another. Within moments, hundreds of the creatures were zooming by and calling out to each other. *I've heard those birdcalls before. They're some kind of sea birds.* He welcomed the chance for a short rest and hunched down to let them pass over.

***

Sara stood helplessly. She was tired and sore after falling so many times and didn't know which way to turn when something flew straight into her face.

She screamed. 'Aaahhh. Help. Get off. Help!'

Sara swiped at the fluttering shape that had somehow gotten tangled in her hair. She clawed frantically till the intruder left, only to glimpse scores more of them passing. Their wings left swirls in the fog as they passed. *Oh creepers, no. It must be the drooling bats!* Now the cry of birds was full in her ears but she was too upset to take any heed; she just sat on the ground with her hands on her head and screamed with all her might.

'Daniel, Daniel, where are you?' She dropped to her hunkers and whimpered, 'Please hurry, Daniel, I'm scared.'

'Where are you?' met Daniel's ears as he crouched in the fog. He quickly cupped his hands to his face and roared with all the strength his lungs could muster.

'Sara, Sara, is that you? Can you hear me, Sara?'

Sara gasped with surprise and relief. 'Yes, Daniel, yes, it's me, where are you? Are you okay?'

Daniel hastened towards the sound of her voice. 'Listen Sara, stay where you are, I'll be there soon.'

But Sara wasn't listening; she was back up and moving towards Daniel, or so she thought she was, for after a few paces she heard her brother shout back.

'I'm fine Sara, what about you? Are you alright?'

Sara's heart sank. Daniel's voice was fainter than before. *Oh no, we're moving in opposite directions.* She immediately stopped and called again. 'Oh Daniel, where are you?'

Daniel panted in the moist air and wiped his brow. 'Sara, please listen carefully. Stay where you are and I'll try to find you. It's no use us both moving around. Sound carries better on the ground, so stay low.'

'Okay Daniel, I hear you. I'll stay here.' Sara nestled against a rock to wait for him. *I'll stay here Dan, but hurry.*

Daniel squeezed his eyes shut for a moment when he heard the fear in his sister's voice. *I never should've left her alone.* With renewed determination he took off across the plateau. He scrambled over rocks and picked himself out of cracks when he stumbled. He angled around boulders and dragged himself across the cold stone. All the while he called to Sara so as not to stray too far.

But to his despair, he searched in vain. No matter how close he seemed to get to Sara, just when he thought he'd find her, her voice would sound farther away again. *It's hopeless. I can't see two steps ahead through this awful fog.*

He stopped and called out. 'Sara it's no use, the fog is too thick, we'll have to stay put till it clears. Do you hear me?' He waited for an answer, but silence greeted him. 'Sara, are you there?'

Sara replied through a fresh wave of sobs. 'I hear you Daniel. I'm tired, cold and scared and it's getting dark Daniel.'

Daniel frowned. *I feel the same, Sis, and I don't know what do either. But you don't need to hear that.* 'Aw Sara, don't you worry, I'm not far away; otherwise you wouldn't be able to hear me. Snuggle up in your fleece and try to keep warm. The mist will lift in no time, you'll see.' Daniel wasn't half as sure as he sounded. *Night time is close at hand, I can tell.* They sat for several moments without a sound till he heard a faint whimper. *That's Sara trying to be brave. She's only twelve years old and she's alone on this dangerous mountain and it's my fault.* Another wave of guilt washed over him. *I have to give her hope, somehow.*

'Hey Sara, do you remember this one?' he called through the mist, and after another moment he began to sing:

'Hush now, my little one, dry away your tears
Even if it's dark and cold, know that I am near.'

'Do you remember, Sis? Mum and Dad used to sing it to us on cold, winter nights to help us fall asleep.'

Sara said nothing and Daniel hung his head. 'Well maybe you were too young to remember. It was a bit babyish, but it's still a nice song.'

Silence followed for a moment but then Sara's soft voice sang across the rocks:

'I will turn the coldness warm right throughout the night
I will make the darkness bright till comes the morning light'

Daniel near leapt with joy. 'Gosh Sara, you do remember! I knew you would.'

There didn't seem anything more to say, so together they joined voice and sang courage into each other's hearts:

'Hush now, my little one, dry away your tears
Even if its dark and cold, know that I am near

I will turn the coldness warm right throughout the night
I will make the darkness bright till comes the morning light

So sleep, my little darling, you're always in my heart
Peace, my little darling, we'll never be apart
You will see how close I am when the sun appears
Be brave now, my little one, and sing away your fears

I will guard you with my love beside you all the while
Come the morning when you wake together we will smile
So sleep, my little darling, you're always in my heart
Peace, my little darling, we'll never be apart'

And so it was that Daniel and Sara spent their second night on Well-Keeper Island, lonely, cold and huddled against the stones of The Rocky Rise. With nothing for comfort but the sound of each other's voices and memories of their parents singing them to sleep.

Chapter 10
Close Shave

Daniel woke from an uncomfortable night's sleep. He stood away from the boulders that had served as a bed and shelter and stretched his weary bones. He looked around and suddenly realised he was standing in broad daylight. *Gosh, the fog has lifted. Sara will be glad. Sara!* He cleared his throat, ready to call her name when a scent in the air caught his attention. A light mountain breeze sailed over the plateau and Daniel sniffed again, inhaling deeply. *Smoke! Who could it be? It's hardly Sara or she'd have called out looking for me.* On high alert Daniel dropped to his hunkers and scanned his surroundings. *Where is it coming from? It could be the marauders Zac mentioned.*

South of his position but some distance away he could make out the plateau's edge. He stepped around the boulders that he'd used as a shelter and could see to the north the mountain face rising before him. The mountain face was an equal distance from his position as it was to the plateau's edge. *Hmm, I guess I'm about half way across the plateau then.* To the west in the distance he could see the curve of a mountain peak and the area of the mountain where they'd exited the tunnel, as well as clusters of big boulders dotted across the plateau. *I really hope Sara is behind some of those rocks.* He gulped. Lastly, he looked to the east. East looked much like the west except in the distance the plateau dipped out of view due to a downhill slope. As he stared, an easterly breeze wisped over the rocks and with it, Daniel saw puffs of grey smoke rising from a distant campfire. Instinctively Daniel dropped to the ground and his breath quickened. *Could it be marauders? Possibly. Might they already have Sara? I doubt it; she'd have kicked and screamed. I'd have heard them catch her at least.* His mind raced. *I can't take the chance; I'll have to get as close as I can to check.*

With sweat on his brow, Daniel squat-jumped, crawled and slid east across the plateau. Fear for Sara's safety urged him to haste, while the caution needed not to get caught told him to tread carefully. Torn, he crept ever closer to the source of the smoke.

The smoke was clearly visible now some thirty paces ahead. Daniel saw a cluster of boulders grouped together on the plateau. *These will do as cover,* he thought as he crept from one to another to stay out of view of the campfire and its unknown company. Just as he was scrambling over a clear area of rock, gruff voices raised from close by.

'Darn and blast. The eggs have burnt.'

Daniel froze for a moment, then ran and dived behind the nearest boulders. He was almost upon the campfire now. He held his breath and listened as another deep voice shouted.

'Fool. They were all we had to eat. Now go catch something for breakfast.'

Daniel exhaled as quietly as possible and took short, sharp breaths, quickened by fear. *Think Daniel. Okay, sounds like all grown men. So far.* He held his breath again to listen.

'It's this blasted mountain air, the campfire blazed up in a flash and the eggs were ruined. Can't we cut a chunk off the deer?'

'No. The venison is to be shared with the men. It's a long trek through the passes and the meat will spoil if we cut it. The going is slow enough with the captive as it is. The meat would never last.'

Captive! Daniel's hearted pounded. *Oh no. please no.*

'Now get hunting or we'll use your carcass as bait,' bellowed the last voice.

Laughter followed from what sounded like a group. Daniel's brow furrowed with concentration. *I count four maybe five voices, all men. Strange accents compared to Zac. No mention of a girl, but who else could the captive be? I'll have to take a look.*

'Go yourself you lily livered mongrel. I'm stayin' put,' replied the man that burnt the eggs.

'Why you, I'm gonna give you the thrashing of a life time,' the other voice snarled back.

The sound of a scuffle broke out followed by more laughter and jeering.

'Ho.'

'Get him.'

'Woo-hoo, good kick.'

'Darn and blast.'

'Hey did you see that.'

'Haa-haa, he got him good.'

Daniel took the fight as his opportunity to risk a look. Ever so slowly he moved his head around the rock till he could see the scene behind. The group were camped in a small crater on the plateau which gave some shelter. In the centre of the crater a campfire burned, surrounded by a circle of stones. Scattered here and there around the crater were bows and arrows, spears, wooden clubs, ropes and travel packs. There were six men in dark, dirty clothes and worn, leather boots. Some had long hair, others wore shabby hats. All the men were scruffy and unshaven. Two of the men were locked together in a scuffle while the others stepped around them, cheering on the fight.

Daniel edged further into view and glanced to the left, past the commotion. *Where's the captive?* There was something on the ground that wasn't moving. It was hard to see through the tangle of legs so Daniel dropped lower. He could just see a dead deer tied by the legs to a pole. *That's the deer but where is Sara?*

The quarrelling men fell and rolled through the campfire. This was followed by more shouting and growling from the others as they made to contain it. The men, distracted didn't notice Daniel stick his head out further and glance right, towards the back end of the crater. Seconds later he withdrew back behind the boulder, completely out of sight. His heart raced with fear and relief. *It isn't Sara, but who is it?* He had seen a man sitting, propped up against the side of the crater. The man was dressed much like the others except his hands were tied behind his back and he had a cloth sack over his head.

Daniel was frantic. *Okay they don't have Sara but they have a captive which means they are definitely dangerous. They must be the marauders Zac saw in the lower passes. I can't worry about the captive, poor man, whoever he is. I must find Sara, but I can't call out for her.* He pressed up against the boulder and shoved his fist into his mouth with frustration. *I've no idea what direction to go to look for her, but they could find her if I don't. C'mon Daniel, think will you.* But nothing came to mind. *Oh she'll wake at any moment, call out and alert the marauders to her whereabouts. I just know it. It's all my fault for leaving her.*

Daniel, sick with fear, despaired and lowered his head into his hands. The scuffle continued close by. With his eyes closed he came to a decision. *All I can do is make my way back to the tunnel, check behind every boulder on the way and hope that they don't see me.* He slumped momentarily. *It's a stupid idea.* But then he thought of Sara. *Still, I've got to try for her.*

Daniel crouched down, preparing to make a dash back the way he'd come, when off to the right a flash of green caught his eye. For a moment he thought it was a plant blowing in the mountain breeze but then thought again. *Hang on, none of the plants and shrubs up this high have that strength of colour.* He quickly glanced around the plateau to be sure. Here and there were desert-brown prickly shrubs. There were a few clumps of pale-green grass poking up between the rocks. He saw an occasional bare tree but for a few faded-yellow leaves, but nowhere on the plateau could he see any plant that full green colour. Still crouched down he stared again to the right and sure enough he could see the little green shape waving, but not in the wind. *It's Bobbin.* Daniel could hardly believe it. *Its Sara's little bonion friend.*

The little bonion was waving her tiny arms, beckoning Daniel over to her position behind another big boulder. Daniel's mind reeled. *It must, she must know where Sara is. She must be aware of the threat. Isn't that what Zac said they do?* With no one to answer the questions in his mind he frowned, then gulped to build up the courage to leave his hiding place and scramble over to where Bobbin was waving frantically. Suddenly the sound of the scuffling marauders came to an end with one of the gruff voices from earlier.

'Enough rough and tumble,' the voice shouted. 'The next man to throw a punch will be thrown down a ravine. Now, both of you go find something for breakfast. *Now!*' he roared.

This was all the courage Daniel needed. He tightened the fleece-pack on his shoulders and dashed towards the boulder and the little bonion. The boulder was some fifty paces away but he made it in twenty-five.

Breathless, Daniel whispered to Bobbin. 'You can,' he paused to breathe in, 'You can take me to Sara, right?'

Bobbin nodded and gestured west across the plateau. She pulled Daniel's trouser leg and Daniel knew what she meant.

'I know little friend, there's no time to lose. Lead the way.'

Together, Daniel and Bobbin scrambled across the plateau, constantly looking over their shoulders. They ducked, dived and crawled as several times the marauders came too close for comfort. Bobbin halted and Daniel after her as there was a moment of silence followed suddenly by the sound of voices from nearby. The marauders were dangerously close and the pair dived in behind the nearest boulders. Daniel could hear clearly what one of the men was saying.

'Check between the boulders, we might find a gull's nest if we're lucky.'

Daniel lay flat on the rocky ground and held his breath. He heard the sound of boots scuffling and exhaled quietly. With the slowest of movements he slid along on his tummy and with one eye he peered around the boulder. A short distance away he could clearly see two of the rough-looking men. Their dark hair and unshaven faces beaded with sweat from the fight. Their clothes where dirtier close up and they both carried knives on their belts. One carried a net and the other a wooden club. They looked dangerous. The marauders were glancing around the plateau and pouncing around each boulder in the hope of catching some quarry. Daniel gulped and slid back out of sight.

***

Sara awoke with a sneeze and opened her eyes to find the source of her itchy nose. Flying busily around her was a pretty butterfly with the colourful pattern of its wings standing out in the sunlight. *The sunlight*, she realised, *the fog has lifted*, as the memories of last night came flooding back to her. Standing up, she stretched and gazed around her. To her back was a big boulder, the same one she had nestled into for the night. *I reckon I'm about halfway across the plateau because I can see the plateau edge is the same distance that direction as the mountain wall is back there.* She glanced south then north again to be sure, satisfied that her calculations were correct, when the sound of voices greeted her ears. *I wonder who that could be. It must be Zac talking with Daniel. He must have come through the tunnel after Bison.* With a sense of anticipation she cleared her throat and raised her hands to her mouth to shout out to them. Suddenly a hand came from behind and roughly clamped her mouth shut. Sara's heart leapt with fright and she froze momentarily in fear; just enough time for a second hand to wrap around her waist and hold her tight.

In a split-second Sara realised she'd been grabbed and a wave of terror brought her from her shock. She struggled to break free and scream, but the hands held her firm.

'Mmmm, grrr,' she forced through the fingers over her mouth and kicked backwards at the shins of her attacker.

'Darn it Sara, would you shush and stay still,' rasped a voice she knew.

Ever so gently the hand around her waist loosened and she turned slowly, wide-eyed with surprise. Daniel looked back into her eyes and still with one hand clamped over her mouth raised a finger to his lips.

'Shush,' he whispered.

A wave of different feelings washed through Sara at once. She was about to blurt out a list of questions when Daniel held her firmly by the shoulders and looked into her eyes.

'Speak quietly Sara. There are marauders hunting close by. *Very* close.'

'But, but,' Sara hissed, 'But where were you?' Her tone was angry. 'I couldn't find you and then the bats came and—'

'Bats, eh?' Daniel interrupted. 'What bats? I was asleep, I smelt smoke and saw the marauders. They're dangerous men Sara, trust me. There's no time to explain. Bobbin led me to you.' His tone was hushed.

Sara scrunched her nose. 'Bobbin? What was Bobbin doing with you?'

But Daniel didn't answer as right in his line of sight a cloud of dust appeared. Sara caught his eye movement and she turned to look. It only took a second for them both to realise something or someone was fast approaching so together they dived back in behind the nearest boulders. A moment later they saw a blur of grey, flapping feathers as a startled gostridge dashed by their position, followed by the grunts and shouts of the two marauders.

'Aaarr. After it man! Don't let it get away.'

'Grrr. Keep up then and help me fool.'

The questers froze to the spot, afraid to move, afraid to breathe. One of the marauders bounded by a moment later with heavy footfalls as his boots hit the ground. They could hear the second man approach too when suddenly he stopped and yelled out.

'Wait up. Wait,' he bellowed.

The voice sounded dangerously close to the questers. They held their breaths. The gruff voice continued.

'It couldn't be gone too far. It'll be hiding around here somewhere. Check behind the rocks.' He kicked some gravel. 'Daft bird,' he added with a grumble.

The questers could see through a small gap between the boulders that hid them. One of the marauders walked into their view. Daniel's heart raced. Sara ducked as low as she could and squeezed her eyes shut, hoping against hope that he'd somehow miss them. Daniel refused to look away. He could see the man's dark beard as he glanced around the plateau. He could see the wooden club in hand. The marauder was all of ten paces away from their hiding place and started making his way towards them.

Daniel ducked down beside Sara but kept his eyes open. He could hear the man approach now and counted the steps in his head. *Three, four, five, six. He must be right next to us. Seven.* Daniel gulped. He could see the man's brown, leather boots through the gap; they were worn and scrapped from mountain travel. One of the boots had a hole in the toe. Daniel picked up a small rock. *I'll break his toe.* It was all he could think of. He raised the rock with both arms and waited for the marauder to step around the boulder and find them. The boots scuffled on some gravel. *Eight, nine!* Daniel gripped the rock tightly, ready to slam it down when suddenly the other man roared from a short distance across the plateau.

'Quick man. I have it cornered. Hurry before I lose an eye.'

The marauder took off at a run and again Daniel counted the steps. *Twenty-three, twenty-four, twenty-five.* When he counted to forty-four, he exhaled and quietly put down the rock to listen. Sara risked a peek from where she crouched and Daniel made the shush motion at her. This time she didn't struggle. The marauders could be heard from not far off.

'Okay I'm ready with the net. When I throw, you club it. Got it?'

'Got it.'

'Aaarr,' one of the men shouted. This was followed by the loud squawking of the gostridge and the heavy flaps of its wing beats.

'Darn it the daft bird is getting away.'

'You're the daft bird you let it jump right past us, why didn't you club it?'

'Shut up fool, you missed with the net. Now get after it.'

The sound of the men's boots and the squawking of the gostridge rang over the plateau as the marauders gave chase to the fleeing bird.

The questers stayed put and listened to the sound of the pursuit as it faded in the distance.

Sara chanced a whisper. 'It's best we stay hidden Daniel, until we're sure their gone.'

Daniel just nodded. He remembered well Zac's warning about the marauders and the captive they held back at the campfire was proof aplenty. *That poor man, tied up with a sack on his head. I can't help him. I must think of Sara's safety, and my own for her sake.* He was still shaken at how close they had come to getting found and taken, or worse. *Hmm, I won't tell her what I saw. It will only frighten her more*—his thoughts were interrupted by the sound of the men, nearby again.

'Ach we've lost it. Dumb gostridge.'

'Dumb you more like it, it out smarted you.'

'Out ran me is all, let's get back. Waste of time this.'

'Come on then, we haven't got all day, we'll take its eggs at least, they're back there in the nest. I left my cloak by the boulder so we'd find the nest again.'

The voices had come and gone past the questers hiding place as the marauders backtracked in the direction they had first come from.

After a very long, silent wait Daniel finally stood up and wiped his brow. 'Phew, *that* was a close shave.'

The fear and tension since the tunnel finally overcame Sara and she jumped up and punched Daniel in the arms. 'I'll close shave you Daniel Taylor.'

'Eh? What do you mean?' asked Daniel, confused. 'I found you, didn't I? And we're safe, aren't we?'

'Found me? You never should have left me!'

'You should have stayed put!'

'Safe you say, for how long? I didn't feel too safe lost in the fog! I didn't feel safe when those bats came or when those creepy men almost caught us. Maybe you feel safe but I haven't felt safe since you made that stupid wish!'

'Hey, you made the stupid wish not me, but what do you mean bats?'

'Well you pushed me to make it, and I mean the bats that attacked me in the fog. They were flying all over the place and screeching like crazy.'

Daniel suddenly realised what she meant and his frown turned into a smile. 'Oh Sara, those weren't bats, those were seagulls is all. Actually if they hadn't arrived, I wouldn't have dropped to the ground, and that's when I heard you call.'

'Well…well,' Sara tried to think of something else to say but her anger gave way to relief and she rushed over and gave Daniel a hug. 'I'm sorry Daniel. I *should* have stayed put. I was just so scared. Thank you for finding me.'

The tension between them melted as Daniel hugged her back. 'Hey now, I'm the one who's sorry,' offered Daniel. 'I never should have left you and I shouldn't have been so horrible to you in the tunnel either. By the way, that idea you had with the flint back there was really clever, I'm surprised I didn't think of it.'

'You did plenty Dan. You can't think of everything.' Sara grinned. 'You did think of that song you sang, even if it was a *bit* babyish! Very uncool.'

'Hey wait a second. You sang it too!'

'Don't worry Dan, I won't tell anyone… Thanks for singing it though.' She lingered for a moment. 'Hey Dan?'

'Yes Sara?'

'Why does everything have to be bigger and fiercer on this crazy island?'

Daniel released from the hug and looked at her. 'We'll just have to be bigger and fiercer too, eh Sara?'

'How can we be bigger?'

'Oh.' Daniel thought for a moment, then punched the air determinedly. 'We'll be crazier, then. Yeah, crazier and fiercer!'

'You're crazy alright.' Sara giggled and gently punched him in the arm. 'Idiot,' she added warmly.

'Numbskull,' replied Daniel. He grinned and lightly returned the gesture.

Chapter 11
Make Haste

Reunited, the sibling's parked the memories of the tunnel and the rough night in the fog to focus on the task ahead.

Sara felt her tummy rumble. 'Gosh, I'm quite hungry. Should we eat something before continuing?'

Daniel shook his head. 'No, we should make haste to the peak.' He stared east. 'It's still quite away from here.'

'It's not like you to turn down food,' said Sara.

'I *am* hungry, believe me. But I'll rest easier once we reach the peak. We'll have to be extra vigilant now for those marauders. Although I don't think they'll be back this way anytime soon, they seemed like they were travelling further and only stopped to camp.'

Sara looked solemn. 'Actually, that's the main reason I wanted to eat now; to let them get well ahead of us, wherever they were going. They seemed like an unfriendly bunch.'

'I know, Sis. But we've lost too much time already. We're well into our third day with only one treasure found so far.' Daniel patted the staff that was fixed through the ties in his fleece-pack. 'The sooner we get the shard of the dragon's tooth the sooner we can get off this big old rock.'

Sara smiled. 'A rock! Don't you mean a mountain?'

'Some say po-tayto, some say po-tato.' Daniel grinned. 'C'mon then, let's get going.'

As Sara hoisted her fleece-pack onto her back she spotted something. 'Daniel, what's that on your leg?'

Daniel looked down to see a green shape cushioned in the crease of his combat trouser-leg.

Reaching down he scooped it up. 'Would you look at that? It's Bobbin and she's fast asleep. I almost forgot about her. She helped me find you when I couldn't call out.'

'*Oh yeah*, you said that. But she was in my satchel with the flint,' said Sara with astonishment.

'I know. It's amazing,' agreed Daniel. 'She just showed up in the nick of time.'

Sara gently placed the sleeping bonion back in her satchel. 'Poor little thing, she must be exhausted.'

'Right,' said Daniel, 'we go east.'

They decided to go along the wall of the mountain at the back of the plateau, and then continue east towards the turn in the mountain that Daniel had trekked towards the previous day. This meant that they would pass far left of the crater were the marauders had camped and hopefully well out of sight, in case any of the rough men still lingered there.

The sun was warm and the breeze light. Occasionally birds could be seen flying overhead. Sara's natural curiosity soon returned but she resisted the urge to talk when she noticed Daniel's face had become grim. *He's been awfully quiet. I guess he's being doubly cautious because of the marauders. Hmm, maybe.* She left her thoughts there as they came around the turn in the mountain.

'Wow,' said Sara. 'It's so very high up, how will we get near it?'

Daniel gazed skyward towards the highest peak of Nightmare Reaches. The tip of the peak sparkled in the sun.

'To be honest, Sis, I've no idea, let's cross these rocks to the base of the peak. We might see a way up when we get a little closer.'

In front of them lay a field of jagged stones with sharp ends protruding up in all directions, and to their left stood a smaller peak, standing next to the one they sought. Crossing through the jagged stones was difficult and here and there a foot got stuck. Daniel stumbled and the fleece-pack on his back snagged on a sharp stone.

'Let me help you with that,' offered Sara as she unhooked the snag. 'You should really watch where you're going. A bad fall here could lead to nasty cut.'

Daniel, his brow furrowed, gave a mumbled reply.

'You're not even listening to me!' said Sara. *He's hiding something, I know it.*

'What's that Sara, eh?'

'You're hiding something Daniel Taylor and I want to know what it is.'

'No, no. I'm just being extra cautious. Marauders, you know, Sis.' He raised a hand above his eyes and viewed ahead. 'Say, look there. It's not actually the base of the peak. There are some large rocks before it.'

Sara was not convinced, *Hmm, I wonder,* but she let it go for now and stared ahead.

Some distance in front of them stood a wall of oval-shaped standing stones. The large rocks stood in a row next to each other and formed a barrier between the questers and the highest peak of Nightmare Reaches. With careful steps they slowly made their way towards the wall of rocks. Caution was necessary if they didn't want to slip and get spiked by the many sharp edges around them. As they got closer, they could see spaces in the wall between each standing stone.

'We'll climb through one of those gaps to see how far we'll have to go on the other side,' said Daniel.

'Shouldn't we stop for a rest?' Sara asked hopefully.

Daniel frowned. *Hmm.* 'If the coast is clear on the other side of the wall, we'll stop for a rest, and some food.'

'Finally,' said Sara. 'I'm starving!'

'Me too, Sis. Just a little further to be on the safe side.'

'Safe side of what? You said the marauders should be long gone.'

Daniel's frown remained. 'Eh…em. Safe side of that wall I mean. Anything could be on the other side. C'mon, stop wasting time then if you're hungry.' *I can't tell her about the captive, she'd be too frightened.* Daniel took off again across the jagged rocks and increased his pace.

It was Sara's turn to frown. *He's hiding something alright. I'll get it out of him.* She made haste after him.

They barely had to duck their heads to climb through a gap between two of the big, standing rocks. On the other side they could clearly see the wall of the peak that held the shard of the dragon's tooth, but to their dismay some fifty paces ahead, they were separated from the peak by a deep ravine.

'Gosh, that's a pretty big gap between us and the peak,' said Sara, as the mouth of the ravine came into view. 'Do you suppose it's Whirlwind Ravine?' she added a little nervously.

Daniel stared across the remaining ground between them and the gaping ravine. 'I think so. It must be, and that means we're on the right track. Mind you, I don't feel any wind.' *Hmm.* He frowned. 'There's only one way to find out. We'll make our way out to the edge, but first we'll stop for a rest.'

Sara gave a sigh of relief. 'At last, my legs are aching.'

'Mine too, and my arms. I suspect the fleeces took in a fair bit of moisture last night in the fog. It adds weight to them,' said Daniel while shaking the fleece-pack off his shoulders.

'That explains it. My arms are about to fall off! Let's roll them out to dry in the sun.' Sara shook hers off too.

'Good idea. And we'll sit under the big rocks to eat and rest while the fleeces dry out.'

They unrolled their fleeces out flat. To their surprise the fleeces were only wet on the outside. The inside lining was bone-dry and the pair realised that's what kept them warm and dry through the cold, dark hours the night before. They sat cross-legged atop a flat stone while eating brown bread and goat cheese washed down with cold fruit juice.

As they sat, Sara noticed the worried look return to Daniel's face. 'So Daniel Taylor, are you going to tell me what's on your mind or I have to shake it out of you?'

Daniel gulped down a mouthful of food. *Oh shoot. Am I that obvious!* 'Eh nothing. Nothing much. I was just thinking about the view of the island from the plateau edge,' he replied unconvincingly.

Sara stopped eating and raised her eyebrows. 'Nice try Daniel. But try again. You've been acting weird ever since those marauders left and I want to know why.'

Daniel pressed his lips. *Hmm, come on brain, think will you. Don't tell her about the captive.* 'You're right Sara. I've been bothered about the time-line. Tobias said five days and four nights. We've spent two whole nights on the island so far and only found one treasure. Like I said earlier, this is our third day. I've just been worried about failing is all.' He looked at his feet.

Sara believed him. 'Hey now, C'mon. Where's the Daniel that's been encouraging me to keep the head up and stay brave? We're trying, aren't we? I've got your back, don't I? Team Taylor, eh?

Daniel felt guilty for not telling her the real reason for his worry, but he smiled at Sara's encouragement. 'Yeah, that's us. Team Taylor, I like it. But don't tell anyone when we get home, *just* in case it sounds a bit silly.'

Sara laughed. 'Deal.'

Something suddenly occurred to Daniel. 'Hey Sara, you were asleep when the goat herders told me about some other strange things about the island. While we wait for the fleeces to dry, I'll tell you if you want?'

'Of *course* I want,' Sara encouraged. 'The more we both know the better. I'm sick of surprises!'

'Zac told me of another legacy. It was how Well-Keeper Island came to have a Great Lake.'

Daniel retold the story as he'd heard it in Zac's words.

Chapter 12
The Vale of Willows

In the time before the coming of the dragon there was a place on Well-Keeper Island known as the Vale of Willows. It was a beautiful area near the south of the island. Its gentle slopes were home to a variety of willow trees. People and animals alike often wandered among them; it was a peaceful place that held an air of tranquillity. But like so many other places on the island, it fell foul to the fury of the black dragon.

Alas, after the dark foe was vanquished, by the time the mighty flying stallion champion of light and hope happened upon the Vale of Willows and saw that it was consumed from one end to the other in the fires of the dragon, it seemed too late. For the fires here had been intense, and neither the lesser horses nor the rain had quenched them. The majestic willows were twisted and gnarled in the flames, and the once fur-soft grass was blackened and sharp as the fires surrounded everything without mercy. The winged steed stalled but for a moment, taking in the scene of the once-beautiful Vale of Willows, now a flaming blur of tortured plants, charred grass, smoke and fire. Craning his neck, the flying stallion spread his mighty wings, shook his silver main, turned in the air, and flew with all speed towards the ocean blue. On-lookers from the grassy plains despaired at the sight of the white horse fleeing the devastation caused by the black dragon. Cries rang out across the island that the Vale of Willows was lost as the stallion disappeared over the distant hills and beyond the dunes of Botanic Beaches.

And so the fires of the Vale raged on unchecked, and many who lost hope shrank in the shadows with fear. But some that stayed and watched on, clinging to a shred of hope that something might be done, found themselves turning towards the ocean as a thunderous sound met their ears.

On the horizon a thick cloud of dust had appeared, and tremor after tremor suddenly shook the island. The cloud of dust moved towards the Vale as though it was driven by a gale, but then to the fore of the cloud the head and the wings of the mighty steed could be seen. His legs flayed in the air and his hooves pounded the ground before him. His mighty strength and the wondrous magic that poured forth from his mane fused, and as he charged, he ploughed up the land, carving a deep channel through stone and soil as he went. Churning to dust the last hill, the edge of the Vale crumbled under the force of the stallion and all at once his mighty wings spread and the skies were filled with his beauty. While below him came a torrent of water that burst along the channel he'd carved, and it gushed down into the Vale of Willows. It only took moments for the water to reach the flames and devour them. The willow trees warped, swayed and twisted as the water rose in the Vale, geysers of spray and steam erupted from the surface and magical sparkles danced in the air. The tips of the willows clawed towards the sky, helpless against the rushing water. Up in the skies the flying stallion oversaw the drowning of the Vale of Willows. Although the trees could not be saved from the dark magic of the dragon, they had been submerged in a magical lake. And as the flame died from the highest twig on the last willow beneath the rising waters, the white steed spread his mighty wings once more and circled the newly made lake. Trails of magical dust poured from his mane and tail, covering the lake in a shower of coloured rain.

Soon after, the flying stallion was retreating in the distance, a blazing sight of shimmering white with the sunlight bouncing off him, and the surface of the Great Lake was almost still but for the gentle ripples playing to the tune of the breeze that whispered across the top. And so the once-beautiful Vale of Willows remains to this day the Great Lake, and twice a day the water rises and drops, ruled by the laws of the ebb and flow of the tide from the ocean blue. At high tide when the Vale is full, the lake shimmers a crystal-blue colour, but at low tide when the waters retreat strange swirls and black shapes can be seen patrolling its murky bottoms. And it's at a time also when the water recedes that a dank swamp can be seen in the middle of the lake. The swamp was once a high mound in the middle of the Vale of Willows and home to an array of beautiful plants. Now it's a mysterious quagmire surrounded by the Great Lake of Well-Keeper Island.

Chapter 13
Cross Over

Daniel, quite pleased with himself, allowed a few moments of silence to follow when he finished the story. *I remembered the tale well if I do say so myself. I wonder what she thinks.*

'Can you imagine it, Sis?' he encouraged. 'The stallion created the tidal lake by carving a channel through the land from the sea to the Vale. He used seawater to put out the fires, clever, eh?'

Sara frowned but made no reply.

Gosh, I must've told it well. She's so impressed for once she has nothing to say! 'Well, Sis, what do you think?' Daniel pushed. 'Pretty amazing, huh?'

But Sara had stopped listening. 'Shush Daniel,' she hissed.

'What do you mean "shush", weren't you listening to my story? Weren't you impressed?'

Sara replied in hushed tones. 'Of course, I was listening. It was a wonderful story, but you listen now.'

'But I can't hear anything.'

'Exactly Daniel, exactly, there isn't a sound. It's creepy.'

Daniel frowned with concentration. He made to stand up but stopped halfway. There he stayed completely still but for his eyes wide and alert. *She's right!*

There wasn't a sound. The air was still, no insects hummed, no birds flew in the sky, no grass or shrub rustled on the wind. There was no wind, the mountain breeze was gone.

Daniel slowly stood and looked around. 'How very strange, I hear nothing. And look, this part of the mountain is barren. Now that I think about it, it's been some ways back the last time I saw a plant of *any* type.'

Sara gulped. 'It's all so very still. Not one sign of life hereabouts. It's such a gloomy place. It just doesn't seem quite right. I didn't notice at first, I guess because I was hungry and just wanted to stop.'

'There's a nervous air to this place. It's still, but not calm and peaceful—more like fearful, do you know what I mean?'

'I do, I think. And where's the wind gone? Since we've climbed the Rise there's always been a breeze blowing at very least. It's too creepy.'

'Let's keep moving before we find out the reason behind it. The fleeces are dry enough. We've delayed overlong and it's my fault for rambling on about ancient legends.'

'Don't be silly. Nobody's to blame. But we *have* been here long enough. Let's follow the ravine to find a way to cross over.'

They quickly rolled up their fleeces and with a lingering sense of dread they continued in the direction of the peak, still determined to somehow get the shard of dragon's tooth that sparkled high atop it.

Side by side they made their way across the last stretch of plateau and towards the gapping ravine. The pair scrambled over the last few rocks and slowed to a stop, for just a few more paces ahead was the edge of the ravine. Close up they saw the ravine was a giant crevice that fell far down the mountain between the peaks, so far down they couldn't see the bottom.

Daniel leaned out and peered right over the edge. 'Gosh, we're so very high up. I feel dizzy looking down there.'

Sara pulled him back. 'Don't look down, it'll make your head spin.' She pointed across the divide. 'Look at the peak on the far side. It's not as smooth as it looked in the distance. With some sure footing we might be able to climb it.'

From their position they could see that the peak had many caves and ledges with plenty of footholds.

'Easier said than done. I don't fancy taking a tumble down that hole.' Daniel risked another look down. 'And anyway, we've to get across the ravine first.'

Sara gestured with her arm to the left. 'Let's continue this way and see where it leads. It's a rising slope, so at least we're going up and who knows, we might even find a way to cross over.'

'Fine then, but stay back from the edge unless you can fly,' said Daniel. Sara laughed, but not Daniel. 'I'm deadly serious, *that*,' he pointed towards the ravine, 'is a bottomless pit.'

Sara rolled her eyes. 'Don't exaggerate Daniel, there is no such thing as a bottomless pit. Oh wait, apart from your stomach!' She giggled.

Cheered momentarily, Daniel smiled. 'Ha-ha, good one. I suppose there's no such thing as Gizords either?' Daniel immediately regretted it when he saw Sara's smile fade. *Oh shoot bad choice of words, I reminded her of Ashar, and just when she was cheered up.*

There was no time to think of Ashar because they were interrupted by the sound of an enormous explosion that came from deep within the ravine. They jumped back from the edge with fright. The explosion was instantly followed by a blast of air up from the ravine that stung them in the face and struck them with such force that they fell flat on their backs. Their fleece-packs broke the fall.

Sara rolled onto her belly and made to stand up but Daniel roared at her.

'No Sara, lay down. Lay down on your belly!'

In shock she obeyed and Daniel lay on his belly too. A ferocious wind had suddenly arrived and the gusts where blasting up from the ravine. Daniel stretched one arm out and held onto to Sara's arm. He raised his head and roared so as to be heard above the gusts.

'It must be the whirlwind. Lay flat and keep your head down!'

The wind whipped up with gusts coming from everywhere at once. Sara gripped Daniel's arm and they both lay with their heads down. It was the only way they could breathe with the gusts blowing over them. An invisible force dragged at them and they had to press hard to the ground so as not to be swept towards the edge of the ravine.

After a short time the gust stopped and the pull of the wind died away to nothing. The siblings rose cautiously and peered around as they stood. Nothing had changed in their rocky surroundings.

'It's definitely Whirlwind Ravine,' offered Daniel, as he straightened the gear on his back.

Sara fixed her fleece-pack. 'Maybe that explains the feeling of dread hereabouts,' she suggested.

'Hmm. Perhaps, perhaps not. One thing we know is it's dangerous. It nearly took us and we weren't even at the edge. Imagine if we'd been in its direct path or had been crossing it!'

Sara gulped. 'Oh but we do have to cross it, somehow.'

'True, Sis, but until then we keep back a bit.'

Sara nodded in agreement and the pair continued along the path of the ravine. The ravine followed the curve of the peaks it sat between, so every few paces another small section came into view.

After a time Daniel looked back. 'Ahead looks much the same as behind, although I can't see the point we started from anymore.'

Sara had gone a few paces in front. 'It's because we're on a gradual bend but—' she gasped. 'But wait, Dan, look ahead. Some kind of bridge.' She broke into a jog.

Daniel spun around. 'Gosh. Wait for me,' he yelled and jogged after her.

Not far in front of them a massive stone spanned the whole width of the ravine and rested on an outcrop coming off the peak on the far side.

Sara had mixed feelings. 'I knew we'd find a way across by going this way,' she bit her lip. 'But I must say I *am* a little nervous about crossing over now that we've met the whirlwind.'

'A little nervous?' said Daniel. 'I'd be worried if you weren't! I'm *a lot* nervous, but cross over we must. Let's check it out.'

Daniel passed her out and led the way to the foot of the bridge. Up close they saw that the bridge was one massive slab of rock that arched right across the ravine and onto the ledge of the peak on the far side. Daniel jumped the two-foot high step onto its end that still rested on the plateau.

'It feels sturdy enough,' he decided as he kicked the rock beneath him and looked across the ravine. 'This side anyway.'

Sara placed her hands on it, fascinated. 'How curious, it's so natural looking yet so perfectly placed. Could people have built it?'

'I doubt it, unless they had giants here to do their lifting.'

Sara raised her eyebrows. 'In this place anything is possible. I'll never doubt again.'

'Okay, give me your arm. The plan is we'll run as fast as we can to the other side. If we make it, happy days, if the whirlwind returns, well maybe *not* so happy.'

Sara giggled as Daniel pulled her up beside him. *Idiot,* she thought. *Funny, but an idiot, I know he's just trying to make light of a dangerous situation so I won't be scared.* 'Thanks Dan.'

Daniel smiled. 'For what? For helping you up? Don't mention it. You can pay me back another time. Are you ready to run?'

Sara nodded. 'I'm ready.'

They held hands and raced across the bridge. The bridge proved stable and they soon found themselves hopping off on the other side.

Daniel sighed with a mixture of relief and surprise. 'I felt no wind whatsoever, did you?'

Standing on the outcrop of rock Sara breathed deeply. 'Not a breeze, unless we out-ran it.'

'You did run fast. I didn't know you *could* run that fast. I could barely keep up.'

'Neither did I! I just imagined those vines from Moody Woods were at my ankles again.' She shuddered and shook her cheeks at the thought. 'Uhhh.'

'Well what now speedy?' Daniel gazed up the sheer face of the peak and something caught his eye. 'Hang on, check it out. It looks like some kind of path. We may be able to use it to climb the peak.'

Sara looked to see a thin pathway at Daniel's shoulder height. The path was carved into the rock and spiralled upward on a gentle slope.

Sara gazed higher. 'It looks wide enough for us to stand side by side, just about. Do you think it will serve? I wonder does it go all the way to the top.'

'Who knows,' replied Daniel. 'But it's going upward so that's further away from the ravine and closer to the shard of the dragon's tooth. Either way we have no other option so after you.'

Sara grabbed the path's edge with both hands and Daniel held her feet and hoisted her up. Daniel then grabbed the path and pulled himself upward and Sara grabbed the fleece-pack on his back and pulled from above. Once up on the path they slapped the dust from their knees and hands and began a slow and steady climb.

Chapter 14
Up and Down

Daniel was in front this time, which didn't bother Sara at all. *After the rats in the tunnel and those marauders I think I'll let Daniel lead the rest of the way,* she thought to herself. The pair looked ahead as they climbed because the path was narrow and the drop was far. For a time they chatted about their journey but the chat soon turned to silence as the effort of the climb required all their energy. With the silence the strange feeling of dread returned. To keep it off the questers tried to think of different things but it only added to the gloom.

Daniel's mind wandered to the marauders. *What a mean-looking bunch they seemed to be,* he thought. *Gosh, lucky they didn't catch us, though what about that poor man they had tied up.*

Sara found herself thinking about Ashar again. *He was such a little fellow, and so brave. I really hope the gizords didn't get him.*

Determined not to let the dread overtake him Daniel shook his head to clear his mind. 'Say Sara,' he called back. 'This is a depressing place isn't it? So tell me, what's your favourite place back home? And if you say school, I'll throw you over the side.' Daniel glanced over the edge of the path. 'Oops, shouldn't have done that.' He reeled where he stood.

Sara caught up with him. 'Ha, serves you right for looking over.' She looked too. 'Oh, I've only gone and done it myself. It's such a very long way down. I'm dizzy just looking.'

The ravine fell deep down below them between the mountain peaks as far as the eye could see. There was nothing much to see but the cold greys and browns of the stone that made the Rocky Rise.

Sara steadied herself. 'My favourite place back home is anywhere flat. The football pitch you play on would do right about now, thank you very much.'

'Ha, good one, Sis. Never thought I'd hear *you* say that!'

'It must be the mountain air. It's making me daft like you! Now keep going and no more looking over the side.'

'Hey, what do you mean, daft like me?'

'Shush Daniel. The quest. Focus now.'

Daniel smiled. *Tease away, Sis, anything that keeps of this sense of dread is good for me.* He set off up the path again but after only a few more paces he stopped suddenly. 'Stop, Sara!' he yelled. Sara reached him as he was taking a step backward. Daniel held a hand out behind him to halt her. 'The path goes no further. We're at a dead-end.'

Sara stepped in front of him. 'Let me see.' Daniel held onto her fleece while she peered over the end of the path. 'You're right, the path leads nowhere, how odd.'

They stood together, bewildered. Their eyes wandered around searchingly. In front of them was the path's end and ahead of that a sheer drop into the depths of the mountain. Behind them was the path they had just trekked up and to their right stood the peak. And to their left lay the deeps of Whirlwind Ravine.

Beyond the ravine still and some ways down, they could see a series of ledges propping out from the side of the mountain. At different levels and sizes the ledges created the effect of a stone stairs. Looking at the ledges, Sara ventured, 'If only those layers of stone were on this side, we could use them as steppingstones up the peak.'

Daniel's forehead scrunched. 'Hmm, I'm not so sure, Sis, they're quite a bit away. I'd say there's a fair drop from one ledge to the next. It's just because we're looking down, we can't see it properly.' The conversation would have continued if not for an unmistakable cry for help that came to the questers' ears from somewhere below them.

The pair froze momentarily. With eyes wide they held each other's arms. There it was again. 'Help, please help me!' The cry carried loud and clear through the mountain air and echoed off the sides of the Rocky Rise.

'Did you hear?' asked Daniel.

'Of course I heard,' gasped Sara.

They quickly dropped to their knees and once again peered down and out across the ravine. The breeze picked up as they scanned the ledges for the source of the voice.

'Do you see anything?' called Sara.

'No I don't,' Daniel called back.

They had to shout just to hear one another as the wind had returned suddenly and whistled up and down the rocks. Daniel dived back across the path and grabbed Sara who rolled with him. A gust so forceful had whipped up from the ravine that it had nearly taken them with it over the edge. Behind the gust came a giant twister, visible by the dust and debris that spun in its trap. The twister swirled up and down the ravine, berserk and untamed, snatching all and everything in its path.

Daniel and Sara crouched down on the path against the face of the peak and clung to each other with one arm and used their free arm as the only other shelter available. There they stayed crouched for some time while the winds howled and the gusts licked up the Rocky Rise.

Quite suddenly the wind stopped and the twister disappeared. The air was still again.

Sara lowered her arm and let go of Daniel. 'Creepers, the whirlwind again. This time there was no explosion. It was nothing like the one earlier. This one was like a tornado. How did you know to dive?'

Daniel blew a sigh of relief. 'It was just luck. I'd just caught a glimpse of something white below on a ledge when from beneath it I saw the twister coming our way.'

Sara was a little shaken. 'Good show bro. It all happened so suddenly.' She shuddered. 'But what did you glimpse?'

'I'm not sure, exactly. It was down there on the second ledge down. At first, I thought I saw a flock of black crows, but they flew away. Then I saw a small horse, or maybe a giant swan!'

'Huh?'

'I know. We'll have to take another look.'

The siblings lay flat on their bellies, diagonally across the path and peered over the edge. At first, they saw nothing but the same series of ledges propping out from the peaks and the gapping ravine between.

'I don't see anything,' volunteered Sara. 'Perhaps the twister took it.'

With his eyes intense Daniel searched the ledge he'd seen the movement on before the twister came. 'There it is,' he cried and hopped to his knees and pointed. 'Down there, look. It's a small horse I think.'

Sara looked to where he pointed and jumped upright. 'I see it now. And you're right, it's a white foal.' She turned to Daniel, eyes wide with astonishment. 'And look closer, it's flapping a wing!'

'Wow, it *has* got a wing,' Daniel realised. 'Just like the stallion in the legend. Thank goodness the whirlwind didn't get it. It must be stuck down there.' Daniel stood and tried to beat the dust off his clothes, without much success.

Sara cupped her hands to her mouth. 'Hey, you down there, are you okay?' Her voice echoed far across the mountain.

'Help, please help me,' the white foal pleaded in a voice full of sadness.

'Gosh, how about that,' said Daniel. 'The foal *can* talk.'

'Yes, amazing,' said Sara, 'just like Ashar.'

Daniel stared down at the small horse. 'I'd hate to leave the poor foal stuck down there. I say we should help him.'

'Agreed,' said Sara firmly. 'If I recall, Zac said that the flying horses still could be seen up on the peaks from time to time.'

'Yes he did. Guardians of good or something like that.'

'So let's help. As we can't go up, we must find a way down, and I think I know who may be able to help us.'

Daniel looked quizzically at her. 'Whom could we possibly ask? We're here alone, or have you forgotten!'

Sara smiled knowingly. 'Not so, Dan.' She quickly opened her satchel and gently lifted out Bobbin. 'Remember, Zac told us bonions came from the far side of the Rise. They helped us the first time we climbed these slopes and Bobbin helped you find me on the plateau. If anyone can get us down to that poor horse, I say Bobbin can.'

Daniel nodded. 'It's certainly worth a try, let's go for it.'

Sara looked at her little bonion and pointed down towards the ledge. 'Well, Bobbin, do you understand? We need you to find us a way down to help that poor foal.'

Bobbin made a series of bubbling noises and wriggled out of Sara's hand. Once on the ground she waved her strange little arms and added a few more bubbly phrases, and with that she disappeared over the side of the ravine and was gone.

Sara watched her go and had second thoughts. *Gosh, she's so tiny. I wonder if it was a good idea to send her.* 'Do you think she understood? Will she find a way down?'

'We'll just have to wait and see,' replied Daniel. 'Let's wait here for a while, and if Bobbin doesn't return soon, we make our way back the way we've come and try and reach it from the far side of the ravine.' Daniel was encouraged. 'Zac trusts the bonions and we can too. Although, it's a pity Zac's cave isn't closer we could just go back and ask him to help.'

Something suddenly occurred to Daniel and his hand shot to his mouth with alarm.

Sara noticed the concern on his face. 'Daniel, what is it?'

'It's Zac, well what he said actually. I just remembered what he had told us. So much has happened since we left the cave I'd forgotten.' Worry lines creased his forehead as he frowned.

'Out with it,' Sara urged.

'Those crows I saw *weren't* crows. *They're* the drooling bats.'

Sara's hands shot to her mouth too. 'Ohh Daniel, it must be them, and I forgot too. They're trying to get the foal!'

'*That's* what the feeling of dread is hereabouts,' Daniel realised.

Sara looked distraught as she recalled Zac's tale. 'No wonder up here is known Nightmare Reaches,' she gulped. 'Let's hope Bobbin finds a way down for us to help, before it's too late.' Her face etched with worry. 'Oh I do hope we can help. We might not get the shard of the dragon's tooth, but at least if we can save that poor animal some good will come of this crazy adventure.'

'Crazy, you said it. Anyway no matter what happens, we have to eat, all this climbing has made me hungry again. While we're waiting for Bobbin, we'll eat the last of the food we have. It'll be something less for those bats to eat if they do come!' he joked nervously.

His voice betrayed how he was really feeling. Sara didn't laugh.

They sat down right where they were, on the narrow path carved into the highest peak of the Rocky Rise. Daniel broke the last of the bread and cheese between them and they drank the last of the fruit juice in silence. The silence was interrupted by the occasional cry for help from below.

Daniel, deep in thought gazed at the dusty path. *Bobbin finding a way is one thing, but could we follow her?* He had just finished his last bite of bread and cheese when he felt something on his neck and he leapt up with fright.

'Aahh, there's something on me,' he yelled. 'Is it a bat?' Frantic, he reached behind and slapped the back of his own head.

Sara stood up and laughed at his antics. 'Hee-hee. Calm down Dan. It's only Bobbin. She wants to get your attention.'

'Well, she's going the right way about it,' said Daniel irritably. The little bonion scampered across Daniel's neck, pulled at his ears and tugged at his hair. Finally he closed his hand gently around Bobbin and relaxed. 'Easy my little green friend, what is it you are trying to tell us? Did you find a way down?'

The bonion wriggled from his grip and stood before him and waved her tiny arms. First, she pointed down the ravine, then to the path and the peak. All the while a babble of bubbling noises came flowing from her mouth.

'She's certainly trying to tell us something. What is it Bobbin? Can you show us?' said Sara.

Bobbin tugged Daniel's leg by the heel of his trousers till he moved in the right direction. When he was standing against the peak, Bobbin raised her tiny arms and pushed once more against his legs.

'I think I get it,' suggested Sara. 'She wants you to stay here.'

Sara had barely finished her sentence and Bobbin once again broke into her bubbly speech. This time she clung to Sara's leg and tried to drag her down the pathway.

'Yes that's it. She wants me to go with her. She must have found a way down. It makes sense, she can only show one of us down at a time.'

Daniel looked at the little creature. 'Is that it Bobbin? You'll lead us down one at a time?'

Bobbin spun around and nodded her approval. Once again, she tugged at Sara's leg.

'Okay Sara, she's eager to get going. I guess you'll have to lead again for a while eh? All I can say is stay steady and be careful. Remember to climb exactly where Bobbin shows you.'

'I climbed up a peak so I guess I can climb down a ravine,' said Sara, trying to make light of the task. She saw the look of worry on Daniel's face. 'Don't worry, Dan, I'll be fine.' *Creepers, I hope.* 'We've come this far, isn't that what you'd say? See you down there.' Without waiting for a response she turned and followed Bobbin, who had already started down the path.

There was nothing Daniel could do but worry and wait. *I hope the whirlwind doesn't return while she's making the climb. If it does, I'm going after her, with or without Bobbin.* He sat again with his chin in his hands and made a silent wish that Sara's good luck would hold.

***

Bobbin scurried along in front and Sara had to jog just to keep up. The little bonion led her down the curved path of the peak till they could no longer see Daniel and then without notice she dropped over the side and down into the ravine. Sara stopped in her tracks for a moment.

'Bobbin, Bobbin, where did you go?' she called out.

When no reply came, she dropped to her knees and gingerly approached the edge of the path. She peered over the side and breathed a sigh of relief.

'Thank goodness, Bobbin. I thought you'd jumped into the ravine.'

The bonion was perched on a small outcrop of rock just big enough for Sara to stand on.

'Do you want me to climb down to you?' Sara asked.

Bobbin replied with a sequence of bubbly phrases and beckoned for Sara to follow. Sara turned around and dropped her feet over first then slid her belly over the edge. Her feet found the outcrop easily. Pleased with herself, she turned once again to face the ravine.

'That wasn't so hard, Bobbin. Where to next?' Her ease soon turned to worry when she looked down. She quickly dropped to her hunkers. 'Oh, we're still so very high up.' Sara took a moment to settle her head. Gosh, *I feel so dizzy. I forgot about looking down.*

Bobbin seemed to realise this, for she waited on the edge while Sara gathered her balance. Once Sara had regained her composure, Bobbin disappeared over the side again. And once again Sara peered over the edge with caution, only to see Bobbin waiting on a similar outcrop a little farther below. Sara learnt as she went. This time she didn't look down, instead she focused on where Bobbin stood, patiently waiting for her. When she reached the second outcrop, she looked again at the bonion.

'A little farther, eh Bobbin?'

Bobbin nodded her tiny head and gave a little turn before she dropped over the edge once more. Sara took courage from the brave little creature and this time with more confidence looked over the side after her. But Bobbin was nowhere to be seen. A moment of panic spread through Sara. *Oh dear, I hope she hasn't fallen.* Against her better judgement she gazed down into the ravine again. Although the dizziness returned, she squeezed her eyes and gripped the ledge, determined to see where her guide had fallen. The rocky mountain and the gaping mouth of the ravine was all she saw. There was no sign of the little bonion.

Sara cupped her hands to her mouth and yelled. 'Bobbin, Bobbin are you okay? I'm sorry, my little friend.' Tears gathered in her eyes. She leaned back on her knees and whispered to herself, 'I'm sorry.' *She's fallen and it's my fault. I never should have asked her. I better go tell Daniel.*

As she turned to climb back up, a flash of green caught her eye and she looked down again. Bobbin was there hanging out of a hole in the side of the peak and waving her to come down.

Sara sighed with relief. 'Bobbin, you're okay. Oh Bobbin, you little onion, don't ever do that to me again. I'd thought you'd fallen,' she wiped away her tears.

Bobbin darted out of the hole and climbed straight back up the peak to the same level as the outcrop. She then reached towards Sara and Sara reached back. Bobbin placed Sara's hand on a bump of rock for grip and scurried back to the hole where she waved again.

'Now I understand, Bobbin.'

Sara dropped her legs off the ledge and secured her feet in the hole that Bobbin had found. As soon as she was stable, off Bobbin shot again to find another hand and foot hold. And so it was that the unlikely pair made their way down the side of the peak, Bobbin leading Sara as she clung to lumps, bumps and ledges, hopping from jutting rocks to rotten stumps and clinging to anything that would offer her a hold.

Sara thought the climb would never end. Her hands were cut and her legs and arms were sore. *Maybe Dan was right, perhaps this is a bottomless ravine. I just hope the whirlwind doesn't return while I'm dangling here.* This thought had just crossed her mind when she looked to see the next step Bobbin had led her to and a wishful smile crossed her face.

'Oh Bobbin, please say we're stopping for a rest. I don't know if I can climb much farther.'

They had reached a platform of stone that jutted out from the peak, with plenty of room to move without fear of falling over. Sara looked around while she caught her breath and noticed that at this particular point the ravine was quite narrow. Then she saw it. At the edge of the platform was a narrow strip of rock that spanned all the way out across the ravine to a ledge on the other side. As she gazed over the windy divide, her eyes fell on two big boulders. Wedged between them was the white foal they had seen earlier.

'Well done Bobbin. You're a clever little plant, eh I mean, clever little thingy…' she hesitated. 'Oh, clever little whatever you are.' She picked up Bobbin, stroked her tiny head and hugged her. The bonion began wriggling from Sara's embrace while Sara called out.

'Hello, can you hear me? We've come to help.'

The foal's head appeared from under his free wing. 'Oh thank you, please hurry,' he pleaded. 'They could be back any moment.'

Sara squeezed her eyes closed for a moment to shut out the pain in her hands, arms and legs that lingered from the climb down. *A little stallion*, she thought. *And he's frightened the bats will return. I can't blame him. He needs my help.* She gulped to swallow her fears, opened her eyes and turned to her guide.

'Quick Bobbin, we must cross over.'

Bobbin, already on the bridge gestured for Sara to hurry. Sara knew better than to look down as she stepped onto the narrow, stone strip. It was just wide enough for her to stand with her feet together. She started to cross with caution. Bits of rock and dust crumbled beneath and around her. The bridge was on the verge of collapsing and she wondered if it would hold Daniel's weight. She could see Bobbin waiting on the other side waving her across as she struggled to keep her balance, and although she didn't know much about bonion expressions, she was sure that her little friend looked concerned. She continued with one foot in front of the other and soon made it the whole way across the ravine. In an instant Bobbin was in her arms and nuzzling her cheek.

'I knew you were worried, my little friend, but I made it. We're safe now,' Sara said softly.

Bobbin stayed for the briefest of moments making a low, bubbly gurgle before slipping from Sara's arms and darting back across the bridge once more. Sara watched as Bobbin quickly disappeared up the peak to fetch Daniel down, then she turned and walked towards the trapped foal.

Chapter 15
Sketch

Sara approached the foal slowly.

'Easy now, white one, we'll soon get you out. My name is Sara. What's *your* name, friend?'

The foal, soothed by Sara's gentle voice replied, 'My name is Sketch. I'm a flying stallion. Well, I'm a flying foal actually. The bats will return soon.'

Stepping closer, Sara could see more clearly how the foal was caught. His left wing and left foreleg were wedged between two sizable boulders.

'However did you manage to get jammed in there?' she asked curiously.

The small horse neighed and dropped his head. After a moment he lifted it and began.

'I was flying my first patrol around the peaks and passes hereabouts. I stopped on this very ledge for a rest. After a short time I began to doze when I awoke to the sudden flutter of leathery wings. Turning to see what approached, I barely had time to stand and run before the drooling bats were upon me. I was still looking backwards as I galloped just a few paces, preparing to take flight, when I ran into these two rocks. My leg and wing got wedged fast between them. I can't move them. It was luck itself that saved me, for the great whirlwind arrived at that very moment. It took a few of the bats with it down into the ravine; the rest of them retreated to their caves.'

'Oh you poor thing, let me see what I can do,' offered Sara.

Sara walked around the side of the inner boulder and placing her hands on two notches, she heaved with all her might but it wouldn't budge.

'I'll try the other one,' she suggested confidently, and marched around the other side to the outer boulder.

Again she gripped the massive rock. She heaved and pushed but there was no movement. Not to be swayed, she dug her feet in and shoved and pulled but still to no avail.

'It's no use, is it?' asked Sketch sadly, 'I'm stuck fast.'

Sara panted to catch her breath and slid down the boulder to sit beside the foal. 'I'm sorry, Sketch, I couldn't move them. But don't you worry, my brother Daniel will be here soon and he'll help, you'll see.'

The white foal fluttered his wing and dropped his head on Sara's shoulder. 'Thanks anyway, Sara. It's not your fault. You're only human after all. You don't even have any wings.'

Sara giggled when the young horse said this, but she couldn't argue with him. 'I suppose you're right there, Sketch.'

Sketch continued; his voice sad. 'No, I've no one to blame but myself. Father will be disappointed...that's if I ever get out of this.'

Sara looked at Sketch sympathetically. 'It sounds like you've had a lucky escape. You should be glad that you're alive and not a meal for those smelly bats.'

Sketch snickered. 'You've a good sense of smell for such a small nose. Those bats do give off quite a stink. Thank goodness the wind carries it away each time.'

'Anyway, what are you doing all the way up here, and alone too?' Sara asked. 'Didn't you know about the whirlwind and drooling bats?'

'I could ask you the same question,' replied Sketch.

'I asked you first, and besides, your reasons are bound to be of greater importance. I *am* only human after all, *and* I don't even have wings.' Sara gave a dramatic wave of her arms for effect.

Sketch, caught between a rock and a hard place, with eyes downcast began his story.

'I am son of Lightning, my father, and Blossom, my mother. They are leaders of our herd since before I was born. We are the descendants of the first flying horses who were servants to The Mighty Flying Stallion, champion of light and hope. Our home, or at least my forefathers' home, is a place somewhere across the Blue Divide known as The Mystery Isles. I've never been there, nor my parents, but it's said that when the time comes, the flying horses know and return across the sea to sit at the feet of their master on the glorious Mystery Isles. It is the duty of our race to act as sentries on Well-Keeper Island. We restore what is broken; we protect the good inhabitants, people, animals and the plant life too. We offer counsel in all manner of situations, but most importantly we patrol the peaks of the Rocky Rise from the dark dangers that lurk on the other side.'

Sara was intrigued. 'I heard of the mighty flying stallion and how he left the shard of the dragon's tooth on the highest peak of the Rise. But you still haven't explained what a foal like you is doing all the way up here on your own.'

Sketch dropped his head again. 'That's just it. I *am* only a foal. I realise that now.'

Sara rubbed his light silver mane. 'But I don't understand. Weren't you always a foal?'

'You see, there's no greater honour for a horse in the flying herd than to patrol the Rocky Rise. Countless times I've asked my father could I accompany him and countless times he has refused. 'You're too young,' he says.'

'I know what you mean; our father doesn't let us go near Appledown Orchards.'

'Where is that?'

'It doesn't matter. Please go on.'

'He always says, "You're only a foal; it's too dangerous; what if something happens? No Sketch, you must wait till you're a stallion. It's not long away, you'll see." And now look, he was right, I'm so ashamed. I'll never be able to fly with the herd again.'

'There-there Sketch, I'm sure everything will be fine.' *Gosh, I hope so at least.*

Sketch neighed aloud. 'All I wanted to do was prove that I was big enough to fly the patrol. I just wanted to make father proud. He's such a brave and respected stallion. I wanted to show him that his son would follow in his wing-beats so that someday when he leaves for the Mystery Isles my mate and I would lead the herd.'

'Who's your mate?' asked Sara.

Sketch hung his head shyly. 'Well she's not my mate yet, but she will be, I hope. I just haven't asked her yet. She's a filly that was on patrol with us. I'll ask her someday.'

Sara could tell he was a bit embarrassed. *I'll change the subject.* 'Sorry, you we're saying about wanting to fly the patrol. Please continue.'

'Oh yes, I was. So my chance finally came yesterday when a messenger pigeon arrived, warning of marauders abroad this side of the Rise.'

'A messenger pigeon?' Sara's eyebrows lifted with surprise. 'Was it from Zac the goat herder?'

'Possibly, or some other sentry.'

Sara looked puzzled. *Sentry? Zac never called himself a sentry, he must mean cave dweller.* She could see Sketch waited for her attention so she dropped the thought.

'Sorry Sketch, don't mind me. I won't interrupt again, do go on.'

'The message was that marauders smoke-fires had been seen in the lower passes. Counsel was held and it was agreed a patrol would cover the area to see what mischief the marauders were up to. I begged Lightning to let me fly my first patrol. He relented and we set off, seven in all including myself. Lightning gave the command to split up so we could cover more mountains and I was given the nearby plateaus to check. We were to locate them and track their movements from above. Everything was fine, my wings were plenty strong to make the climb and the distance didn't bother

122

me at all. My problems began when a thick fog rolled across the mountains. At first, I flew above the fog and circled, waiting for it to clear. But the fog lingered and I grew tired. I decided to land and stop for a rest. The mistake I made was landing blind. I just flew down through the fog till my hooves found rock and there I stayed. When I woke up, the fog was gone. That's when the drooling bats came and I got stuck. They've come again since and were right at me the second time before the whirlwind drove them away. It would have taken me too but that I'm sheltered here behind the boulders. They're getting closer each time. If they come again, I fear I'm done for.'

Sara put her arm around his neck. *Poor fellow. Let's hope we can free him. Hurry Dan.* 'What about the other six horses? Won't they be looking for you?'

Sketch shook his silvery mane and answered forlornly. 'Patrols can often take two or three days, but they will look for me eventually. And when they find me, I'll be so ashamed. I've let the herd down, and my father.'

Sara frowned. 'I don't see what you've to be ashamed of. It's not your fault the fog came. Come to think of it I got lost in it too.'

'You don't understand. Dealing with fog is part of a stallion's training. We're never supposed to land blind on the Rise, but I forgot.'

'You can't remember everything you're taught. I know I don't.'

Sketch looked at Sara for a moment. 'You're very nice with your kind words. Tell me, what's a small girl doing up the Rocky Rise? And all alone too.'

Sara turned to look Sketch in the eye. 'I'm not *that* small. First of all, I'm leading a quest.' *Well partly leading.* 'And secondly, I'm not alone. I already told you that my brother Daniel will be here soon.'

'Sorry,' said Sketch, 'I really didn't mean to offend you.'

Sara's voice softened, 'It's okay Sketch, I didn't mean to raise my voice. It's just that we've been through so much in the last few days, far too much for a girl of my age, or any age for that matter.'

'Really?' Sketch asked, interested.

'Really,' Sara replied. 'It all began in our back garden.'

And so to pass the time while waiting for Daniel, Sara told Sketch all that had happened to them since leaving the garden. While telling him she made a silent wish that neither the bats nor the whirlwind would return before Daniel arrived.

Chapter 16
Batter's Up

Daniel landed with a jump on the same ledge Sara had a while before. His journey down had mirrored hers, Bobbin led him to the same grips and footholds all the way down. Sara noticed them first from the far side of the ravine and called out.

'Daniel, Daniel, you've made it. Come quickly, the wind is picking up.'

Swirls of dust from the mountain and the whistle of the breeze crept up from the ravine. Daniel hurried over to the stone bridge where Bobbin stood. The bonion seemed unwilling to cross.

'What are you waiting for? Go on. Little climber, after you,' said Daniel and gestured for the bonion to lead. But for some reason Bobbin wouldn't budge. She turned around and pushed against Daniel as though she wanted him to retreat.

The wind started to howl and Daniel grew anxious. 'What is it Bobbin? We must cross now before the wind picks up.'

Daniel was determined to cross but Bobbin refused his passage and stood in the way. They stayed deadlocked like this for a few moments when suddenly a high-pitched screech came from the far side. Shocked to stillness, the screech sent a chill through Daniel and Sara both.

Sketch brought them from their shock with a shout. 'Here they come, it's the drooling bats. That's the noise they make coming up through the caves. They'll be here any moment!' Sketch made a desperate attempt to shake free. 'You must flee now, flee for your lives,' he cried while twisting and turning.

'Take cover, Sara,' Daniel shouted.

Sara was frightened but she swallowed her fear and shouted back. 'I'm not leaving Sketch.'

'That's it,' said Daniel, 'I'm crossing, Bobbin, whether you're coming or not.'

Bobbin frantically waved her tiny arms, stopping Daniel once more. She turned towards the narrow stone isle and approached the strip with caution. She very gently placed her tiny legs on one at a time.

Daniel's browed creased with worry. *Don't blow away little climber, but please hurry. Sara's over there.* 'You must hurry,' he urged.

Bobbin raced across the divide. She reached the other side, swivelled and once again started waving frantically while shaking her head from side to side. Mistaking this as encouragement, Daniel placed his right foot forwards heavily onto the bridge and pulled it back just as quickly. To his dismay and horror a section of the stone collapsed in front of him. A cloud of dust followed that was quickly carried off by a strong gust.

Sara watched from the boulders with despair and cried out. 'Oh Daniel, I forgot to warn you that the bridge was weak.'

Sketch was distraught. 'Oh we're doomed,' he neighed.

'Never say it, Horse,' Daniel roared back.

He quickly removed the hag's staff from the fleece attached to his shoulders. The screech of the bats was louder now, and as Daniel placed the staff across the collapsed section of bridge, the fierce beasts appeared on the ledge.

Daniel gulped to steady his nerves. *Okay magic of the heart, if you're in this stick I need you now.* With that thought he went forwards slowly, using the staff as a tightrope he began across the gap. *If I fall, I fall to my death, and the bats get Sara… I can't fall.* He concentrated on balancing.

The drooling bats gathered around the mouth of the caves for the briefest of moments and then as one they flew in the direction of Sara and the trapped foal. The screech was deafening. Sara burrowed in under Sketch's wing and the pair hugged against one another in a desperate attempt for cover.

Daniel struggled to keep his balance on the staff. He swayed on his perch as the wind whipped under and around him. Looking to the ledge he could see the bats now clearly approaching his sister. He could see their pig-like snouts, their pointy fox-like ears and, most terrifying of all, their fangs bared and hungry for flesh. Anger swelled within him at the sight of the hideous creatures advancing towards the boulders. He reached the end of the staff and at the same moment a gale force blasted up from the ravine. He dropped to his hunkers, grabbed the staff and raced across the remainder of the stone strip, all thoughts of losing his balance forgotten. He jumped the last five paces and landed on the ledge with a tumble. The stone strip crumbled to dust in his wake.

Daniel bounded towards the boulders and reached them just as the first three bats swooped in to attack. Still clutching the hag's staff he swung it in an arc and smashed it into the three bats, sending them crashing into the ravine.

'Batter's up,' he roared and got ready to swing again.

More bats arrived. Daniel swung. Bats fell. Spinning his weapon this way and that, Daniel was swatting bats all around him. The battle raged. All the while the whirlwind was brewing and it howled across the battle site.

Sketch risked a peek to see Daniel thrashing bats out of the air with the hag's staff. But he was hopelessly outnumbered and in the thick of the fight he let the staff fall. With no weapon to fight with he started swinging his arms with all speed, fists clenched, trying to defend the group with his bare hands. Many bats got punched. Any that came in low got kicked. He fought with all his might, but the drooling bats were too many and he soon fell to his knees. Then with nothing left but his own body, he threw himself on top of Sketch and Sara to cover them, trying somehow to protect them from the fatal attack of the drooling bats.

But the attack never came. Instead, the mountain rang out with howling gales that blasted up from Whirlwind Ravine. The questers and the foal were sheltered from the force of the whirlwind by the boulders. The bats that could escape retreated to their caves. Many left it too late and were caught in the gusts. Some tried in vain to fly against the force of the whirlwind but they had no chance. The whirlwind swallowed them up and carried them to their doom, down into the depths of the ravine.

Silence descended across the ledge but for the heavy breathing of Daniel, still breathless from the battle. Little evidence of the scene moments before remained except for the small group tucked in between the boulders and the hag's staff lying where it fell. There was no screeching, no drooling bats, no howling wind, the air was still.

'Are we alive?' asked Sara, still with her head under Sketch's wing.

'Ask me in a little while,' replied Daniel as he removed himself from atop the others.

Sara stood and patted down her clothes which by now were very crumpled and dusty. 'Daniel, meet Sketch, the flying foal…I mean flying stallion.'

Sketch shook his silvery main. 'It's okay Sara, I'm no stallion, not yet.' He turned to Daniel. 'Daniel, that was the most courageous thing I've ever seen, and from one so small. Are you sure you don't have wings?'

Puzzled, Daniel looked from Sketch to Sara. 'Huh?'

Sara giggled. 'It's true. Sketch quite rightly points out your lack of wings.'

'Have you gone mad?' Daniel asked her.

'Ha, it's a private joke.' Her voice became serious, 'As I said, this is Sketch of the flying herd.' Sara quickly retold Sketch's story for Daniel.

When Sara had finished, Daniel patted Sketch's nose in sympathy. He felt sorry for the trapped horse and tried to sooth him. 'It's not as bad as it seems, Sketch. The herd might be proud of you for trying to prove yourself.'

Sketch hung his head again. 'You're kind like your sister, and courageous, but you don't know the ways of the herd.'

'That's true,' admitted Daniel. 'But we've been in many sticky situations since arriving on this island and come through them all.' *So far.* 'This is just another one for us to get through. Now let's see what can be done.'

Chapter 17
Snapped

Daniel quickly circled the big rocks that held Sketch trapped. He didn't want to delay any further for fear that the bats and whirlwind would return again.

'I tried pushing from every angle,' said Sara.

Daniel nodded. 'Okay then, let's both of us try it again.'

Together they set to work trying to find some give in the boulders. Working both boulders, they tried heaving from the bottom, pulling from the top, shoving from the middle, all to no avail. When that failed, they tried digging with their hands but it was no use as the ground was too hard. The rocks wouldn't budge. The three sat in silence. Worry settled amongst them once more and the feeling of dread returned. Each of them was aware of the passage of time and what it meant.

As Sara rested against the boulder she looked out over the ravine. 'Sketch is right, you know, Daniel, the way you crossed the canyon and fought the drooling bats; it *was* very daring.'

Daniel waved away the praise. 'If I hadn't had the staff, I never would've made it across, nor would I've been able to fight the bats. It was the hag's staff mainly, not me. It's got magic of the heart in it you see. I suspect the well-keeper knew we'd need it, that's why he told us where to find it.' *Hmm.* 'Well, kind of told us.'

'But you dropped it and fought on,' Sketch reminded him.

Daniel frowned. 'Well, no matter. We've more important things to think about. Like getting you unstuck.'

Sara suddenly leaped up from where she sat. 'That's it, of course, the hag's staff. We can use it as a lever to move the boulders.'

Daniel eyebrows shot up. 'Leverage. Great thinking, Sis.'

Sara quickly retrieved the staff, and Daniel fetched a large stone from across the ledge. Sketch watched with curiosity as they put the stone a few paces away from him and jammed the hag's staff in under the nearest boulder.

'What're you doing?' the foal asked.

'Leverage,' the questers chorused together.

'Leverage?'

'It's something the goat herder taught us,' explained Daniel.

'It saved us. *He* saved us,' added Sara.

'Right then, no time to lose. Let's get to work,' ordered Daniel.

They rested the staff onto the stone. With everything in place, the pair held tightly to the top end of the staff and dug in their feet. Daniel and Sara looked at each other determinedly.

'On three,' said Daniel.

'One, two, three, now!'

On the signal the pair pulled down with all their might. Their faces turned red with the effort. Daniel let out a roar as he used all the strength in his body. Sara groaned with the strain. The boulders hadn't budged. Despair washed over Sketch as he watched the siblings struggle to free him. Forlorn, he let out a wail. Determined, the questers tried again. They pulled so hard they looked like they would burst.

'*Aaahhhh,*' they roared aloud with the effort.

The roar choroused over the mountainside. Holding their grip they pressed with all their strength. Suddenly everything shook. A loud crack rang out followed by a deafening snap, then an enormous thud and a cloud of dust. The force of the movement knocked the questers to the ground.

Daniel coughed and spluttered from where he sat. 'Oh no,' he wailed. 'The hag's staff has snapped; it's shattered in bits.' He held up the small piece that had remained in his hands. 'So much for magic of the heart,' he groaned and rested his head in his hands.

Sara wasn't listening to him. She had landed beside Sketch and as the dust cleared, she saw the toppled boulder.

'The boulder has fallen. Sketch you're free,' she called with excitement.

Sketch lifted his head in wonder. He stamped his feet and flapped his wings. 'I'm not stuck. I *am* free, *I'm free,*' he shouted with joy. 'I'm free, oh thank you, my friends, I'm free.'

Momentarily cheered, Sara gave Sketch a warm hug. 'I told you we'd get you out of there, didn't I? Are you hurt?'

'My leg is fine. My wing is sore, but definitely not broken.' Sketch flapped his left wing, but grimaced with the effort.

'Hey Daniel, come and give Sketch a hug,' said Sara. She looked towards Daniel. 'What is it Daniel? What's wrong?'

Daniel looked sideways. His voice was full of despair. 'Didn't you hear me? The hag's staff has split into pieces. It's broken beyond use.'

Sara let go of Sketch and reached for Daniel's shoulder. She looked around and saw the splintered remains of the hag's staff scattered across the ledge.

'Oh, I see. I never noticed, I thought the snap was the boulder giving way and then dust came and we fell, and, and...' she trailed off.

Sketch had stopped his trotting to listen.

Daniel pushed Sara's arm off. 'Now you get it. The first treasure we're charged to find and we've destroyed it.' Daniel suddenly roared, '*Aaarrrr,*' and threw the small piece of the broken staff against the side of the peak.

Sara and Sketch jumped with fright. Daniel caught their motion from the corner of his eye and his tone softened. 'I'm not angry at you guys. I'm angry at myself. After all we've been through to get this far and we've failed.' Despair washed over him afresh and he kicked the dust where he sat. 'We've failed the quest. It's all been for nothing.'

Sara gently returned her hand to his shoulder. 'Hey now, c'mon Dan. Maybe we did fail the quest, but what hope had we? We're just a couple of kids. Maybe we'll wake up tomorrow and this will all have been a crazy dream.'

Daniel grunted. 'Humph.'

Sara had enough. 'Humph yourself Daniel Taylor. You're not a quitter and you're certainly not quitting now while I'm still stuck on this ledge. Need I remind you of the drooling bats?' A fresh breeze blew her hair across her face. She fixed it behind her ears and continued. 'Not to mention the whirlwind.'

Daniel looked thoughtful. *Hmm.* 'What about magic of the heart? Isn't that what we needed the staff for?' He raised his voice to a shout, 'What's any of this for?'

'I don't have the answers Daniel,' Sara shouted back. 'But we're here for a reason, whatever it is.'

'Oh yeah, what reason?'

They were standing and yelling now.

'I said I don't know, didn't I? We freed Sketch didn't we, maybe that's the reason.'

Daniel softened. 'I guess.'

'So stop feeling sorry for yourself and find us a way off this ledge.'

Sketch, who had been quietly watching the exchange from a few paces away, jumped between them and scrapped his right fore-hoof in the dust. 'Wait,' he neighed.

The questers stopped, surprised by his forceful tone.

Sketch looked from one to the other. 'Please stop quarrelling,' he continued more gently. 'The drooling bats will return anytime now. Even with your scent downwind the noise of your bickering is enough for them to know a meal still awaits them out here.'

The siblings looked at each other with regret and shared the same thought. *Sketch is right.*

Sketch neighed again. 'You saved me and I won't forget it. I will fly you both to safety.'

Daniel put aside his despair. 'You can't Sketch. You'll never take our weight.'

Sketch held his head high and stamped his forelegs. 'You don't know the strength of the flying herd.'

Sara looked concerned. 'We don't doubt you Sketch, but you're injured. You said yourself your wing is sore.'

Sketch was determined. 'You lost your treasure saving me. I won't leave you now, with no way off this ledge. You can't go back across the ravine. The stone bridge has collapsed and your staff has shattered. I'm taking you, one at a time if need be.'

Daniel rested a hand on Sketch's mane.

'You mean well friend. I'll tell you what, you rest your wing while we take a look around the ledge. If we can't find any way to climb off, we'll agree to let you take us.'

Sketch lowered his head in thought.

'One at a time that is,' added Daniel.

'Okay,' agreed Sketch. 'But please hurry, the—'

'We know, we know,' Daniel interrupted. 'The bats and the whirlwind. C'mon Sara, we'll take a quick look around while Sketch rests his wing.'

Sketch stayed by the boulders and Daniel and Sara walked to the back of the ledge to examine the wall of the peak that the ledge protruded from. As they passed the piece of the hag's staff that Daniel had thrown, he bent to pick it back up.

'I might as well keep this,' he said uncertainly, 'just as proof that we did actually find it.'

'Good idea,' Sara encouraged. 'Pop it in your satchel for safe keeping.'

Together they eyed the stone rise for notches and holes that might serve them for climbing, but there were none to see. The next ledge visible above them appeared far too high for them to reach.

'We'll have to check the other side of the ledge,' said Daniel pointing. 'You know what that means?'

'Yep,' Sara gulped. 'We have to pass the mouth of the caves.'

Ever so carefully they began across the ledge. When they reached the back and centre, they stayed close to one another, not daring to breathe. Unable to look away they stared in as they passed the dark entrances to the caves. Images of the drooling bats filled their minds and with every step their hearts raced. They shared a look of relief when they reached the far side of the ledge.

'Thank goodness we didn't disturb them,' whispered Sara.

But their relief was short lived as they studied the rock face before them. It was too smooth for them to scale. There was nowhere to hold on.

Daniel groaned. 'Not even Bobbin could lead us off this ledge. We're truly trapped.'

'Never say it friend.' The questers turned to see Sketch land beside them. Sketch continued. 'You're not trapped. I can take you one at a time. One of you must get on now.' He knelt on all fours and folded his wings in.

Daniel was stern. 'You're supposed to be resting your wing Sketch.'

'There's no time for that. Even if you could climb it's too late. Take a look over there.' Sketch swung his head in the direction he had come from. 'Do you see that haze? It's a creeping breeze. I've seen it already. It clings to you. It will make you feel tired and distracted. The bats sense it somehow. They try to get you first. Then the whirlwind comes.'

The adventurers watched with growing horror as an eerie haze crept up from the ravine and spread out across the ledge. It moved slowly and reached out in long finger-like motions through the air. They stared, bewitched.

'What's it doing?' asked Sara.

'Searching,' said Sketch.

Then they heard it, the combined screech of the entire host of drooling bats. The screech was so piercing that Daniel and Sara stuffed their fists against their ears. The bats halted at the mouth of the cave and hovered in a black cloud of leathery wings. The screech stopped.

Sketch roared. 'One of you on now, they're gathering to a swarm.'

Daniel shouted. 'Get on Sara, go.'

Tears welled in Sara's eyes. 'I'm not leaving you Daniel. Sketch, fly yourself to safety.'

'You saved my life, I'm not leaving you,' replied Sketch. 'You must get on now if I'm to make it back for Daniel.'

'Get on, Sara, now,' Daniel snapped.

'But—' she tried to object but Daniel roared over her.

'Shut up, Sara, and get on Sketch.' He pushed her towards the waiting foal.

Sara made to mount but quickly ran back and hugged Daniel. He returned the hug then pushed her away.

Daniel nodded at Sketch as Sara mounted. *Take care of her,* was his unspoken thoughts. Sketch nodded back and Daniel took it that he understood.

Sketch unfolded his wings and Daniel slapped him on the rump. 'Go,' he yelled.

Daniel watched as Sketch flew quickly away with Sara clinging to his neck, her eyes stinging with tears.

Chapter 18
Fire Wall

The screech of the bats brought Daniel's attention back to his own safety. The host came forwards, a frenzied black cloud of ravenous, drooling bats. Bats of all different sizes, young and old alike swarmed from the caves towards him. Twenty steps to his right lay a big rock that curved round in an arch. Daniel dashed over and dived in behind it. As quick as his hands would move, he emptied out the contents of the small pouch he'd been carrying on his belt. *Okay Zac, precious moments in a fight you said. Don't fail me now.* With that thought he scooped up some of the flint-balls, stood and waited for the bats to get closer. They arrived within seconds.

Daniel raised his arm above his head as the bats to the fore of the swarm approached. He gripped two flint-balls tight in his hands and called out to himself to steady his nerves.

'Hold...hold.' The bats were almost upon him. 'Fire,' he roared at the top of his lungs and flung the flint-balls to the ground.

On contact with the rock the flint-balls exploded in a blast of crimson fire. The flames spread out in a line and leapt high in the air. Daniel didn't wait to see if they stopped the bats. The heat was such that he dropped down behind the arch-shaped boulder to avoid getting scorched.

The boulder was only waist high to Daniel so after a moment he climbed to his knees to risk a peek over the other side. The flames had quickly weakened but as they shrank, they gave off a thick black smoke. He saw the charred remains of a few bats smoking on the ground. One bat was still alight and flapped desperately where it fell. Daniel picked up a stone and with a practised aim he put it out of its misery. He looked again through the smoke as it thinned and he could see that the swarm of bats had retreated a short way back. His heart raced and he took deep breaths to control his fear. *Oh creepers. That's what Sara would say if she were here. Hurry back for me Sketch. I don't think I can keep these monsters back any longer.*

The smoke cleared to a light haze and the bats advanced again. Their screeches filled the ravine. Daniel gulped with fear. He scooped up the remaining flint-balls, six in all and flung them at the last possible moment. The explosion was great this time. Again Daniel dived behind the boulder. Bats screeched and fell and the smell of scorched leather filled the air. A tall wall of fire stood between Daniel and the drooling bats but he knew he did not have long left. He crouched down from the intense heat and collected his thoughts.

That's it. I've no staff to fight with. I've no flint-balls left and Sketch hasn't returned.

I'm done for. I just hope Sara's okay. It was then he noticed the haze coiling around the boulder. Up close he could see its substance. *How odd, it's actually dust moving along on a breeze.* He watched as the breeze swirled in strange patterns, visible by the dust it carried. He shook his head to clear it. *What a thing to be thinking of when I'm about to die.* He peered once more over the boulder. The flames had died away and the smoke was almost cleared. The swarm of bats still hovered just beyond the smoke line but Daniel noticed they were now engulfed by the strange haze. He looked down again and saw that he too was surrounded by it and then he recalled Sketch's warning. *The whirlwind will follow. If the bats are going to get me, they'll do it now.* The bats came as one.

Daniel stood and raised his fists over his face, but he was tired and hopelessly outnumbered. In moments he was overcome. The bats swooped in at him from all directions and he fell down behind the boulder again. Tears burst from his eyes as he lay crouched on the rocky ground.

'I'm sorry Sara,' he said aloud. 'I hope you make it home safely.'

It all happened in an instant. He squeezed his eyes shut and felt the bats land on him. He waited for the killer bite. Suddenly the battle cry of a warhorse rose above the screech of the bats. Daniel opened his eyes as the bats that had been on him scattered. And there was Sketch hovering above him with wings outspread and hooves flaying.

Sketch neighed again and his battle cry rang out aloud and echoed off the mountainside. Using all his strength the young foal drove the drooling bats back. He trampled and kicked them with his hooves, caught and flung them with his teeth and used his wings to hurl them in numbers back the way they had come. A battle-frenzy was upon him and his tail and mane swung wildly.

The bats retreated to regroup for another attack. Sketch landed beside Daniel, amidst the dying smoke of the flint-balls and dusty haze.

'Quick, jump on,' shouted the foal.

Daniel pulled himself up and lay across Sketch's back just as a gale burst up from the ravine and whipped across the ledge. The bats screeched in chaos, torn between retreat and attack. The whirlwind was upon them. Sketch was already in the air beating his wings with all his might and Daniel clung to him for dear life. Against the odds they rose upward. The whirlwind exploded across the ledge and howled with a monstrous force. It drowned out all other sound and sucked everything in its path towards the gapping ravine.

Daniel looked down as they rounded the peak just beyond the reach of the twisting whirlwind. He saw a cloud of black tumbling amongst the gusts, drooling bats, trapped beyond hope. Still Sketch beat his wings, up and up they flew until they flew around the peaks and the ravine was no longer in sight.

Finally they landed on yet another small ledge jutting out from the highest peak on the opposite side to the Whirlwind Ravine.

Chapter 19
The Flying Herd

Daniel was vaguely aware of white shapes approaching at speed from different directions, though his eyes were trained on the fleece bundle nestled among the rocks some twenty paces ahead.

'Sara, Sara!' he called as he slid off Sketch's back.

The bundle of fleece turned and jumped up.

'Daniel? Daniel you made it!' Sara cried out.

Brother and sister raced across the ledge and hugged tightly. Both were crying.

'Sara, Sara you're okay. Thank goodness. I thought I wouldn't make it. But Sketch came.'

'I was so worried Daniel. I thought it was all over. I thought the bats got you and Sketch wouldn't be back and it's so cold up this high and, and...oh Daniel.'

'Sara, I thought I'd lost you. We're not splitting up again.' Daniel's tears fell freely.

They hugged harder. A fresh mountain breeze sang across the ledge so the siblings turned sideways to block it. It was then they noticed the other flying horses. There were six in all.

'We've got company,' said Daniel as he let go of Sara and wiped tears from his cheek. Five of the horses were clearly adults and one was in between, bigger than Sketch but smaller than the others.

Sara dried her tears too, looked at the horses and back to Daniel. Daniel's face was smeared black from smoke and tears, and his hands and clothes were caked in dust.

She leaned up to his ear and whispered. 'And you look awful.' They both laughed. It was the giddy laughter of relief.

The horses stood silently by, watching the questers reunion.

Daniel turned to Sketch. 'Sketch, thank you so much for taking us to safety.'

But it was the biggest of the flying horses that stepped forwards and spoke. 'Sketch, what passes here?'

His voice rumbled like thunder and the questers shuddered. He stood twice the size of Sketch, his body firm, muscular and snow-white all over.

Resting on his shoulders where two giant wings. His mane and tail where silver and both hung down in flowing waves.

'I'm sorry father. I failed. I forgot my training. I wasn't ready.' Sketch hung his head in shame.

'Go on dear,' said another of the horses in a sweet, feminine voice.

Sketch looked at her forlorn. 'Yes mother. I forgot my training. I landed blind in the fog and got trapped beside the Whirlwind Ravine.' He turned his head towards the adventurers. 'These humans freed me, and saved me from the drooling bats.'

Sketch's mother looked much like his father, but she was smaller and her body had a softer look, less muscular. Her tail and mane where white as her coat and the hairs curled in a slender curve. She had beautiful, long eyelashes.

'Did you not then fly yourself to safety?' asked Sketch's father.

'I couldn't leave them father. You see they had no way off the ledge.'

'*He* saved *us* in the end,' said Daniel as he looked from the big horse to Sketch. 'He was very courageous. He fought off the drooling bats alone and flew us both to safety even though he had an injured wing.'

Sketch neighed and shook his mane. 'I took my example from you two. It was your bravery in rescuing me in the first place.'

The horse Sketch called mother examined him with concern. 'What's wrong with your wing?'

Sara, much relieved at Daniel's safe arrival and Sketch's parents too, joined the conversation. 'His wing and leg were wedged between two boulders, it looked ever so sore.'

Sketch shrugged away from his mother while looking at the next-smallest horse. 'My wing is fine mother. It was just a bit sore from being stuck is all.'

'Now-now Sketch, let me look. You don't have to be embarrassed in front of Isobel, she has a mother too.'

'Mother,' said Sketch, exasperated.

The young filly turned her head shyly away.

'Aren't you going to introduce us to your friends?' asked his mother, indifferent to Sketch's discomfort at being mothered.

'Of course,' said Sketch. 'Daniel, Sara, this is the patrol from the flying herd I told you about.' He nodded to the biggest stallion, 'My father, Lightning,' then to his mother, 'My mother, Blossom. Leaders of the flying herd.'

Unsure how to greet them the questers just nodded.

Sketch continued. 'And these stallions are the Twin Stallions, Rainer and Glide.'

Two of the big horses nodded in union. They looked almost exactly like Lightning but that Lightning was slightly larger and wore a sterner expression.

'And these two mares are Elsa and, and Isobel,' Sketch said the last name shyly.

Elsa was an adult, equal in size and similar in appearance to Blossom. Isobel was smaller, closer in size to Sketch; her mane and tail fell in beautiful curls and her long eyelashes blinked rapidly as Sketch said her name.

Elsa and Isobel flapped their wings and bent their knees slightly in a curtsey.

'Nice to meet you all,' said Sara. 'We're Daniel and Sara, we, we...' but she trailed off not quite knowing what to say.

'We're here on a quest,' helped Daniel. 'At least we were, but we seem to be failing.' He hung his head.

Lightning spoke with an authority not to be disobeyed. 'A quest that takes you to the peaks of the Rocky Rise is no small thing. We will hear it. But first we deal with Sketch. Sketch, step forwards.'

Sketch came forwards gingerly, his head downcast. 'I'm sorry I forgot my training father. I've failed the herd.'

'Enough,' bellowed Lightning. The questers jumped with fright.

Sketch shuddered but stood his ground.

Lightning stared intensely at his son. 'You are no longer my foal.'

The questers drew a sharp breath, their faces shocked. Sketch, filled with despair, buried his head against his mother's side.

Lightning continued, 'As we scoured the Rise on patrol, we each heard the battle-cry of the herd and thought that one of our own was in trouble. We flew here with all haste but it seems we arrived too late to help. You Sketch, did not flee danger when others needed you. There *is* no greater good in this life than to risk your own life for another.'

Blossom nudged Sketch out with her head so the young horse was standing in the middle of the group.

'You have grown today son,' boomed Lightning. 'You are no longer my foal. You have attained the rank of colt, a stallion in training. Stand and be proud.'

Sketch lifted his head and shook his mane with surprise. Each of the adult horses congratulated him in turn, even shy Isobel. Sketch looked pleased.

'Well done brave horse,' said Daniel while patting Sketch's nose.

'I'm so happy for you Sketch,' said Sara as she closed her eyes and gave him a big hug.

Lightning neighed for attention. 'Now then young humans, to this quest of yours, begin at the beginning.'

So there, on the ledge among the stones and boulders, the adventurers recounted their journey so far. The flying horses listened quietly from when they started back home in their garden right up till Sketch flew Daniel to safety. The only interruptions came from the stiff mountain breeze and from Sketch, who retold in detail of the questers courageous rescue of him from the Whirlwind Ravine and the drooling bats.

After hearing all that had passed, Blossom said, 'It's clear that you pair have had an extraordinary journey so far and a few lucky escapes too.'

'I know,' agreed Sara. 'Even before we met Sketch, I thought we were done for with gizords chasing us, then those awful rats.' She shuddered. 'Uuhh. Not to mention the marauders.'

'Indeed,' said Lightning. 'No doubt the same band of men we were searching for.'

'Did you spot them? Did you discover what they were up to?' asked Sketch.

'Alas no son, not this time,' said Lightning. 'They must have passed over the Rise, or else lay well hidden. The purpose of their presence here is not known *this* time.'

Daniel had been listening intently. He looked at Sara and gulped.

Sara raised her eyebrows as a guilty look spread over Daniel's face. *I know that look.* 'What is it Daniel?' she asked. 'What's wrong?'

But Daniel turned to Lightning to answer. 'One more thing about the marauders, I em…' he hesitated and looked at the ground. 'They had someone with them who I guess wasn't one of them.'

'What do you mean someone?' interrupted Sara impatiently. 'Who?'

Daniel looked at her and spoke quietly. 'A prisoner. A captive.'

'A captive? You should've told me Daniel!' she shouted.

Daniel frowned. 'Yes Sara, a captive, that's who! A man tied up with a sack on his head. I saw him when I went looking for you on the plateau!' he shouted back.

The horses appeared to be alarmed at the mention of the captive. They shuffled and looked to one another. But neither Daniel nor Sara noticed.

Sara's anger flared. She walked over and pushed Daniel. 'I knew you were hiding something from me back there. Stop treating me like a child Daniel. We're in this together!'

'You *are* a child, and we wouldn't *be* together had those marauders found you!'

'That's nothing to do with it and you know it. You're just angry because you feel guilty for lying to me!'

'I was only trying to protect you. That's all I was trying to do. It could have been us next Sara, *that's* why I didn't tell you!'

The siblings squared up to each other.

'Enough!' bellowed Lightning.

The questers jumped again.

'Enough,' repeated Lightning, quietly. 'Sara is right Daniel. The best way to protect her is to prepare her. The island is wrought with danger. You *must* trust each other on your shared quest.'

Daniel frowned. Sara glared back.

Lightning continued, 'Now, about this captive, tell me everything, leave nothing out. How tall was he? What was he wearing? How many men guarded him? What weapons had they? Which way where they headed? Everything, do you understand?'

Daniel gulped and nodded. He gathered his thoughts and told the horses everything he could recall.

When Daniel had finished, all eyes rested on Lightning. The big stallion stared at the ground intensely. He spoke deeply, as though to himself, but the questers overheard him.

'With each crossing they raid further into the lowlands. And *so* it continues.'

Sara's brow knitted. *What continues? I wonder.*

Her thoughts were interrupted when Lightning rose up on his hind legs and uttered a loud cry.

'Neiiiiiighhhhhhhhhhhh.'

His wings flapped and his forelegs circled in the air as his battle cry echoed over the mountainside. Rainer and Glide, Elsa and Isobel, Sketch and Blossom all joined in.

What is it? Daniel shouted to Sketch.

Sketch stopped to answer. 'A mission. We prepare to fly.'

The other horses stopped too, first Isobel, then Elsa and Blossom, next Rainer and Glide and finally Lightning.

As his fore-hooves landed on the rock and his wings came to a stop the leader spoke his command. 'Rainer, fly east to Botanic Beaches. Glide, go west to Cascade Falls. Elsa and Isobel, you stay together, cover the plains from Moody Woods, through the Dales to Hawksdale village. Gather any news abroad and watch for pigeons.' The urgency in Lightning's tone was clear.

Rainer flapped his wings and spun in a circle. 'What of you?' he asked in a deep husky voice.

'We'll see to Sketch's companions here,' he nodded towards the questers, 'and make for the Tor-Folk settlement.'

The twin stallions exchanged a quick nod of understanding with Lightning then took to the skies with mighty flaps of their wings.

'Fly well friends, with all haste,' said Lightning; the twin stallions were already flying fast in opposite directions.

'Come Isobel, we have much to do,' said Elsa, her voice soft as she flapped her white wings in preparation of flight.

Isobel did likewise but before she took off, she turned back to Sketch. 'Bye Sketch,' her eyelashes fluttered. 'Be careful.' Saying the last she rushed off and with wings flapping took to the skies after Elsa.

Sara was still annoyed with Daniel, but watching the exchange between Isobel and Sketch made her smile. 'She's very beautiful,' she whispered to Sketch. 'I think she likes you.'

'I hope so,' Sketch shyly whispered back.

The questers watched as Elsa and Isobel flew over the ledge in the distance. As the mares disappeared from view, Lightning stamped his hoof off the rock; the loud crack brought them to attention.

Chapter 20
Top of the World

'Now brave adventurers,' began Lightning, 'the flying herd are in your debt for freeing Sketch. And for your acts of bravery you will be rewarded with the shard of the dragon's tooth.'

'Really?' asked Sara in disbelief. Daniel's face shared her surprise. They gazed up at the high peak where the shard of the dragon's tooth sat twinkling in the sunlight and shared the same thought. *It's ever so high up.*

As though hearing their thoughts, Lightning said, 'We'll collect it together. Daniel, climb on my back. Blossom will take Sara.'

The horses lowered to let them mount.

Sara wrapped her arms around Blossom's neck as the mare said, 'Sketch, you will join us.'

Sketch nodded, flapped his wings and the group of five took to the skies.

Within moments they were soaring high in the air, up through the tallest reaches of the Rocky Rise. The whole island was in view below them, but as they were so high up all the questers could make out were blurred images in the greens, blues and browns of nature.

'It's spectacular,' said Daniel to no one in particular as he clung tightly to Lightning's strong neck.

Sara forgot for the moment that she was mad with him. 'It's amazing, just amazing, and so high. We never would've made it up here by climbing.'

The horses flew up and around, following the curve of the highest peak. Passing through swirls of mist and clustered cloud and still they soared higher. The siblings had been looking down but raised their heads when the ascent stopped. Their mounts hovered in the air.

'There it is,' Lightning's voice boomed. 'The last known shard of the dragon's tooth.'

Daniel and Sara gasped in wonder. The shard sparkled like a diamond and rays of bright light bounced off it in every direction. They had to shield their eyes for a moment.

'Reach out and take it,' ordered Lightning.

'Would you like to?' Daniel asked Sara.

'No. No thanks. I mean you do. It *is* beautiful and all, only we're on top of the world here and I think I'd like to stay holding on with two hands.'

Daniel gulped. *She's right. Oh well here it goes.* He reached his arm out ever so slowly and placed his fingers around the shard. There was a crackle of colourful flakes and sparkles that made his fingers tingle, but the shard gave easily. It was diamond in shape, with one end thinner than the other and was the same length as Daniel's hand from his wrist to the tip of his forefinger. His hand shook as he withdrew it back towards the safety of Lightning's neck.

Lightning seemed to sense Daniel's unease. 'Sketch, come now and take the shard. We'll return to the ledge below.'

Sketch flew over and Daniel placed the shard in his mouth. Once Sketch closed his mouth over it, using both hands Daniel quickly clung back to Lightning's neck.

Daniel sighed with relief. 'Thanks Sketch, I was worried I'd let it fall is all.'

The flying horses spread their wings wide and glided back down the way they'd come. The questers clung tightly on the decent.

Daniel was smiling. *I can't believe I'm gliding down from the top of the world. Gosh, it's so high, I better hold steady.*

Sara's hair whipped out behind her. *This is breath-taking,* she thought, *what amazing views. I'll never forget this. Just don't fall girl.*

They landed back on the same ledge as before. Sketch trotted to centre of the group and gently dropped the shard from his mouth.

'Daniel and Sara,' began Lightning, 'behold the last known shard of the dragon's tooth. Take it, it's yours.'

The siblings gazed, awestruck, as the sparkles from the shard danced in the evening sun.

'Wow. It's beautiful,' said Sara again.

Daniel mesmerised by its appearance, echoed Sara. 'Wow, it *is* beautiful. It's like a crystal or a diamond or something. Although I *did* think it would be bigger. Still though, see how it shines.'

'It contains pure magic of the heart,' said Blossom gently. 'It *is* but a shard of the great dragon's tooth. The whole tooth was many times larger.'

Lightning touched his nose to the shard and it crackled with bursts of white-light.

'Our ancestors have patrolled the Rocky Rise and the island for generations. The shards of the dragon's tooth have ever been beacons of goodness and hope. This was our destiny, till such a time that the shards and the magic contained within could be passed on for some greater good.'

'What became of the other shards?' asked Sara.

'Many have adventured here over the centuries, some on quests for magic of the heart, some for reasons of their own. Not just humans, other creatures too. Some succeeded, some perished, some stayed and some went home. The other shards had their purposes, each to their own, there is but one remaining after this one but *its* fate is unknown.'

'But if this is the last known shard, surely, we cannot take it?' said Daniel.

The shard caught the sunlight and twinkled in the evening sun as it rested on the rock. Lightning nodded his big head towards it.

'I believe that time has come for this, the ninth shard. Take it now and continue your quest.'

At the mention of the quest Daniel frowned. A look of despair returned to his face. 'I don't see the greater good in us having it. The hag's staff is broken. There's no point in trusting us with this, this…' he hesitated, 'this magical piece of your island's history. We don't belong here. We've already failed in our quest.' He sat on the ground. 'Maybe you could just take us back to Tobias and the well? That would be payment enough. I think it's time we went home.'

Sara joined him. 'He's right you know,' she said sadly. 'We're just a couple of kids in a strange world. We'd lose your precious shard for sure. Home sounds nice right about now.'

'Come now,' soothed Blossom. 'You *are* far from home right now, but you have each other.'

The questers looked at each other and Sara scowled. 'Humph,' she said, and looked away. *Not much use having each other if he treats me like a baby all the time.*

Daniel watched her with a pang of guilt. *She's still mad at me I guess.*

Blossom continued, 'After coming so far and surviving so much to be here, it would be a pity to give up now.'

'But what's the point anymore?' pleaded Daniel. 'We needed the hag's staff but *it's* lost, back there broken on the ledge with the drooling bats. Let's face it, we've failed.'

Lightning shook his mane and spoke with authority. 'Things happen in our lives for reasons that we may not understand at the time, but know that one thing leads to another, and everything makes sense in the grand design of destiny. The purpose of all events, great *or small*, unfold in the fullness of time; things become clear in the end. But for now, we must each play our part as best we can, as *you have* been doing. Think not of it as failure. So I say again, take the shard now and continue on your quest.'

Such was the force of the Lightning's words that the questers believed him.

'Okay, we'll take it,' said Sara. 'But what will you do now? The flying horse herd I mean.'

Blossom answered. 'We will still patrol the Rise. There are strange tidings afoot and much work for the herd to do. While the shards of the dragon's tooth have been part of our heritage, it was foretold that the day would come in which they would all serve some other purposes. Our work continues nonetheless.'

Daniel stood and looked at the flying horses. 'You make it sound like all this,' he gestured around him, 'us here, this quest, us having the shard was meant to be. And though I can't see how, we'll take it. If it has magic of the heart like you say, I guess that can't be a bad thing. We'll go on with it and see where it takes us.'

The shard was aglow with shining white-light. Daniel picked it up and rested it on the palm of his hand. With his other hand he gently pressed his finger against the thinner end.

'Ouch,' he cried, pulling back his finger and sucking it. 'It's needle-sharp,' he explained and held out his finger to show the group a red dot of blood where the shard broke his skin.

Curious despite herself, Sara reluctantly looked. *Ha, serves him right,* she thought.

'Best put it away,' said Lightning.

'I will,' replied Daniel. He tore a piece off his fleece and wrapping the shard in it he unbuttoned a pocket on his combat-trousers and popped it in there for safekeeping. 'And thank you,' he added, 'thanks to all of you. If not for you three, Sara and myself would never have made it this far and—'
He was interrupted by a loud gurgle from his own stomach. Daniel placed his hand over his belly and his face blushed.

'We haven't eaten since early today,' explained Sara.

Lightning nodded his long nose and his white mane shook as he done so. 'Enough thanks where none is needed. So before you find the nourishing stone you need nourishment yourselves. There are creatures on the island that *may* be able to help you. We'll take you as near as we can and hopefully get you fed along the way. Climb up friends, it's time to fly.'

Chapter 21
Descent

With Nightmare Reaches to their backs the questers, still high in the sky, clung tightly to their mounts.

Daniel glanced back over his shoulder for a last look at the Rise. 'I'm glad to be leaving that place,' he called out from his position on Lightning's back. 'Tunnels, rats, bats, crumbling pathways across ravines, it's just not for me!'

'I suspect it's not for most people!' said Sara from Blossom's back. 'Except maybe cave dwellers!'

Without turning his head, Lightning's deep voice rumbled over the high breeze. 'Those crumbling pathways you speak of were long ago built by the good people of the island and once served a great purpose.'

'What purpose?' Sara asked.

Continuing the descent they soared into a glide and Lightning explained.

'In the early days following the great battle of the horse and dragon, the good inhabitants of the island were very nervous. There was no way of knowing if more dangers lurked on the dark side of the Rise or what might cross to wreak havoc once more upon the island. A great counsel was held of man and beast. It was agreed there that humans would patrol the lower slopes of the Rise while the flying herd would guard the higher regions that were unreachable by man. So men carved the pathways into the mountain-side and placed stone bridges across ravines to allow sentries easier passage to the best watch posts.'

'But we saw no sentries,' Sara interrupted. 'The pathways were unused and the bridges were crumbling.'

Lightning went on. 'Alas, Youngling, that is the way of it with humans. Your memories are short by our standards.'

'And they don't have wings,' said Sketch, as he flew alongside Blossom.

Daniel and Sara giggled, but a frown in Sketch's direction from his father signalled that he wasn't finished explaining.

Lightning continued. 'People forget easily. As time passed with no sign of threat from the Rise, their fear soon turned to caution and then caution turned to carelessness. Till eventually the watch posts were abandoned altogether. Most of the pathways collapsed in ruins and with no one to repair them many crumbled to dust. Those that remain are too dangerous for use.'

Blossom flew to the front and took over the telling. 'The only sentries that remained were the cave dwellers. They kept vigil long after the lowlanders forgot.'

'You mean to say Zac and Gertie are sentries?' asked Daniel, surprised. 'They never said!'

'The cave dwellers were among the best sentries. But alas they are too scattered and too few. They have suffered most in recent times from trouble on the mountain, but they linger on defiant and proud. The good people of the island owe the cave dwellers much.'

Lightning took the lead once more. 'The great white stallion and the black dragon became the stuff of legend. But we of the flying herd continued our patrols, and still do till this very day. For this is our calling, to protect and maintain peace and harmony this side of the Rocky Rise. The mountains have become a dangerous place again. There are strange tidings afoot. Raids and kidnappings happen often and rumours of worse. With the marauders taking captives and fell creatures crossing the Rise the flying herd and the cave dwellers must be ever vigilant.'

The questers threw a last glance back towards the mountains, now far in the distance, and this time Sara said it.

'I'm glad we're leaving!'

Silence followed for a time. The group flew in a southeast direction with a beautiful sun setting in the west. The questers gazed down at the rivers, meadows and woods far beneath them. As Sara took in the breath-taking sights below something caught her eye.

'What's that?' she called out while pointing off to her right.

'*That* is the village of Hawksdale,' said Blossom.

Holding tight with both hands, the siblings turned their necks hard to look at the village, far in the distance.

'I can see smoke and cottages. I think I even see people!' cried Daniel.

Lightning made a noise that sounded like a chuckle. 'Naturally, it's a human settlement.'

Daniel and Sara continued to stare towards Hawksdale but the horses didn't change course and the village was soon shrinking in the distance.

'Aren't you taking us there?' asked Daniel expectantly. *I suspect they'd have some food.*

'The village is not our destination,' replied Lightning.

'Pity,' said Daniel quietly. *I'd consider eating garlic right about now.*

'Where *are* you taking us?' asked Sara. *If I'm this hungry, I can imagine how Daniel is feeling. Humph, serves him right.*

Blossom slowed up slightly, allowing Sketch to catch up before she answered.

'The Tor-Folk in the east are good people. We must speak with their elders. It's our hope that they'll feed you and aid you on the next part of your quest.'

'Do you think they know where the nourishing stone is?' Daniel asked.

Lightning circled around to bring up the rear. 'The nourishing stone is not of this land. We of the flying herd are taught the lore of Well-Keeper Island. The lore is passed from generation to generation. Never before has this nourishing stone been mentioned. Not in the histories or in the prophecies, if it was we would know. This is the way of things.'

'Then how will we ever find it?' Sara asked.

'Ah, humans, ever doubtful and ever impatient,' grumbled the stallion. 'In the heart of the shining Great Lake lies a tiny island, no more than a swamp, but home to the strangest creatures in this realm. The swamp itself is only visible at low tide, but it's there just the same. The creatures are known as mowlers, and like many on Well-Keeper Island, they owe their strange existence to the magic's of the Horse and Dragon.'

'Zac mentioned them briefly,' said Daniel. 'You were sleeping Sara.'

'Tell me they're friendly,' pleaded Sara.

Lightning cleared his throat with a chesty rumble. 'The mowlers were a primitive people. They once spent their days sitting in the trees of the Vale of Willows, sleeping on the ground and eating insects, bird eggs and any edible plants. When the dragon set the Vale alight, the mowlers were trapped. Smoke, fire and the black beast's magic engulfed them. But the mowlers were strong of body. So when the flying stallion brought the flowing sea to the Vale, the mowlers rose up and swam to the centre for sanctuary from the raging fire and the rushing water. Following a downpour of colourful flakes from the flying horse's mane, the mowlers, like so many others on the island, transformed into something different. Something magical.'

Lightning described what the mowlers looked like before flying to the front of the travelling group. After a few more wing-beats the stallion turned his head and called back with pride, 'Look now, all behold the Great Lake created by our master, in all its glory.'

'Wow,' the questers chorused together.

'Isn't it beautiful?' said Blossom softly. On the horizon lay a golden plain. It was the Great Lake with the evening sun reflecting off it. The dazzling sight transformed the landscape with wondrous beauty.

Gazing towards the lake Lightning continued, 'In its centre, there the mowlers reside, but no longer the basic creatures they once were. Since the time of the horse and the dragon, they have become something much more. They understand all spoken tongues. Many have sought their counsel over the ages, for their gift is prophecy.'

Sara strained her eyes, willing her vision to stretch beyond the glare of the lake to its centre. 'I can only see the lake.'

Blossom spoke mildly. 'Don't strain your eyes youngling. You'll see the mowlers soon enough, for it is to them you must go to seek the location of the nourishing stone.'

Daniel's brow furrowed. 'I thought you said it was the Tor-Folk that knew the whereabouts of the nourishing stone.'

The group were approaching the shores of the lake, and as one horses changed direction to due east. They flew close to the lake's edge but stayed over land.

'That's not exactly what we said,' said Blossom. 'The Tor-Folk may aid you in your quest, but it's the *mowlers'* wisdom that you must seek in order to find your treasure. The Tor-Folk are the best boat builders in this region. It's our hope that they will help you cross the lake.'

'Listen carefully Daniel,' said Lightning. 'When seeking the mowlers wisdom, the seeker must be ever wary.'

Daniel gulped. 'Sorry. I will. But, eh…' he hesitated. *How can I say this without sounding rude?*

Lightning seemed to sense his discomfort. 'You have something to say. Now is the time.'

'I was just wondering why you don't just fly us across the lake,' said Daniel, 'especially when we're so close.'

'A wise thing to wonder,' replied Lightning. But they stayed flying over land. Sketch flapped his wings with all haste, determined to keep up with the adults. 'Steady now, Sketch,' ordered Lightning in a voice not to be disobeyed. 'You've proven that you can keep up. Save your energy. As a stallion you may have to carry a passenger at a moment's notice. Remember your training, this is the Great Lake. Fall back from the edge.'

Blossom flew alongside Lightning and spoke. 'To the untrained eye it may look calm and peaceful, but the Great Lake is fraught with hidden dangers. One must be ever vigilant on and over its surface, for the slightest disturbance can unleash dark forces lurking on the lake bed.'

'Oh I remember,' said Daniel, 'Zac called them the bottom-claws.'

'That *is* what they are called,' said Lightning. 'But not just the bottom-claws, other creatures of the deep reside in the Great Lake.'

'Oh I don't like the sound of them,' said Sara. 'Anything with claws in the name can only mean trouble. What exactly are they?'

Lightning looked to the fading sun. 'We still have time yet so I will tell you. The bottom-claws were once beautiful willow trees, the same bows that the mowlers climbed and rested on. When the fires of the black dragon ravaged them, the dark magic soaked into their trunks and down to their very roots. The magic fused with the trees, turning them into something monstrous. Their branches stretched and twisted into hideous claws.'

'Creepers,' said Sara. 'And we've to cross the lake alone?'

Lightning shook his shimmering mane and went on. 'The magic that created the Great Lake came from our master, and a piece of this magic still resides in us of the flying herd. Because of this, we cannot cross its waters. The magic of light within us and the dark magic submerged in the lake are ever drawn to one another, for this is the nature of strong magic. Our presence above the waters would awaken the bottom-claws, much to the doom of any who may be using the lake. And so we avoid crossing at all costs, for the sake of those lives that would be at risk. So now you see why we can't carry you over.'

Not for the first time the questers exchanged a worried look.

Besides all of that, it's late,' said Blossom gently. 'You'll need rest and food before you cross any lake.'

The descent from the mountains continued in silence for a time until Sara noticed the change in the light.

'Gosh,' she said, looking at the last rays of the sun. 'It's late evening already,'

'So it is,' agreed Daniel. 'I didn't realise how long we'd been flying.' The sun disappeared on the horizon, giving way to twilight.

The travellers rounded a bend and entered a group of low-lying hills and shortly afterward the dwellings of the Tor-Folk could be seen in the distance. It was night time when they reached the outskirts of the village.

Chapter 22
Tor-Folk

The flying steeds and their riders descended over a low earth embankment marking the border of the Tor-Folk settlement. Torches were just being lit at points along the mound as the group landed lightly on soft, brown clay. Lightning and Blossom stood tall and straight, waiting with patience to be greeted, but the questers and Sketch could not help staring all around at the bustle of activity going on about the village. The surroundings were dotted with small structures, huts made from dried mud with thatch roofs. Each hut had a circular window carved into the wall, and many of these windows had woven reeds hanging over them serving as a curtain to keep out the night air. Rising from the centre of the village, atop a high hill, was a much larger wooden building with light pouring out from its many windows. There was a constant troop of people pacing back and forth carrying jugs, platters and instruments of every description.

Daniel and Sara shared a glance at one another. Both wore a look of surprise, for the tallest of the Tor-Folk were not much taller than Daniel, and some were a good deal shorter. Despite their short size though, they were stocky in appearance. The men had broad chests and muscled arms. The women looked strong too but were fair of face. Sure-footed children raced around the village laughing, shouting and crying aloud.

Blossom gave Sketch a stern glance.

'Sketch, you know it's rude to stare.'

The colt quickly dropped his gaze. Daniel and Sara's cheeks reddened as they realised that Blossom was scolding them too.

'They're smaller than I expected,' whispered Daniel from the corner of his mouth.

'State the obvious why don't you,' Sara whispered back. 'They seem to be preparing a feast of sorts.'

'Who's stating the obvious now, genius,' Daniel whispered again.

'Small people, I grant you, but with big warm hearts,' said Blossom quietly. 'They stand a head shorter than the other people of the island, but their strength is renown throughout.'

The questers reddened afresh as they realised they'd been overheard.

Lightning turned his long face towards the skies. 'And right you are, youngling. They *are* preparing a feast, the feast of the crescent moon.'

The siblings followed his gaze towards the night sky and sure enough, there was a crescent moon low on the horizon.

Daniel rubbed his stomach. 'I've never heard of that feast, but any feast sounds nice right about now.'

'Can you tell us about the feast?' asked Sara. 'It'd be nice to hear about something that's not threatening for once.'

With the fullness of night descending, more torches flared to life, lighting up the village. As the preparations continued around them, Lightning explained the feast.

'An ancient race, the Tor-Folk are known as such because of the gentle tors that surround their lands. Rich with knowledge of the land they live off, they are at one with nature. They cherish the earth, in which they grow their crops and the grass from which their flocks graze. The water is precious to them, a source of nourishment, health and life. The sun, too, is praised; it brings warmth and heralds growth. The Tor-Folk give thanks to the elements, those forces of nature that they rely on for their daily survival. And so this is the festival of the crescent moon, a guide for them in the night skies marking a point in the season. They have many such feasts. The people gather together and celebrate, and a great counsel is held with the whole community involved. This is the way of the Tor-Folk.'

They stood for a few more moments till one of the Tor-Folk appeared beside them. He was dressed in a colourful robe that covered him from shoulder to ankle and he held a staff of sorts with feathers and beads hanging from its top.

'Come,' he said simply, then turned and walked towards a large hut not far from the main hall.

Curious bystanders stepped aside as the steward led the way. Side by side Blossom and Lightning followed behind, while the questers and Sketch brought up the rear. The group passed oven-houses, fires and roasting spits and the smell of baking and meat cooking filled the air. Daniel's tummy groaned. As they approached the large hut a group of elders had gathered outside the entrance.

'You must wait here,' said Lightning, turning to Daniel and Sara. The elders entered the hut with the adult horses following. Lightning just about fit through the door. Sketch trotted after them but Lightning stopped him. 'You must wait outside too, Sketch. We're very honoured to get a private counsel with the elders of the Tor-Folk. Their wisdom is great and their time is precious, especially on a festival night. Stay here with the steward. We won't be long.' Lightning passed through the entrance and the wooden door slid shut.

The steward stood to the left of the door and looked straight ahead. He held his staff through folded arms. Daniel frowned, deep in thought. *I wonder what they're saying. Perhaps I can listen at the door.* He took a step towards the door and glanced at the stern expression on the steward's face. *Eh, maybe not then.*

Sara glanced sideways at the steward. *These Tor-Folk are a serious lot*, she thought to herself. As there was nothing else to do, they sat on the ground and waited for the counsel to end.

Not long after, the door of the hut slid open and the horses trotted out followed by four elderly Tor-folk. Two were men and two were women. They all wore colourful robes with feathers hanging from the sleeves.

The questers hopped off the ground and brushed the dirt from their clothes.

'What news?' Sara asked.

The elders stood silently by and let Lightning answer.

'The Tor-Folk have ruled in your favour. It's settled, you'll feast with them tonight. When first light arrives, the Tor-Folk will give you a boat and take you to the Great Lake. From there you'll continue your journey alone.'

The prospect of being alone again did not sit well with Daniel or Sara. A look of gloom washed over their faces but the moment was interrupted by a loud shout from the village watchtower.

'*Pigeeeon incoming!*' roared the voice above the din of the preparations.

All heads turned towards the watchtower and a moment later a flutter of blue-grey wings came zooming across the village. One of the Tor-Folk elders raised his arm above his head and stretched the palm of his hand out flat. The pigeon slowed its approach and came in to land on the outstretched hand. With a sense of urgency in the air the horses and elders crowded around the pigeon. The questers stood close too, eager to watch this curious development.

'May we?' asked Lightning.

'Please do,' replied the elder that was holding the bird.

'Sketch, come forwards,' said Lightning. 'Where has the messenger pigeon come from?'

Sketch studied the pigeon closely. There were pieces of brown cord tied to each of its legs. Tied to the end of one piece of cord was a twig with strange symbols carved on it. There was a small feather tied to the end of the other.

Sketch nickered softly as the group watched him expectantly. 'The cord is woven from roots of dale-ivy and the feather is eh…em,' he hesitated.

'Remember your training dear,' encouraged Blossom.

'Let me see.' His eyes opened wide. 'Black-brown feathers with sharp tip, it's a hawk's feather. The pigeon has come from Hawksdale!'

'Good,' said Lightning. 'You did well son. But the message is not good. See the double cross on the twig with a circle in the centre? That's a tied net and is the symbol for a captive.'

Daniel and Sara gulped.

'What else does it say?' asked Sketch.

Lightning spoke low and deep. 'The bow without an arrow means it was a lone hunter. The apex is the symbol for a home, which means he has a family. The marauders have taken a father from Hawksdale.'

'It must be the one you seen, Dan,' said Sara, alarmed.

'Oh no,' cried Daniel. *And I did nothing to help him.*

'Do not despair,' said Lightning, as though he read Daniel's mind. 'You are not at fault.'

'But what will become of him?' Daniel asked, distraught.

'I guess we won't be staying for the feast then,' said Sketch.

'No,' Lightning replied firmly. 'We've stayed overlong already. It's time to fly.'

Lightning nodded to the Tor-Folk elder. The elder raised his hand in a quick gesture and the pigeon flew off into the night.

Lightning turned to the questers. 'Daniel and Sara, may magic of the heart guide you.' And before they could respond the flying stallion uttered his battle cry.

'*Neiiiiiighhhhhhhhhhhh.*'

The questers leaped with fright; such was the suddenness of Lightning's cry. They turned their faces away to shield from the force of his wing-beats.

When the battle-cry stopped, Sara turned back to say goodbye to Sketch but he was gone. So too were his parents. The sound of their wing-beats was quickly fading as the flying horses disappeared into the night skies.

The questers gazed at the empty sky where the retreating horses had been only moments before.

'Nobody answered my question,' said Daniel. '*And* we never thanked them properly.'

'I wanted to give Sketch a hug,' added Sara sadly.

The elder that had held the pigeon stepped forwards. 'Welcome to our lands. I am Turlock, chief elder of the village council. The flying herd have urgent matters to attend elsewhere this night. They've told us much of your quest, a very brave endeavour.'

The questers shook hands and introduced themselves to each of the elders.

Turlock continued, 'Tonight is the Feast of the Crescent Moon, you will feast with us and sing and talk, for there is much to discuss this night.'

The elder was interrupted by a small girl tugging at his robes. He stopped and stooped down to hear her whisper something. When she finished, he straightened up and laughed good-naturedly. The small girl shyly hid behind his legs.

'This is Bluebell, my granddaughter. She's quite taken with your appearance and wants to know if she can sit next to you at the feast.'

Sara smiled down to the shy girl. 'Of course you can, and what a pretty name you have, just like a flower where we come from.'

'We have the same flower here. In fact that's what she was named after,' said Turlock.

Daniel winked at Bluebell. 'And what a lovely name it is,' he said.

This brought a delighted giggle from the small girl and she raced off shyly behind the nearest hut.

'We don't get many visitors hereabouts,' said Turlock. 'Bluebell has never seen people of your Race, nor have many of our tribe. Tonight will

155

be a double celebration, the welcoming of guests and the Feast of the Crescent Moon; let us begin.'

Daniel and Sara were led to the great hall by the group of elders. As they entered Sara felt a small hand close around her finger. She looked down and there was Bluebell smiling up at her. Sara smiled back and in they went. The village gong sounded, and that was the signal for all to sit.

Daniel wore a broad smile. 'Things are finally starting to look up. Our first feast.'

Sara rolled her eyes. 'Trust you, Daniel. You'd eat plate and all if you got your way.'

'Maybe I would eat the plate, with a little dollop of butter and honey.'

This brought a burst of laughter from the Tor-Folk around them.

They were seated at one end of a large oval table, and Bluebell had positioned herself right beside Sara on the long wooden stool. 'Can he *really* eat plates?' she whispered up to Sara. She was overheard by some of the adults, and this brought more laughter.

'Do you know, it wouldn't surprise me if he could!' said Sara.

Bluebell gazed at Daniel, fascinated. But when he didn't bite his plate, she turned her attention back to Sara and the two of them fell into a merry chat.

Meanwhile Turlock had begun to explain the various dishes on the board to Daniel. Daniel too was fascinated as he took in all around him.

'So much choice,' he muttered, 'and they all smell delicious.' His mouth watered.

At either end of the board there were two great vats of broth, mountain herb at one end and the other was flavoured forest delights. Next to the soups were three different types of bread: one rolled, one white and one brown. Beside the breads came baskets of fruit, apples, pears, grapes, plums and a good many that the questers had never seen before. Approaching the centre from both ends of the table sat a circle of bowls overflowing with steaming-hot vegetables, and placed in the middle was a wooden platter with juicy cuts of meat mounded high atop one another.

Daniel was dizzy with the smells and the sights. 'Where does one begin?' he asked Turlock.

'Where does one end? Is the question I usually ask,' answered the grinning elder. 'Wait till you see the pastries and pies that come after.'

Four serving stewards appeared from behind a bead curtain pushing a long cart. Daniel's eyes grew wide and his stomach groaned. Atop the cart lay a delicious assortment of pastries. There were cream muffins, lemon pies, sweet trifles, buns, cakes and tart slices, enough for everyone in the hall twice over.

'Where does one end?' said Daniel as he stared, enchanted.

The Tor-Folk watched on and laughed with merry delight.

I was wrong, Sara thought to herself, *they really are a friendly people, so lively, nothing at all like the steward we met first.*

Turlock stood and raised his arms for silence. 'Greetings all on this night, our feast of the crescent moon, made doubly joyous by the welcoming of guests. Before we begin, as is our tradition, we will have a story. Any requests?'

Many voices cried out from the hall.

'The chief's beard,'

'The Vale of Willows,'

'The bent dagger,'

'The long fog.'

But the most calls came for a story called the Parched Valley.

Turlock raised his hands again for silence. 'Very well, very well. We will hear the story of the Parched Valley. Chief Maeve and second elder of the Tor-Folk will do the telling. Rise Chief Maeve and work your art.'

Chief Maeve stood from where she sat next to Turlock and her long auburn-red hair fell down over her shoulders. She gazed around the hall with her deep-green eyes and when she had everyone's attention, she swung her colourful shawl over her shoulder and began the tale.

Chapter 23
The Parched Valley

The great battle between the giant flying stallion and the great black dragon had ended. Victory was the stallion's but much work was still to be done to restore tranquillity and order to the land. The mighty steed flew with all haste over the hills and glades that were home to the Tor-Folk tribes. And farther east still he flew till he happened upon a valley that was once the most beautiful valley in all of Well-Keeper Island. But alas, he was too late. The valley once teamed with a rich tapestry of life, but what met the eyes of the stallion was a smoking ruin. Everything lay charred and black with no sign of life, for the dragon's fires had blazed here unchecked. Without counter measures from the stallion or his minions, the ferocious fires had laid waste to the valley. All was destroyed. The white steed landed gracefully, hoofing the crumbling soil and sniffing the air. It was at this very moment that a low growl came to his ears. Raising his head, the horse saw that he was surrounded by a pack of fevered wolves.

The wolves had left their den in the northern end of the valley and had been hunting in the meadows when the dragon arrived and unleashed his deadly fires. With nowhere to escape to, the wolves were engulfed in the flames and changed forever by the dark magic of the dragon.

Their eyes were wild and blood shot, their tongues hung sideways from their mouths and spit hissed between their snarling fangs. Swinging his neck, the stallion circled in a measured dance so as to keep all the wolves in his line of vision. All the while the hounds inched closer. The horse knew these creatures were doomed. The dark magic of the dragon had seeped into the very fibre of their souls, and they could not be saved from madness. An army of fangs flared as the wolves crouched, ready to pounce. The white steed raised himself to full height and spread his wings. The wolves attacked as one; leaping from all angles, closing their circle of death. In the same instant, the flying horse was transformed into a vessel of golden light. He shone so bright and dazzling that it was as though the sun itself poured forth from his body. The leaping wolves fell away from the shining horse, blinded by the magical shield of light. The golden light pierced their eyes and threw them into a rolling frenzy. Rubbing their heads in the charred clay and squirming on their backs, the wolves howled and screeched. This was the effect the golden light had on their disturbed minds. For the golden light was pure magic of the heart. Soon the stallion settled from his magical dance and was once again visible as a white flying horse. But not visible to the wolves, for the light had blinded them and they scattered in every direction whimpering and yelping. And as the wolves made a feeble retreat, the stallion beat his mighty wings and took to the skies and flew off into the sunset.

Unlike much of the Island the great stallion chose not to restore the Parched Valley. He left it bare and desolate so that other creatures would not dwell there. The valley is devoid of life but for the blind wolves, this was their home before that fateful day, and so it remains. The wolves are bound to the Parched Valley and it's there they live out their doom. Only on dark nights the wolf pack leave the valley to hunt; Still blind and still ferocious. On those nights watch out!

Chapter 24
Dog Fight

The great hall was silent. Maeve's audience were captivated by her chilling and haunting tones. Somebody sighed and the spell was broken. A great cheer followed and loud applause.

Wearing a warm smile Turlock leaned over so Daniel and Sara could hear him above the din. 'Maeve's art is storytelling. It never fails to win the crowd. But now it's time for *my* favourite part. Listen for the second gong, that's our signal to eat!'

The questers smiled back. A loud gong sounded in the hall. *Finally,* thought Daniel, *sweet, sweet food,* as he prepared to swallow a soft bread-roll in one bite. Turlock snatched the bread-roll from his hand.

'Quickly! No time for food, we're under attack!' shouted the elder. 'You two must hide with the children.'

Tor-Folk were jumping up from the table and dashing for the door, all the time the bell was ringing out across the village.

Daniel had been so focused on eating the bread-roll he suddenly found himself confused with all the commotion. 'What's happening? Is this another part of the feast?'

'That's not the feast bell! It's a warning from the watchtower! Blind wolves have breached our borders!' shouted Turlock.

Hunger quickly forgotten, Daniel and Sara charged from the hall with everybody else. Amidst the panic, Daniel stopped and turned to Turlock. 'Where are your weapons? I can fight.' Turning to Sara he added, 'You go with the children, Sis. I don't want anything to happen to you.'

Sara's brow crinkled and her face reddened. 'No Daniel!' she screamed as she pushed him in the chest with both of her fists. Daniel stumbled backward. His face froze, shocked to silence. 'No Daniel!' Sara shouted again. 'We're not splitting up again. You fought the bats, you fought the rats and you lied about the marauders. All to protect me! Well I'm part of this too and I'm not leaving your side.' Daniel, still stunned by the force of her protest, just nodded. Sara turned to Turlock. 'I can fight too!'

Turlock looked back to Daniel.

'We're both staying,' said Daniel, his face set. The elder didn't argue and quickly led them across the village towards the weapons keep.

Tor-Folk were running to-and-fro with torches, spears, bows and swords. Children could be heard crying above the chaos as their mothers tried to calm them. Men shouted to one another, and it was soon learned that the wolves were advancing from the east. Suddenly a chilling howl sounded through the village.

'Ow ow ooooooooowwwwwwwww!'

Many Tor-Folk froze to the spot, the howl frightening them to stillness. Several wolves could be glimpsed in the shadows approaching the centre of the village. The red of their sightless eyes and their dripping, yellow fangs were illuminated by the torchlights. The people broke from their shock as the pack advanced. Women screamed, trying desperately to usher the children into huts and hide-a-ways. The men fired arrows and spears into the night, hoping to slay the attacking beasts. It was difficult to aim amidst the fear and confusion of the frantic, fleeing crowd. Everything was blurred and confused. Not many throws found their mark.

Daniel and Sara had not yet reached the weapons keep when a ferocious snarl sounded dangerously close. They turned as one to see the wolves now spread through to the centre of the village. The blind beasts were attacking closed huts by digging, climbing on the roofs and clawing at the doors. They snarled and snapped at the villagers who were struggling to fend them off. Not enough tor-folk had gotten their weapons.

Turlock beckoned to Daniel and Sara. 'I hope all the children are secure. Come, we must get to the keep!'

A child screaming in terror rose above the noise of the battle. The three watched as a blind wolf burst from a hut with a small child held by her simple, cloth dress between its teeth.

Turlock's face knotted in shock and horror. 'Bluebell!' he roared with all his might. 'They've got Bluebell!'

The Tor-Folk fighters turned to see a daughter of the hills held in the ravenous jaws of the blind wolf. The pack bunched together around the wolf that held Bluebell. The fighters watched on helplessly while the snarling beasts made their escape from the village towards the safety of the Parched Valley.

The Tor-Folk villagers stood still, horrified at the sight of sweet Bluebell being carried away by the vicious beasts. Daniel broke into a sprint after the pack.

'There's no time! To me!' he screamed and grabbed a spear from the nearest warrior as he raced by. He wailed a screeching battle cry and charged the pack. 'Aaayyyeee!'

The wolves sensed his approach and turned to face him. Planting the spear in the earth, Daniel pole-vaulted through the air and into the heart of the pack. This daring advance startled the pack and they scattered momentarily. Daniel frantically scanned the pack for the little girl.

'Daniel! Daniel!' Bluebell cried out in a terrified voice.

Daniel turned and there she was still hanging by her dress from the teeth of the wolf. The wolf had to sway its head this way and that as Bluebell kicked and screamed. Daniel bolted straight for the beast. Slamming into the wolf from the side he threw his arms around its neck. Such was the force of Daniel's attack that the wolf dropped Bluebell and tumbled to the ground. Daniel stayed clinging to the wolf's neck as the two rolled along the dirt in a fierce embrace.

Turlock appeared from somewhere and scooped up Bluebell then dashed back towards the safety of the village and the watching warriors. The wolf struggled to its feet, but Daniel stayed clinging to its neck. His mind raced. *If I let go now, I'm open to attack.*

Sara watched with the rest of the Tor-Folk as once again the blind wolves re-grouped and continued their escape away from the village. 'Daniel! Someone has to help Daniel!' she cried.

The other wolves were closing in around the wolf that Daniel clung to. They sniffed, snarled and snapped blindly. All the while putting distance between themselves and the Tor-Folk settlement. From the corner of his eye, Daniel saw Sara break away from the crowd and then the wolves were upon him.

Sara dashed to the nearest fire and snatched two burning branches, one in each hand. She raced towards the pack that now enclosed Daniel and running up the crest of a hill she leapt towards the beasts. She screamed as only twelve-year-old girls can scream.

'Get away from my Brother!'

The wolves heard her scream and felt the heat of the fire. Sara waved the burning branches in looping arcs. She scattered the wolves for a few precious moments. Frenzied by battle she spun the flaming sticks in circles and sparks flew through the air. Daniel saw his chance and released his grip from the wolf. He tumbled once, jumped up and raced to Sara's side. Without a word, she handed him one of the burning branches and together they faced the wolves. The pack, desperate for a kill, quickly surrounded them again.

'Sweat teamed off Daniel's brow. 'Sara, what're you doing here?' he gasped.

'Thought you'd get to fight these dogs alone did you?' Sara replied through heavy breaths.

Daniel nodded. 'Okay, Sis, stay beside me then.'

'We stand as one,' said Sara determinedly as the nearest wolf attacked.

The wolf leapt at them both with mouth open and dripping fangs bared. The siblings swung their weapons at the same time and smacked the beast square in the side of the head. It fell to the ground squealing. An instant later a second wolf attacked from the side. It was barely inches from Daniel's throat when he parried it away with the flaming branch. The wolves were growing fearless, and although Sara and Daniel fought bravely, the beasts were just too many.

Launching a full attack, the wolves sprang from every direction, fangs bared and claws swiping through the air. The siblings fought wildly, swinging their branches this way and that. Some wolves howled and raced off into the night, their coats aflame. Others rolled in the dirt only to spring back up and charge the questers again.

It seemed that at any moment Daniel and Sara would be overcome when suddenly a hoard of Tor-Folk warriors came charging to their aid. Turlock led the charge, brandishing a sword high above his head.

'Attack!' he roared at the top of his lungs.

The attacking warriors met with the blind wolves full on. Metal and fangs clanged, wolves howled and blood spilled.

Still fighting with a burning branch Daniel locked eyes with Turlock. 'Bluebell?' he asked through desperate gasps.

'She's safe,' Turlock managed to reply before cutting down another snarling beast.

Others from the village began grabbing any weapon they could lay their hands on. Taking courage from the bravery of Daniel and Sara, they ran to the fight and the battle was joined.

The Tor-Folk soon outnumbered the wolves, and the tide of the battle turned. They drove the pack back with force and determination. Followed into the night by armed scouts, the blind wolves took flight. The battle was over.

Chapter 25
Tor-Folk Heroes

The scouts had not yet returned from the pursuit of the wolves. While waiting for word that the village was safe, those that fought sat on the ground and tended to their wounds. Daniel and Sara suffered some scratches and a few light burns. One of the Tor-folk healers gave the questers special ointment to rub on their wounds.

'Wow,' said Daniel, 'It really soothes the pain of the burns.'

'It's an ancient Tor-Folk remedy passed down through generations. The ointment can draw poison from wounds, and scars too will heal quickly,' said the healer, before moving on to the next injured group.

When the healer moved on, Daniel turned to Sara. 'Hey, I'm glad you were nearby back there, I don't mind admitting I was a little frightened.'

Sara raised her eyebrows. 'A little eh? I was more than a *little* frightened. But it's okay, you'd have done it for me. *Have* done it for me even.'

'Well thanks anyway, Sara, about back there on the mountain, the marauders and all,'

'Yeah, I know Dan, you don't have to say it. You're forgiven.'

'Thanks, Sis. No more secrets, eh?'

'No more secrets.' Sara smiled. 'Idiot.'

Daniel grinned. *I'll give her that one.*

They sat for a short time under the clear night sky till the scouts returned from the chase. The front man jogged straight over to where Turlock sat, close to the questers.

'The Blind Wolves have fled. They've gone beyond the borders of the Parched Valley,' said the front man. Sara looked at him. *Oh, he's the steward that brought us to the elders earlier on.* Her eyes widened when he turned to her and fell to one knee.

'Fire wielder and daughter of the light, you shame us with your valour. We are forever in your debt,' he said, with his head bowed. Turlock wiped blood and dirt from his face before joining the steward and knelt to face Daniel.

'And you also, son of the light and champion of the Tor-Folk, your courageous deeds will never be forgotten. Your deeds will be recounted in our lore from this day forth. Your names will live on, and tonight's victory will be retold in song for many generations to come. I myself will compose the first this very night.' The elder stood before the questers and raised his palms skyward. 'Arise Daniel, arise Sara, Tor-Folk warriors, Tor-Folk heroes.'

Daniel and Sara stood hesitantly, and as they did so, the remaining Tor-Folk warriors joined the steward on one knee to pay homage to the brave questers. Daniel and Sara were embarrassed by the gesture but nodded respectfully to the kneeling crowd.

Turlock clapped once. 'Right then, our young guests are modest, nevertheless we shall return to the village and continue the honours.'

The journey back to the village was a short one. The sibling's walked either side of Turlock who led the way.

'Do you get many attacks like this?' Sara asked.

'We've had many over the years, but never as fierce as tonight,' said Turlock. 'The wolves never entered the village like this before. They're pack has grown and hunger makes them bold.'

'What will you do?' Daniel asked. 'If it happened once, it could happen again.'

'What will we do?' Turlock winked. 'You'll see young warrior, you'll see.'

Word went ahead that the blind wolves had been defeated. Relieved faces appeared from out of hiding places. Adults and children alike gazed at the Daniel and Sara as they returned with the warriors. Turlock led the way to the village heart. On reaching the centre the elder raised his hands and the gong sounded once. Complete silence followed. Not even a whisper dared to break the stillness and suspense hung in the air. Turlock waited till he judged the moment right and cried out:

'Here ye all friends and kinsmen, as you all know we have lived in constant threat of attack from the hounds of the Parched Valley. And this has been so for many ages past. We have often lost part of our flock to these wolves, and worse—a lot worse, we've lost members of our tribe the same way. Now with our sheep penned up for a late lambing season, we'll have more lambs than ever before, the largest flock in our tribe's history. This brings us great joy, as nature has rewarded us in plenty. However, with such bounty we must show extra caution to protect our lot. Till now we've been content to drive away the blind wolves only for them to return another night, and this has been our downfall. For the wolves too, have grown in number. They seek more hunting territory and have more hungry mouths to feed. Tonight was proof of this, for never before have they breached the heart of our stronghold. Never before have they taken a child in their ravenous jaws. A daughter of the Hills! Children, our blood wealth, our future and our happiness. My very own granddaughter Bluebell.'

Turlock paused to gather himself again, and not even a breeze disturbed the silence. The tribe waited on his every word. Taking a deep breath, he continued aloud. 'If not for the sheer bravery of our young guests Daniel and Sara, our precious Bluebell would be lost and our grief would be great. Against hopeless odds, against vicious beasts far greater in size and greatly outnumbered, these courageous youngsters ran to her rescue. They charged our foes and fought like warriors. Daniel turned from boy to bear and wrestled the wolf for Bluebell's life. Sara joined the battle wielding flaming sticks, and she swung those burning embers like swords forged from the sun. These who are children themselves in their own land risked their lives to save ours, and save us they did. Let a great cry go out across the land That Daniel bold as a bear and Sara shining like the sun were victorious, Tor-Folk warriors, Tor-Folk heroes.'

A great cheer went up from the gathered crowd, and their shouts and applause echoed off the surrounding hills. Sara and Daniel stood next to Turlock and blushed but held their heads up high. The elder smiled warmly and allowed the din to continue for a few more moments before raising his hands to signal quiet.

'Not only did these brave warriors win the day, they've won our hearts also. And through their courageous deeds they have thought us to conquer our fears and inspired us to action. No longer will we hide behind our walls fearing attack night after night. Come the end of the lambing season, we will arm ourselves with fire and steel and take the fight to the blind wolves. Although it was the dragon's fire that made these wolves such vicious creatures, fire is our greatest defence against them. They fear the light as it still burns in their minds. Fire is what the blind wolves fear most after daylight. So we will seek them out by day, find their caves and remove this threat from our lands. We will not stop until every wolf has fled or has been slain. Our children will be safe and we will sleep soundly in our beds. I, Turlock, chief elder of the Tor-Folk, declare it. Are we united?' A shout of approval rose up from the gathering, and as the excitement grew, he shouted again, 'Are we united?' This time a great roar sounded. Every member of the Tor-Folk tribe cheered as their hearts filled with hope and courage.

It took longer for the noise to die down this time. Turlock was content to let the villagers cheer and shout and chat among themselves.

Daniel turned to Sara. 'What a night!' he said.

Sara shook her head in wonder. 'You can say that again.'

Turlock overheard them. 'And the night is still young, my friends!' He winked, swirled his robes and clapped the noisy crowd to attention once more. 'Listen now, one and all. Now we shall begin the Feast of the Crescent Moon. But we shall make it a double celebration, for tonight we honour our guests Daniel and Sara with the Ceremony for Heroes. This time the noise reached fever pitch as the delighted tribe cheered and hurried to begin the feast. Turlock turned to the questers and smiled. 'This will be a *long* night!'

Chapter 26
Fond Farewell

A new day dawned in the East. Sara woke to the sunlight spilling in the window and spreading through the hut. She shielded her eyes from the beams and stretched while looking around. Her dungarees, t-shirt and cardigan had taken quite a battering in the last few days, and one of the village ladies had given her a soft woollen nightdress to sleep in. Now her clothes lay clean and folded at her feet. *Someone must have tended to them while I slept,* she thought, while yawning. *That was one long night!* Smiling, she shook Bluebell gently to rouse her. The little girl had insisted that Sara sleep in her hut after the feast, and Sara had gladly accepted. *I was so tired last night I would've slept standing up.* Bluebell had nodded off still wearing her colourful frock. The celebrations had gone on late into the night. There was feasting, singing, the telling of tales and of course, dancing. During the Ceremony of Heroes there was an exchange of gifts. Daniel and Sara were given wood-carven crescent moons, each inset with a tiny green gem. In return they gave some pieces of flint from the Rocky Rise as tokens of thanks for the honour they received.

Rubbing the sleep from her eyes, it only took moments for Bluebell to spring to life. 'Sara, what a wonderful night. Do let me see your necklace again,' she said excitedly. Sara smiled and removed the cord holding the carving over her head.

'Here you go, Bluebell. Do you know you're quite a dancer? You kept me on my toes half the night!'

'*You* are a wonderful dancer, Sara, even if you do wear the strangest clothes.' The pair looked at each other and burst out laughing. 'Come along, we'll go find Daniel. I'm hoping he'll eat a plate at breakfast.'

Deep in thought, Daniel sat on a wooden stool in the corner of the hut that he'd slept in. He was so tired the night before that he'd fallen asleep without undressing. *That was a long night. Three nights have passed since we got here, time is passing. Still, I feel rested and refreshed. Our journey continues. But to what end?* He stroked the carving between his thumb and finger and let his thoughts wander back to the night gone by. With his eyes closed he recalled the Feast of the Crescent Moon and the Ceremony of Heroes. Turlock had placed the leather cord holding the gem carving around his neck and spoke for all to hear:

'Rise, Brother Daniel, boy to bear, son of the light, warrior true and champion of the Tor-Folk,' and the gathered tribe went wild in a frenzy of cheering and clapping. With the memory of the Tor-Folk music fresh in his ears, he smiled and went outside.

Bluebell saw him from a distance and came racing across the village. 'Daniel, Daniel, you're awake, come with us. You can sit with me and Sara for breakfast if you like.'

Daniel laughed. 'I'd be delighted.' *Where's the shy little girl we met yesterday?*

Bluebell raced ahead towards the village hall just as Sara reached Daniel. 'To think, just last night she was in the jaws off a wolf, and today she's full of the summer.'

Daniel nodded. 'I was just thinking something like that.'

Bluebell turned and shouted back. 'Hurry, you two, or it will soon be time for dinner!' Daniel and Sara laughed aloud and broke into a sprint after her.

There was a buzz of excitement in the main hall as plans for the next stage of Daniel and Sara's journey were discussed over breakfast. Most of the tor-folk tribe had volunteered to accompany the adventurers to the edge of the Great Lake. Everyone wanted the honour of leading the heroes beyond the Tor-Folk borders. Daniel and Sara sat at the top of the table with Turlock in between them.

In the end, it was decided that only the steward and Turlock would show them the way till a little voice cried out from the back of the hall.

'Oh Granddad, please let me go with you. I'll be ever so good.' It was Bluebell standing on a stool for all to see.

'Ah my precious Granddaughter, the way is long for your little legs, and the Great Lake is no place for a small girl,' said Turlock.

'I'll take twice as many steps to keep up.' Bluebell jogged on the spot to prove her worth. The on-looking tribe laughed. Bluebell planted her hands on her hips. 'Sara is a small girl in *her* own land and she's going!' Turlock looked to Daniel and Sara.

'We don't mind if she tags along,' said Sara. Daniel nodded his agreement.

Turlock raised his hands in submission. 'Okay my young flower, I can see you're determined. But no running ahead. You must stay close and don't be bothering the travellers with too many questions!'

Bluebell squealed with delight. 'I won't say a word starting now.' Bluebell sealed her lips tightly together. But one moment later, still standing on the stool she asked Sara, 'Can I walk beside you?' Instantly realising her slip, she clasped her hands over her mouth. 'Oops,' she said. The entire hall erupted in a roar of joyous laughter.

The whole village turned out to see the group off. Some clapped and cheered, others wept, and some watched and waved silently. Younger members of the tribe followed them a short distance till their mothers called them back. Leaving the village, Daniel and Sara turned and waved goodbye while taking one last look at the Tor-Folk settlement.

Daniel was thoughtful. *Although I've not known them long, I've become fond of the Tor-Folk. I'll miss them.*

Sara smiled as she waived but her eyes were sad. *They're a wonderful people, it's sad that we've to leave our new friends so soon.*

The steward led the group. Resting on his head was one end of a long, narrow boat. He was followed by Turlock who held the other end of the boat, also on his head. The boat was made of a light timber frame surrounded by leather hides and held together with a strong pitch. Turlock explained that the pitch was a mix of nature's bounty known only to the elders. Daniel and Sara carried their fleeces on their backs and Bluebell skipped along beside them. Daniel still carried the rope given to him by Zac, and Sara the satchel, still containing two pieces of flint and their tiny helper Bobbin. They had other provisions too, provided by the Tor-Folk: two canteens of fresh drinking water and some slivers of dried meat sandwiched between thick slices of brown bread. Sara brought the sandwiches in the other satchel that Daniel had carried since the Rocky Rise. The elders had prepared them more healing ointment in a small clay jar that Daniel carried in one of his combat-trouser pockets.

Winding over and around hills covered with ferns, grass and other plants, the group moved ahead at a steady pace. Daniel was eager to help carry the boat, but Turlock advised him to keep his strength for rowing across the lake. Spirits lifted along the way, as it was impossible for them to remain sad with merry Bluebell in their company. She had managed to stay quiet till they were out of sight and sound of the Tor-Folk village, but as they crested a colourful slope, she could no longer hold it in.

'Wow-wee, look at all the beautiful wings,' she said, for the hill was covered with a myriad of colourful butterflies. 'Do you have butterflies where you come from?'

'We do indeed,' said Sara.

'I *do* like butterflies,' continued Bluebell. 'They only come out in the good weather, you know. I wonder why they are called butterflies, do they like butter? Have you got butter where you come from? Do you like it, butter I mean? I wonder, are we near the lake? Granddad, are we near the lake? I think I see it, oh wait no, it's just the sky, what colour is the sky where you come from?'

'Hoe-woe, easy now my young flower,' said Turlock. 'If you talk any quicker, you'll run out of words before we get there!' Daniel and Sara laughed heartily, and even the steward managed a smile.

'Sorry,' said Bluebell, looking up at Turlock. But a moment later she gave a little leap of joy, giggled and said, 'It's all so exciting, my first time out of the village.' She fell silent for a few more paces before turning to Sara and asked, 'Is this your first time out of your village?'

'No Bluebell. No it's not, but *it is* my first time to Well-Keeper Island.'

'Gosh,' said Bluebell. 'Do tell me how you got here, please tell me all about it.'

'Of course I will,' promised Sara, 'I'll begin at the beginning.'

And so as they walked Sara recounted their adventure, starting in the garden back home right up to landing in the Tor-Folk settlement. It was the quietest Bluebell had been since they met her.

'That is the most amazing story I've ever heard,' said Bluebell. She looked at Daniel and Sara, eyes wide. 'Perhaps when I'm older I'll go to your world and have just such an adventure.'

'Perhaps you will, my dear petal, but for now stop troubling our travellers,' said Turlock.

'It's no trouble at all,' said Sara. 'Would you like to see Bobbin, my bonion friend?' she asked the little tor-girl.

'Could I please?'

Sara reached into her satchel and lifted out Bobbin on the palm of her hand. Stroking her head gently, Sara said softly, 'Hey there, brave climber, I've missed you. Come and meet Bluebell, you'll like her.'

Sara extended Bobbin out on her palm and the bonion gurgled softly. Bluebell put her nose right up to the tiny creature.

'Hello Bobbin, you are a cute little green, eh,' she hesitated not quite sure what Bobbin was, and then added, 'cutie.' Bobbin made more soft bubbly noises.

'She likes you, I'm sure of it,' said Sara, much to Bluebell's delight. 'But we'll put her back in the satchel for now. She likes it there when she's not in the ground.' Sara popped her friend back in the satchel and closed it.

Daniel unbuttoned one of his pockets and rummaged around. 'Take a look at this, all the way from Nightmare Reaches,' he said.

Bluebell gasped as Daniel unrolled a piece of fleece-cloth and held aloft the shard of the dragon's tooth. Bright beams filled with colour danced off the diamond-shaped shard in all directions.

'Wow-wee,' said Bluebell, 'It's beautiful.'

Turlock suddenly turned on them. 'Put that away lad, quickly now.' Shocked at the urgency in the elder's tone, Daniel shoved the tooth back into his pocket. Turlock inhaled sharply and spoke calmly this time. 'It's the lake, you see, we're very close. The shard of the dragon's tooth is charged with raw magic. We don't know what fury may awaken in the presence of such power. Thread with caution, my brave warriors for where the light shines, dark ever follows in the shadows.'

The remainder of the journey was sombre as Turlock's words frightened Bluebell. His warning weighed heavily on Daniel and Sara's mind too and although they said nothing, their faces showed it. The group soon rounded a shrubby hill, and they found themselves before the Great Lake. Turlock and the steward put down the boat.

'This is as far as we go,' said Turlock. 'Bold Daniel, courageous Sara, we give you every Tor-Folk blessing. May magic of the heart guide you.'

Sara and Daniel's faces were sad as they shared the same thought. *I'll miss them.*

The steward stepped forwards. 'It was a great honour to walk with you this while. It was a great honour to fight at your sides. It was truly a great honour to meet you both, Tor-Folk warriors, Tor-Folk heroes,' He said as he dropped to one knee and bowed his head.

Daniel by now was familiar with the ceremony of the Tor-Folk way, so he stepped forwards after their fashion. 'Rise, brave steward, the honour was ours to meet people so trustworthy and wise.'

Sara stepped forwards to stand beside her brother. 'So friendly and spirited, you can do now us an honour, master steward, by giving us your name, that we could remember forever one so loyal and noble.'

The steward looked stunned for a moment, for never before had he been spoken of so highly. He looked to Turlock, who just nodded kindly. The steward stood and his face broke into a broad smile. 'My name is Broud, son of the Hills and steward to the elders of my tribe.'

'That is a fine name indeed,' said Daniel, 'You honour us Broud. We shall never forget you and your people.'

The mood lightened with the honours exchanged, and next it was Bluebell's turn. 'You two are so wonderful. I'm going to miss you so much. I knew this time would come when I'd have to say goodbye. Here Sara, you should take this back.' She returned the carving that Sara had let her wear that morning. She turned to Daniel and from somewhere she produced a fruit tart. 'I took this from the stores this morning because I know you like them. Please say you'll eat it.'

'I will Bluebell, I'm sure I'll love every bite.'

'We'll miss you too,' said Sara. 'And I'll never forget how good a dancer you are.'

Daniel scooped up Bluebell and gave her a big hug. 'You were so brave in the jaws of that wolf. If we have half your courage along the way, I know that we'll be fine.'

Sara hugged her next. 'Goodbye Bluebell,' said Sara. Tears welled in her eyes.

'Goodbye Sara,' said Bluebell, through little sobs. Turlock allowed them a moment and then nodded to Broud. The steward took something metal from his robes.

'Till now you've fought with fire, stick and stone. Now you will have steel should further danger await you,' said Turlock. Broud handed two metal blades each to Daniel and Sara. They looked at them top to bottom.

'These are tor-folk swords,' said Turlock. 'What they lack in length they make up for with strength.' The swords were short with pronged guards above the handle. The blade was narrow and pointed. Daniel swished one of the blades. It quivered through the air. 'Careful now, they're sharp enough to cut through bone,' said Turlock. Daniel gulped and quickly copied Sara by hanging the swords to his fleece.

'Thank you, Turlock,' said Daniel. The elder waived away the comment and gestured towards the lake.

'You must row southwest in that direction to find the swamp.' Daniel and Sara looked to where he pointed. 'That's where the mowlers reside.' The elder raised a finger of caution. 'Be careful and pay close attention, for the wisdom of the mowlers isn't always clear.'

'We'll be careful,' said Sara.

Turlock picked Bluebell up onto his shoulders. 'Farewell adventurers, till we meet again.' With that he turned and left, followed by Broud. The three tor-folk disappeared around the shrubby hill and were gone.

Daniel and Sara shared the same thought. *We're alone again.*

Chapter 27
Blinded

The questers pushed the small boat through some rushes at the edge of the lake. As it entered the water Sara climbed carefully in and Daniel gave it another shove before hopping in beside her. With their fleeces placed in the middle of the boat the pair sat at either end. The boat wobbled in the water.

'Will it hold us?' Sara whispered.

'It should do. It *is* light but it's sturdy too.' Daniel patted the side of the boat, then handed Sara an oar. 'Can you row?'

Sara shook her head from side to side.

'Don't worry, it's easy,' Daniel kept his voice low. 'Move the same time as me. Bring the oar forwards and dip the head in the water, drag it backwards and lift it out when it reaches the rear of the boat.'

Sara prepared to make a practise stroke but stopped short. 'What if we disturb the bottom-claws?'

Daniel took the oar from her and held it up to his face. 'Try not to fret, Sis. These are what the tor-folk use.' He ran his finger along the shaft. 'Just feel that timber. It feels like the hag's staff. Worry lines creased Sara's brow. 'Tell you what, let me show you,' Daniel offered. He placed the head of the oar into the lake and pushed it back. The boat glided along the water soundlessly. 'See, it barely makes a ripple on the surface.'

'Okay then. We'll have to row gently though, just to be on the safe side,' said Sara.

Daniel gave her back to oar. 'Move the same time as me, that way the oars will do the work.'

Sara picked it up quickly, and after just three goes they had a rhythm with even strokes. The day was clear with the sun high in the sky. Daniel kept his eyes peeled on the lake despite the glare of the shining surface. Sara kept her eyes on Daniel's oar strokes to keep time. Every so often Daniel would look straight ahead then back at the retreating bank they'd left behind. The going was good and it wasn't long before he spotted something in the distance. He stopped rowing and pointed.

'I see it Sara. Look, it's the swamp!'

Sara, who had been concentrating hard on the rowing, gave a startled jump. 'Daniel, keep your voice down.' She placed her oar down and turned to look. Some distance ahead the lake was interrupted by a tuft of growth. They could just make out the green of bank-rushes through the shimmering glare bouncing of the lake.

'It's strange how it quivers,' said Sara, staring hard. 'It's as though it's floating on top of the lake.'

'The edges of swamps are eh,' Daniel paused to think, 'They're oozy, that's all.'

Sara turned to him and raised her eyebrows. 'Oozy? Are you sure you know what you're talking about?'

'Oozy, Daniel repeated. 'Let's just get closer. I can't see properly with the sunlight blinding me.' He picked up the pace.

Sara matched his strokes and allowed herself a smile. 'Oozy,' she said again.

As they got closer the shimmering effect of the lake lessened and the swamp became clearly visible.

Daniel pointed again. 'See I told you, it's just an island like any other.'

Sara turned. She saw a dense cluster of strange plants surrounded by a border of rushes. 'I don't recall you calling it an island like any other, you said it looks—'

Daniel slapped his oar into the lake hard. 'C'mon, almost there let's hurry it up. Less talking,' he said.

Sara finished the sentence in her head. *Oozy.*

Suddenly the boat wobbled and small waves lapped around it in all directions. Startled, Daniel and Sara stopped rowing and stared at each other, alarmed.

Daniel spoke through his teeth without moving his lips. 'I think there's something underneath us.'

Sara set her face tight. 'It's *your* fault. Could you've slapped the oar in any harder?'

'Shush,' rasped Daniel. *She's right though.* 'Let's look.'

They each held onto the sides of the boat and very slowly leaned to look over the edge. Daniel looked to one side and Sara to the other.

'I see it!' they hissed at the same time.

'What did you see?' asked Sara as they straightened up.

'A dark shadow, it was moving along the edge of the boat. What'd you see?'

'Dark shadow, moving along the edge of the boat.' Sara gulped. Very slowly the pair peered over each side again. The shadow was coiling in circles around the boat, visible by a grey outline against the blue of the water.

'Stay still,' whispered Daniel.

Sara pressed her lips tight and nodded. The shadow broke the surface beside the boat and a thick, green, scaly body arched out of the water before disappearing under again.

'Could *it* be the bottom-claws?' asked Daniel, still whispering.

Sara sat tensely in the boat. 'Must be, what'll we do?'

'It's not how I pictured them, somehow,' said Daniel uncertainly.

Sara glared at him. 'Who cares how you pictured them, what're we going to do?' She pointed downward. 'It's *right* underneath us.' Daniel leaned over the side but the shadow had gone.

He breathed a sigh of the relief. 'It's gone, whatever it was. Some kind of water serpent I suspect. Nothing to worry about, Sis.'

Sara suddenly tensed.

Daniel noticed her turning pale as the blood drained from her face. 'Hey, Sis, I said don't worry, it's gone.'

Sara's eyes were fixed to a point above Daniel's head and she raised a shaky finger upward. 'It's...it's behind you Daniel. It's a—'

Daniel turned quickly to look and leapt back with fright. He fell over the fleece-packs in the middle of the boat and landed at Sara's feet.

'Monster,' finished Sara, in a voice gone hoarse with fear.

The creature's neck snaked out of the water in an S curve. It was as thick as the boat. It's green and yellow head was even bigger. The questers gazed up in horror. The monster stared back through one yellow eye with a large black pupil in its centre.

Sara managed another hoarse whisper. 'What is it? What's it doing?'

Daniel answered through the side of his mouth. 'It's sizing us up. It's only got one eye. The eye on the left is missing.'

'I can see the scar,' hissed Sara, 'but who cares, *what's* it sizing us up for?'

The creature opened its jaws to reveal four long fangs. The fangs were coated in slime and a red pointed tongue darted between them. The siblings trembled.

Sara gripped her brother's shoulder. 'Daniel, I think it's going to attack!' The creature's pupil shrank to a small dot and trained directly on Daniel.

'Get down Sara!' Daniel roared. The creature's head jolted back slightly before lunging towards the boat.

Sara saw the enormous jaws open wide enough to snap Daniel in two and the fangs bearing down on him. She screamed.

'Daaaaniel.'

In the same instant from out of fleece-pack in front of him Daniel pulled a tor-folk sword and drove it deep into the creature's only eye.

The creature's massive head bolted backwards and its body shot up, high above the lake. It let a piercing cry that screeched across the lake. Daniel and Sara clung to the sides as the boat rocked from the waves. They never took their eyes from the beast. Blood poured down its head from where the sword still sat. With another surge the creature rose higher before crashing backwards beneath the surface of the lake. A pool of blood remained where the head went under.

'Did you kill it?' Sara shouted as the boat thrashed amidst the water rings that followed.

'Don't know,' Daniel roared back, *'don't care, just row like crazy!'*

Daniel grabbed an oar and took his own advice. Sara did likewise. They no longer cared about disturbing the lake's surface. Throwing caution to the wind the oars smashed and splashed with every turn as they rowed with all their strength away from the pool of blood.

The boat suddenly stopped with a soft thud. The questers looked up, breathless. They'd rowed right onto the swamp's edge. A shallow mud-bank held the boat and the pointed heads of some swamp rushes brushed over the sides.

Daniel gulped and wiped his brow. 'My heart is pounding, *that* was...' he searched for words. 'That was close.' He stayed sitting in the boat.

Sara hopped out. 'You're in shock. Now get out of it, *and* out of the boat,' she said. 'It *was* close, and thank goodness you thought of the sword or we'd been done for. Now help me pull the boat through these rushes and off the mud bank.' She was still breathing hard from the effort of rowing.

Daniel moved slowly. 'Weren't you scared Sara?'

Sara stopped pulling the nose of the boat and looked at him. 'Scared? No, I was terrified, absolutely terrified. *That's* why I'm trying to get us off the lake and onto dry land Daniel! Now give me a pull with this will you.' Daniel joined her at the front of the boat and helped her pull.

His nerves settled. 'Okay, Sis, okay. It was frightening, but now that I've gotten my breath back it wasn't *so* bad. I mean it could've been worse. That bottom-claw thing could've capsized us.'

'Get your priorities right. *It* could have eaten *us!*'

Daniel paused. *Hmm.* 'You're right, I guess. Still, nothing's eaten us yet, so let's get going.' He gave the boat another pull through the thick of rushes.

'Exactly, *nothing yet!*' Sara hurried after him.

Chapter 28
Muddled

The questers left their fleece-packs and supplies in the boat and tucked it in amongst the rushes out of view. With a final glance at their position they moved away from the lake's edge. All around them were different sorts of swamp vegetation. Some plants had huge leaves while others had thin shoots with small spikes dotted from base to tip. One bed of plants they came to had large yellow petals with orange centres.

'How pretty,' said Sara. 'Sunflowers growing in a swamp.' But just as they passed it a low hiss came from the flower head, followed by a pungent stench. 'Uuhh, I take it back.'

Daniel grabbed his nose and waved a hand across his face. 'Sara, please.'

She thumped him in the arm. 'It was the flower Daniel, and well you know it.'

'*Sure* it was,' Daniel mocked.

'Shut-up idiot, said Sara firmly. 'And watch where you're going. The ground is quite soft. Have you noticed how soggy it feels?'

Daniel, who had been leading, looked back and smiled. 'So what you're saying is it feels *oozy!*'

'Ha-ha, very funny, *not*. I'm saying be careful where you thread.'

'I know what you're saying, but what I'm hearing is… *I* was right!' Daniel turned back around to continue and let out a loud roar. *'Aaaahhhhhhhhhhhhhhhhhh.'* The ground before him was liquid mud and had swallowed him up to his waste. *'Sara, help. No don't, get back.'*

Sara had seen it all happen in an instant and hadn't taken a step. Her words came quickly. 'Daniel, gosh Daniel, one moment you were there, then you were gone. I looked down and you were stuck in the ground.' She ran towards him but when she got within reach her foot sank ankle-deep. She yanked her foot back out and the mud squelched. 'Daniel, it's so sticky, can you get out?' her tone urgent.

'I don't know, but it feels like I'm sinking. Stand back just in case.' Daniel tried to wade in the mud but it sucked him down further.

Sara bit her lip. *Oh no, if he panics, he could sink.*

Daniel looked at her. 'Don't worry Sara, I'll be out in a tic.' His face betrayed his feelings though. *I'm in a sinkhole on a floating swamp, not good. Not good at all!*

The sinkhole belched and squelched as it slowly swallowed Daniel. He struggled to keep calm. Suddenly in one quick motion he was sucked in up to his chest. Sara jumped with fright and clasped her hands to her mouth. Daniel started thrashing frantically.

Sara screamed. '*Stop Daniel, stop moving, you'll sink quicker!*'

He stopped thrashing. *Your right, Sis, I'll still sink though, just slower.* He tried to block out his thoughts but couldn't. *I won't escape this; I'm going to drown right here in the mud.* Tears came to his eyes and he gulped. 'Sara, I'm done for—' but she didn't let him finish.

'*Shut up, Daniel, just shut up and don't move and don't sink,*' she shouted. She turned while wiping tears of her own and ran back the way they'd come.

'*No Sara, wait, I—*' but she wasn't listening. The noise of the squelching mud was stuck in her ears and she ran. Her thoughts raced with her. *Get back to the boat, get the rope. Gotta save Dan. Run girl, run.*

Daniel watched her go. He knew her plan. *Hurry, Sis, please hurry.* He sank a little further.

Sara got to the boat and fumbled with the fleece-packs. Her hands shook with fear. *C'mon on rope, c'mon. I'll be too late.* She loosened it and sprinted back into the swamp as fast as her legs would take her. The air burned in her chest as her breath struggled to match her determination. Tears stung her eyes as she passed the pungent sunflowers. They hissed at her but she didn't care. *Almost there. Hang on Daniel.* She decided to shout.

'*Hang on Daniel, I'm close.*' She skidded to a stop to avoid running into the sinkhole herself. Daniel had sunken to his shoulders with just his arms held high out of the mud. He kept his head tilted upward. He was trying to gulp air.

'Sara, you're back... I'm going to drown Sara... It's hard to breathe.' His words came through gasps and tears ran down his cheeks.

'Don't talk, save your strength.' *Think Sara, what to do.* She looked around and spotted a low hanging branch close to the sinkhole. As quick as her hands could move, she tied a knot in the end of the rope and tossed it over the branch. *I hope this works. It's got to work.* Taking the end with the knot she threw it to Daniel. 'Catch the rope. Catch it.' The knotted end hit Daniel on the head before falling between his arms. He grabbed it.

'Got it,' he managed to rasp.

'Good, now hold on. *Don't* let go.' Sara took the other end of the rope and pulled with all her might. The sinkhole bubbled and gurgled but Daniel didn't move. With his arms outstretched, Daniel did his best to hold on.

Sara wiped away her tears and took a tighter grip of the rope. *Please don't drown Daniel.* 'Don't give up Dan, I can do it. I'll get you out.'

Daniel didn't answer aloud as he was weakening, but set his mind with Sara. *I'll hold on, Sis, I'll hold on for you.*

Sara turned away from the sinkhole and put the rope over her shoulder. She bent her knees and pulled. The rope was strained and the branch above the sinkhole bent. She squeezed her eyes shut and pulled harder. Through gritted teeth she grunted and growled as the rope dug into her hands. Daniel too, shut his eyes and held on tight as he felt the sinkhole bubble around him. Suddenly a powerful surge pulled on the rope causing Sara to fall flat on her face. Daniel came launching out the sinkhole. He landed with a splat just beyond it. Sara quickly rolled over to look back at him. Relief washed over her.

'Daniel, you're out, you're free.' She let go of the rope and ran to him. 'Are you okay?' she said as she wiped the mud from his face.

Daniel groaned. 'I'm, I'm okay. Just winded.' He was gulping the air. 'Thanks, Sis, thanks for—'

'Shush Daniel, shut-up. Get your breath. Thanks goodness, I thought you'd, it doesn't matter, you didn't.' Sara gave him a hug and continued wiping mud from him. Daniel lay there catching his breath and gathering his thoughts.

'Sara, I'm okay, really I am, thank you. Okay now that is. I was really scared, I thought—'

Sara heaved a wad of mud off his chest. 'Shush Dan, I know. It's okay, everyone gets scared sometimes, even you.'

'I guess.' *Hmm.* 'But I wasn't scared of the bottom-claw, *that* was just shock. Even you said.'

Sara smiled. 'I know bro, *that* was just shock. *This* was scary. Come to think of it I don't know where I got the strength to pull you out, it came from…' She trailed off and shrugged. 'It came from somewhere. Magic of the heart, maybe?'

With Sara kneeling beside him Daniel made to sit up. As he did so his face became alert and he grabbed Sara by the arm. 'Look Sara,' he pointed into the swamp. 'Perhaps your strength came from there.'

Sara turned and gasped. Before them stood a big creature covered head to toe in thick grey fur. It held the end of the rope in one of its massive hands.

Daniel slowly got on his knees beside Sara. 'Is it a yeti?'

Sara gave him a bewildered look. 'A yeti? No, what're you talking about. Clearly, it's a mowler. It's just like Lightning described them. The hunched shoulders, the muscly arms and legs, deep-set eyes, remember?'

'Oh. Oh yes, you're right.' Daniel rubbed his hands to his face. I must've swallowed some mud, I'm a bit muddled.

Sara rolled her eyes. 'Clearly, or mud between your ears more like.'

'But what's he, *it* doing?'

'*It* is standing there holding the rope, *watching* us.'

'I agree, on both points. It must've pulled on the rope.' Daniel looked at Sara. 'You still saved me though, you get the credit.'

'I agree on both points. Now wake up Daniel, it's time for you to lead again. I think you left your brains in the sinkhole.'

Daniel looked back towards the hole. 'Maybe but I definitely left a shoe there.' His legs were caked in mud and one of his trainers was missing. A deep, guttural rumble from the mowler got the questers attention. They stared unashamedly.

'I don't think he cares about your trainers,' said Sara, quietly.

'*It* Sara, it doesn't care about my trainers.' Just then the mowler lifted a giant hand. Its wide fury fingers bent and beckoned them to follow. It dropped the rope and turned to go.

'Should we follow?' said Sara.

'I guess we should,' said Daniel. 'He helped you rescue me. I won't get my trainer back but we can ask him about the nourishing stone. Isn't that why we're here?'

'We can ask *it*, Daniel. And yes, that's why we're here. I almost forgot what with you not watching where you were going and falling into sinkholes at every opportunity.' The pair got up and followed.

After a few paces the mowler suddenly spun around and raised its palm to signal a halt. Daniel and Sara trembled with fright. The mowler pointed back at the sinkhole. They cautiously turned to look back.

'What's he pointing at?' said Sara.

'Don't know,' said Daniel. The sinkhole erupted and a geyser of mud shot high into the air. The siblings watched on when suddenly something hit Daniel in the head with a thud. He stepped back in surprise. 'What on earth, hey wait, look, it's my trainer.'

Sara giggled. 'A mud ball more like. I guess he *does* care about your trainers after all.'

Once again, the mowler beckoned for them to follow and turned to go. Daniel was still scooping mud from his trainer.

'C'mon Dan,' said Sara, as she wound the rope around her shoulder. 'Walk beside me.' *This rope may come in useful again.*

Daniel sighed. 'I wasn't finished.' He put the trainer on anyway and groaned. *Yuck, it's all over my toes.*

They followed the mowler further into the swamp.

Chapter 29
The Dance

Deeper into the swamp the vegetation changed to clusters of rushes and small willow trees. The trees had lush green leaves and their bark was coated with a damp slime. Insects of all shapes and sizes buzzed constantly. Daniel and Sara fell silent as it was enough for them to swish the bugs from their faces and keep to the path that the mowler was leading them on.

Sara frowned. *I wish he'd slow down, wherever he's taking us.*

Daniel hardly noticed the discomfort of his mud-soaked clothes as he too struggled to keep up. *Why won't he walk in a straight line, doesn't he know we're not native swamp dwellers!*

The mowler was several paces in front of them and kept disappearing out of view only to reappear in a different place a moment later. The further they went the further ahead the mowler got and the pair started to get nervous.

Sara risked a whisper. 'It's creepy how he keeps doing that. I mean creepers.'

'I know,' Daniel whispered back and looked around. 'It's *even* creepier these shadows that keep moving over and back across our path.'

Sara glanced around and linked Daniel by the arm. 'I *hadn't* noticed, till you said it. *Now* I notice.'

'Stay close,' Daniel drew her arm tighter to him, 'for your own peace of mind that is.'

Suddenly they heard muffled laughter as though coming from many strange voices at once. They stopped, alert and listened. The voices changed to a loud cackling before changing again to a soft mumble. Daniel and Sara looked at each other but words failed them so they looked ahead. The mowler that had been their guide was standing beside a row of willow trees. It beckoned for them to follow then disappeared beneath the low-hanging branches. The pair slowly crept towards the row of trees, uncertain now as the strange mix of voices continued nearby. Still linked at the arm, they reached the trees at the same time and with a nod of determination to each other they parted the low-hanging branches and stepped through to the other side.

Daniel let out a deep sigh. 'More swamp. More rushes, more willow trees and *more* swampy ground.'

Sara relaxed. 'You sound disappointed. What did you expect?'

'I don't know. I was hoping for,' he paused to think. 'I was hoping for mowlers to be honest, creepy as they are. Some kind of settlement or something. There's nothing different here. Just more swamp. Where's he gone anyway?' The mowler had disappeared again.

Sara had her arm resting on her chin. 'Think about it Dan, the swamp *is* their settlement.' She let her arm fall and her eyes roamed the trees. 'And there is something different here, total silence. It's eerie.'

Daniel looked and listened. *She's right. No strange voices, no insects, no wind, not a sound.* They linked arms again.

The pair stood still, looking around nervously as the total silence filled the swamp. Daniel gulped. *Hmm, why not.*

'I have an idea,' he whispered.

'What is it?' Sara whispered back.

Daniel cupped his hands to his mouth and yelled. *'We've come to seek the wisdom of the mowlers.'*

Sara got a fright when he yelled, but stayed put. 'Shout? Brilliant idea brains! *Now* what?'

'Simple. We wait,' said Daniel. *But what we're waiting for I've no idea.*

They were not waiting long when out from the shadows appeared the mowlers. Some crouched down on all fours, others strode upright while others leapt from side to side. Daniel and Sara could only stare at the strange creatures that approached them. Although the mowlers were many different sizes, all were large compared to Daniel and Sara. All of them had muscular bodies and hunched backs, and despite their wide hands and feet none of them made a sound as they advanced through the swamp.

Sara tensed as they approached. *I'll count them to distract myself. One, two, three…* But suddenly the mowlers huddled together into a bunch. Their bulky shape and grey fur had the effect of blending them, making it impossible to tell how many of them there were. Unnerved she hissed at her brother. 'Daniel, they read my mind, I'm sure of it, I tried to count them but they stopped me by,' she paused, unsure and pointed at the bunch of mowlers. 'By doing that!'

The mowlers had formed a circle with their arms over one another's shoulders and their heads bent inwards. As they spun around in clockwise circles, every few moments one of the mowlers would raise its head and look at the questers with eyes that flickered with silent intelligence.

'What're they doing anyway?' Sara hissed again

Daniel gulped. *I haven't got a clue.* 'They're eh,' *Hmm,* 'They're spinning.' The mowlers suddenly changed to spinning in an anti-clockwise pattern.

'Oh wait, said Daniel, I think they're dancing, maybe.' He looked at Sara questioningly. 'Spinning and dancing?'

'You're an idiot,' decided Sara.

Daniel brightened up. 'I know, it worked last time I'll just ask them—' he was interrupted by a sudden combination of loud chattering, giggling, growling and groaning that came from the mowlers.

Daniel frowned. *What was I about to do? I can't, hmm, I can't remember.*

Sara too found it hard to concentrate. *I've forgotten what I was thinking. Oh, oh well.* The pair were mesmerised by the strange creatures as they watched them shuffle round and round.

After some time Daniel blinked and remembered his surroundings. He looked at Sara and gave her a tap on the arm. She jumped, startled.

'Sara, how long have they been doing it? The dance.'

'I don't, gosh I don't know. It feels like I've been in a trance, sort of.'

'Me too. Strange. Well we're out of it now, so let's just ask them a few questions and see how it goes. How weirder can it get?'

'We've thought that before!'

Daniel cleared his throat to speak when suddenly the mowlers stopped their dance, faced the questers and spoke as one:

Far from home you have come to find enchanted lands
Accept you did the keeper's quest, it now lies in your hands
Seek you now our wisdom to aid you with your task
Speak it now, for one question only can you ask
Daniel and Sara looked at each other with surprise.

Daniel found his voice first. 'I heard them, but I didn't see their mouths move,' he whispered.

'Same here,' said Sara, 'telepathy.'

'Tell a who? What're you talking about?'

'Mind speaking, it's called telepathy. *That's* what the mowlers just did.'

'Oh *that* telepathy. I knew that.'

'Sure.'

'Anyway, shut-up about the mind speaking, you might annoy them. They want us to question them, didn't you hear?' The mowlers remained still and continued to stare at the siblings. Once again Daniel cleared his throat, 'Ahem,' and looked directly at the mowlers. He spoke loudly. 'Well we need to know a few things: the first is why—'

Sara snapped in. 'Daniel wait, wait Daniel.'

He turned back to her, 'I'm beginning with the bottom-claws. We need to know for sure if that serpent back in the lake *was* one.'

'No Daniel, it seems like you're the one who didn't hear *them*. 'Only one question can you ask'; that's what they said in my head anyway. We must find out about the nourishing stone.'

'Oh yes,' replied Daniel, 'They did say that.' *Hmm, here it goes.* He turned to the mowlers again.

'As you say, we have travelled far and have undertaken a difficult charge, a charge to locate three treasures, two of which we've found and one of those we've broken; the third we cannot find. We've been counselled by Lightning, leader of the flying herd and Turlock, elder of the Tor-Folk, to seek your wisdom. You might have the answer we seek.'

A sudden shuffling of the mowlers position caused Daniel to lose his nerve.

'Em, eh,' he hesitated.

Sara took one step forwards, raised her chin slightly and called aloud. 'Can you tell us where we must go to *find* the nourishing stone?'

'I was trying to say that but the words wouldn't come out,' Daniel whispered to her.

'It's okay. They mind-spoke to me and told me to ask. I heard their strange voices say "speak girl".'

'Gosh, I didn't hear that.'

'You aught be worried if you did, you not being a girl and all.'

Their whispering was interrupted by the mowlers as they once again began their strange dancing and chattering. It went on for some time, so much so that Sara leaned over and whispered in Daniel's ear.

'Maybe they've forgotten us. Perhaps we should interrupt them?'

Daniel nodded. 'Off you go, as they selected you to ask the only question.'

Sara frowned at her brother and started forwards reluctantly. As she got closer to the dancing mowlers she stretched out her hand slowly but halted and quickly returned back to where Daniel waited.

'Maybe you should do it, brother. You *have* led most of the journey.'

Daniel would have turned down the offer but he heard the nervousness in Sara's voice. 'Your right of course, I *am* the leader. Stand aside.' He puffed out his chest and approached the chanting mowlers, but when his head was turned away from Sara he gulped. *If she wasn't my sister, I wouldn't be doing this.* Daniel mimicked Sara's advance with his hand outstretched too. He was almost upon them when he jumped with fright. For quite suddenly the mowlers stopped their strange ritual and another rhyming chant filled the questers' minds.

Return across the lake you must, great peril you may face
The stone you seek rests within in most unlikely place

Make haste you must to grasses tall, great loss you may endure
Kindness to those in need will show in deed your heart is pure

The words trailed off in the minds of the questers and the whole swamp was silent. For some moments there was not a sound, no leaves rustling, no insects buzzing, no breeze stirring, and the mowlers stood statue-still with their eyes closed.

'Do you suppose they're finished this time?' Daniel whispered.

'I couldn't really say,' said Sara. 'They appear to be.'

The pair stayed looking on for what seemed an impossibly long time. Eventually, when the mowlers still hadn't moved Daniel turned to Sara.

'I guess they *have* finished. They've fallen asleep, or something. We should get going. We can solve their riddles on the way to the boat.'

'Shouldn't we thank them first, or something?' said Sara.

Daniel frowned. *Hmm.* 'I guess, but if I wake them up and they mess with our minds it's your fault,' he raised his voice slightly. 'Emm-ehh, well, thanks very much for your wisdom. I'm sure it'll be a great help, once we work out what you meant of course. Anyway we better be off. Thanks again.' When the mowlers didn't budge, Daniel let out a sigh of relief. 'We'd best get moving Sara.'

Sara nodded agreement. 'I just didn't want to insult them by leaving without saying thanks,' she whispered.

The pair turned on their heels to go, when suddenly the growls and chattering began once again. Startled, the questers stood still, but for the turn of their heads back towards the sound. The mowlers were splitting up and withdrawing back into swamp and the cover of the willow trees. As they retreated their departing words echoed in Daniel and Sara's minds.

Take heed now searching travellers, from the sky beware
The gathering of the gulls is nigh and so you may despair
Spoke we have of good and bad away your journey on
No more we have foreseen and so we will be gone

And so they were gone, except one. The same mowler that had led them here, now stood right in front of them.

'What do we do?' Sara hissed.

The mowler charged towards them. The siblings frightened by the charge, back-stepped and fell over each other. They stood awkwardly and looked at each other, confused. The mowler was gone. Only willow trees and swamp plants could be seen where the creature had stood moments before.

'I guess we've overstayed our welcome,' said Daniel.

'Or they want us to hurry,' replied Sara. 'Either way, they want us to go.'

'Let's go then.'

Chapter 30
Riddles

The adventurers hurried back through the soggy swamp, careful to avoid the sinkhole from earlier. The afternoon heat dried the mud into Daniel's clothes and caked it in hard. Despite the discomfort he wanted to get back to the boat as quick as possible. When they reached it, they decided to stop for a short rest and think over the mowlers words.

'If we break it into parts, we've a better chance of understanding their message,' suggested Sara.

Daniel shrugged and replied confidently. 'I've been thinking about it. Sounds straightforward enough to me. We cross the lake, something about a great pearl, that's probably the shard of the dragon's tooth, *which* I have in my pocket. Go to the tall grass and there we'll find the nourishing stone, simple.' Sara glared at him. 'What?' he asked.

'You must *still* have mud between your ears. They said great *peril*, as in danger, not pearl. They were warning us, remember, "great loss you may endure", "beware the gathering of the gulls", "You may despair", etc., etc.'

Daniel wore a puzzled expression. 'Oh, let me think a moment.' *Hmm.* 'Ah yes, now I see, but they obviously speak in riddles and I know what they meant. The gulls, we've already encountered them when that fog surrounded us on the Rocky Rise. We've already endured great loss too; we lost the hag's staff, didn't we? And then some. *And* we've despaired many times since getting to the island. Eh?'

Sara looked annoyed. 'Why would they tell us to heed their warnings about events that already happened?'

'Why does anything happen Sara, tell me that? I've said my piece and I'm sticking to it.'

'I'm being serious Dan; we best be cautious.'

'Fine, Sis, you can be cautious for both of us. As for me, I'm fed up being cautious. I think we'll have the nourishing stone real soon. I can feel it, we're close.'

Sara threw up her arms in surrender. 'Fine Daniel, everything will be tickety-boo. Let's just sail back across the lake and find the stone then.'

'Row Sara, not sail.'

'Whatever.'

They pulled the boat out from where it was hidden in the rushes and dragged it to the lake's edge. Sara looked at Daniel, who had suddenly stopped and wore a thoughtful look.

'You'd forgotten about the bottom-claws, hadn't you?' said Sara.

Yes, yes, I did. 'I took care of one already, didn't I?' *If it was one.* 'I'll do it again if I have to. Remember how to row?'

Sara nodded.

'Good. Less talking, more rowing.'

Chapter 31
Troubled Waters

Pushing the boat out silently, the questers hopped into it as it moved away from the bank. The vessel glided smoothly along the surface. The oars moved with even strokes and barely made a ripple. The afternoon sun bounced off the lake. As Sara looked at the shimmering surface, she thought it was hard to imagine that anything dangerous lurked beneath, only the earlier crossing proved otherwise. A plopping sound and splash close to the boat caught her attention.

'Daniel, did you throw something in the lake?' she asked while quickly lifting her oar into the boat.

'It wasn't me,' Daniel answered quietly. 'Look there.' He pointed to rings that appeared in the water just off to the side of the boat. Daniel lifted his oar in too. Another splash broke the water surface right where the oar had been. The boat slowed to a stop as the pair looked on with worry at the growing water-rings where the splashes had taken place. They continued in hushed tones.

'It's not like earlier with the serpent,' said Daniel, unsurely. 'These are just small splashes.'

'Something *is* happening though; do you fancy waiting around to see?' asked Sara.

Daniel shook his head from side to side. 'Nuh-uh.'

'Let's get rowing then!'

'Okay, but keep it nice and steady. Let's not draw unnecessary attention to ourselves.'

They started rowing again as quickly as their rhythm would allow. The splashes were appearing everywhere now. Water-rings rippled behind, to the sides and in front of the boat. Suddenly the sky overhead seemed darker.

Sara looked up and cried out. '*Look*, it's a flock of birds Daniel. It's the gulls the mowlers warned us about!'

Daniel turned his eyes skyward to see a mass of wings and feathers blocking out the sun and descending towards the lake. The gulls were diving into the lake in ever increasing numbers and reappearing with small fish in their beaks. The lake surface was a flurry of splashes and feathers.

'If our rowing didn't disturb more of the bottom-claws, these birds certainly will,' said Daniel, anxiously. 'Let's row!'

Ignoring the need for rhythm they rowed as fast as they could, frantically thrashing the oars in and out with all their strength. The flocks of gulls were so thick that the sky grew even darker. No longer calm, the lake surface was sloshing around in turmoil, such was the number of diving gulls.

Trying not to panic, Sara kept her eyes on the sloshing water, but with every added splash she feared another snaking neck would appear. She looked up to see the far bank in the distance.

'Daniel,' she shouted. 'I'm frightened. We still have a long way to go.'

Daniel looked over his shoulder as he rowed. 'We can do it Sara, just row, row with all your—' his words were drowned out as the lake surged and its waters erupted, exploding high into the air in all directions.

The boat rocked violently. All around the lake huge claw-shaped digits were piercing the surface from below. Daniel and Sara grabbed the sides of the boat and gazed in horror at the bottom-claws. They looked like leafless trees, except that where branches and twigs should be there were razor-sharp claws. The bottom-claws rose and fell in a vicious frenzy, blindly snatching at the diving gulls. Suddenly one of the bottom-claws came crashing up beside the boat.

Daniel and Sara screamed. 'Aaaaaaahhhhhhhhhhh.'

The jagged talon sliced through the water and snatched a flying bird. The gull with a fish in its beak, flapped desperately, trying to escape the raging terrors. Some of the claws were small, just snapping for one gull at a time, others were enormous, big enough to scoop the whole boat.

Daniel and Sara swerved this way and that, throwing their bodies over and back as they desperately fought to control the swaying boat.

Daniel's brow furrowed with concentration. *If one of those big things grabs the boat, we've no chance.*

Sara was numb with fear. *Oh creepers, I preferred the serpent.*

The diving gulls dived and the bottom-claws snapped. Time rolled on.

'Will it ever end?' screeched Sara.

'Hang on, Sis. Once we don't capsize. We're not far from the bank,' Daniel roared.

The boat thrashed up and down uncontrollably as three massive claws broke the surface nearby. Huge waves came crashing over the side as the questers fought to balance the craft. Trying to avoid the waves, Sara leaped towards Daniel, but the water smashed into her chest and knocked her over the side.

'Daniel, Daniel!' screamed Sara before her head disappeared beneath the frothy surface.

Daniel stared at the spot where she went under, his eyes filled with terror. A moment later she reappeared in the thrashing water beside the boat, waving her arms and screaming.

'Daniel, help me.'

Unbeknownst to her, a bottom-claw had risen up behind her and opened its claws. Daniel didn't waste a second. With steely determination he picked up his oar and swung it with all the strength his arms could muster. The oar smashed into the bottom-claw, shattering two of its talons. The bottom-claw slashed wildly in the air before crashing into the lake behind Sara. Two more went for her, and both times Daniel hammered them with the oar. Sara somehow managed to stay afloat but as Daniel fended off the attacks she had drifted out of reach of the boat.

'Hang in there,' Daniel roared, willing his sister to fight the raging waters. She thrashed her arms and gulped for air as the waters smacked her in the face. Daniel rummaged in his fleece and loosened the rope. He tied one end around his waist and threw the other towards his sister.

'Grab on, Sara, I'll pull you in,' he screamed out to her.

Sara's hands found the end of the rope and she hung on for her life. Daniel wedged his feet against the floor of the boat and pulled her to the boat's edge. She threw her arms over the side. Daniel grabbed her and hoisted her in.

The pair sat breathlessly for a few moments while the lake ragged on around them. Sara, soaked through, looked at her brother and without speaking he knew that her teary eyes we're saying, 'Thank you.' Daniel pressed his lips and nodded. *Glad to have you back, Sis.* Still catching their breath, the pair clung to the boat. All direction lost now; the boat rocked violently in the troubled waters.

Daniel recovered first and gazed across the lake. He shouted above the noise of thrashing lake. *'With all this mayhem it's hard to see the edge. We'll have to try and wait it out. Fix your fleece-pack across your shoulders. I'll do the same. We don't want them falling overboard.'*

Daniel carefully wrestled his fleece on. Sara followed suit, her body was numb with fear and exhaustion. She moved mechanically and shivered as the weight of the fleece-pack pressed her wet clothes against her.

Daniel saw the defeated look on her face and tried to encourage her. 'If the gulls stop diving and if the sky clears and if the bottom-claws return to the bottom, we might just be okay.'

'That's a lot of ifs,' Sara called back through chattering teeth.

'I know, Sis, but we have to hope, and from now on we stay together.' With his face set he took the other end rope and tied it around Sara's waist.

'Thanks Daniel, at least if we go, we'll go together.'

194

Daniel nodded. He stood and bent low, intent on returning to the other end of the boat, but as he did so a diving gull smacked off his shoulder. He swung his arms wildly trying to gain his balance and dropped down again beside Sara.

'*That* was a close one,' he said, relieved.

A loud cracking sound suddenly rattled the boat, caused by an enormous bottom-claw that came ripping through the boat the opposite end to where they sat. The questers only had seconds to see half their boat shred into splinters before it split in two and the lake closed in around them.

Unable to talk, unable to think, tied together the pair spun in the water. They held their breaths when they went under and gasped for air when their heads re-surfaced. Struggling to keep upright they treaded as best they could. It was all they could do to stay afloat in the swirling and choppy waters of the lake.

Daniel spat out a mouthful of water. 'Keeping treading Sara, keep treading.'

Sara, almost too tired and frightened to speak saw Daniel struggling himself. 'You too,' she managed to call back. All around them the lake raged.

Finally the gulls began to depart from the lake. In vast numbers the birds flew north and the sky above brightened somewhat. The bank was clearly visible now, although the questers were still a long distance from it. All around them menacing claws were gnashing blindly. Still, the pair made progress, slowly treading their way to dry land.

Daniel felt a pull on the rope and turned to see Sara struggling to keep up. '*Wait Sara,*' he yelled, '*I'm coming back to help.*'

She was exhausted and her arms and legs were gone numb in the cold water. 'Okay,' she replied weakly.

Daniel swam to her and quickly wrestled the fleece-pack off her shoulders.

'Oh thank goodness,' said Sara, once the extra weight was removed. 'That's much better.'

Treading beside her, Daniel nodded. 'Okay, good. Now let's make for the shore.' They took off again.

Without the weight of the fleece-pack the swimming became easier for Sara and she passed ahead of Daniel. Time and time again they barely avoided the snatching talons of the bottom-claws that sliced through the lake all around them. They inched on determinedly.

At last the bank was within reaching distance. *Not far to go, a few more strokes,* thought Daniel, but tiredness overwhelmed him and he slowed.

Sara swam on closer to the lake's edge when she felt the strain on the rope. She looked back to see Daniel slowed to a stop and barely able to stay afloat. She shouted back to him. *'Daniel, take off the fleece, it's the only way you'll make it!'*

Daniel gasped for breath. *'No… We'll need, we'll need it later. We're almost there,'* and calling on the last of strength he surged forwards through the water.

Most of the gulls had departed and the lake was a torrent of rage as the bottom-claws thrashed, sliced and grabbed at the last few stragglers. Even in the midst of the turmoil, the questers could hear the lake's edge lapping and slapping against the bank. They knew they were close.

'We're going to make it,' Sara shouted but Daniel didn't answer. She looked back and her eyes filled with horror. A giant bottom-claw had sliced through the surface just missing Daniel, but one of its talons had pierced through the fleece on his back. The bottom-claw shot upward. Daniel was skewered above the lake.

He just had time to roar, *'Swim, Sara, swim!'* before the bottom claw dropped down and crashed back into the lake.

Sara, still tied to him, saw Daniel disappear below the surface. With a sudden jerk she was dragged under too. Under the water she saw everything in slow motion. She saw the bottom-claw retreating towards the bottom. She saw Daniel sinking, trapped by the talon that snagged his fleece. She saw the talons folding in, the claw slowly closing. She saw another bottom-claw rising directly below her, digits extended, and knew that she herself was the target. She saw the air bubbles escape her brother's nose and float past. Her own lost air followed. She saw Daniel's arms outstretched to her and his mouth open in one final, silent scream. She saw the approaching talons of the other bottom-claw advance in her direction. She saw Daniel tumble as the talons of his captor closed like a fist. She saw something bright fall out of Daniel's pocket and glow momentarily. She saw the lake erupt in an explosion of white-light.

Daniel tried to scream to warn Sara about the bottom-claw but his throat filled with lake-water and the talons closed around him. He felt the shard of the dragon's tooth come away from his pocket and saw it glow to life. In that instant he saw countless more claws race towards him, drawn to the ancient magic. The claws reached out to contain the power. The moment the nearest talon touched the shard, the magic contained within it was released. Pure white-light pierced through the entire lake and the sky above lit up. He saw the shard send forth a surge of elemental energy that consumed the bottom-claws in a flash-wave. The whole lake glowed in the shimmering essence of the shard's brilliance.

The waters erupted in spectacular waves with the magical white-light coursing through every drop. The questers came blasting forth to the surface on the crest of one such wave and landed with a splash at the lake's muddy edge.

Complete silence fell. The lake was still, its waters crystal-clear. The bottom-claws were destroyed and the magic contained within the shard of the dragon's tooth returned to nature from whence it came.

Chapter 32
Screeching

Daniel and Sara coughed and spluttered on the muddy bank where they'd been washed up. Together they crawled through the mud and lay on the dry grass. The lake sat silent and still, but this was of no comfort to them, as they were soaked through, the evening sun doing little to dry their clothes.

They rested unmoving for a while till eventually Daniel sat up. 'I must've left my pocket unbuttoned when I showed Bluebell the shard of the dragon's tooth,' he said in sad tones.

Sara stayed lying in the grass and answered quietly. 'At least it saved us from the bottom-claws. Magic of the heart, I guess.'

Dejected, Daniel hung his head. 'Yeah, but now *it's* at the bottom of the lake and the hag's staff is shattered to pieces back on the mountain. It was all for nothing.'

Sara still ached all over but she sat up too. '*No* Daniel, don't you dare say it was all for nothing. How many times have we almost lost our lives?' her voice raised, 'That's the problem with you. You always talk first and think later.'

'Hey, no need to shout. Just tell me what could we've done that would've made any difference?'

Sara's anger flared and her voice rose to a screech. 'Let me see, for a start you could've have listened to the mowlers message and been more careful. Then you could've taken off your fleece and the bottom-claw wouldn't have snagged you. And I'll shout if I want to!' She burst out crying.

Daniel's temper rose and he shouted back. 'Well maybe if you hadn't of fallen over board we'd have made it all the way in the boat. Maybe if I didn't have to tie us together for your safety I could've stayed in the lake and you could've swum ashore carefree!'

'That doesn't even make sense.'

'You don't even make sense.'

Sara's voice changed to pleading. 'Daniel, I'm exhausted, soaking wet and can't take any more. Don't you tell me it was all for nothing!'

Fear and fatigue had overcome them. They sat silent for a few moments.

Daniel frowned and looked at the ground. *I shouldn't be fighting with her.* His voice broke in a whisper. 'I'm all those things too Sara.'

Sara sobbed. 'I'm sick of being frightened, I'm sick of the dangers and I'm sick of this quest. The nourishing stone can stay where it is, we'd only lose *it* too. I just want to go home.' A fresh flood of tears spilled down her cheeks and she buried her face in her hands.

Daniel's felt his eyes welling with water. He put his arm around Sara and drew her close so that she rested her head on his shoulder. He looked out to the lake and spoke quietly. 'Me too, Sis. Me too. Let's just get back to the well somehow, and ask Tobias to send us home.'

'Yes, let's. I'm sorry Daniel, I didn't mean to blame you,' said Sara, still sobbing.

'I'm sorry too, for the things I said and for being an idiot.'

'You're not an idiot, really. Well, maybe sometimes, other times you just pretend to be.'

Daniel dried his eyes and smiled. 'Yeah, maybe sometimes, but most of the time you're just cleverer than me.' He stood and stretched out a hand to help Sara up. 'C'mon, let's see if we've any supplies left. Something from the boat might've washed up with us. We'll need anything we can find if we're to make it to the well by tomorrow.'

'Why tomorrow?' asked Sara, taking his hand.

'Tonight will be our fourth night on the island. Tobias said return to the well in five days. *With* or without the treasures I don't want to be late. He's our only way home.'

Sara's brow furrowed with concern. 'Gosh, I'd forgotten about the timeline.'

'No sense in worrying now. Hopefully the dangers are all behind us.'

'Somehow I doubt that.'

'You said you'd never doubt again. Back on the mountain, you said it.'

'I take it back. What was said on the mountain stays on the mountain.'

'Agreed, and *it's* behind us so let's look forwards, after we look around that is.'

Together they walked back to the lake's edge to search the area.

'See anything?' said Sara.

'Nothing,' said Daniel, gloomily. 'Water, mud and grass. Oh, and here's a bit more mud right here.'

Sara shared his gloom. 'We've lost everything. No fleece-packs, no ropes, no food.'

Daniel looked at her and his eyes widened. 'Hey, you've still got your satchel.'

Sara looked down at it and back to Daniel with surprise. 'You too. I never noticed mine around my neck.'

'Me neither, it was stuck to me with the wetness!' said Daniel as he eagerly untied the leather clasp. He fumbled his hand into it and Sara did likewise. 'Look,' he cried, taking out the jar of tor-folk ointment. 'We still have this. Pity we can't eat it.' He put it back and took out a small piece of wood. 'And this, it's the piece of the hag's staff I kept. Pretty worthless to us now though—'

'Bobbin!' Sara cried out, interrupting Daniel. 'Oh Bobbin, shame on me, I'd forgotten all about you. Thank goodness you're okay.' The little bonion climbed out of the satchel and onto Sara's hand.

'However did she survive the lake?' said Daniel.

'Oh, it doesn't matter how,' said Sara, 'Once she's okay. My sweet little friend.' Sara nuzzled the small creature against her cheek. Bobbin responded with gentle bubbling noises.

The ground suddenly began to rumble and Bobbin quickly darted back into the satchel. The questers looked up just in time to see two giant boars burst through the long grass and bear down on them. Their faces froze with fear as the boar advanced. The thudding hooves left big holes in the mud but did little to slow down the giant creatures. It seemed like the boars were not going to stop. Daniel and Sara back-stepped several paces till their feet were standing in the shallows of the lake.

Finally the boars stopped with their massive snouts just inches away from Daniel and Sara's faces. The questers inhaled sharply and drew their heads back further, trying somehow to put more distance between them and the giant creatures. The bigger of the two boars faced Daniel and he closed the inches between them by leaning forwards.

'Friend or foe?' the boar rumbled in a deep, throaty voice.

'Friend, we hope,' said Daniel, nervously.

'Not all humans are friend to the Boar,' said the beast.

Sara turned her head sideways, swallowed for courage and risked an answer. 'Not all those we've met on our journey have been friends to us, but those who have talked with us *have* been. We hope you are too.'

The boar was silent for a moment, as though he was considering Sara's words. Sara took a breath and a closer look at the giant boars before her. Their tough-looking skin was different shades of dark-brown, the bigger boar slightly darker than the other. Long bristles spiked up from their backs. Their legs were thick and stumpy and their haunches bulging and muscular. Sara gulped. *Creepers, I've seen boars before but these are the size of elephants, tusks and all!* She kept her thoughts to herself.

The bigger boar snorted and looked to his right. The two giant tusks that pointed up from the boar's lower jaw swung by Daniel's face as the massive head of the boar turned. A blob of spit from the big snout brushed Daniel's face. He bit his lip but didn't dare move. *Those tusks are as long as me. Who'd be a foe to this thing!*

The giant boar looked behind him at the mud where he had trodden. Daniel and Sara followed his gaze. Out of the mud glints of light sparkled in the evening sun.

'Tor-Folk steel. Where did you get it?' said the giant boar. Two of the tor-folk sword handles were visible in the hoof-holes behind the boars.

Daniel's thoughts raced. *His hooves must have uncovered the swords from the mud. Honesty is the best option here, I think.* 'Turlock, chief elder of the Tor-Folk gave them to us.'

The boar shifted his weight and Daniel and Sara trembled.

Sara gestured towards the blades in the mud. 'He, Turlock felt we might need them on our journey.'

The two boars looked at each other and retreated back a few steps.

The bigger one spoke again, 'Tor-Folk are friend to the Boar. The elder was right to share his steel if you planned to journey in the Fens.'

Relaxing slightly Daniel and Sara stepped out of the shallows.

'The Fens, where are the Fens?' Sara asked.

The big boar snorted. 'Here, these tall grasses are known as the Fens. Have you seen any mantes?'

Sara shook her head. 'No we've not seen any. Well at least I don't think so. I don't know what they look like actually.' She leaned into Daniel and whispered. 'Does he mean praying mantes, the little-small things that eat other insects?' She made a small gesture with her fingers.

The giant boar turned to her with surprising speed and snorted. 'I mean spraying mantes. And there is nothing small about them I assure you, not by human standards. A full-grown mantis stands at twice your height, young human, and could kill you with one spray.'

Sara trembled. 'Creepers, what do they spray?'

'It's a poisonous slime,' said Daniel. Sara looked at him, questionably. 'Zac told me about them, back in the cave,' Daniel added. A distant look crossed his face. 'It seems so long ago.'

Sara, exasperated, waved her hands. 'Daniel, a bit of focus here. The spraying mantes, tell me about them!'

Daniel shook his head to clear it. 'Oh yes, of course. Well he didn't tell me much. All he said was they look a bit like crickets and—'

The giant boar interrupted him. 'Enough, you'll know all about the mantes should we encounter them, which we plan to. We've stayed overlong here already. The mantes have taken one of our own, we need to find her by nightfall. You will come with us, there's power in numbers.'

Forgetting herself Sara burst out. 'How did they take one of *you?*'

'You ask as lot of questions, young human.'

'You can call me Sara, if you like that is. And he's Daniel.'

The giant boar snorted. 'Sara, Daniel, yes. In human speech my name is Crunch and my quiet friend here is Stomp.'

Stomp snorted. 'Greetings, friends of the Tor-Folk,' said Stomp.

Crunch continued. 'Our sounder was watering by the lake's edge. We always water in large numbers, taking turns to have a drink while others stand guard. We keep the piglets close, always wary of mantes. Suddenly the lake erupted when the bottom-claws rose to feed on the gulls. The eruption startled our group and many scattered into the Fens. We quickly re-grouped only to discover one of our young was missing, a little piglet named Tess. For a moment we thought it was the bottom-claws but then we caught the scent of spraying mantes.'

'Oh no,' said Sara. 'That's awful. What will happen her? What will you do?'

Crunch trod his hoof into the muck. 'The boar army have split up into groups to search. If we find her by nightfall, she has a chance. Our hides can resist the poison spray for a while, but *only* for a while.'

Daniel and Sara marked the urgency in Crunch's tone and exchanged a knowing look.

'Can we help? We want to help,' said Daniel.

Crunch nodded as he snorted. 'As I've said, there's power in numbers. Bring your tor-folk steel, you'll need it. And no more screeching, we aim to find *them* before they find us.'

Daniel and Sara looked at each other, embarrassed. Without another word they pulled the tor-folk swords from the mud and followed the giant boars into the tall grass.

Chapter 33
The Fens

The grass was summer-green and stood as tall as the giant boars. As evening fell, a constant buzz of insects sounded from all around. Crunch led the group with the questers in the middle and Stomp brought up the rear. The two boars kept their snouts high, sniffing the air in all directions. After trekking silently for a short while, Crunch spoke.

'The deeper we go, the thicker the grasses get.' Crunch flattened the grass as he trod, but it was still an effort for the questers to pace through the flattened clumps.

Trudging over a clump of grass, Daniel whispered to Sara. 'Well I guess we're going deeper; the grass is getting thicker.'

Sara nodded in agreement but she had other things on her mind. 'Tell me now what you know about the spraying mantes,' she whispered back.

'Like I said earlier, big crickets, but they kill and eat most things.'

'Most things, like what?'

'Like anything that moves.'

Sara's brow creased with worry. *And we're entering their lair. So much for getting back to the well and home.*

'Their spray paralyses their victims, leaving them helpless,' said Stomp from behind. The pair looked back, surprised at being overheard.

'Creepers,' said Sara.

'Yikes,' Daniel said at the same time.

Crunch stopped abruptly and turned back to face them. 'Spraying mantes don't like their food fresh. If it's big, they'll leave it where it is and return later to feed when the catch is long dead. If it's small like a piglet, they'll carry it off to their nests. The boars normally avoid the nests, but *not* today. This Zac you speak of is right. Mantes will eat anything. They even eat each other if there are no other creatures to eat.'

'So what you're saying is they *might* eat us?' said Sara.

'No,' said Crunch with a snort. 'I'm saying they *will* eat you, given half a chance.'

Daniel and Sara shuddered.

Crunch raised his snout high and sniffed through the grass. 'Stay alert. I smell mantes, close.'

Daniel and Sara gulped and tightened their grips on the tor-folk swords. A moment later, they walked into a circular clearing. The grass was completely gone down to the bare, damp earth, except for round bunches of grass woven into nests and dotted around the clearing.

'A nesting lair, but empty,' said Crunch.

The nests closest to the group suddenly buzzed to life, and before Daniel and Sara knew what was happening, they were surrounded by small, brown creatures.

Sara jumped in behind Crunch. 'I thought you said the nests were empty,' she said nervously.

'Empty of grown mantes. *These* are the young mantes,' said Crunch.

'What did I tell you, just like big crickets! Mind you, they're not as big as I pictured, they're not even up to my knee,' said Daniel, feeling a little relived.

'These are only new-borns,' said Stomp, 'Mantis nymphs.'

The nymphs jumped up and down and back and forth without getting too close to the group. Daniel regarded the small creatures. *Quite like crickets,* he thought. *Although I'm not sure if crickets have so many eyes.* Their small triangular heads swung around in arcs with their tiny eyes constantly moving.

Sara peaked around Crunch for a closer look. *Their wings look like leaves,* she thought. *And with all those legs, it's hard to tell one from the other, they just blend into a swarm.*

Crunch sniffed the air again. 'The full-grown are not far.' The nymphs hopped closer.

Daniel held his sword out towards them. 'What about these small ones?' he asked as he swished the sword. The nearest nymphs scattered.

'Their fangs grow later,' said Crunch. 'Until then, their slime is harmless. They stay close to the nests while the adults hunt.'

'Fangs?' said Sara.

'Fangs,' said Crunch. 'I believe humans call them razor-sharp. This is how they devour their catch, by tearing it to pieces.'

Sara shuddered again. *They'd have to have fangs, wouldn't they?*

The nymphs began jumping and spitting small blobs of black slime. Daniel and Sara back-stepped further behind Crunch to avoid the oozing blobs. Stomp snorted and trod past them to stand beside Crunch. Sara could not hold in a scream when a blob splattered on her knee. The moment she screamed, the nymphs stopped their attack, and as one, they buzzed back to their nests. An eerie silence fell on the clearing.

'I guess I scared them off, eh?' said Sara, uncertainly.

'It wasn't you,' said Crunch. The two giant boars lowered their heads and charged across the nesting lair. The ground shook as the boars galloped towards a spot in the tall grass the far side of the clearing. Daniel and Sara watched, bewildered, as the giant boars charged with tusks lowered into the Fens and out of sight. They stared at the spot where the boars had disappeared.

'Em, wait for us, maybe?' said Sara, pointlessly. She turned to Daniel. 'What'll we do now?' Daniel didn't answer but slowly looked around the clearing. Sara did likewise. It was a bright evening and an early moon had just come out. The questers caught some movement at the edges of the nesting grounds where the grass was long. A chill ran through them as they watched the grasses sway and shadows dance in the early moonlight. They shared an urgent look of trepidation.

'Let's get after them,' said Daniel. They ran. They reached the far side of the clearing and slowed their sprint to a jog.

'You saw it, didn't you, the movement in the grass?' said Sara, anxiously.

'The twilight can play tricks on the eyes,' said Daniel, unconvincingly.

'Yeah right, *that's* why you ran?'

'Okay, I saw it. Let's just hope it plays tricks on the mantes' eyes too; after all, they have more eyes than we have.'

Sara looked at him desperately. 'That hope gives me *no* comfort, the Fens is their home. We're sitting ducks.'

Daniel stopped jogging. 'No, Sara, nothing like ducks. We've got tor-folk steel, that meant something to the boars, didn't it?' He swung his sword for effect and it whistled through the air. 'Have a go.' Sara swung hers half-heartedly. 'Harder,' said Daniel, 'You can do it.' She tried again and the blade sang on the evening breeze. 'You've got it.'

'Okay, if you say so,' said Sara. 'But stay close. And we stay on this path made by the boar, agreed?'

'Agreed.'

Daniel and Sara held their swords in battle readiness and kept their eyes peeled on the grass either side of the path. The grass was slightly thinner than before so they were able to see several paces into the growth. When they rounded a bend, the path forked off in two directions. Daniel looked from one path to the other.

'So much for sticking to the path. Which path is *the* path?' he said.

Sara glanced over her shoulder and screamed, '*Aaahhhhhhhhhhhhhhh.*'

Daniel spun and found himself staring into the five eyes of a yellow spraying mantis. A bubble of black slime gathered at the mouth of the creature. Daniel was still with fear. His shock was broken when a blade whizzed by his face. The head of the mantis flew through the air and the creature's body collapsed at his feet. Daniel turned again slowly. Sara was standing behind him, wide-eyed, breathing hard and holding her blooded sword in both hands.

Daniel nodded in admiration. 'Yes. You've got it.'

Sara nodded back, her lips tight. 'Got it.' *I can't believe I just did that.*

They studied the head of the fallen creature. On the triangular head sat five eyes, two big outer eyes and three smaller ones in between. A long neck had joined the body to the head before Sara cut it off.

Daniel pulled his gaze away from the kill and looked down one path, then the other. He pointed with his sword. 'Let's go left.' They hurried on but didn't run fearing that they'd run into a trap. Movement in the grass next to Sara caught Daniel's eye. '*Ambush,*' he roared. Four mantis legs shot out of the grass and knocked Sara over.

Sara screamed, '*Aaaahhhh.*' The legs had short spikes on them that pinned her to the ground.

This time Daniel was ready. He swung the tor-folk sword with all his might and cut the front legs off from the joint. The yellow bodies of the two attacking mantes fell forwards out from the long grass and collapsed beside Sara. With a quick hack, Daniel removed their heads. He stopped to wipe his brow and held his hand out to help Sara up.

Sara didn't take his hand; she pointed and screamed again. *Behind you, Daniel.'*

Daniel spun, swinging his sword at waste height and severed another spraying mantis in two. The dead creature's yellow wings were caught on his sword. He used his feet to pull them off.

Sara had recovered and stood beside him with her sword ready. 'Three together. There could be more nearby.'

'Let's not wait to find out,' said Daniel. Together they ran as fast as their legs could carry them.

With no sense of direction, they simply followed the path flattened by the boar, but the farther they ran, the thicker the flattened grass underfoot became, slowing them down. All the while the tall grasses on either side of the path rippled and swayed with deadly movement. Another yellow mantis reared up just in front of them. The questers swung their blades and killed it in one blow without even stopping their run. Another appeared and again they cut it down with tor-folk steel. Twice more with alarming closeness, the yellow mantes appeared only to fall to the slicing blades. Tired and breathless, the siblings paused for a moment.

Daniel panted. 'Their numbers are growing. We'll have to keep going.'

Sara rested her palms on her knees to catch her breath and shook her head from side to side. 'No, I think we're going the wrong way. The mantes keep appearing in front or from the side, never behind. What if we are running towards them? Let's go back and take the other path. We might find the boars.'

Daniel nodded. A flash of colour caught his eye. He tensed up and grabbed Sara's arm. He gestured upward with his head and spoke through gritted teeth. 'You're right, look ahead.'

The pathway was blocked by dozens of spraying mantes, their yellow bodies clearly visible in the full light of the moon. Some stood tall, propped up on their hind legs with their front two legs held in the praying position. Others moved their forelegs over fangs that oozed and glistened in the moonlight. Others still knelt on the ground with two of their hind legs bent upward, ready to pounce.

There's too many, thought Daniel. *'Run,'* he cried, turning where he stood. They raced back the way they'd come.

Leaping over the still body of a dead mantis from an earlier encounter, Sara risked a glance back. *'They're gaining on us,'* she screamed.

A moment later, they reached the fork in the path, and without looking back, they turned down the other track. The grass was well flattened on this path and they somehow found the strength to sprint. For what seemed like an age, they ran, barely aware that it was night time, barely aware of their hunger and thirst and barely aware of their own exhaustion. Their only thought was to put as much distance as possible between them and the oozing fangs of the spraying mantes. Side by side, they raced into a wide-open space.

Chapter 34
Green Lights

The questers looked around wildly, breathing hard. It was another nesting lair, circular in shape.

'Seems empty, just like the last one,' said Sara through gasps, 'except bigger maybe.'

Daniel pointed with his sword. 'Let's make for the far side and see if we can pick up the track trampled by the boar.'

They took off again, running just slow enough to avoid the grass-woven nests clustered around the clearing. No nymphs greeted them this time but that was of little relief to the pair, knowing what pursued them. They ran again side by side, but as they reached the centre of the clearing, they split up to run around a nest blocking their way. The moonlight was directly overhead, lighting up the clearing.

Sara leapt over a mound on the ground and skidded to a stop. 'Daniel, come back her quick.'

Daniel hurried back from the far side of the nest. 'What is it?'

Sara was standing over the mound she'd just leapt. 'It's a piglet. It must be Tess.'

The small boar lay still but for the slow rise and fall of her side.

'She's still breathing,' said Daniel. Unsure what to do next, they stood over the injured boar. The piglet was brown all over, with short hair, small ears and big black eyes. Her hide was stained with black streaks. Daniel studied the streaks from her head to her tail. 'Look! It's black slime, see here,' he pointed to a patch close to where the piglet lay. 'It's a pool of black slime, it *must* be from the mantes. She managed to slither out of it. Just about that is.'

Sara looked at the cute, curled eyelashes and the glassy eyes of the little boar and fought back her own tears. She put her hands over her mouth. 'Oh, Daniel, it's only a baby. We've got to help her, somehow.' They desperately looked around the nesting lair while trying to decide their next move.

Daniel dropped to his knees and took off his hooded top. 'I'll have to carry her.' Standing in his vest, he looked at Sara. 'You know what that means?'

Sara gritted her teeth and nodded. 'Yes, I fight the mantes if they come.' She picked up Daniel's sword. Her face was an angry scowl. 'Let them come. How could they hurt this poor defenceless baby? We've fought gizords, rats, bats *and* wolves. We've even survived trees that turned into murderous monsters!' her voice raised to a screech. *'If these insects think I'm scared of a few overgrown crickets, then let them come!'*

'That's the spirit, Sara, but still, let's hope they don't, eh?' *I can't protect her if I'm carrying the piglet.*

Sara didn't answer. She knew what he was thinking. *You don't need to worry about me this time, Dan, I'm mad!* She trained her eyes on the borders of the nesting lair and held a sword ready in each hand.

Daniel wrapped the small boar in his hoody, leaving her head free, and very carefully picked her up. 'Okay, let's try and find the boar's path,' he said. As he stood up, they heard the thumping sound of heavy hooves approaching. They looked up to see Crunch and Stomp pounding across the nesting lair at full speed.

'You found Tess,' grunted Crunch loudly, still several paces away. 'Does she live?'

'She's alive, but her breathing is shallow,' Daniel called back. The boars skidded to a stop, raised their snouts in the air and trumpeted a thunderous snort that rang out across the Fens. After a moment, the boars stopped and trotted quickly over to Daniel.

'Put her down,' said Crunch. 'Let us see her.' Daniel lowered Tess to the ground, and using his snout, Crunch rolled her out of the hoody. Crunch and Stomp immediately started licking the black streaks of slime off her hide. The questers watched on anxiously. When the boars were done, they spat the slime off their tongues, licked the dusty earth and spat again. There was no change to Tess; she lay quiet and still. 'She's cold, wrap her up again now,' said Crunch.

Daniel marked the urgency in his tone and quickly rolled the hoody back around Tess. 'What will happen to her?' he asked.

'She has some time, but not a lot,' said Stomp. 'She needs heat and something to drink soon, or she *will* die. It's the poison, it zaps the moisture from her body and the cold paralyses her.'

Tears came to Sara's eyes but she spoke through gritted teeth. 'Blast those yellow mantes; we should've stayed and killed the lot.'

Daniel looked at the boars to explain. 'When you left us, we tried to follow your path. We were attacked by some yellow mantes. We killed eight of them but a swarm came and we ran; that's how we got here.'

'Were they all yellow?' asked Stomp.

'Yes, as far as we could see.'

'The yellow mantes are trackers, still only adolescents, said Crunch. 'You did well to slay eight and were right to run. The adults follow after. You were being hunted. We left you because we saw mantes and caught Tess's scent from them. We gave chase and met them nearby. They're dead now. Your screeching led us here.'

Sara reddened. 'Sorry about that, again.'

Alert, the two giant boars stiffened.

'Sorry for what?' said Crunch. 'You led us to Tess, and just in time.'

'In time to take her to safety?' asked Daniel.

'No,' said Stomp urgently. 'It's too late for that, the full-grown mantes are upon us. Get ready, they approach now in numbers.'

Sara set her face hard and gripped the tor-folk swords. *Let them come.*

Daniel looked around the nesting lair frantically. 'I can't see them? Where are they?'

'Watch for their eyes,' said Crunch in deep, hushed tone. 'They glow in the moonlight.'

The eyes appeared. Luminous-green dots appeared all around the edges of the nesting lair.

Sara gasped. 'Their eyes, they light up!'

Daniel gulped. 'And so many!'

'All the more to kill,' said Sara. The eyes were appearing from everywhere now, at ground level, from above the tall grasses and within, in numbers impossible to count.

'Get ready,' repeated Stomp.

The tall grasses swayed and the mantes came into view. Daniel and Sara took a sharp intake of breath at the sight before them. The mantis's eyes stared straight ahead while their fangs oozed and glistened in the moonlight. The questers circled in a slow turn. The creatures were appearing around the entire perimeter of the nesting grounds, some of the adolescent mantes yellow in colour, but most of the others were twice their size and green, their bodies barely distinguishable from the grasses behind them but for their heads towering high above the stalks. Their triangular heads poised on long necks arched back and forth, heads mostly made up of bulging eyes. The glowing eyes regarded the group in the heart of the nesting lair with a predatory glare.

'We're surrounded,' said Daniel. 'What will we do?'

'Fight,' snorted Crunch. 'We'll charge. You protect Tess.'

Daniel carefully placed Tess into the empty nest beside them. 'Give me a sword Sara and—'

'I know,' Sara interrupted. 'Stay close.' *Likewise, brother, this fight is mine!*

Some of the mantes reared up on their hind legs and rubbed their forelegs over their bigger outer eyes in anticipation of the kill. More crouched on the ground in a squatting position, baring fangs and ready to spring. Others fluttered their wings and hovered momentarily before landing again.

Daniel gulped. 'We saw their wings earlier, but they weren't flying then.'

'In the Fens, their prey hears them approach if they use their wings, only in the cover of the grass can they stalk silently,' said Crunch. 'But here in the nesting lair, they *will* fly.'

A strange clicking noise started, low at first but then grew louder as more mantes joined in. It sent a chill down the spine of the questers.

Sara shuddered. 'I've heard that noise before from crickets, but never so loud.'

'Never so sharp,' added Daniel.

Crunch snorted. 'That's the formation chorus of the spraying mantes. Here comes the attack.' The giant boar turned to the questers. 'Protect her, protect Tess!'

Crunch and Stomp trumpeted another thunderous snort, lowered their tusks and charged.

Chapter 35
Inner Circle

The spraying mantes swarmed into the nesting lair while the boars ran. Crunch and Stomp charged in opposite directions, breaking the front line of the attacking mantes that split to meet them. Daniel and Sara watched on from their position in the heart of the lair as the two foes met. The mantes attacked the boars from the front and sides, flew over them to attack from above and circled around to attack them from behind. Both boars quickly disappeared amidst a cloud of green, only to reappear an instant later in the swirls of battle. The boars thrashed and bucked, knocking the mantes off their backs, and as the giant insects tumbled to the ground, they were crushed by the boars' giant hooves. More mantes replaced the fallen. The questers remembering their task to protect Tess resisted the urge to run to the aid of the boars. The clicking chorus of countless mantes echoed around the nesting lair as the battle raged. Lifeless mantes sailed through the air, walloped by the massive heads of the boars that swung wildly to-and-fro. Other mantes flayed dead or dying, skewered at the ends of the boars' tusks. Still the mantes came in wave after wave. Daniel and Sara gripped their swords in both hands and braced themselves for the fight to come. Crunch tumbled to the ground.

Daniel's heart sank. 'Oh no, Crunch has fallen,' he cried. That is all he saw. Some of the yellow mantes had reached the heart of the lair and were almost upon the questers.

Sara raised her sword aloft and screeched at the top of her voice. *'Let them come. Aye yeye yeye!'*

The young mantes closed in from all directions. Hopelessly outnumbered, a strange fearlessness came over Sara. She greeted their foe with a strength that should have long left her. She swung the tor-folk sword with all her might and cut down the first three mantes within her reach. Four more took their place.

Daniel, emboldened by Sara's courage, raced to her side and screamed a howling battle cry of his own. *'Aahhhrr!'* With two quick strokes of his sword, the four nearest mantes collapsed, headless.

They had no time to celebrate first blood for the mantes had multiplied. The giant insects were all around them now, with their bulging, green eyes glowing in the moonlight. In a blur of fangs, legs and black slime, Daniel and Sara hacked down the spraying mantes. Just as they cleared some space around the nest, an adult mantis that had been hovering overhead dropped from the air and knocked Daniel over, and using the spikes on its forelegs, pinned him to the ground.

'Sara!' Daniel screamed as he watched the fangs lower and the blob of black slime gather at the creature's mouth.

Sara spun, rolled on the ground and in one fluid motion, she picked up Daniel's sword with her free hand. The fangs were an inch from Daniel's throat when both swords criss-crossed through the body of the creature. It landed in a heap beside Daniel. As Daniel stood, Sara swung around again and hacked another flying mantis from the air. With a wild look in her eyes, she threw Daniel his sword. *I hate these beastly insects*, she thought, and charged at another group that approached, crawling along the dirt. She took out two, but even in her battle frenzy, there were too many and the others pounced, toppled her and closed in for the kill. Daniel was at her side and cut his way through before they could manage to bite her. The remaining adolescent mantes nearby hesitated briefly, sensing the threat of getting too close.

The short break gave the questers a chance to catch their breath. Panting, Daniel wiped the sweat from his brow and glanced around the nesting lair.

'Crunch has fallen,' he repeated, 'and I can't see Stomp,' he added frantically.

'No, he hasn't,' said Sara through sharp breaths, 'they're over there.' She had her free hand resting on her knee and pointed with her sword to a distant point across the lair. Daniel looked and there were the two giant boars fighting with fury. The spraying mantes were still attacking the boars from every possible angle. The broken bodies of the mantes were everywhere and black slime shot through the air.

'I thought he'd fallen, I had seen him fall,' said Daniel, bewildered. Both boars fell again but this time, Daniel got a better look. 'They're doing it on purpose!' he shouted to Sara. The boars had fallen on their sides and rolled several paces across the ground before jumping up and fighting on. 'Did you see it, Sara, how many mantes did they crush as they rolled? Thirty each, forty maybe?'

'So fast for their size,' said Sara, 'and each time they roll, the dirt cleans the slime off their hides.' They had no more time to be impressed.

Daniel glanced back towards the nest and realised that something was wrong. *Where is Tess?'* he cried.

Sara scanned around frantically and spotted some yellow movement off to the right of the nest. Her mind and body raced. 'Over there, quick.'

A group of adolescent mantes were dragging the baby boar off towards the tall grasses of the Fens. In the heat of battle, the questers hadn't noticed the group stealthily raiding the nest. As Sara ran, she thanked her lucky wishes for the moonlight. Daniel was a step behind her. The young mantes sensed their approach and picked up speed, but as they did so, they dropped their prey. Tess hit the hard ground and the shock woke her momentarily. She somehow found the strength to let out a high-pitched squeal. The squeal rose above the din of clicking chorus and the adolescent mantes hesitated. It was all the time Daniel and Sara needed. They fell upon the group and hacked them to pieces.

Tess lay still under a yellow mass of tangled legs and bodies. She'd used her final strength for the squeal and now lay very still.

Wasting no time, the questers began to free Tess. They rolled the dead mantes out of the way and pulled apart the spiked legs of the others that had managed to pin the little boar down to the ground when they fell. It didn't take them long to clear the bodies off her, but when they looked up, they were completely surrounded by the adult, green spraying mantes. The adolescents that weren't dead had scattered. The questers stared into the glowing eyes of the numerous mantes that circled them. The creatures less than a few paces away on all sides attacked again.

Daniel and Sara had no plan and no time to make one. They simply fought with all that was in them; they fought for their lives. They swung their tor-folk swords in a frenzied dance, connecting as often as missing. More mantes were dying than Daniel and Sara were killing. They became vaguely aware of an onslaught close by. When Tess had squealed, Crunch and Stomp had retreated back to their positions, fighting as they moved. The two giant boars were within striking distance of Daniel and Sara, mauling, bashing and crushing all and any mantes that they could. But the circle was closing as the mantes still came in hundreds and thousands.

Sara darted in and out between the long green legs, hacking and slicing. Daniel spun his blade in curving arches. Mantis fell. The boars were beside them now killing mantes by the dozen. Time and again black poisonous slime was sprayed; Daniel and Sara dodged it and the boars ignored it landing on their thick hides. Often the slime landed on another mantis.

Still the mantes attacked. It was getting harder to dodge the slime as more and more flew through the air and splat all over the ground in thick black globs. Daniel and Sara were tiring.

The greens aren't falling as easily as their yellow offspring did, thought Sara, *they're getting harder to hit and even harder to kill.*

Daniel just about dodged the fangs of a pouncing mantes. *Either they're getting quicker or we're getting slower*, he thought as he cut the pouncing insect down in flight.

Sara back-stepped, tripped and came dangerously close to getting snared by a mantis's spike wreathing and flaying in another's slime. Daniel grabbed her out of the way. The shock of seeing her come so close to death sent Daniel into a rage. He screamed at the top of his voice and charged forwards swinging the tor-folk steel in a deadly assault.

'*Aahhhrr!*' he wailed and drove the sword between the eyes of the nearest mantis. It fell down dead and another took its place.

Sara was beside him again. '*Aye yeye yeye,*' pierced the night air as she cut another mantis down. The battle frenzy was on them once more, and the boars joined them, trumpeting another loud snort that filled the night air.

Together, the four companions fought on, rolling, crushing, hacking and slicing, unwilling to give up the other to the poisonous predators. They fought bravely, but hopelessly outnumbered; they were losing the battle. Any ground won was quickly lost. The mantes filled the nesting lair now and had closed in tightly around the group, trapping them in an inner circle. As though sensing victory, the mantes suddenly stopped.

There was no escape. Crunch and Stomp stood firm, with heads lowered, snorting with each breath and foaming at the mouth. Their hides were smeared with blood and black slime. Between them were Daniel and Sara. They stood over the still body of Tess. Their bodies trembled but theirs jaws were set tight and they held their swords aloft, ready to fight to the death. The front line of mantes was within touching distance of the boars, with the rest of the swarm packed tightly behind them. Countless glowing eyes stared at the group trapped in the inner circle. Those mantes nearest rubbed their forelegs over their bulging eyes. The clicking chorus started again. When it reached fever pitch, the spraying mantes attacked. Mantis poured into the circle from all sides. The ground began to shake.

Chapter 36
Drove

The earth beneath them rumbled. Daniel and Sara lost their balance and fell on the ground beside Tess. Something had startled the mantes. They were scattering in all directions. The boars were going berserk, attacking the mantes as they fled and as Sara looked around, she realised it wasn't only Crunch and Stomp.

'Daniel,' she shouted above the din, 'it's the giant boars! *There's hundreds of them, the lair is full of them.'*

Daniel nodded. *'Stay close, stay close or we'll be crushed.'* The adventurers, exhausted, huddled together over the still body of Tess, watching nervously as the carnage continued around them.

Countless mantes were thrown through the air, their bodies snapping in two like twigs. Countless more were trampled by giant hooves. Crippled mantes slammed to the ground, their lifeless bodies twitching. Poisonous blobs of spray lay everywhere. The thick legs of the boars pounded to-and-fro in thunderous charge.

The moonlight beamed down on the nesting grounds. Gaps were appearing in the battle when the questers caught sight of a boar larger than any other. The creature had massive tusks sticking up from his jaw, attached to his equally massive head. The massive head was swinging left and right, tossing the spraying mantes into the air, skewering them on his tusks and trampling them into the ground.

'Gosh,' said Daniel, 'He's the size of Crunch and half that again.'

'He's bigger,' said Sara, 'He's Crunch and Stomp rolled into one. He's tossing those mantes like leaves in gale! He's—'

Daniel cut her off. *'He's coming this way!'* he roared. The enormous head of the biggest of the giant boars was bearing down on Daniel and Sara. With tusks lowered, the giant charged at full speed.

'Aaaaaaaaahhhhhhhhhhhhhhhhhh,' Daniel and Sara screamed together as they watched, wide-eyed with horror.

The tree-trunk legs tore up the earth as the boar charged. There was nowhere to run, there was no time. Daniel and Sara held each other and closed their eyes tight, waiting for the impact that would surely kill them. They hadn't stopped screaming.

'*Aaaaaaaaahhhhhhhhhhhhhhhh.*'

But a louder roar drowned out theirs. '*Hooolllllld,*' a deep voice boomed across the nesting lair. Daniel opened one eye to see the giant of giant boars skid to a stop and halt just an inch from his face. He felt the warm, moist breath of the boar on his skin. Daniel gulped.

'Hold,' the deep voice said again from close by. The questers recognised the voice as Crunch's and opened their eyes fully to see him trotting towards their position. The battle was over, most mantes left in the lair were dead and shuffling among them were numerous giant boars. Daniel and Sara didn't dare move, though, under the watchful eyes of the biggest creature they'd seen since they'd gotten to Well-Keeper Island. A brief silence fell on the nesting ground but for the faint clicking of some dying mantes and the rustling grasses as others fled. Crunch trotted to Daniel and Sara's side and spoke quietly.

'Tusks, *they* fought with us. They protected Tess with tor-folk steel.'

The giant boar, called Tusks, snorted and nodded his great head. 'Friend of the Boar,' he said in a voice even deeper than Crunch's. With a gentleness that surprised the questers, Tusks lowered his great head down to Tess and closed his eyes. After a moment, he licked her hide. The baby boar gave a weak shudder. Tusks lifted his head quickly. 'She lives. Boy, have you strength enough to carry her?' Daniel just nodded. 'Good,' said Tusks. 'The spraying mantes will re-group in the grasses and return in greater numbers. We leave now. Crunch will carry you boy, and Stomp, your companion.'

Daniel shook the tiredness from his eyes then gently picked up Tess and held her to his chest. 'I could walk, if it was easier on Tess,' he said.

'No,' said Tusks. 'The Fens are vast and time is of the essence. You are still weak from battle, that much is plain. If Tess is to have any hope of survival, we must leave the Fens now. You will ride on the Boar.'

Sara, relieved to be leaving the nesting grounds, whispered to her brother. 'If we could ride a flying horse, I'm sure a giant boar will be a piece of cake.'

Daniel sighed. *Don't talk about cake. I'm famished,* he thought, while Crunch dropped on all fours beside him. Stomp did likewise for Sara. Once they mounted, the giant boars stood.

Tusks snorted a loud command. 'Drove, assemble.' The rest of the boars began forming a line with Tusks in the middle.

Daniel and Sara were a little unsure which way to sit.

'Don't worry,' said Crunch, 'you won't fall off. We travel fast, but you're safe on the back of a boar.'

Sara settled herself and tried to relax. 'Where did they all come from, the other boars I mean?'

Tusks swung his massive head around to her. 'The drove main were spread many leagues throughout the Fens when we heard the call of the Boar. As we got close, we heard a piglet squeal; we knew it to be Tess. Your human scent led us the rest of the way.'

Sara frowned momentarily. *Why must everyone here get our scent, do we really smell so bad.*

'The drove, what's that?' Daniel asked, while watching the line of boars form under the moonlight.

'Humans call us the Boar Army. We are the Drove,' said Tusks.

'You certainly drove the mantes away,' said Daniel, allowing himself a smile. Tusks snorted. 'I think I made him laugh,' Daniel whispered to Sara.

'Idiot, you made him snort, there's a big difference,' she whispered back.

'It was definitely a laugh.'

Tusks snorted again. 'Yes, we drove them away, with your help, but not for long. Now we make for the edge of Fens.' Daniel reddened at being overheard. *I forgot they had such good hearing.*

The giant of giant Boars looked up and down the assembled line of boars and roared at the top of his voice.

'Boars, let's move out.'

The line, as one, charged into the night.

Chapter 37
Surprises

The Boar Drove charged at full speed through the tall grasses of the Fens, leaving a trampled plain of green in their wake. Daniel leaned low, clutching Tess to his chest with one hand and holding onto Crunch's ear with the other. Sara's hair flew out behind her in the wind as she leaned low with a firm grip on both of Stomp's ears. They'd been charging for some time with no sign of stopping.

Daniel had to shout over to Sara to be heard above the force of the charge. 'I'm surprised how fast they can run, given their size.'

Sara looked to the side and her hair flayed across her face. 'Let's just hope they're quick enough to save Tess.' She thought for another moment and went on. 'I know they said the Fens were vast, but I'm surprised just *how* vast. And you were going to walk!'

Crunch interrupted them. 'The Fens *are* vast.'

Despite being jostled on the back of a charging giant boar, left to their own thoughts, weariness crept upon the pair once again. Trying their best to ignore the hunger and tiredness both their minds turned to the baby boar in Daniel's arms.

I hope we get where we're going soon, she feels so fragile, thought Daniel.

Sara looked over and shared his concern. *Poor little Tess, hang in there*, she thought, *the drove will know what to do.*

Finally when it seemed like they'd never stop charging, the Boar army burst out of the Fens and into a meadow of short grass that was dotted with shrubby growth and rushes. They pounded on a few more paces and slowed to a stop.

Stomp and Crunch knelt on their hind legs so that Daniel and Sara could slide off. It was late in the night and the clear sky was lit by the bright full moon. Sara gave a shiver to fight off the cool night air.

Daniel hugged Tess close. 'She feels so cold,' he said as Tusks approached them.

'Put her down so we can see her,' said the giant boar.

Any of the giant boars that could squeeze their heads in circled around them to see the little piglet. Tess lay very still. Her hide barely rose and fell with each shallow breath. After a few moments, Tusks raised his head and the gathered boars took a step back.

Tusks spoke with urgency. 'Tess is very sick. She's been bitten by an adolescent mantis. If it'd been a full-grown, she'd be dead by now. The wound is not deep but the poison has set in.'

'Oh no,' cried Sara, raising her hands to her mouth. 'What can we do?'

'She needs heat first, warmth to fight off the cold; we cannot wait till the morning sun. And she needs something to drink.'

Daniel's brow furrowed with concern. *I wish we could help, but how?*

Tusks went on. 'Crunch, Stomp, make haste to the river. Return with all you can carry and don't swallow a drop. The rest of you will dig. Go.' Crunch and Stomp charged off into the night.

'Dig?' asked Daniel.

'Dig for water,' said Tusks. 'The river is a long way from here. They may not be back on time. Water runs underground hereabouts between the lake and the river; we might find an underground spring.'

'Will she make it?' asked Daniel, his voiced etched with worry.

'Time is short,' said Tusks.

Sara's face suddenly set with determination and she ran a few paces into the meadow.

'Sara?' Daniel called after her.

'Over here, Daniel. Help me gather some of these,' she shouted back. Between them, they pulled a cluster of dry rushes from the ground and Sara arranged them in a neat row to form a mat on the short grass. 'Now, Dan, you go get Tess over here.' She raced back to the edge of the Fens and began tearing out long strands of the tall grass. A blade of grass cut her hand. 'Oochh,' she cried and went back to work.

Tusks appeared beside her. 'Let me help.' With one swish of his tusks, he felled a sheaf of grass so big, Sara needed both hands to pick it up. She raced back to the mat. Tusks joined her. The rest of the boars continued digging furiously.

Daniel carried the baby boar over and gently placed her down on the makeshift bed. Tess began to shake. 'The poor little thing; look, she's shivering. We'll have to warm her up,' he said.

'That's the plan,' said Sara. She split the sheaf of grass in two, putting half on the ground and divided the rest between herself and Daniel. 'We'll rub her down. This grass is nice and soft. It should bring some warmth. You do the top half and I'll do the bottom.'

Bunching the grass around their hands, they set to task, gently working the grass up and down the baby boar's hide. Fresh tears came to Sara's eye as she regarded the baby boar again. *What a lovely shade of brown her short hair is. Her small ears are so cute and look at her curled eyelashes. And her big black eyes, they're so lovely, but she seems so sad.* 'Don't worry, little one, we'll have you warm in no time,' she said, and began to gently rub the piglet's underbelly. Tess winched in pain. Sara and Daniel were startled by the movement and stopped rubbing.

'Oh no,' said Sara, 'I've hurt her.'

'No,' said Tusks. 'It's working; as you warm her, she fights the poison. Please continue.' They started to rub again, faster but just as gently.

After a time when Tess hadn't moved again, Daniel despaired. 'She's still so cold, if only we could—' He stopped abruptly. 'Wait, the tor-folk ointment, I still have it!' He quickly pulled it out of his satchel. 'Will it work on the bite?'

'Only one way to find out,' said Sara urgently. 'Give it here and help me turn her on her side.' Under the watchful eye of Tusks, ever so carefully, they turned Tess over.

'Oh,' the questers gasped together. Visible on Tess's underbelly were two bite-holes made by the fangs of a mantis. Yellow puss streaked with trickles of red blood oozed out of the wounds.

'That looks nasty, it needs to be washed, *somehow*,' said Daniel. Tusks lowered his massive head between Daniel and Sara and they moved aside to let him through. He ran his thick, pink tongue across the bite marks and licked away the puss and blood.

'It's clean for now,' said Tusks. He spat the ooze across the field. Sara quickly removed the lid of the jar and using her fingers, began rubbing the ointment onto the wounds.

'What made you think of it?' she asked Daniel.

'The tor-folk healer told me it draws out poisons. I hope it works on boars,' he said, and glanced unsurely at Tusks.

Tusks nodded. 'The Tor-Folk are friend of the Boar.'

Tess soon started to breathe more easily. Sara continued rubbing in the ointment while gently stroking the small boar's head.

'It seems to be working, but she's still so very cold,' Sara said with a shiver, 'I'm feeling chilly myself.' She was interrupted by a flow of bubbling sounds. Bobbin appeared, poking her tiny head out of the satchel hanging at Sara's side. 'What is it, Bobbin?'

The Bonion borrowed into the satchel and reappeared a moment later trying to hold a small piece of black flint in her tiny arms. The weight was too much for the little creature and she dropped it again back into the satchel.

'Oh Bobbin, well done, only for you,' said Sara. She rubbed the little Bonion on the head and took out the small piece of flint. She held it up to Daniel and Tusks. 'It's just an edge off one of the pieces of flint. It must've broken away and got caught in the seam of the satchel. I'm surprised it survived the lake crossing.'

Daniel took it from her. 'Let's be glad it did. There's enough to make a spark. Tusks, can you get me a big dry rock?' The giant boar pounded off and returned with a big flat rock in his mouth. Sara had stayed with Tess while Daniel had gathered some dry leaves and grass, twigs and a few shrubby branches. He rested the flint on the flat rock and added a small bit of the tinder on top. 'Here it goes,' he said, and using a smaller stone, he cracked it off the top of the flint. A bright spark flared up and he quickly blew the spark to flame. He added more tinder, then the twigs and last the branches. In a short time, a hot fire blazed beside them.

They moved Tess closer to the heat. Sara had used all the ointment so she took the rest of the sheaf of grass and laid it over Tess for a blanket. Daniel put his hoody back on, surprised that it was clear of mantis slime.

The questers and Tusks sat beside Tess and waited anxiously for the precious water to come. Daniel and Sara hugged their knees, silently willing the baby boar to recover, while Tusks' unreadable face stared into the flames as the night ached on. Tess gave another shiver so Daniel got up and added more wood to the fire. The other boars had not found a spring but continued to dig.

Tusks got up and nuzzled Tess with his nose then turned to the questers. 'With heat and the tor-folk ointment she has gained *some* strength, but the poison was deeper than I thought. We've bought her time only, without moisture soon she will still pass in the night.'

Sara burst out crying.

'Pass?' Daniel asked quietly.

'Die, Daniel. He means she'll die,' Sara blubbered through her tears.

Daniel gulped. *Oh no, it can't be, we've got to do something.* His brow furrowed, then without a word, he dropped to his knees and began frantically digging the clay with his bare hands. Sara immediately fell beside him and did the same. Tusks knelt beside Tess and breathed warm air over her hide. Daniel and Sara's fingernails were soon scratched, broken and full of dirt. Their arms ached but still they dug, desperate to find water for Tess.

The first signs of dawn were appearing on the horizon as a pale pink outline spread on distant clouds.

Tusks stood. 'They're back,' he said. Daniel and Sara heard the thumping of hoof on earth and moments later Crunch and Stomp pounded into view. 'Daniel, you hold Tess's head up,' ordered Tusks. 'Sara you open her mouth if you can.' They did as instructed and one after the other, the giant boars opened their mouths and gushes of water flowed down their tongues and out into Tess's mouth. Tess gulped as the water flowed down her throat. 'Now we wait and hope,' said Tusks.

Daniel laid Tess back down on the mat and Sara gently stroked the piglet's head.

'There-there little Tess,' said Sara, 'you'll be okay, I promise.' *I hope.* The baby boar lay still for a time. Her breathing became calm and even.

Finally, Tess spoke. 'Thirsty,' she rasped through quivering lips.

Astonished, Sara clasped her mouth. 'Oh, she's awake! She's looking for another drink.'

The assembled boars snorted loudly and trotted in beside the fire. They nuzzled and licked the little piglet. Tess had recovered enough to try and stand. She very slowly stood but as she straightened, her small legs wobbled and collapsed underneath her. To comfort her, the giant boars nuzzled her again till Tusks moved them back.

'She's gained *some* strength, but she's still too weak to continue,' he snorted loudly, 'She needs more to drink or something to eat, something moist.' He didn't need to give the order; the boars immediately began to dig and forage.

The early light of dawn peeped through the clouds. Tess rolled on her side with the bite marks facing upward. The questers were surprised at the speed the tor-folks' ointments had healed the wounds, which were already turning to faded scars.

Sara knelt on her hunkers and spoke softly to Tess, 'Hi Tess, I'm Sara. No need to be frightened, you're safe now.' Tess whimpered. Sara continued, 'You're hungry aren't you, me too. I'm sorry we've no food to give you.' She pointlessly checked her satchels again.

Daniel rummaged aimlessly in his pockets for any morsel that they might be able to give Tess to help her recover. 'Those hideous bottom-claws,' he said, 'we lost almost everything when, oh, what's this?' His fingers closed on something deep down in one of his combat-trouser pockets. 'What do you know, look, Sara, it's the plum I kept from Appledown Orchards, I'd completely forgotten about it.'

'I'm surprised it's kept its shape after all we've been through since then,' said Sara.

'Well, it *is slightly* mushed,' said Daniel, turning the bruised plum over. '*I'm* surprised it didn't fall into the lake; it was in the same pocket as the shard.'

Tusks examined the fruit in Daniel's hand. 'It will serve,' said the giant boar, 'If you will spare it, for I know you young humans' hunger also.'

Daniel's tummy grumbled. 'We're okay for a while yet,' he lied, 'Aren't we, Sara?'

Sara nodded agreement. *I feel sick with hunger but Tess needs it more.* She took the plum from Daniel, slowly reached down and pressed it between Tess's lips. 'Here you go, Tess, we've found some food. I'm sorry it's not much at all.'

Tusks swung his mighty head to face the questers. 'It's everything.'

Tess's nose scrunched as she slowly squashed the plum in her mouth. A little trickle of juice rolled down her face but her tongue darted out and licked it up. Her throat gulped as she swallowed the entire plum. With Tusks by their side, the questers watched on with concern. Tess lay still for a few moments.

'I'm sorry it wasn't more,' said Daniel quietly. Tess started to shudder. Her whole body shook with a ripple of movement through her hide. She jumped up and shook one leg, then another and another. She swung her head quickly from side to side. The questers jumped with fright as the baby boar let out a squeal.

'*She's having a fit,*' cried Sara.

'No,' said Tusks, who had relaxed his stance. 'She's happy, it's a squeal of delight.'

'Huh?' said Daniel and Sara together. They looked at each other, confused.

Tess rolled over on her back then leaped into the air with a sprightly jump and ran around in a circle. She was completely whole. Her soft hair glistened smoothly and she bounded around, full of energy.

'It's all tingly,' she squealed happily. All the boars snorted loudly and thumped the earth with their hooves in celebration.

'Amazing,' said Daniel, 'She's better, I think.'

'Unbelievable,' said Sara, 'I don't know a great deal about piglets but she appears fine. Could it be?' she hesitated and rested her hand on her chin in thought.

'What?' Daniel asked.

'Well I was just wondering could it be magic of the heart, or something? I don't know.'

'Hardly that,' said Daniel. 'It was the heat, the tor-folk ointment, the water and the plum. Exactly the things Tusks said she needed.'

Tusks trundled up beside them. 'You're both right, it was all those things and more. It was thanks to you two, Friend of the Boar.' The gathered boars snorted again and thumped the earth. Daniel and Sara looked at each other and smiled.

'Glad we could help,' said Sara. She was interrupted by Tess who started coughing loudly. The baby boar sat on her hunkers and started to shake. 'Oh no,' Sara gasped, 'She *is* having a fit.' The questers raced to her side. Tess swung her head forwards and coughed up the seed of the plum. The seed bounced and rolled to a stop close to Sara's feet.

'I'm okay, I'm okay,' said Tess in her soft squeaky voice. 'The plum seed got stuck, is all.'

'Oh,' said the questers together, relieved. The gathered boars chortled in deep grunts.

'I think they're laughing,' whispered Sara.

'At us or at Tess?' Daniel whispered back.

'At both,' said Tusks loudly. 'And now we'll assemble and make for the river, it's been a long night for all.' The boars started forming a line. 'I will carry Tess, as before, Crunch and Stomp will take the humans.'

The giant boars knelt so their passengers could climb up. Tess raced up Tusks' back and curled in a ball between his giant shoulder blades. Sara began to mount Stomp when a sparkle from the ground caught her eye.

'Wait, wait a moment,' she said and slipped off Stomp's back.

Daniel joined her. 'What is it, Sis?'

Sara stooped and picked up the plum seed. 'I thought I saw it sparkle.' The plum seed was brown in colour and hard to the touch. The surface was dotted with tiny holes. Sara turned it slowly around in her fingers and gasped.

'Oh, Daniel, look. There's something stuck in it, something shiny.'

'Give it here a moment,' said Daniel, 'let me have a closer look.' Sara handed it to him and he carefully examined the seed. The boars, now assembled, stood patiently by. Daniel's face filled with wonder. 'Sara, it's a piece of the shard of the dragon's tooth. It must be!'

'But how,' said Sara, bewildered.

'I had them in the same pocket, the shard and the plum I mean. The point of the shard must've got stuck in the plum and a tiny piece of the tip broke off.' He held it up to the light. 'Can you believe it? I'm going to keep it *too*, as proof that we had the shard.' He popped it into his satchel where he kept the piece of the hag's staff.

'Good idea,' said Sara. 'Hey, maybe that's what helped Tess, the magic of the heart from the point of the shard I mean.'

'Yep, must've been,' said Daniel, still astonished at the find. 'I'm surprised you spotted it, it's so tiny,' he said as he climbed back onto Crunch's shoulders.

'Yeah me too,' said Sara, now sitting firmly on Stomp's back. 'There have been a lot of surprises tonight.'

Crunch, who had been waiting silently, spoke. 'Young humans, *it* is the morning now.' The assembled boars chortled and Sara laughed with them.

'So it is—' said Sara, but she was interrupted by a loud snore that echoed across the scrubland. Tess was fast asleep.

226

'Boars, move out,' snorted Tusks. The drove began to trot across the scrub. Sara noticed Daniel's frown.

'Dan, what's the matter?'

'It's the morning,' he said, his voice full of worry. 'It's the fifth day of our quest. We have to get to Botanic Beaches before sunset, wherever that is. *And* we don't have the nourishing stone.'

Sara heard the strain in his voice and thought of all they'd been through. 'Yes, I'd almost forgotten, what with the Fens and then Tess. Didn't we agree back at the lake to forget the quest? Let's just get back to the well with what we have. We tried, right?' Daniel remained silent and downcast. *Poor Daniel, he hates to give up on anyone or anything*, thought Sara, *the sooner we get home the better for us both*. She leaned over and shouted to Tusks. 'Excuse me, Tusks. Is it far to Botanic Beaches? Maybe you could point us in the right direction?'

'Its many leagues as the pigeon flies,' said Tusks with a snort.

'Oh,' said Sara, disappointed. *Oh dear, a league sounds far. I was hoping they had miles or kilometres here.*

Tusks swung his massive head and snorted loudly. The Boar drove burst into a charge. The questers swung on their mounts and had to grab onto the boars' ears to steady themselves.

Daniel, startled out of his despair, called out, 'What's going on? I never thought to ask where we're going.'

'Our river territory is closer to your destination. We're taking you with us. Its many leagues from here, so get some rest while you can,' said Crunch.

Sara tried to object. 'We don't mind walking if you'd only show us the way.' *A league couldn't be that far, it's only an island.*

'You're delirious with tiredness young human,' said Crunch. 'You'd be three sunrises going on foot. Now, get some rest.'

'Oh that far,' said Sara, 'okay then, we'll take the ride.' She looked at Daniel as they shared the same thought. *How are we supposed to rest on the back of a charging boar?*

But rest they did. Lying on the back of the charging boars, dirty from head to toe, aching all over, hungry and thirsty, they finally surrendered to exhaustion and slumped into a deep sleep.

Chapter 38
Plum Apples

Daniel woke with the sun on his face. He yawned and used the motion to shield the light from his eyes. Suddenly he wobbled as what he thought to be the ground moved beneath him.

'Wo,' he cried aloud. Feeling the tough hide beneath him, he realised he was still on Crunch's back. 'Gosh, where are we?' he said to no one in particular.

'This is the river territory of the Boar,' said Crunch.

'Oh, I see,' said Daniel as he looked all around him.

Sara lay asleep next to him, still on the back of Stomp. The ground below was matted with short grass, the blades soft and deep green with the strength of summer. Far to the right rose the high peaks of the Rocky Rise. To the left and in front of them lay fields of yellow, green, brown and gold that ran far off into the distance. Behind their position, a long distance away, the Great Lake was visible as a sheet of white, gleaming in the sun. Much closer, only fifty paces to their right, the drove of giant boar was gathered by the side of a big river. The river meandered its way through the plains towards the lake. Daniel had never seen so many swine in one place. *Gosh, there must be two hundred of them,* he thought. The boars were all different sizes, from as small as Tess to as large as Crunch. Many of the boars were chewing on wild turnips and river cabbages while others stretched out lazing in the sun. Some of the smallest ones were right on the bank of the river enjoying a mud bath. The largest boars, however, were not joining in the activities of the others. They stood in groups of fours and fives on the perimeter of the gathering, facing away from the main drove. Daniel noticed how rigid they stood with their snouts held high to the wind. *They're so tense,* he thought, *Maybe the biggest don't like to relax. Although I guess with spraying mantes as neighbours, relaxing isn't so easy.* With this thought, the memories of their journey since the lake came flooding back to him. *Those mantes, they were horrible, if I never see one again it'll be too soon. And poor Tess, I just hope she's okay now. She almost died and would've too if not for, well lots of things. So much has happened since we started this quest. Our quest!*

'Sara,' he shouted. '*Sara, wake up.* Crunch, what time is it? I mean how long have we been asleep?'

'Huh?' said Sara, 'What's wrong?' stirred from her drowsiness by the urgency in Daniel's tone.

Crunch snorted. 'You've slept since dawn. High sun approaches, midday in human tongue.'

'Thank goodness,' said Daniel, turning to Sara. 'It's still the fifth day. With *or* without the treasures we've got to get back to the wishing-well before sunset. The well is our only way home!'

'Are Botanic Beaches far from here?' Sara asked while rubbing the sleep from her eyes.

'Many leagues,' said Crunch as he and Stomp lowered their hind legs. 'Dismount, and wait here,' he added.

'We really should get going,' said Sara.

Daniel nodded. 'If only we hadn't slept so long.'

Crunch and Stomp had started to walk away but they stopped. 'Tusk's orders were to let you sleep until you woke yourself,' said Crunch. 'You needed it. Now you're awake. Wait here.' The two boars turned and thumped hastily over and joined separate groups of the biggest boars on the perimeter of the gathering.

When they had gone out of earshot, Sara turned to Daniel. 'How far *is* a league?'

Daniel's brow crinkled. 'Well, hmm, it depends if you're a pigeon or a boar.'

Sara raised her eyebrows. 'You don't know.'

'Yes I do, it's just not something I can explain.' *I wonder how far it is,* Daniel thought.

'I see,' said Sara. *He doesn't know.*

'Anyway,' said Daniel, 'It's far, we know that much. We should leave soon.' His tummy groaned. 'I'm famished with hunger and could do with a drink too.'

Sara put her hand on her tummy. 'Me too, I can't remember the last thing I ate, not to mention drank. My throat feels like old socks.' She smacked her gums together in vain efforts to moisten her mouth. 'Hey Daniel, I bet you're sorry you didn't eat that plum yourself.'

'Too right.' *Hmmm.* 'Well maybe not, as it *did* help Tess and all. Speaking of the plum, let's take another look at the point of the shard.' Daniel rummaged his hand in his satchel and took out the plum seed. He held it on the palm of his hand and they examined it together. Daniel turned at the sound of heavy thudding footsteps. The sun shone down on the plum seed and a thin beam of light shone back from it.

'Wow,' said the questers together.

'It really gives off a bright light for such a tiny piece of shard,' said Sara.

The footsteps were from Tusks. They turned to meet him, with Daniel still holding the plum seed. The giant of the giant boars approached them with purpose. The questers regarded him with a touch of fear. He had looked big the previous night, but in the light of day, he was absolutely enormous. The great bulk of his frame reminded Daniel of a rhinoceros, but he wouldn't dare suggest the comparison aloud. Although his approach was not threatening, his head appeared as menacing as the first time they saw it, massive and solid with spear-length tusks protruding from a jaw made for crushing.

'Put your stone away,' said Tusks with authority, 'we've far to travel and leave very soon. I will take you both. We'll wait by the river. Come.'

'What are we waiting for?' said Daniel as he put the plum seed back in his satchel.

'Apples,' said Tusks, 'first you'll drink. The water is fresh.' He turned and strode towards the river.

'Apples?' said Daniel, confused, and made to follow Tusks. Sara stayed standing where she was, her face frozen. Daniel hadn't noticed.

'Apples,' snorted Tusks again, already several paces ahead. 'You have to eat as well as drink I'm sure.'

Daniel smiled at the news. 'Did you hear that Sara? Food,' he said, turning back. 'Hey, what's the matter?'

'Daniel,' said Sara, wide-eyed, 'did you hear what Tusks just said? He said put your *stoooone* away!'

'And I did, now hurry will you.' He made to turn back again but stopped suddenly. 'Oh, I see what you're getting at.'

'Exactly, some people call a plum seed a stone. That's it! We've got the nourishing stone!' Sara strode hastily over to join him. 'Let's have another look.'

Daniel took it out and they examined it again. 'I'm not so sure,' he said. 'I mean it doesn't look like much, except for the tiny piece of shard in it.'

'Think about it,' said Sara, taking the plum seed from him and holding it between two fingers. 'See how quickly Tess recovered, *that* was from the nourishment from the stone.'

Daniel frowned. *Hmm.* 'I don't know, Sis. There was the heat from the fire, the ointment and the water that helped Tess too. Besides, you can't *eat* a plum seed. She got the nourishment from the plum, *not* the seed.' Tusks had reached the bank of the river and stood waiting patiently.

'Listen Dan, the mowler's message said we'd find it in an unlikely place, right? Neither the flying horses nor the tor-folk ever heard of it, why? Because *you* brought it from Appledown Orchards. It *is* the nourishing stone, I just know it is.'

Sara's eagerness began to rub off on Daniel. 'Yeah, yes you're right. And that means we've got the three treasures, in part at least!' They smiled at each other. 'C'mon then, we might still make it to the Botanic Beaches before sunset and get going home.' He put the plum stone back in his satchel, and together they hurried over to waiting Tusks.

The riverbank sloped gently down to the river's edge. The top of the bank had a grass verge broken by a mud trail dotted with countless hoof prints, and thin, pointed reeds grew in clusters right next to the water.

'Drink deeply, friend of the Boar,' said Tusks, 'for we ride fast and far to make Botanic Beaches by nightfall.'

Daniel and Sara dropped on their knees and washed their hands in the river, then they cupped their hands to lift water to their mouths and drank scoop after scoop. The water ran down their chins and onto their clothes, but they didn't mind as their clothes were already tattered, battered and stained. After taking a long, refreshing drink, they washed the grime from their faces.

'Oh that feels good,' said Sara as she slapped handful of river water against her cheeks. *So much water here and so lovely and fresh. To think how we needed some so badly for Tess last night. Tess! Shame on me.* She jumped to her feet and turned to Tusks. 'I'm so sorry, I never asked you,' she blurted quickly. 'How *is* Tess? Did she, is she okay? Is she well?' Daniel stood too and dried his face off with his sleeve.

'Tess is fine,' said Tusks. He grunted and stepped to his left. 'See for yourself.' A big female boar approached. The questers gasped.

'*That*, that's Tess?' Daniel asked, bewildered. The boar that trotted up next to Tusks was up to his shoulder in height, had a light-brown hide and no tusks. Her black eyelashes were long and curled up at the end. She held a large piece of tree bark in her mouth and resting on the bark were ten red apples.

'This,' said Tusks, 'is Bess, Tess's mother.'

'Ah,' said Sara.

'Oh,' said Daniel. 'And *you* thought she was Tess,' he whispered to Sara.

Sara whispered back, 'So did you, idiot.' Tess, as small as ever, trotted out from behind her mother's leg. She held a smaller piece of bark in her mouth and was struggling to balance two apples on it. The questers couldn't help but smile. Tess and Bess placed their bark plates down beside Daniel and Sara.

'Apples for you,' said Bess, quietly. 'Tess,' she added, more firmly. Tess gave a little cough before speaking.

'Thank you for,' she began in her soft squeaky voice. She scrunched her nose, trying to remember something rehearsed. 'Thank you for, em, eh.'

'Tess,' said her mother encouragingly. Tess scrunched her nose again and then gave up trying to remember her lines.

'We brought you some apples. Are you having a mud bath?'

Daniel and Sara laughed good-naturedly.

'No,' said Sara, 'we're in quite a hurry.' She dropped to her hunkers and stroked Tess on the head. 'We were just having a drink before we leave. Thank *you* for the apples, we're ever so hungry. It's just what we need.'

'I love apples,' said Daniel.

Tess gave a squeal of delight. 'Me too,' she said, and with a spritely jump she joined her mother.

Tusks strode forwards. 'Collect your apples and secure your tor-folk steel, we ride out now.' The giant of giant boars dropped his hind legs so the questers could mount. Using their clothes as a pouch, Daniel and Sara quickly gathered the apples and climbed onto Tusks back. They were barely aboard when Tusks stood and strode up the riverbank.

'Goodbye, Tess,' the questers called back. Tess ran alongside Tusks' massive legs and looked up at them.

'Are you sure you can't stay for a mud bath?' she asked pleadingly. The questers smiled.

'Maybe next time,' said Sara. 'Bye-bye Tess.'

'Bye,' said Tess, meekly. Tusks had broken into a run. The questers waved for a moment then Bess beckoned Tess back to her side. As the little boar returned to join the drove with her mother, the questers aboard Tusks were racing through a plain of rich, green grass.

After a short time, the questers looked back the way they'd come. They could see that they were following the path of the river and the boar-drove gathering was a shrinking sight in the distance. It didn't take them long to find their balance and they soon got stuck into the apples as they ran. Famished with hunger, they quickly ate four each and would have eaten them all only that Tusks cautioned them.

'Our journey ahead is a long one. There'll be no time to stop for more food again,' said the giant boar as he thundered through a patch of reeds and bulrushes. So they saved two apples each for later.

'Is it really that far?' asked Daniel. *Now that we can prove we had the treasures, I really want to make it back on time. We might just succeed on our quest.*

'It is,' said Tusks.

'Let me guess,' said Sara. 'Many leagues?'

'Indeed,' snorted Tusks and picked up speed again. Shadows of wings suddenly appeared, darting along the ground. The questers looked up and a moment later, two blue pigeons and one white flew across their path and were gone again as quick.

'Wow,' said Daniel, 'And I thought we were travelling fast.'

232

Tusks snorted. 'We're travelling as fast as carrying two allows.'

Daniel's face reddened. 'No, I didn't mean anything, I mean *we're* going fast too, I just meant the pigeons can fly super-fast.' Daniel looked over at Sara unsurely.

Sara glared at him and put her finger to her lips. *Shush Dan*, she thought, *he'll think we're ungrateful for the ride.*

Daniel raised his hands and pressed his lips. *What did I do?* He thought.

'Nothing in our skies can fly as fast as the messenger pigeon,' said Tusks, 'but they can't carry you to Botanic Beaches.'

Sara suddenly felt bad. 'We're sorry to burden you Tusks. Would it have helped if maybe Crunch or Stomp had come too?'

'*No,*' Tusks roared. The questers jumped with fright. The giant boar skidded to a stop, digging big lumps out of the ground with his hooves as he did so. 'No,' he said again, calmly this time. He turned his massive head to look back at his passengers. 'You misunderstand. You're no burden; *you* are friend of the Boar.'

Daniel and Sara exchanged unsure glances.

Tusks continued. 'The scent of hog hunters is in the air, so Crunch and Stomp stayed back to protect the drove with the others.'

Daniel frowned. *That explains why the biggest boars were uneasy back there; they were standing guard.*

Sara looked down at Tusks. 'Hog hunters, what are they? They sound awful, are they anything like the spraying mantes?'

Tusks grunted and shuffled the earth with his hoof. 'The hog hunters are humans,' he said and looked ahead. The questers gasped, horrified. Tusks sniffed the air. 'Not *all* humans are friend to the Boar.'

Sara found her voice. 'Tusks, I don't know what to say. I'm really sorry. Maybe we should make our own way, you shouldn't be helping us.'

'You should go back to the drove, we're so sorry,' said Daniel.

'What are you sorry for?' said Tusks. 'Are *you* hog hunters?'

'No, but—'

'Well then you've nothing to be sorry for, so enough of your nonsense. Do you know where we are right now?' He didn't wait for them to answer. 'Here marks the edge of the Boar territory. It's very rare that we would travel beyond these borders, only in a time of great need. Our need was great in the Fens and you came to our aid, now your need is great. So, shall we continue?'

Daniel and Sara looked at each other, both their faces set.

We've come a long way and been through so much, let's finish this crazy quest, thought Sara.

We're so close now and just maybe we'll succeed, thought Daniel, *get the treasures to the well and home. We can do it.*

'Yes please,' the siblings said together.

'Good,' said Tusks, 'good. So you think the pigeon flies fast. Now you will see how fast the leader of the Boar can run. Hold on, young humans for until now we were only trotting.'

Tusks burst into a sprint. The questers almost tumbled from his back but the giant boar kicked up his hind legs and the movement tossed them back between his shoulders. They grabbed him by the ears, braced themselves for the ride and lay low. Within moments, the landscape of Well-Keeper Island was whizzing past them in a blur.

Chapter 39
River Race

Running close to the river, Tusks raced across the island. While Sara tried to hold on, she thought about the creature beneath her. *His hide is so tough, almost like wood but not altogether uncomfortable.* She could feel the enormous strength harnessed in his muscles with every step they took. *I wonder how fast we're travelling, very fast at any rate!* Tusks pounded the earth beneath with every footfall. He tore through meadows, leaped over ditches, ploughed through gorges, waded through ponds and never missed a step. The questers saw thin wisps of smoke in the distance and were surprised when a row of cottages came into view off to left. They were even more surprised when around the next bend, they saw ordinary people out tending to the fields. Almost without warning, the skies overhead filled with shadows and the calls of a thousand gulls. The questers tensed.

'Fear not the gulls,' said Tusks.

'It's the third time we've seen them,' said Sara with a shudder, 'it's just that they bring back bad memories.'

'We met them in the fog on the mountain,' said Daniel, 'and again at the Great Lake. It wasn't so nice.'

Tusks grunted. 'Choice words, young human. I sense you had an unpleasant experience, but no fault lies with these harmless birds. They nest on the mountains, but they cross the island once a day to feed at the Great Lake when the tide is at its highest. That is all they do; the gulls carry no ill will.' Hearing this from the giant boar, the questers relaxed and watched the gulls with a new wonder.

'The sheer number of them, it's incredible,' said Daniel.

'It's breath-taking,' said Sara as she craned her neck to watch them passing overhead. All the while Tusks raced along the course of the river.

Now and then, they passed man-made bridges and on one occasion, an otters' dam. The otters with fish in their mouths watched furtively as Tusks and company charged past. They came to a big, meandering bend so Tusks cut across through a wooded area that filled the bow in-between. When they came out the other side, they were next to the riverbank again. The stretch of river ahead was a long straight stretch with flat grass plains either side. The questers looked into the deep, clear waters. Shadows appeared in the river just beneath the surface and darted along close to the water's edge. The questers watched them curiously. The shadows broke the surface then and zoomed along the top, flicking the water to the side as they swam.

'*What* are they?' said Daniel, as he marvelled at the strange sight.

'That's a school of flicks,' said Tusks.

'Flicks?' said Sara while watching the tunnel-shaped wave that crested up from the river.

'The young of flicker fish,' said Tusks, 'the fastest creature in our waters.'

'Do they grow big?' asked Daniel, fascinated. *I bet they do.*

'Let me guess,' said Sara, 'They grow to giant size.'

Tusks chortled. 'Well, let's just say you don't want to be in the river when a flicker fish is passing.' The small wave continued to turn at the same pace Tusks was running until the giant boar veered left and pounded several paces into the grassy plain. He reached a safe distance inland from the river and straightened the direction of his charge when suddenly the river erupted in a spectacular wave.

'Wow,' chorused the questers together as the wave arched high in the air and came crashing down close to their line.

'Flicker fish,' said Tusks by way of explanation and without warning, he lowered his head and burst into a faster sprint.

'Wo,' said the questers together, grabbing a tusk each to hold on. They both smiled, excited with the rush of speed and marvelled by the massive wave that was still tunnelling along the top of the river and crashing down just beyond their reach. Tusks charged at full speed in line with the long, straight stretch of river. The siblings gasped to catch their breath.

Awesome, thought Daniel. '*This is awesome,*' he shouted to Sara.

'*Wooo-hooo,*' Sara roared into the air, enjoying the thrill.

Tusks kept up with the speeding wave until another big bend in the river came into view. As they approached the bend, he slowed, raised his snout and trumpeted a loud call. The wave suddenly collapsed and shrank back into the river. Daniel and Sara gazed in wonder when up from the river rose a fish that was as long as Tusks and half his width. The flicker fish had silver scales dotted all over with yellow and red spots. It spun in full circles as it rose, flicking two big fins out either side. For the briefest of moments the flicker fish stopped in the air with only its tail in the water. Tusks trumpeted another call and the flicker fish disappeared into the river.

'*What* was that all about?' Sara asked, still tingling with excitement from the full-speed charge.

'The flicker fish salutes us,' said Tusks.

'Why?' asked Daniel, gazing at the place in the river where the flicker fish had just disappeared.

'We raced,' said Tusks. The questers drew in their breath sharply and looked at each other wide-eyed. Tusks seemed aware of their surprise and chortled. 'It was a draw,' he added.

'*Hooray,*' roared Daniel. *That was the most fun I've had since, since I don't know when,* he thought.

'*Wooo-hooo,*' shouted Sara again. *That was so wild. Wooo-hooo.*'

Tusks had only slowed down slightly, to the pace he was running before he'd raced the flicker fish. He bent his neck back and called back to his passengers. 'Friends of the Boar, we've not many more leagues to travel now before we can see the ocean, and *then* Botanic Beaches. With no more delays, we'll make it before dusk.'

The earliest signs of evening had just begun to creep across the landscape. Insects began to hover around the plant-life. The heat of the strong sun had faded and it turned a darker orange as it slowly sank from overhead to a point on the horizon. The questers sat safe on Tusks back, exhilarated from the river race and cheered at the news that they were close.

Sara's hair flew out behind her. Excited, she smiled at Daniel, her heart full of renewed hope. 'Do you know, Dan? I think we're going to make it. I really do.'

Daniel, with his combat-trousers flapping in the wind, beamed beside her. 'We *are* going to make it,' he said determinedly. 'We've *got* the treasures, we'll *be* there on time *and* we'll fulfil the quest.' His eagerness made him giddy and he broke into a big smile too. 'Nothing can stop us now, Sis.' *Nothing.*

Up ahead, a wide, deep ditch lay across their path. The ditch took drain water down to the river. There were some short weeds growing on the side they approached from, while on the far side, a thick of tall bulrushes and reeds grew. Preparing for the leap, Tusks picked up speed as they got close. He had already made many much bigger jumps since they set out. Tusks launched into the air in the last moment before they reached the ditch. The questers braced themselves as the giant boar sailed through the air, and just as before, they easily cleared the gap.

Chapter 40
Hog Hunters

When Tusks landed, there was a loud smack accompanied by the sound of something snapping. The questers sailed through the air, barely with time to think.

'*What's going oooooooonnnn?*' shouted Daniel.

'*Aaahhhhhhhhhhhh,*' shouted Sara.

They hit the ground hard and lay among the reeds, dazed and slightly winded.

Daniel gathered his thoughts while he caught his breath back. *What just happened? Nothing feel's broken.* 'Sara, are you okay? He stood and helped her up.

Sara clutched her arm as she stood. 'I'm okay, I think. A bruised shoulder maybe. *What* happened there?'

'My thoughts exactly,' said Daniel. 'One second we were landing and the next we were thrown off Tusks' back.' He put a hand to his ear. 'Listen. That must be Tusks. Let's go see.'

Following the sounds of loud grunting and snorting, they parted a cluster of bulrushes to see Tusks hanging upside down from thick planks of wood. The questers gasped. The giant boar's neck and legs were snared in thick ropes. He thrashed and pulled, trying to free himself.

'Oh no,' cried Sara. 'What is it, Tusks?' The giant boar stopped thrashing and looked at them.

'This is a trap of the hog hunters.' So saying this, Tusks pulled again but with each pull, the snares closed tighter. Blood began to spill from the giant boar's legs where the ropes had tightened.

'We've got to get you down,' said Daniel.

'No,' said Tusks. 'You *must* flee. Our time together ends here.'

Daniel ignored him. He circled around Tusks, trying to make sense of the contraption. The wooden planks had been hidden under some chopped reeds with a hole dug underneath. The planks were fixed onto a pivot bar. *The planks must flip if weight is added,* Daniel thought, *And those ropes, they're as thick as my legs.* When Tusks landed, he was catapulted by the planks while at the same time, his neck and each of his legs were caught in the waiting snares. Tusks shook furiously, pulling on the ropes that held him fast.

Sara became frantic. 'Tusks please stop thrashing. You're making it worse. You're bleeding.' Trickles of blood appeared around Tusks' neck too and ran down his hide.

Tusks stopped again and looked at the questers. 'What're you still doing here?' he said with urgency. 'Flee! Flee I tell you, before it's too late.'

'But...but we've got the tor-folk swords,' said Daniel hesitantly. 'We can cut you loose.'

'What if the hog hunters get you?' added Sara. Tears welled in her eyes.

Tusks snorted. 'I fear not the hog hunters, but *you* should. If they catch you, they'll trade you to the men that cross the mountain.' A look of horror fell on the questers' faces.

'The marauders?' asked Daniel in disbelief.

'So they are called,' said Tusks. 'Not all men are friend of the Boar, and not all men are friend to *other* men.'

'But the hog hunters will get *you!*' cried Sara.

'If they do, so be it,' said Tusks forcefully. 'I didn't get to my size by fearing the hog hunters. I'm caught by my own fault, I should've smelt their trap but in my haste, I dropped my guard.' Suddenly, the distant shouts of men could be heard. 'Go, go now,' said Tusks.

Daniel ignored him again and began hacking at one of the hind-leg snares with his tor-folk sword. The snares were fixed to big posts made from tree trunks and hammered deep into the ground. Sara circled around frantically to see which direction the men were approaching from.

'You owe the Boar nothing,' said Tusks to Daniel.

'You were helping us,' said Daniel. 'That's why you're trapped.' He continued to hack at the nearest rope.

Sara reappeared beside them with her tor-folk sword at the ready. 'There's a bunch of them, I can't make out how many,' she began hacking at another of the snares while she talked. 'They're coming from behind us. They must've been hiding in the woods back there.'

The platted cord that made the rope frayed easily but to the questers' dismay, they discovered that the hog hunters had woven thin strands of copper through it to make it stronger.

'There's wire in it,' said Daniel, unable to hide the fear in his voice, 'it's taken longer than I thought it would.'

'No wonder it's cutting into him,' said Sara.

The shouts and roars of the approaching men suddenly sounded much closer. Sara ran to the edge of the ditch to look back the way they'd come. She saw a band of vicious men charging towards her. They were dressed all in brown, laced boots, britches and tunics.

'Oh no,' she cried in panic, 'they must've sprinted, they'll be here any minute, *and* there's loads of them *and* they've got weapons!' She raced back to join Daniel, her mind full of the images of the hog hunters. *They look so fierce with their long hair and beards, and everything they're wearing is made of boar-skin. Everything!*

'There's no time to cut me loose, flee friends,' shouted Tusks. For the third time in a row Daniel ignored him and continued to hack at the ropes. Finally the rope snapped and one of Tusks' hind-legs was free. *Thank goodness for tor-folk steel*, thought Daniel and made to start on another snare.

'Leave me, nowwww,' the giant boar roared. The questers fell to their knees with fright. 'Now. Not another word,' Tusks added, quietly but firmly. 'May magic of the heart guide you.'

Daniel and Sara stood shakily and picked up their swords. With tears in their eyes they took a last look at Tusks and ran away from the hog hunters' trap.

Using the bulrushes as cover, they crept along the riverbank. Tears stung their eyes and caused a lump in their throats.

Why wouldn't he let us help him, thought Sara.

We might've freed him, thought Daniel, *we might've.* They heard the sounds of Tusks struggling violently followed by the threatening calls of the hog hunters, dangerously close.

'First blood gets the rump,' shouted one.

'The hide is mine,' roared another.

'We've got to kill 'em first,' yelled someone else.

The questers stopped in their tracks.

Daniel closed his eyes for the briefest of moments. *No, we're not leaving him to die.* He opened them again, ready and alert.

Sara was looking at him with the same look of determination. 'We're going back?' she asked hopefully.

Daniel nodded once. 'We're going back. They kill Tusks they'll have to kill us first.'

They raced back as fast as their legs could carry them and reached Tusks as the hog hunters were reaching the ditch on the far side. Tusks bled badly from where wire in the snares dug into his skin.

'Hurry Dan,' screamed Sara. 'There's more chance if we work together.'

The approaching hog hunters stopped for a moment and stared in disbelief at the questers. Daniel and Sara ignored them, and working as one, they timed their swings to perfection. They hacked at the snare holding Tusks nearest front leg. After just three chops, the snare broke. Tusks swung his leg and snorted loudly. The sight broke the hog hunters from their shock and some of them threw their weapons while others scrambled into the ditch. Two spears, a pitchfork and a net landed just inches from the trap. The questers frantically hacked at the second snare and in a moment, both of Tusks front legs were free.

240

'*The neck, Daniel*,' screamed Sara. '*We need to free his neck.*' Several of the men climbed out of the ditch. Clutching their weapons, the hog hunters advanced on them, looking angry and menacing. The questers raised their swords aloft.

'*Stay still Tusks*,' shouted Sara.

'*Now*,' roared Daniel and questers swung with all the strength they could muster.

The tor-folk swords sang through the air straight and true. Both blades hit the neck-snare in the same spot and sliced right through it. The questers fell to the ground with the effort and Tusks tasted freedom in his throat. He trumpeted the call of his kind, and with monstrous force, he pulled on the final snare that still held his hind leg. Earth flew in all directions as the post that held the snare ripped from the ground. A dozen hog hunters back-stepped with fear but they were too late. Tusks swung his whole body in a wild circle and the wooden post, still fixed to his leg, was flung their way. Daniel and Sara watched from the ground as the post sailed over their heads and smashed into the nearest hog hunters, knocking them senseless. Many more hog hunters were climbing out of the ditch and brandishing their weapons.

Tusks stopped for the briefest of moments and yelled to the questers. '*Mount!*'

Daniel and Sara scrambled up the giant boar's back just as the second wave of hog hunters advanced. The hog hunters, with their faces twisted in rage shouted and roared towards the trio.

'*Stop thieves.*'

'*That's our catch.*'

'*We'll cut you up along with beast.*'

With the questers mounted, Tusks spun again sending the post swinging towards the men. This time, the hog hunters were ready and jumped back into the ditch to avoid it. This won Tusks a few precious seconds to escape and he burst into a charge along the riverbank.

The hog hunters quickly gave chase. Tusks' charge was hampered by the big post trailing out behind him and the questers looked back to see their attackers gaining on them. With weapons held aloft, the hog hunters roared and growled as they ran.

'*Aaaaarrr.*'

'*Stooopppppp.*'

'*Grrrrrrrr.*'

'*We're gonna get youuuu.*'

'*Faster Tusks, faster*,' screamed Sara, when a double-headed axe thrown by the nearest hog hunter lodged into the trailing post.

Daniel returned fire by flinging back his tor-folk sword. The hog hunter wasn't expecting it and the sword came down on his boot. He fell to the ground clutching his foot and howled in pain. Two of his band fell over him and in the confusion, Tusks got further ahead.

They came to an inlet on the riverbank when suddenly Tusks plunged into the river. 'Hold on tight. It's deep,' he snorted and quickly swam towards the other side.

The river was wide and deep with the water coming up close to where the questers sat. Tusks, holding his snout high above the water, was three-quarters way across when the first of the hog hunters reached the inlet. The men threw their spears. Sara turned and parried them away with her tor-folk sword.

Tusks reached the far bank and lumbered out of the river, still pulling the wooden post behind him. Turning to the sounds of splashing the questers gasped.

'*They're still following us,*' shouted Daniel.

'*Oh creepers,*' added Sara.

The hog hunters were taking daggers from their belts, placing them between their teeth and jumping in to swim across the river.

'Fear not friends,' said Tusks. 'Aid is near.' The giant boar looked back downstream to a point in the river that suddenly erupted in spectacular waves. Astonished, the questers gazed at the wall of water zooming up the river. The hog hunters still on the far bank saw the approaching waves and shouted warnings to the others in the river.

'*Look out.*'

'*Flicker fish.*'

'*Get out quick.*'

Those hog hunters still at the river's edge raced back up the bank followed quickly by the last few men that had just entered the water.

'Could it be?' asked Sara as she watched the remaining hog hunters, many of whom had reached the centre of the river, frantically swimming back the way they'd come.

'Flicker fish,' said Tusks in a voice deep and calm. The wave approached much faster than the hog hunters could swim but encouraged by their fellows, with desperation in their strokes most of them made it back to safety before the rolling waves arrived.

The hog hunters shouted and roared to those still in the river.

'*Hurry!*'

'*Get out, get out!*'

'*Here they come!*'

Two of them didn't make it out and the wall of water hit them side on. Those hog hunters closest to the edge jumped back to safety as the waves arched out and soaked them.

The questers watched on speechless at the two hog hunters still in the river. They were pushed along the river at the head of the wave by unseen forces. The wave surged by with such speed that soon two the hog hunters were out of sight, far up river.

On the far bank, some of the hog hunters stood shocked, staring up the river after their lost men. Others stared across the river at Tusks and the questers with a mixture of fear and relief on their faces.

Tusks glared back and whispered low and menacing. 'We'll meet again hog hunters. I have your scent!' Suddenly he snorted loudly and startled the staring men.

Soaked and defeated, the hog hunters gathered themselves and retreated, trudging in small groups back the way they'd come. The evening sun, burning dark-orange, hung low in the sky.

Daniel turned to Tusks. 'What now?'

'Cut me loose of this log,' said Tusks, and shook his hind leg. '*Now*, we run like the wind!'

Chapter 41
Howlers

With the wind at their backs they entered broad open plains of green and gold-coloured grasses.

'Look yonder,' said Tusks loudly, so as to be heard above the thumps of his pounding hooves. 'Ahead are the dunes of Botanic Beaches. It won't be long now before we reach them.' Daniel and Sara strained their eyes trying to make out the gentle slopes of the dunes ahead.

Sara beamed. *We did it,* she thought, *we've made it on time.*

Daniel grinned. *Almost there.* Their hearts soared.

'I think I can see them,' called Sara excitedly, as her hair whipped out behind her.

'Me too,' shouted Daniel, 'there're boulders up ahead, and those purple hills beyond them must be the dunes.'

Tusks snorted. 'What boulders?' he said, still charging at full speed.

Daniel pointed. 'Those big shapes dotted across the plains, aren't they boulders?'

'No,' said Tusks, but said no more.

Daniel and Sara gazed curiously as they approached the big shapes and together, they gasped with surprise.

'The boulders,' cried Sara, 'They're moving.'

'They're not boulders,' said Tusks, '*They* are howlers.' With Moody Woods off to their right, shimmering in a myriad of colours, the giant boar pounded right towards the roaming herd.

'Wow,' said the questers as they got closer to the strange creatures.

'They're like nothing I've ever seen before,' said Daniel. 'They're enormous.'

'They're beautiful,' said Sara, and made a quick count. *Twenty-four, I think.*

The howlers stood twice as tall as Tusks. Their bodies were pear-shaped and covered in faun fur. The herd plodded along at a slow space, stooping here and there to pick flowers and eat them, petals first then stems. The massive creatures ignored the trio as Tusks ran around and between them. Up close, the questers could make out their features clearly.

'Their big brown eyes are so bright and happy,' said Sara.

Daniel nodded, fascinated. *And the way their mouths curl in a gentle smile, they seem so content. Not a worry in the world,* he thought to himself.

The howlers' legs were thick and muscular and ended in huge feet with three bulbous toes. Their arms were thinner, and they supported three nimble fingers.

Look at those fingers, thought Sara, *perfect for picking flowers. Ashar did say that Harry ate flowers.* She gasped and put her hand to her mouth. *Ashar! Harry!*

'Stop, Tusks,' she wailed loudly. Daniel leapt with fright and the nearest howlers bounded off a few paces. The giant boar skidded to a stop, tearing up earth as he did so.

'What is it?' said Tusks.

'Tusks,' said Sara urgently. 'Can you take us into Moody Woods?'

'Why Sara?' said Daniel, frowning. 'What do you want to go back there for, of all places?'

'Ashar, Daniel,' said Sara, 'we promised him we'd come back for Harry.' Daniel's eyes widened, and with his mouth open, he nodded slowly. *She's right, we did. I'd forgotten.*

Tusks looked at the sky. The heat had long since left the evening sun; fading, it dipped low on the horizon.

'Friends,' said Tusks, 'we're but a league away from Botanic Beaches, but sunset approaches. There's little time for further delay if we're to make it there by dusk.'

'Sara's face filled with anguish and she hung her head. 'So if we go to Harry, we fail the quest.'

Daniel looked at his sister with pride. *After all we've been through, she still thinks of others. Good for you, Sis, succeed or fail you're a hero to me.* 'No Sara, you're right, a promise is a promise and *we* promised Ashar,' he said determinately.

Sara looked at her brother and brushed away a tear that had just gathered in the corner of her eye. She nodded and leaned over to look at Tusks face. 'There's a howler somewhere in Moody Woods, do you think you can find him Tusks?'

The giant boar turned right in the direction of the woods. 'Hang on,' he said and burst into a full charge. Leaving the howler herd behind, they quickly reached Moody Woods.

Crashing through the brush, the questers had to lean low to avoid getting struck by low-hanging branches. The woods around them danced in an ever-changing display of colours. Sniffing the air, Tusks swerved to his left and continued the charge, leaping over an orange log, trampling a red, thorny bush and bursting through a patch of purple nettles. The giant boar planted his hooves into the earth and stopped with such suddenness that

245

Daniel and Sara almost fell off. Sitting in front of them, throwing pebbles in small stream was Harry the howler.

Daniel said the first thing that came into his mind. 'He looks just like the others.' The questers slid off Tusks' back and walked slowly towards Harry.

Sara held her palms up in a gesture of friendliness. 'Hello there,' she said. Harry acknowledged them with a side glance from his eyes but did not look straight at them. He stopped throwing pebbles and stood, shyly awaiting their approach.

Daniel stared up at the giant creature. 'You're a big fellow.'

'Howlers do not speak,' said Tusks, 'not in a language we would understand. Stroke his fur gently and he will accept you as a friend.'

Daniel and Sara together placed a hand on the furry leg of the howler.

'Oh so soft,' said Sara. Harry responded by sounding a soft coo.

'Gosh,' said Daniel, 'it sounds like a pigeon.'

'Hey Harry,' said Sara, 'we don't have much time. We came to tell you that there are howlers roaming close by, your own kind.' Harry cooed again and sat back down, his mouth curved in a gentle smile. Sara's face dropped. 'He doesn't seem to understand. Tusks, can you tell him?'

Tusks shook his head from side to side. 'Howlers do not speak,' he repeated, 'not in the tongue of human or boar anyway.'

'Oh no,' cried Sara, her anguish returning. 'What're we going to do?'

Daniel clicked his fingers. 'Didn't Ashar say that the call of his own kind would help? We need to get him to howl. Quick Sara, help me find some flowers.'

Sara raised her eyes with hope. 'Will it work?'

'It's worth a try,' said Daniel and together they started to look around for any type of flower they could find.

'Make haste,' cautioned Tusks as he sniffed the air. 'Time is short *and* these woods aren't safe.'

All too aware of the dangers in Moody Woods, the questers searched frantically.

Sara looked behind the trees and in bushes. 'Oh no,' she said, 'there's none around here.'

Daniel returned, having scoured a few paces away. 'These will have to make do; they're all I could find.' He was holding a bunch of yellow-head dandelions. He handed them to Sara and she slowly extended her hand out to Harry. Daniel made a silent wish. *Let's hope dandelions are flowers to howlers.*

Harry the howler took the dandelions in his nimble fingers and swallowed them in one go. His throat gulped and he let out a mighty howl that echoed throughout all of Moody Woods.

All the trees and plants around them shimmered in a display of bright colours. Before the final echoes of the howl faded, it was answered in kind by another howl, followed by a second then a third. Harry stood and his head shot up, alert and listening. Within a few moments, a whole chorus of howls sounded through the woods. Harry, with eyes wide and happy, arched back facing the canopy and howled at the skies so loudly that the questers blocked their ears to drown out the sound. The entire woods exploded into a rainbow of brilliant colours as the delighted howler turned where he stood and ran in the direction from which the howls were coming.

Harry charged in a straight line on his way out of Moody Woods. Bushes got squashed, nettles trampled and trees pushed aside with no effort at all to the giant creature. The trio watched him go.

'You've freed the howler,' said Tusks. 'Now *we* must leave, for danger is near.' The questers heeded the warning and scrambled up Tusks' back. They couldn't see the gizords that had gathered in the bushes just beyond the stream.

Chapter 42
Monkey Business

The questers had barely mounted when a chorus of high-pitched screams rang through the woods. Daniel and Sara leapt with fright. Tusks bolted to a charge along the track that Harry had left behind. The trio were assailed from the trees. Creatures jumped down atop them screeching wildly as they landed.

Sara screamed. *'We're under attack, help!'* Something had landed on her head and was pulling her hair.

'Aaaaahhhhhhh,' shouted Daniel, *'They're trying to topple me!'* There was a creature on either side of Tusks pulling at Daniel's legs. Daniel managed to kick one of them off when suddenly another landed on Tusks' head right in front of him. *'They're monkeys!'* he shouted, *'Just like Ashar! We're being attacked by monkeys!'* The monkey in front of him was black all over except for an orange face. The monkey, baring small pointed teeth had grabbed him by the nose and pulled hard.

'Aaaaaaaaaaaaahhhhhhhhhhhhhh,' Daniel roared in pain. Using its long tail, which ended with pointed shanks, the monkey slapped Daniel in the face and let out a piercing scream. Others rallied to the call and sailed down out of the trees.

Sara yanked the monkey by its tail off her head and threw it to the ground but two more landed on her shoulders and pulled at her arms. *'Daniel, help,'* she screamed, *'they're going to knock me off.'*

But Daniel had troubles of his own. Several monkeys, all looking alike, had landed on and around him and were pulling at his ears, nose, hair, arms and legs. One even swung from the satchel that contained the treasures from their quest. The screeching of the monkeys was deafening. Tusks swung his head this way and that, trying to dislodge monkeys that swung from his tusks and bounced on his snout. He was unable to do much without also throwing Daniel and Sara off his back so instead he kept running.

A monkey came summersaulting from a tree and cannoned into Sara knocking her backwards. She fell off Tusks' back and screamed as she fell.

'Aaaaaaaa, heellp.'

Daniel saw her fall and screamed.

'Sara, nooo.'

Filled with fear and worry he flung off his attackers and leapt back to catch her, his arm outstretched. Sara reached to catch Daniel's arm but all she managed to grab was the bone-whistle from around his neck. Sara hit the ground hard and lay there stunned. Daniel was about to leap off Tusks when he was stormed by a fresh onslaught of monkeys. They attacked him violently from all sides. Some slapped and punched him, others pulled and scratched him.

Lying between Tusks' shoulders, Daniel roared at the top of his voice.

'Stop tusks, stop, Sara fell.'

The giant boar stopped still in his tracks and spun around. He made to charge back for Sara when several gizords crawled out from the underbrush and blocked the path. Tusks spun again to discover more gizords filling the track behind him. They were completely surrounded. He lowered his head to point his tusks forwards and snorted menacingly. The scaled creatures spread their claws and hissed through their teeth at the giant boar.

Sara's head cleared and using her arms, she propped herself up. Her eyes filled with horror at the sight of the gizords up ahead. Shaking, she felt something in her hand. *Zac's bone-whistle.* Trembling, she raised the whistle to her lips and blew with all her might.

The shrill tune of the whistle rang through the canopy and momentarily sent the monkeys scampering back to the trees.

Daniel sat up and looked back at Sara, his eyes full of dread. *Sara!*

Tusks with foam bubbling from his snout snorted loudly. 'Hold on, Daniel, this fight is mine.' The leader of the giant boar lowered his spear-like tusks and spun in a wild circle as gizords closed in from all sides.

The last thing Daniel saw was a lone gizord slithering up the path behind Sara. *'Behind you, Sara,'* he screamed. The monkeys attacked again.

Hearing Daniel's warning, Sara turned her head quickly to see the yellow eyes of a gizord inches from her face. Its forked tongue darted in and out between its long teeth. The gizord opened its mouth and recoiled, ready to pounce. Terrified into action, Sara rose to her knees, drew her tor-folk sword and slashed the blade forwards. The gizord's tongue flew through the air, sliced clean off. Hissing and squirming, the scaly creature darted back into the undergrowth. Sara flung the tor-folk sword after it. Wild rasping and hissing followed as the sword found its mark. Sara found herself defenceless. *I shouldn't've done that!* she thought. She looked up the path towards Tusks and Daniel and saw them bombarded by an onslaught of gizords and monkeys. She looked back down the path again and her heart sank. *Oh no, I'm dead, we're dead.* She sat on the ground and burst into tears. Dozens more gizords w—ere crawling up the path towards her, hissing and spitting as they came.

Tusks spun in a frenzied circle. Using his tusks, he lifted gizords and flung them far into the woods, others he impaled and skewered. Those that attacked low were trampled by his giant hooves and crushed into the ground.

Daniel was frantic. *Hang on Sara, if only these blasted monkeys would get off so I can come back for you.* He kicked a monkey away that pulled from his neck and another took its place. *The monkeys want the satchel!* he finally realised. The monkeys jumped at him in wave after wave. It was all he could do to stay on and not let the monkeys take the satchel. They beat him on the head, scratched his face and bit his ankles. Daniel clung to satchel with both hands as several monkeys pulled at it.

Sara took a last look up the track at Daniel and Tusks, fighting off their attackers. She stood slowly, shaking at the knees and picked up a rock as she went. Using her sleeve, she wiped the tears from her eyes and turned to face the many gizords that were almost upon her. *This is for you Dan, if I can even kill one, it might buy you time to escape.* She swallowed her fear and threw the rock. The gizords pounced. Sara braced herself for the oncoming claws. The rock sailed through the air and landed among the scaly bodies and hissing tongues. The gizords exploded through the air, some were flung into the trees and others off to the sides. Sara fell backwards with shock and disbelief. *One rock did that?* A familiar growl snarled amidst the chaos, and there was Bison. The rockwilder was grabbing gizord in his mighty jaws, flinging some into the woods and crushing the throats of others.

Overcome, Sara burst into tears again. 'Bison, it's *you*, you came.' She scrambled to her feet and ran back up track towards Tusks. Sara took a last look back to see many more gizords arrive and turn their attack on Bison. *Oh Bison, you brave, brave dog. I wish I could help you but I must get to Daniel.* Bison stood his ground and continued to fight.

Further up the track, Tusks fought furiously. Gizords bit into his legs and dug their claws into his haunches. But Tusk's hide was thick and tough. He slammed the gizords against the nearest trees then trampled them. Daniel tried his best to hold onto the satchel while wrestling with the monkeys but suddenly the strap broke and he felt his grip on it loosen.

'No,' he roared, '*we fought to get these, and we'll fight to keep them.*' A monkey came leaping from the canopy, screaming louder than the rest.

'*Aye aye aayyyyyyyye. You'll not fight alone pink human.*' The monkey landed next to Daniel and immediately grabbed two other monkeys, knocked their heads together and flung them off Tusks' back. Daniel was speechless as it took him a moment to realise what was happening. Meanwhile, the screeching monkey punched, bit and slapped at the others that were still attacking Daniel.

Daniel finally realised. *Could it be?* 'Ashar is it you? Are you alive?'

The small monkey continued to fight his fellow creatures. 'Course it's me, in't it? Who else would it be? What trouble you get yourself in this time boy?' asked Ashar as he summersaulted into three more monkeys and sent them flying.

'Ashar, Sara, have you seen her?' said Daniel urgently.

'Back there with the puppy ain't she,' said Ashar, as he grabbed the last of the attacking monkeys by its shanked tail and bit it hard. The monkey screeched in pain and leapt back into the trees.

Daniel stared back down the track to see Sara running towards them, wobbling as she ran. *'Sara!'* he roared, *'We're coming.'* Tusks flung off the last gizord, and free from attack, he ran back towards Sara. Tusks reached her, skidded to a stop and lowered his hind legs. Sara was breathless and through eyes stinging with tears she stared at his back.

'Ashar, is it really you?' she managed.

'It's me sure as it's you little lady,' said Ashar.

Daniel stuck out his hand. 'Quick, climb on Sara, the gizords and monkeys could be back any moment.'

Tusks suddenly flicked his rump and Daniel tumbled to the ground. 'No,' said the giant boar. 'Carry on alone. Follow the howler's track out of the woods. Go, as fast your legs can take you, for dusk is upon us. Go now!'

'But Tusks,' said Daniel confused, 'won't you come with us.'

'No,' said Tusks, 'I stay to fight with the hound.' Without another word, Tusks charged down the track towards Bison, who had just disappeared under a swarm of countless gizords.

Sara watched him go, her eyes filled with horror. *'Ashar, won't you come with us?'* she called pleadingly.

'I stay to fight with the hog and the dog!' the hanging monkey shouted from where he still sat on Tusks' back. *'Run my friends, run!'*

Daniel made to go but Sara leaned over and cried aloud. *'Nooo, no please come back. Ashar, Tusks, Bison.'*

Daniel pulled her by the arm. 'C'mon, Sara, we've got to go.'

'But we have to help them, we have to,' Sara protested.

Daniel grabbed her tightly by both arms and looked into her eyes. 'Listen to me Sara, we can't help them, and if we don't go now, it will all have been for nothing.'

Sara closed her eyes for the briefest of moments and swallowed her grief. She opened them again, squeezed on Daniel's arms and nodded. 'Let's go then,' she whispered.

Holding hands, the questers raced towards the last rays of the failing sun that shone down the track.

Chapter 43
Failure

Leaving the sounds of battle behind them the questers, burst out of the woods at full sprint. They were vaguely aware of the howlers bunched together in greeting, far off to their left. Up ahead to their right, the purple dunes of Botanic Beaches were still visible in the last shadows of the fading sun; they raced towards them. As they ran, their thoughts raced with them.

They're still fighting back there, Daniel thought. *So tired, but can't stop now, almost there.*

Sara was one step behind him. *Can't breathe,* she thought, *need to stop. It looks like the place up ahead, hard to tell, it's getting dark. Hope we make it, hope our friends back there make it. Creepers.*

Sara stumbled and fell. 'Sorry Dan, so...' she caught her breath, 'I'm so tired.'

Daniel stopped to help her up. 'Me too, Sis,' but it's almost night time, we've got to find the wishing-well.' He helped her to her feet.

They took off again but only made it a few paces when Daniel tripped and tumbled along the ground.

Sara helped him up. 'C'mon Dan, it's around here somewhere. I recognise the meadow we're in. It looks like the one we started out from when we got here five days ago.'

Daniel stood, breathless. He frowned and looked around. 'Five days ago, seems like five years ago. You're right, though, this looks like the place but I don't see the wishing-well *anywhere.*' An edge of panic had entered his tone.

'Oh no,' said Sara, clasping her hands to her mouth. 'What if we're too late?' The pair scanned around the meadow desperately. Their search became frantic until Sara noticed something off to her right. *'Here Daniel look, quick,'* she called as she ran. Daniel joined her beside a big saucer-shaped rock resting in the grass. They stared silently at the rock for a moment till Sara spoke quietly. 'It's the same rock, isn't it? We've made it back.'

'Yes,' said Daniel quietly, staring down. 'We must be...' he hesitated, 'we must be too late,' he barely whispered the last. He swallowed, trying to control his feelings but couldn't stop his eyes filling with water.

Sara remained still for a moment but despair washed over her and putting her hands on her head she fell to her knees. *'Oh no,'* she cried aloud. 'We...we...we,' she struggled to find the words, 'we failed. We *are* too late! *And* it's all my fault.' She burst into tears.

Daniel, overcome with grief, covered his face. His tears leaked through his fingers. 'It's *my* fault,' he said from behind his hands. 'I knew the stupid plum seed wasn't the nourishing stone.' He began to sob. 'And we've only tiny pieces of the other two treasures. I was a fool to think we had a chance to fulfil the quest.'

Daniel's words only made Sara weep all the louder. 'It's *my* fault we're late,' she said, distraught. 'I insisted we go back into the woods for Harry. We might've made it here on time if not for me.' Her voice rose to wailing. 'Our friends back there could be *dead* because of me. We've no way home because of me!' She squeezed her eyes tight and cried uncontrollably.

Daniel wept openly and knelt down beside her. 'After all we've been through,' he whispered hoarsely.

The memories of their journey came flooding back to them: The excitement, the wonder, the frights, the chases, the battles, the danger, the friends, the foes, the fun, the fear, the pain, the losses, the victories and last, the failure. Anguish overtook them and their tears flowed freely down their cheeks. They put their arms around one another and as they sobbed, their shoulders shook. Unaware of the passing time, the night slowly crept upon them and still they sat crying, alone and forlorn.

Eventually, Daniel sat up, shivered and dried his eyes. He looked up at the skies. 'Thank goodness for the bright moon, otherwise we'd be sitting in the pitch dark.' He criss-crossed his arms across his chest. 'Brrr, it's getting cold, eh Sara?' Sara kept her head down and sobbed quietly. Daniel looked at her and his heart melted. 'Hey, Sis, c'mon now. It's not your fault, it's not anyone's fault. Tobias said *before* sunset, but he didn't say how long before sunset. He could've meant noon, he could've meant first thing this morning!'

Sara glanced up at Daniel through glassy eyes. 'But *what're* we going to do Daniel?' her voice croaked, strained from all the crying.

Daniel punched one hand into the palm of the other and spoke determinately. 'We're going to...eh we're going to,' he hesitated and began to pace. 'I'll tell you what we're going to do, we'll...' he looked around searching for an idea but when nothing came, he stopped pacing. A frown creased his brow and he slumped back down beside Sara. 'I don't know what we're going to do,' he said, 'but I do know things always look better in the morning.' He looked away and gulped. *Although I can't really see how.* 'Why don't you get some rest, I'll keep watch.'

Sara caught the look on Daniel's face and her sadness turned to anger. She jumped up and slapped him on the arm. *'You don't fool me Daniel Taylor,'* she shouted. *'Don't you think I know when you're worried? You've no idea what we're going to do, do you?'* she hit him again.

Daniel jumped up and shouted back. *'Yes, Sara, I am worried, I'm frightened actually.'* He threw his arms up in air and leaned towards Sara. *'For all I know, we're stuck on this crazy island forever. Satisfied?'*

Sara burst out crying again and covered her face in her hands. 'I'm scared, Daniel, I'm really scared.'

Daniel stared at her for a moment then drew her to him in a hug and leaned his head on hers. 'Me too, Sara,' he said, straining his voice so as not to cry again, but his eyes betrayed him and the tears returned. He squeezed his eyes tight and whispered again, 'Me too.'

A flash of bright light snapped across the air accompanied by a sharp crackling sound. The questers jumped with fright and stumbled as some unseen force knocked them over. Before they had time to think, the ground shook with loud thumps. They sat up and looked warily back across the meadow to see Tusks trotting towards them and Ashar sitting between the giant boar's shoulders.

Sara's eyes bulged wide. 'Could it be?'

'It *is*,' said Daniel. 'It's them.' He jumped up and rushed to meet them with Sara at his heel. They ran until they slammed into Tusks and threw their arms around the boar's neck.

'You're alive, thank goodness,' cried Sara, still hugging the boar. 'Ashar, Tusks, it's so good to see you.'

Relief washed over Daniel and after a moment, he took a step back. 'Those monkeys, friends of yours, Ashar?'

'No friends of mine,' said Ashar. 'Those there are shank monkeys, new to the woods they are. Up to no good they are, that's why old Ashar was following them. Good thing too as I found you humans.'

'I think they were after the treasures in the satchel,' said Daniel, patting the small bag by his side. 'What happened to them?'

'Fled,' said Ashar.

'And the gizords?' Daniel asked.

'Dead,' said Tusks.

Sara let go of Tusks. 'What of Bison?'

'Fierce hound,' said Tusks and Ashar together. Ashar jumped off Tusk's back and landed on Sara's shoulders.

'I'm so glad you're okay,' Sara said gently. Ashar nuzzled into her before jumping back onto Tusks. 'But is Bison *okay?*' she added anxiously.

'The puppy is fine,' said Ashar, 'he ran off into the woods when the fight was over.'

'You guys have no idea how happy we are to see you,' said Sara, 'we were just, hey wait a minute,' she glanced around with a puzzled look on her face. 'I've just noticed it's...it's so bright.'

'Yeah,' said Daniel, looking around. The meadow was lit up by a strange bright, white light. 'There was that crackling noise, then a flash, but then you guys came and,' he pointed at Tusks and Ashar then turned back in the direction they had ran from. He gasped and grabbed Sara's arm.

Sara saw it too and stood there wide-eyed. Beside the saucer-shaped rock, right in the spot where they had sat moments before, now sat the wishing-well. White light gushed out of it up into the air before spreading over the meadow in a mushroom cloud. Suddenly, there was a hiss of mist and within it, the silhouette of a man appeared. The mist cleared and there stood Tobias Wells.

The well-keeper turned his palms upward and spoke, 'Greetings well travellers, and friends.' The questers stared, mesmerised by his enchanting voice that sounded from far and near at once. 'Come closer,' said Tobias, beckoning with his long white fingers while his words echoed around the meadow.

Daniel and Sara started forwards slowly. As before, Tobias was dressed all in black and as he stood patiently amidst the mystical white light, his clothes crackled of magic. He still wore his top hat above his bushy silver eyebrows. The lapels of his coat swayed gently in the night breeze.

As the questers got closer, they were drawn to his face and Sara found herself confused once again at the timeless look to his mystical face. *He could be as ancient as the mountain or just a young man, it's so hard to tell,* she thought to herself.

Daniel was captivated by Tobias's intense stare. *I forgot how tall he was,* he thought, as he craned his neck up to meet Tobias's piercing eyes, *could he be reading my mind?* He gulped nervously.

The questers stopped a few paces in front of Tobias, vaguely aware that Tusks and Ashar had joined them and stood quietly behind.

Silence followed for a brief moment till Tobias spoke in a commanding tone. 'Speak now of your quest,' he gestured with his palm outward, 'how did you fair?'

Uncertain, Daniel and Sara exchanged glances. Sarah nodded urgently to Daniel. Daniel frowned and fumbled with his fingers. 'Let me see, it's hard to know where to start,' he said uncertainly.

Tobias's jet-black eyes twinkled. 'The beginning is always a good place to start, I find.'

'Gosh,' said Daniel, 'the beginning seems like a life time ago, so much has happened since then. We got off to a good start anyway. We found the hag's staff pretty quick.' He turned back and gestured to Ashar. 'Actually, it was all thanks to Ashar really. But then,' Daniel lowered his head and looked at the ground, defeated. 'Then we broke it on the mountain. He looked at Sara but she kept her lips tight so he looked back again to Tobias. 'I kept a piece of the shattered staff.' He took it from his satchel and held it on the palm of his hand. Tobias stared at him but remained silent. 'I guess it was a lame thing to do, now that I think about it,' Daniel finished quietly and closed his hand around the piece of staff. He looked again to Sara for help.

Sara tried to take over. 'We got the shard of the dragon's tooth as well. We had it for ages, but,' she hesitated as the feelings of defeat returned to her too. 'But we lost it in the lake,' she said in sad tones.

Daniel took over again, speaking low. 'We foolishly thought we had the nourishing stone but it turned out to be just a plain old plum seed. I kept it though, as the point of the shard got stuck in it. I thought if we made it back, I could show it to you as proof.' Daniel took the plum seed from the satchel and held it out to Tobias, but when Tobias didn't respond, he quickly put it back in the satchel again along with the piece of staff.

Tobias stood straight and spoke aloud. 'Is that it?' The questers trembled as the well-keeper's voice boomed and echoed across the night sky.

'We tried our best to get the treasures for you,' said Daniel, sadly.

'We tried to get back here before dusk on the fifth day, we really tried,' added Sara pleadingly.

'Is this all you have to tell me after five days and four nights on Well-Keeper Island?' said Tobias, his face bright and unreadable.

Daniel and Sara looked at each other, trying to think of something to add, but all that came back to them was the despair, emptiness and the feelings of loss. Sara started to cry, and although Daniel tried not to, he couldn't hold back tears of his own. Sara buried her hands in her face and wept, while Daniel looked at the ground sorrowfully.

'We're truly sorry, Mr Wells,' said Daniel as he choked back his tears. 'We really *did try* to fulfil the quest but we failed you, and we failed so many others too.'

'Such a short account of your stay here,' said Tobias in a curious tone. 'Were you not guided by magic of the heart?'

Through teary eyes Daniel and Sara looked at each once again.

'Maybe we were,' said Daniel quietly, 'but we still failed, we weren't worthy of the task,' he finished with a whisper.

Tobias spun and reached the wishing-well in one big stride. 'So much talk of unworthiness and failure, but so little of your journey. Let us take a look and see.' He clapped his hands and suddenly the well bubbled up full of water. The water, crystal-clear, spilled over the tilted rim and splashed onto the ground. The questers watched uncertainly. Tobias beckoned to them. 'Come join me.' And so saying he dipped his finger into the well. The well water rose up out of the well and funnelled through the air in an arch, cascading down again onto the saucer-shaped rock nearby. Tobias withdrew his finger then and the water arching through the air collapsed to the ground with a splash.

The questers reached Tobias's side just as the water on the rock settled into a still, clear pool. Tusks, with Ashar on board trod over too and the ground vibrated with his approach, causing ripples in the clear pool atop the rock.

'Gather round now,' said Tobias, 'and let us bear witness to your quest on Well-Keeper's Island.' He regarded the questers through his intense eyes and with a slight tilt of his head he spoke in a voice as strange and magical as the island itself. 'Behold your ordeal, for *only* then can we see wherein the failure lies.'

The ripples in the pool stilled. Astonished, the questers' faces lit up, for suddenly a blurred image appeared in the water pool. The water shimmered with colours and the image took shape; it was Daniel and Sara standing together in Appledown Orchards.

Chapter 44
Magic of the Heart

'Two young people on a journey you were, wishing for adventure.' Tobias's voice filled the night. 'To Well-Keeper Island you came and undertook a daring and difficult charge.'

Daniel and Sara stared into the rock pool, astounded, as they could see themselves five days ago, happily picking fruit in the orchards.

Tobias continued. 'That charge was to search this island fair for treasures three, and return to this place we now stand, with all that you have found.'

Daniel's brow twisted to a frown. *Not that we found a whole lot.*

Sara saw him and her thoughts followed his. *We returned, but with no treasures and no nothing.* Her face became sad.

The questers exchanged a brief look of defeat before their attention was drawn back to the rock pool by the loud boom of Tobias's commanding tone.

'One more instruction you were given, *but* was it followed?'

What instruction? Sara thought, alarmed, *I don't recall any other.*

Daniel shot her a worried glance. *What's he talking about.*

Tobias swept his arm through the air. 'Be guided by magic of the heart, *that's* what you were told. *But...*but were you?' he said in hushed tones. Silence briefly fell. 'Let us see!' Tobias roared and clapped his hands once. The skies echoed back the sound and white light flashed.

The questers watched, speechless, as suddenly the image in the rock pool changed again. They could see themselves holding hands, their faces filled with surprise, flying through the colourful clouds as they travelled through the wishing-well. Tobias's voice soared,

'Magic of the heart is Wonder, the *wonder* that comes with new experiences and discoveries.' The pool swirled and the image shifted. When it cleared again, the questers could see themselves in a tunnel, deep within the Rocky Rise. Daniel is hanging over the side and Sara is pulling him upward by the staff strapped through his fleece. Their faces filled with wonder as Daniel floats upward. The scene quickly changed to Daniel standing in the meadow that borders the tall grasses. He's got the plumb seed in his hands, his eyes are wide with discovery and he speaks, 'Sara, it's a piece of the shard of the dragon's tooth. It must be!'

The questers stared into the rock-pool mesmerised, as they could hear themselves talk from the reflection, but their voices trailed with echoes and sounded far away. The image changed again, this time it was Sara standing near the Boar drove and the river, her face was alight with wonder. She was saying, 'That's it! We've got the nourishing stone!'

Once again the colours swirled before they cleared to show the questers sitting on the back of the flying horses. They were soaring high over the Rocky Rise while viewing the island far below. Daniel was saying, 'It's spectacular,' and Sara, 'It's amazing, just amazing.'

Tobias's voice sent ripples over the images.

'Magic of the heart is Awe, the *awe* we feel at seeing great and beautiful sights.'

Still on the backs of the horses, the scene shifted to them flying across the island with the stallion Lightning speaking, 'Behold the Great Lake created by our master, in all its glory,' and the questers saying, 'Wow,' together as they stared at the golden lake on the horizon, lit up in the evening sun.

The image changed again to show the questers atop Tusks' back, staring in awe up to the skies at countless gulls passing overhead. And then again to the riverside when the giant flicker fish jumped in the river. Shocked, the questers took a step back as it appeared as though the flicker's head rose out of the rock pool before the image changed again.

'Magic of the heart is Curiosity,' said Tobias, '*curiosity* in things strange and unknown.'

The rock pool showed the questers in Moody Woods looking at the silk-trail spider web and Sara saying, 'Let's follow it to see where it leads.' The waters rippled, and suddenly, they saw themselves standing amongst the shrubs at the foot of the Rocky Rise. Sara is asking Zac about the bonions, 'And you say they talk, Mr Zac; is that what they're doing when we hear that bubbling noise? And do you know what they're saying?'

'Magic of the heart is learning, *learning* from what we see and hear.'

The rock pool showed Zac using his hook and the hag's staff to loosen the rocks to topple them down on top of the climbing gizords. The image blurred momentarily then cleared to show the questers using leverage to move the boulders that held Sketch. An instant later, they were sitting in Zac's cave and Sara was listening intently to Gertie, her voice sounded sweet and far away, 'I believe everyone has magic in their lives if they just take time to realise it. It exists in people's hearts and minds and is full of never-ending mystery.'

Tusks and Ashar remained standing behind Daniel and Sara, silently watching the scenes of the questers adventure. Light pouring from the wishing-well filled the meadow and Tobias's voice filled all the space around them,

'Magic of the heart is Caring. Caring for your friends; caring for those less fortunate than you; *caring* for those in need.'

The image in the pool changed to show the questers standing in Moody Woods, watching after Ashar, Sara was biting her lip and saying, 'Will he be alright?' The water swirled and images started to change quickly now, flashing from one scene to the next. They were in the mountain cave with Gertie patting the blanket around Sara's shoulders. They were at the mouth of the tunnel and Daniel turned to hug Gertie goodbye with a warm embrace. They were pointing down the ravine towards Sketch. Next Sara was struggling down the face of the ravine. The image blurred and they were standing in the Tor-Folk settlement to the sound of the alarm bell, Sara was shouting, 'No, Daniel, we're not splitting up again! You fought the bats, you fought the rats and you lied about the marauders! All to protect me! Well I'm part of this too and I'm not leaving your side!' The scene changed again to show the questers kneeling over Tess, rubbing grass over her hide to keep her warm, Sara's eyes filled with tears. The pool swirled and there they were, once again in Moody Woods and Sara was handing Harry, the Howler, the dandelions.

The gentlest of breezes disturbed the night air and the magical white light that filled the meadow shimmered. The water in the rock pool stilled and settled. Daniel and Sara looked away from the pool and looked at each other uncertainly. Sara's lips were pressed tight and Daniel's brow was creased in a frown.

Tobias Wells stepped in between them. 'You still don't see? Then *let us* see more,' his voice crackled from the earth and sky.

'Magic of the heart is Wisdom. The wisdom in wise words; the wisdom in good ideas; the *wisdom* in sensible choices.'

The scene in the pool suddenly flashed to life, startled, the questers jumped back a step. Once again, they stared into the water, this time to see themselves deep in the tunnels of the Rocky Rise. Daniel was saying, 'The opposite of brave is not scared, it's cowardly, and you're no coward. If you do something that puts yourself in danger even though you're scared, it makes you even braver than if you weren't scared in the first place.' Still in tunnel, the scene changed to Sara crawling along in the dark while banging the flint off the rock for light. The pool fogged up and Daniel appeared in midst of it, kneeling on his hunkers on the Rocky Rise, they could hear his voice coming from far away, 'Sara, please listen carefully. Stay where you are and I'll try to find you. It's no use us both moving around. Sound carries better on the ground, so stay low.' Suddenly, Lightning was there on the Rocky Rise talking to Sketch and the questers, 'There *is* no greater good in this life than to risk your own life for another.'

'Magic of the heart is laughter, the humour we see in little things that make us *smile* and lift our hearts.'

The pool flashed and there was Sara in the meadow trying to pick up the disappearing bonions, and Daniel next to her laughing, 'I guess they don't like you either' came his muffled voice from the pool. The water swirled and there they were eating stew by the cave dwellers fire, warm laughter filling the cave. Suddenly, the questers were among the tor-folk in their great hall at the feast, next Sara and Bluebell where in the small hut, and then back to great hall with Bluebell standing on a stool with her hands clasped over her mouth. In each of the scenes, the rooms were filled with joy and laughter.

Quite suddenly, the light pouring from the wishing-well vanished and the questers found themselves standing in the dark of night. They could see nothing while their eyes adjusted. Sara was just reaching for Daniel's hand when with a bright flash, the light blasted from the well again. Tobias was standing over the rock-pool with his arms held high in the air. His voice boomed.

'Magic of the heart is bravery, the courage that comes from within *when* we need it most.'

The rock-pool spun and spiralled before settling to show Ashar leading the gizords away, using the questers' clothes as a scent trail. The pool rippled again and there was Zac swinging his hook at the hissing gizords. The images started to race by, Sara leading the way through the tunnel. Daniel, diving for the torch against the on-coming rats. Daniel, peering around the boulder to see if the marauders had Sara, next he's tightrope-walking across the ravine, then he's diving on Sketch and Sara to protect them from the bats. Sara, racing across the tor-folk village after the blind wolves while spinning, burning branches in each of her hands. Daniel standing alone amidst the wolves, then on the Great Lake driving his sword through the serpent's eye. Sara in the Fens, cutting the head of the first mantis, then she's in the nesting lair, surrounded, 'Let them, come,' she says, the mantes come. Sara meets them in a battle frenzy and Daniel too. The last image shows the questers hacking with all their might at the cords that bound Tusks, to sound of the angry hog-hunters.

The questers could barely draw breath after watching themselves in action from afar, but reliving it from the safety of memory. They gazed into the pool, spellbound.

'And *that* is but a glance,' said Tobias quietly. 'And *now* the last,' his voice rose to fill the night.

'Magic of the heart is Love, the *love* we show to those who mean the most to us.'

The light pouring from the wishing-well seemed to brighten as the images in the rock-pool took shape once again. The scene showed the questers as they entered Moody Woods five days ago when they were startled by rustling and they reached out to hold hands. The water bubbled and a moment later, they could see Daniel leaping off the wall on the Rocky Rise to aid Sara, where she was lying on the ground before the oncoming gizords. Small waves lapped over the pool and settled to show the goat herders sat by their cave fire holding hands and smiling as they explained their life on the mountain to the questers. Suddenly, the water turned grey and murky, Daniel and Sara looked at each other, puzzled, then looked at Tobias but were drawn back to the pool by the sound of singing. Their eyes lit up, for as the water cleared, they could see it was themselves singing to one another in the fog on the Rocky Rise. Tears came to their eyes as they relived the moment and they put their arm around each other's shoulders. Almost like a reflection, the pool swirled and the image showed them embracing with relief on the plateau after just avoiding the marauders. Suddenly, a great wind blew up from the rock-pool and the questers' hair whipped back behind them. The scene within was beside Whirlwind Ravine and as the whirlwind whipped across the rocks, Daniel outstretched his arm to protect his sister. The images flicked quicker now, the questers were in tears, embracing after Sketch had flown Daniel to safety after rescuing him from the drooling bats. The wind stopped suddenly to be replaced by smoke rising out of the pool, there was Sara charging with burning branches towards the blind-wolves that surrounded Daniel. The smoke melted away and the scene was of the questers standing amidst the Tor-Folk after battling the wolves. Daniel was apologising and Sara's was saying, 'You're forgiven.' The scene shifted to show Daniel stuck in the sinkhole and Sara racing back to the boat for a rope. The pool rocked violently and through it they could see themselves in the middle of the Great Lake, Daniel had a rope around his waist and was pulling with all his might with Sara on the other end, thrashing in the raging waters. There was a bright flash and suddenly, the scene in the pool showed the questers sitting on the bank of the lake, their clothes soaked through and their eyes glazed over with tears. As they sat their forlorn, Daniel put his arm around Sara and drew her close so that she rested her head on his shoulder.

The light pouring from the well dimmed ever so slightly as the final images in the rock-pool faded. The water was still but for the gentlest of ripples caused by the night breeze.

The questers felt the cold of the breeze and shuddered. They became aware of the noises around them and turned as one to look behind. Tusks was there looking back at them, his breathing coming in deep quiet snorts and on his back still sat Ashar. The little monkey was busy worrying through a nut.

Sara, overwhelmed at all she saw wiped her tears and turned to Tobias. 'I think I get it,' she said. 'Magic of the heart was with us all along?'

Tobias chuckled and stretched out the palms of his hands. 'Yes, yes you're right Sara, magic of the heart *was* with you, but more, much more than that.'

Daniel, overcome from the scenes in the rock-pool, sniffled and cleared his throat. 'We still failed though, even *with* magic of the heart to guide us we couldn't fulfil the charge.' His face was crestfallen.

He's right, thought Sara and her eyes fell to the ground too.

With one great stride, Tobias was next to them and gently raised their chins so they were looking straight at him. His face was spread in a broad grin. 'Speak not of failure brave questers. Your only failure was not realising that magic of the heart came from within *you*. Magic of the heart *was* with you and as it came to the fore through your words and deeds, it spread all around you, leaving its mark everywhere you travelled.'

Sara's frown softened, 'So…we didn't fail?' her words caught in disbelief. 'We succeeded?'

Tobias laughed heartily. 'Succeeded and more, your journey was a true triumph.'

Tusks snorted loudly and Ashar back-flipped while applauding.

'Ooh, ooh, ahh, ahh,' cried the monkey, mid-turn, 'I knew you'd do it, din't I.'

The questers' expressions went from puzzlement to wonder to delight all in the space of a moment.

Sara smiled and grabbed Daniel in a bear hug; she couldn't help it and burst into tears again. They were tears of joy. 'We did it, Dan, can you believe we actually did it.'

Daniel not knowing whether to laugh or cry did both at the same time. 'We did…I mean I can't…I mean I can,' he hesitated, stuck for words. 'I don't know what I mean, but I'm happy we did it. Everything we've been through, it wasn't for nothing, it *meant* something.' He hugged his sister back.

'Meant something?' said Tobias. 'It meant more than you know.'

The questers looked at the well-keeper curiously. With questions forming in their minds, they began to speak at the same time.

'But wha—' said Daniel.

'How abou—' said Sara.

They laughed at each other and both tried again. 'You first,' they said together.

Dark shadows suddenly zoomed overhead and the questers looked skyward to the sound of heavy wing-beats.

Chapter 45
Reunion

The questers gazed up, their faces lit with surprise, for there hovering overhead was Lightning, leader of the flying herd, and perched on his back was Zac of the Rocky Rise. Another shadow swooped across from the side, and the questers spun again to see Blossom gliding towards the ground with Gertie on her back. A squeal of delight broke through the air. Coming through the skies was Sketch, and on his back, he carried Turlock, chief elder of the Tor-Folk. Daniel and Sara circled where they stood.

'Who squealed?' said Sara, looking around. And there was Bluebell, clutching to the main of Isobel, as the young mare came in to land.

Bluebell waved with merry delight. 'Daniel, Sara, up here, I'm flying; we made it. I'm flying, can you see me?' the little tor-girl called out. The questers smiled.

'We can see you,' said Daniel, '*and* hear you.' The adults chuckled.

'How…I mean why?' Sara searched for the words. 'What're ye doing here?'

The older ones dismounted slowly from the flying steeds, but Bluebell jumped down and raced over to them. 'Sara,' she squealed happily and ran into her arms; Sara returned the gesture with a big hug.

Daniel picked up Bluebell and spun her around, 'You found us,' he said.

Bluebell hugged him too. 'I did, and I flew; so did the others. This is Sketch, oh you know him already, silly me,' she blurted out excitedly, all in one breath. Sketch had made his way over to the reunion.

Daniel could sense that something was different about Sketch. He didn't hug him but patted him on the nose and said, 'Hello Sketch, I see you've arrived with passengers, all the way from the Tor-Folks' territory; that's quite a journey.'

Bluebell blurted out, 'He carried us, all the way across the island, never stopped once.'

'Never stopped once, eh,' said Daniel, impressed.

'Greetings, Daniel,' replied Sketch, while stamping a hoof and beating his wings. 'I wasn't alone,' he moved his nose to the right, 'Isobel was with me,' he added more shyly. The filly tossed her mane at the mention of her name. Lightning and Blossom stood proud and tall watching the exchange.

Sara broke the moment as she rushed to Sketch and gathered him around the neck in a big warm embrace, 'Come here, you big cuddly stallion, I missed you.'

Sketch neighed, wrapped a wing around her and said back, 'I've missed you too.'

Zac, Gertie and Turlock had joined them now, and the questers were shaking hands and hugging them each in turn.

'How did you fair lad?' Zac asked Daniel.

'Well we made it back here anyway,' he answered bashfully.

'It's so good to see you alive and well,' said Gertie warmly. 'Is the quest fulfilled?'

'Lucky to be either, if we're honest,' said Sara. 'If not for the help of our friends,' she gestured to Tusks and Ashar, 'and you lot, we wouldn't be here today, that's for sure.'

'The quest?' asked Turlock.

'Eh, Tobias, this is Tobias Wells,' said Sara, gesturing towards him. Tobias stood quietly next to the wishing-well while the reunion took place and nodded silently towards the new arrivals. Sara continued. 'Tobias says we succeeded; he says it was a true triumph, but...' she trailed off, not sure how to finish.

'But we can't really see how,' said Daniel. He was interrupted by the sound of the ground shaking beneath them.

Thump-thump-thump came the sound of something enormous and fast approaching. Sara spun to see Tusks was still beside them. *He's not the cause then, but who then?* Her thoughts were answered when suddenly Crunch the giant boar came thundering around the dunes with Tess sitting solidly between his shoulders.

Crunch ground to a halt directly beside Tusks. Turning to him, Tusks simply grunted, 'You made it.'

Crunch, by way of reply snorted back, 'As always.' Tess slid off, and it was her turn to run to greet the questers. Daniel and Sara were overwhelmed by the arrival of all their friends.

Tears of joy fell from more than one face while others fought to contain them, Sara had no intention of holding back hers and they spilled happily down her cheeks. 'What're you all doing here?' she asked aloud.

'I have summoned them,' said Tobias in a commanding tone. He stepped forwards and the gathered crowd fell silent.

'But how?' said Daniel.

'But why?' said Sara at the same time.

Zac placed a hand on Daniel's shoulder and spoke quietly. 'The ways of the well-keeper are known only to him, lad.'

Tobias turned to face the crowd and as he did, white light crackled over his black coat. He raised his hands aloft and spoke aloud.

'The how is not important brave questers, and as to the why, well that is very much so. We are gathered here today to bear witness to the true triumph of your journey and to convene the first meeting of our new order.'

This was followed by the humans clapping and the sounds of wing-beats, snorting and hooves on earth. Daniel and Sara, both wearing looks of puzzlement looked at the gathering and then back to Tobias.

'You've told us we succeeded in our quest, but what about the three treasures you asked us to find?' said Sara.

Tobias smiled broadly. 'Ah yes, the treasures, give them here.' He extended his long palm.

Daniel handed him the piece of the hag's staff and the plum seed. 'There's not much left of them,' he said hesitantly, 'like we said earlier, we broke the staff, and there's a tiny piece of the shard of the dragons tooth stuck in the plum seed.'

'We thought we'd found the nourishing stone, but maybe we didn't,' added Sara uncertainly.

'Didn't you?' said Tobias mischievously, as he took the items. He pressed his thumbs into the side of the plum seed and pried it open.

Everyone gasped, for there sitting inside the outer shell was a purple amethyst. As the light fell on it, a purple beam glowed out from the stone and shimmered in Tobias's hand.

'Wow,' chorused Daniel and Sara, both wide-eyed. 'It *is* the nourishing stone,' they said in union.

Tobias closed his hands around the three treasures and continued. 'The treasures, each had their uses, that's for sure, but they too were merely instruments of a greater cause. The true victory of your journey was the Magic of the Heart that came to the fore. Magic of the heart is the magic upon which our island once thrived, and because of you, Daniel and Sara, and your brave deeds, this magic has awoken once again.'

The gathered crowd stared in awe at Tobias, for as he spoke his hands, still closed around the treasures, glowed white then purple and finally green. Beams of colourful light burst out between his long fingers. The well-keeper opened his hands and the treasures were gone; fused together by magic and in their place sat a small tree sapling.

The sapling was little more than a thin branch with two twigs on either side, supporting three purplish-green leaves. He continued speaking and his voice filled the air,

'Magic of the Heart is alive in you brave questers and awoken once again among the great and good of Well-Keeper Island, may it spread and flourish before darker days befall.'

Suddenly, Lightning rose on his hind legs, neighed, flapped his wings and sounded the cry of the herd, quickly followed by the other flying horses. The boars trumpeted their call and the humans clapped and cheered.

Louder than them all was Ashar. 'Whoop-whoop-whoop,' he yelled, while leaping high in the air. The crowd closed in around Daniel and Sara.

'Well done young man,' said Zac, firmly shaking Daniel's hand.

'I just knew you'd do it,' said Gertie to Sara while giving her a gentle hug, 'somehow I just knew.'

Turlock appeared and placed a hand on the questers' shoulders. 'So brave, my brave friends, we're in your debt,' said the elder.

'Warriors,' said Tusks.

'Heroes,' added Crunch.

Not to be left out, Bluebell squeezed in between the two giant boars and said, 'Well travellers.'

Sara turned to them all, her face awash with feelings of joy and disbelief. 'I don't know what to say, you've all been so kind and helpful.'

Daniel was red-faced from the praises and just said, 'We couldn't have done any of it without all of you.'

'Sure you would've, pink human,' said Ashar, matter-of-factly.

Lightning stepped forwards. '*He* is right, brave friends,' said the white horse in his deep rumbling tone. 'No matter the help or the hindrance, you faced every danger and conquered every challenge. Your hearts are true and so is your legacy.' Lightning and Sketch then gently touched their heads to Daniel's while Blossom and Isobel did the same to Sara.

Tobias watched these exchanges all the while smiling quietly. When there seemed nothing further to say, he called their attention, 'And now to our new order,' his voice carried from all places at once. He stood tall holding the tree sapling aloft above his head. 'Behold this sapling, born from magic of the heart it will grow into a mighty tree.' Tobias knelt on one knee and gently placed the sapling on the ground. There was a blinding flash that caused everyone to look away. When they looked back, the sapling was routed firmly in the ground. A faint purple light shimmered off the leaves as they gently swayed on the night-breeze. The well-keeper stood ceremoniously and turned to the onlookers.

'A tree will grow here to mark this sacred gathering, for here we've held the first Magic of the Heart Council.' The white light pouring from the wishing-well suddenly vanished to reveal a starlit sky and a bright, full moon lighting up the night. From where the gathered crowd stood it looked as though Tobias stood directly under the moon. He reached down slowly and gently touched the closest leaf on the sapling. A faint purple glow travelled from the leaf and up his long, white finger. Daniel and Sara with the others watched on spellbound at the strange ceremony. Tobias withdrew his hand then and beckoned them forwards. 'Come,' is all he said.

Lightning shook his mane, trotted over to the sapling and gently touched it with his nose. The purple glow shimmered briefly from the leaf to his nose. The stallion stood aside and after him came Blossom, Sketch and Isobel, all of whom touched the leaf in turn. Zac and Gertie went next and then stood beside the horses. Tusks nudged Tess forwards, and when the little boar touched the sapling with her snout, it glowed purple and she squealed a happy sound. Ashar had found his way onto Turlock's shoulder and the elder approached the sapling holding Bluebell's hand. They each touched the leaf and as with the others, there was a mystical purple glow each time. Those who touched the sapling formed a semicircle behind it. Only Daniel and Sara were left and the others watched them expectantly. The questers looked at them, then at each other then back to their waiting friends.

'Us too?' asked Daniel, raising his eyebrows and pointing at his own chest. Sara said nothing but shared Daniel's look of surprise.

Tobias' face spread in a broad smile. 'Especially you two,' said the well-keeper and his voice echoed off the dunes. Daniel and Sara held hands and touched a leaf each. The sapling glowed bright purple and the magical light spread out in an orb that completely surrounded them. The questers gasped as the power surged through them.

It feels like when we floated down the well, thought Sara.

This reminds me of when the shard exploded in the lake, thought Daniel.

Images suddenly flashed through their minds: A high wooden wall lined with fire-lit torches, Appledown Orchards, a dagger, a girl and a boy both strangers, smoke bellowing over the Rocky Rise, a mighty plum tree filled with luscious fruit, a black dragon, an army on the march, a deep-dark cave, a spear and a shield.

The purple glow faded and Daniel and Sara looked at each other, confused and speechless. They turned to the crowd but no one offered any explanation so they turned to Tobias.

Daniel tried first to make sense of it. 'I felt...I felt a strange, hmm, I don't know what I felt...magic I guess.' His brow furrowed. 'And I saw things...strange things.'

271

Tobias nodded knowingly but offered no reply.

Sara shook her head as the images faded from her mind. 'I felt it and saw stuff too, strange stuff. Stuff from here, but not here, not from now.' She looked at the well-keeper, her face a mask of confusion.

For the briefest of moments Tobias and Lightning exchanged a look before Tobias turned back to the questers. He waved his arm in a sweeping gesture and spoke aloud. 'Curious you are and no wonder, for magic of the heart fills this night. We each have had our own experience and it has given us much to dwell on. And so it is for me as well-keeper to declare the first meeting by the Magic of the Heart Council come to an end.'

Chapter 46
For Now

'Wait a moment…wait please,' said Daniel. 'Before our meeting ends, I'd like to know something, if I may.'

Tobias gestured for Daniel to continue.

'I was just wondering, what will become of the captive we saw on the Rocky Rise?' Daniel asked in concerned tones.

Sara nodded. *Good question Dan,* she thought. 'Yes, and Lightning, one thing *you* said back there on the Rise was, "It continues." I was wondering *what* continues?' she asked curiously. 'And Tobias, what did you mean, "Till darker days befall?"'

The well-keeper placed a hand on the questers' shoulders and looked at them earnestly. 'Good questions, friends, important questions indeed. *But* not for this night, this night is a night of celebration when magic of the heart has triumphed, and *thanks* to you, our two heroes.' Tobias gently turned the questers to face the others and continued, 'Although you will be dearly missed, the time has come for us to part ways.' He turned to the others and gestured to them, 'Come, let us say goodbye to our brave adventures, Daniel and Sara.'

The semi-circle quickly came apart. Bluebell broke away first and ran over to hug Daniel and Sara. Tess quickly followed and soon most of the gathering encircled them. Just Tobias and Lightning kept back while the others said their goodbyes. Each had something kind to say and it wasn't long before many of the gathered were watery-eyed again. Tears flowed down Sara's cheeks.

'Are you okay dear?' asked Gertie warmly.

Bluebell took Sara by the hand and gave her a square of soft cloth to dry her eyes. 'You can keep it,' said the little tor-girl, smiling. 'I can make another.'

Sara couldn't help but smile back. 'Thank you, Bluebell, and thank you also, Gertie. I'll be okay,' she said while drying her eyes, 'I'm just sad because you've all been so wonderful and I'm going to miss you all.'

'You're the one who's wonderful, and we'll miss *you* more,' replied Bluebell.

Daniel was quite overwhelmed with the occasion and spoke with a lump in his throat. 'Goodbye my friends and take care. We wish you all the best.' Smiling, though with sad eyes, he waved and as he did, so Lightning trotted over beside them.

'On behalf of all creatures great and small that dwell here, we thank you,' said the stallion, 'for all of your brave deeds throughout your quest and for the good you've left in your wake. Our inhabitants will speak of you for many generations with renewed hope and joy in their hearts.' Tobias appeared beside him although the questers hadn't seen him move.

The well-keeper stretched out his arms and his voice soared, 'All that remains is for I, Tobias Wells, well-keeper of this fair Isle, to thank you, Daniel and Sara, for fulfilling your courageous quest and returning to us this night triumphant, true champions of magic of the heart.'

Once again, the gathered crowd cheered and applauded, each in the manner of their kind.

Daniel put his arm around Sara's shoulder and they smiled at one another. 'Thank you,' they said together.

'So what happens now?' Sara asked Tobias.

Tobias turned his top hat by the rim and tilted it slightly. 'It's time for me to send you home.'

Daniel turned to Sara. 'Hey Sara, can you believe it? We're actually going home.'

'I know,' said Sara. 'After all we've been through, it's hard to believe.'

Tobias clapped once, spun his hat and the air exploded in a rain of colourful crystals. 'Home, yes, home for now, that is!' his voice boomed.

The questers turned as one. 'For now?' they chorused together.

The well-keeper spun his top hat again and shared his broad smile amidst a sudden blizzard of multi-coloured flakes. The magical shower surrounded the questers and lifted them into the air; it carried them along and swept them into the wishing-well.

Multi-coloured streaks flashed past them as they zoomed through the rainbow tunnel.

Here we go again, thought Daniel as he spread his arms out wide.

Sara's hair whipped out behind and she smiled. *Home at last,* she thought, already forgetting Tobias's parting words.

The colours started to fade quickly and Daniel grabbed Sara's hand. 'We'll be exiting into the Orchards any moment. Get ready to roll when we land,' he called out.

Sara nodded her agreement just as the multi-colours turned to white. They braced themselves, leaned forwards and tumbled straight ahead.

Just as planned they came out of the wishing-well and rolled along the ground.

Daniel sat up, his head still spinning. 'Huh?' he said, looking around.

Sara felt the short, freshly cut grass beneath her and held her head waiting for the dizziness to stop. 'This isn't Appledown Orchards,' she said, looking around at the lawn they'd landed on.

'No,' said Daniel, confused, he scratched his head. 'It's our back garden.'

Their heads stopped spinning and their minds worked as one. 'The wishing-well!' they shouted together and spun around to look behind them. The well was gone.

Daniel crawled back and forth feeling the grass. 'Where's it gone?' he said in disbelief, 'It was here a moment ago.'

Sara looked around the garden while shielding her eyes from the evening sun. 'Stop, Daniel,' it's gone, the well is gone. It's just us.'

Daniel stood slowly and looked around too. His brow furrowed. 'Yeah, you're right.' His eyes widened. 'Hey, look at your clothes, mine too, they're exactly as they were before we set off five days ago.'

Sara looked at herself and Daniel over and her mouth fell open. 'Amazing, it's *just* simply amazing.'

But for a few grass stains, their clothes were clean, there was no signs of the burns and tears or the muck and dirt they suffered on their journey.

'Magic…I guess,' said Daniel quietly. 'What else could it be?'

They sat back down on the lawn and stayed there for a while saying nothing, both deep in thought, occasionally looking around the garden or at one another.

After a while, Sara broke the silence, 'It all seems so strange, Daniel, like another world altogether.'

'I guess it was another world,' said Daniel.

Sara paused for a moment and then looked Daniel in the eyes. 'Daniel, did it all really happen, were we *really* there on Well-Keeper Island?'

Daniel quietly returned the stare but his reply was slow in coming. 'Hmm…' he hesitated, 'you see…' he started again and stopped. His brow furrowed. Searching his mind, he linked his fingers then scratched his head and patted his chest. His face suddenly lit up. 'Wait a minute,' he said and reached inside his top.

Sara watched curiously. 'What is it?'

Daniel slowly lifted out the moon-shaped carving that was given to him at the Tor-Folk ceremony. Sara gasped, quickly felt around her neck and found her own carving held in place by its cord. Stunned to silence, they stared with open mouths, first at the carvings then at each other.

Daniel finally found his voice. 'Well there's your answer. 'What more evidence do we need, eh?'

Sara shook her head in wonder. 'None…none at all.'

Suddenly they both jumped, startled by the sound of their mother's voice.

'You two, stop rolling on the grass now and come in for your tea. You've been outside all day.' At the sight of her walking down the garden towards them, Daniel and Sara quickly tucked the Tor-Folk tokens out of sight. Their mother continued. 'An early night tonight, with school starting back next week. You'll need to get in the habit again of going to bed a little earlier.'

Sara threw Daniel a quick smile. *She really has no idea how long we've been gone,* she thought, *thankfully!*

Daniel grinned. *If she only knew where we've been!* He kept his thoughts to himself.

Their mother seemed completely unaware of anything different in her children and continued talking, 'That woman next door can sure talk; she's only just left. I should have called you an hour ago. Come in for your tea now before its cold.'

The questers shared a final secret look and replied in chorus, 'Yes, Mam.'

As the back door closed behind them, nobody noticed a small, green plant settling in amongst the bushes that grew beside stream.